KAI

Gwyneth Jones is a writer and critic of science fiction and fantasy: she's been called the most exciting UK science fiction writer (*Guardian*). Her essays and reviews appear in *Foundation*, the journal of the Science Fiction Foundation; *Interzone*; and *The New York Review of Science Fiction*. She has been featured on radio and tv, discussing futurist and scientific issues. Her novels, set in the future and typically exploring gender roles and the effect of new technology on everyday life, have been nominated for the Arthur C. Clarke award four times, the fourth time for *North Wind* (Gollancz, 1994). The first novel in the same series, *White Queen*, was co-winner of the James Tiptree Award for science fiction on sex and gender issues, 1991.

She was born and educated in Manchester and went to Sussex University. Having spent some years in Singapore and South East Asia, she now lives in Brighton with her husband, son and a fierce Burmese cat, writing and planning further tropical expeditions.

KAIROS

GWYNETH JONES

VICTOR GOLLANCZ

LONDON

First published in Great Britain 1988
by Unwin Hyman Ltd

Revised edition published in paperback 1995
by Victor Gollancz
An imprint of the Cassell Group
Wellington House, 125 Strand, London WC2R 0BB

A catalogue record for this book is
available from the British Library

ISBN 0 575 06067 0

Printed and bound in Great Britain
by Guernsey Press Co. Ltd, Guernsey, Channel Isles

for my brother David,
in memory of The Forty Years
and the
Land of Ghosts and Witches

Contents

First Angel

Second Angel

Third Angel

Fourth Angel

Fifth Angel

Sixth Angel

Seventh Angel

∞

FIRST ANGEL

1

Viscount Melbourne's Door

It was as cold as an August day can well be. Faint glimmers of sunlight lay like ice on the puddles outside St Paul's. The hawkers of snacks and souvenirs were miserable, the huddled up tourists looked smug: forewarned and well protected against the rigours of this climate. Sandy Brize threaded her way between the groups and past the news vendors' placards of war news, rubbing her eyes and coughing in the bitter city air. She walked slowly into the great church, showing her Benefit card with a perfunctory gesture at the turnstile, and was swallowed up in a deep, shadowy whispering immensity.

There were marble plaques on the distant walls, there were two thousand five hundred straightbacked chairs set out in the nave. Her card didn't cover the crypt or the galleries. Vcs whirred faintly, and the voices of tourguides buzzed like bees. Crowds of brisk footsteps hurried over the pavement: stopped, and the buzzing started again. She was glad to be out of the cold. She had been prowling the streets of London for hours: an unhealthy occupation. Whenever she came up here Sandy wondered how Londoners managed to breathe at all.

Prowling and thinking: thinking mainly about her lover.

They had been together for more than ten years, lovers since Sandy was twenty-three years old. And the matrix of friendship out of which their love had sprung went back further than that. Sandy had not thought of herself as a child when she left Brum to seek her fortune in the dazzling promise of a place at university. But looking back she saw that her time with Otto covered the whole of her adult life. Take that relationship away, and there would be nothing left of the person she was now.

It might have been all right if things had turned out differently. Unfortunately, the revolution, which had been struggling bravely

1

against the odds when they were all young, had faded ignominiously away. This was the age of sanitised newscasts, of a tough-minded acceptance of poverty and squalor as part of life's rich tapestry; of pragmatic revival of the gender roles. Otto Murray was not a rebel nowadays, she was a crank, no more regarded than any old bloke in sandwichboards who wanders up and down Oxford Street ranting about the antichrist. Sandy had not had a chance to die on the barricades: she could have managed that. She could not manage, could not sustain any longer, the long drawn war of attrition with the evident and inescapable facts of her life. She had traded her determination to escape for a set of luxury ideals, and had spent the last ten years unemployed and hopelessly in debt. She was on the scrapheap, stuck there for life: and tired, tired, tired, of trying to share the poses of a disaffected aristocrat.

I married her for her money, thought Sandy. Which is a brutal way to put it: but once you've said it obviously true, and then everything else collapses.

It was as if a rocking balance had finally settled. One possible interpretation of events became fact. The others vanished.

Staccato footsteps drifted around her. She stared up at the coruscating *lamé* ceiling of the choir: strawberry and cobalt and emerald like a rich woman's evening dress. She was preoccupied, but not so as to be oblivious of her surroundings. Instead she felt an ironical sympathy with St Paul's. Here it stood, still complete but empty as a vast fluted shell. There was no trace of the former occupant, only hissing echoes and a damp, faintly briny smell. She looked at the small board giving details of services which only sightseers would attend, and thought that this place was like herself. It had tried and failed to do something impossible. Now it was just waiting for an overdue announcement.

One of the memorials along the north wall took the form of an ornate doorway. Larger than life, its dark panels and lintel inlaid with polished metal, it had a substantial early Victorian presence. It looked like the kind of door that might open to your touch one day, though for a thousand years on either side it was only a façade with blank stone behind. Sandy studied the three-metre white angels flanking it. The one on the left was on guard, leaning on a great naked sword. The other angel slept, with half-shut eyelids drooping over blank alabaster eyes. She noticed that the wakeful angel was male, the sleeping one clearly female.

Isn't that the truth, thought Sandy. This is a man's world: always was, and will be until the end of time. It is so stupid, so *tedious*, trying to pretend that anyone can change that.

She was wondering *is this the way something ends?* Pain, sorrow, the appalling business of disentanglement. The loss not only of a partner but of a complete mind and soul...A shiver ran though her. After months, maybe years of simmering unease, she knew that she was really contemplating this death. She stared at Viscount Melbourne's memorial. Around her failing love affair the failing world gathered: started and spoiled, tried and failed, until Sandy could scarcely tell the two apart. On the face of it nothing dramatic had happened. Things could go on getting a little bit worse day by day for a long time yet, before any final crisis. But the balance had fallen. What purpose was there in acting out the rest of the charade? It would be no bad thing if that right-hand angel, leaning on her lily trumpet through all the ten thousand million years, were to wake this very afternoon: and lift the brazen stem and blow...

Either there was a service going on far in the eastern recesses, or else the choir was practising for a sound and vision show. Tour groups sat down to listen to the music. Sandy joined them, at the end of a row so she could watch her angels. A party of young Italians beside her started to make too much noise. A man in a long black skirt came out to quiet them – SSSh! Somebody nudged Sandy in the ribs, she turned to see a rosy, tanned face grinning at her: one rebellious youth expecting sympathy from another. Sandy glared. Don't count on me, she muttered. I'm just a poor native. But she was annoyed at having to seem to support the churchman. She returned to her angels in time to see a tall, shining, winged figure walking away down the aisle, towards St Paul's Churchyard and Ludgate Hill. Involuntarily, she glanced to see if both white statues were still in place: looked back in time to catch a last glimpse as the figure disappeared behind a large group of dark clothed Japanese. She sat a while longer. The hallucination did not surprise her. She was used to symptoms of this kind. Sometimes she thought perhaps everybody was suffering them, only people didn't care to admit it. There were plenty of possible causes - clinical depression, air pollution, contaminated food. It was nothing to worry about.

She noticed as she passed them on the way out that the Japanese were all wearing full-face smog masks, with goggles. Cheek, thought Sandy. You're better off here than you'd be at home. You could die

3

from walking down the street barefaced in Osaka, according to the news on the cable. She wondered, amused, if they were protected from seeing angels.

Outside, London seemed to be carrying on as usual. If anything exciting had happened it had not spread to the City yet. On a bench in the Churchyard gardens under a bower of gritty laurels, she put on her sunglasses and then took them off again – a gesture meaning, I don't care what happens to me. She was better dressed for the weather than some, because Sandy's wardrobe did not allow for half tones. The coat was the coat, a thick square black garment in the style of about fifteen years ago. She drew her knees up and wrapped its folds around her, humming faintly under her breath.

Dove sono i bei momenti
Di dolcezza e di piacer ...

Sandy was very white skinned, with small delicate features and a cap of fine dark hair that lifted and fluttered in the wind. Her old coat and her bare head made her look young: a pretty girl indulging the perennial youthful fashion for nostalgia. But there were reproachful lines around the orbits of her blue eyes, and her mouth was set forever now in an etched frame of fatigue and hope too long deferred. Sandy's looks were turning sour along with everything else, so that even mirrors told her it was too late. *Where have they gone, those lovely moments of sweetness and pleasure?* They are worse than far away, they are undone, they never were. It could be, she thought, frightening herself. I'll go home tonight, oh yes, and I won't start packing my bags. But it must be just a day like any other when the end begins.

The City of London went bustling on, apparently still full of life. Sandy watched the passers-by listlessly, half dozing in a chilly dream. Killing time.

2

Sodom and Gomorrah I: Fireworks for a Prince

Sandy Brize emerged from the tower block of the hospital into cold darkness, huddling her big black coat around her. The door of the Stag opened as she walked up and she clambered in. She clenched her teeth to stop them from chattering: she felt dizzy and lost. It was only a few minutes ago but she could not remember leaving Otto. She was sure now she ought to have stayed, or else somehow brought her lover away. *Did I kiss her? Did I dare, in that public place? I don't think I did.*

The two young men in the front seats turned their heads eagerly, bright Luci and dark James.

'What's it like in there?'

'Did she get my hamper?'

'I didn't see any cockroaches. Yes, it arrived. She promises not to eat any hospital food.'

'Damn right,' muttered Luci. 'If you'd seen those kitchens...'

He had worked as a porter, last summer.

'We could go back in, and try to get to see her?' Luci and James lived in London these days. Sandy had summoned them many hours ago: *Flag at Beckfoot, start for the Pole sort of number*, as James described this arrangement. They'd been waiting at Sandy and Otto's house for news. Sandy had taken over all the telephoning, it seemed the least she could do: but she was afraid she had let herself be intimidated by the Ideological State Apparatus again. Otto wouldn't have had the boys waiting in the car park. She'd have insisted on having them up to see her, never mind what the hospital thought.

Her suggestion caused a silence, in which all three of them thought of meeting Otto for the first time in this new mode; and

5

though Sandy had been with her in the midst of it all – still, it would be different with the accomplished fact.

'No,' said James softly, at last. 'We'll come back tomorrow. I mean later.' He stared broodily into his own dark eyes in the driving mirror. 'Did you phone Colin?'

'Yes. She didn't want to speak to him, her only sign of weakness. Otherwise she's ready to take on the world.'

Colin was the child's father, the obliging donor. He had left Brighton shortly after finals and lived on an organic smallholding in Devon.

'Um – is the display still in order?'

'Of course it is. What do you take her for?'

'It does sound like your piston rings,' remarked Sandy as the Stag roared showily up the hill. 'I *told* you not to buy this thing.'

It was November. The waste ground above the racecourse had been suppurant with bonfires since well before the fifth and was still covered with smouldering mattresses and old tyres. The suburban riding horses in the field across the road snorted and thumped noisily to their gate when they heard a car draw up. Luci turned towards them as if drawn by a magnet. Poor bloody gees, he muttered. Out in all weathers, half crazy with lead poisoning. There oughter be a law...

Black broke to red underfoot as if they were walking on crusted lava. They took the graffiti-splattered tunnel and settled with their backs against the mesh fence: a white moon above, the constellations of Brighton spread below and the sea a darkness beyond.

When Sandy Brize had first arrived at Sussex University she used to blush any time she ever heard the word lesbian, or even thought of it (which was frequently). Meanwhile, Jane Murray (Otto) was the epitome of campus cool. Sandy watched them from afar – Otto and her great friend James Esumare, and his great friend who came down for weekends, with the shining platinum crop and the amazing eye make-up. Mysterious lines of connection brought her to the edge of Otto's sphere. She went on watching, pressing closer or being drawn in, it was hard to say which, until at last she was over the boundary and they were rushing and falling together, merging into one lovely, unlikely whole...

Sandy was still a little frightened of James, not only because of his public school accent but because he was black. Whenever she spoke to him she could feel her parents and her brothers trying to climb out of her mouth. He was Nigerian, his parents were dead: he lived in Hampshire with his guardians in a house that was practically a stately home. He refused to have anything to do with black consciousness, the same way as he crossly resisted Otto's attempts to bully him into gay activism. But even so safe and so aloof, he made her nervous...[They smell funny, they take our jobs, they breed like rats: when are you going back to Africa, nignog?]

She was wary of Luci for different reasons. He had lost the accent, or cunningly never acquired one. He was defiantly weird in every way that James was defiantly normal, sharp in every way that James was gentle. Luci laid traps. When they first met he used to call her Alexandra (her name was Sandra). What's Luci short for, she countered: Lucifer, he told her. Sandy, who was at that time as innocent of Judaeo-Christian mythology as if she had been an Ancient Egyptian, called him it for weeks before she found out what everyone thought was so funny...

They were not often alone together, these three. Otto was the missing connection: lost leader. They glanced at each other shyly in the moonlight. It is so strange, thought Sandy. Not my class and not my world but I belong here with these people, as I belong nowhere else on earth.

'Yours truly will be i/c fireworks!' cried Luci suddenly, and leapt away with a tall package and a clinking binbag of empty bottles.

'What does eyecee mean?' asked Sandy.

'In charge of. It is a structuralist term, I believe.'

'Ah. I thought it was some more middle class homosexual slang. I'm trying to improve my vocabulary.'

James snorted. 'Still having trouble with those chips on your shoulder, Brize?'

'Not a lot, Sir. They're very tasty really.'

Luci flapped about in his black PVC vampire cloak and the genuine Courrèges boots, planting firedrakes. He was a research assistant now, and James was being in an advertisement on the telly: something he was not proud of but the money would set him up while he was getting into real acting. The boys were both very *sensible* about their careers. It made Sandy laugh. She couldn't stand the idea of a straight job herself. She wanted simply to live this good life she had discovered: books, music, drugs, sex, nice food – in whatever order and if possible all at once. She giggled, and at once, from nowhere, her eyes flooded with tears. Otter! Otter! How can I go home without you?

James was watching her, very kindly.

'I expect that was quite an experience.'

'It was, James.' Her voice wobbled dangerously.

He wrapped his arms round his long legs: a meditative black spider.

'Are you still signing, Sand?'

He was changing the subject to spare her feelings: terrified of emotional outbursts himself, he assumed everybody felt the same way. She fished in her pocket, and scrubbed her eyes with a dirty tissue. James had never been happy about Otto's decision. He hated changes.

'Course.'

'I wish you wouldn't.'

'Got no choice James. You can't do much with a third-class degree in Business Studies, if I even wanted to. And if I don't pay off something on my cards every month, I'll be in dead trouble anyway.'

'How much do you owe? I mean altogether.'

'What, you mean counting the loan-grant? None er your business, James.'

'Sorry.'

He heaved a sigh.

'Sandy, why did she do it? I mean really ?'

Oh, it's never going to be the same…   Sandy took a can of strong lager out of one of the carrier bags and cracked it.

'Don't get morbid James. I hate it when you get morbid. Have a drink.'

He didn't like the taste of any kind of beer. He opened a bottle of Burgundy instead.

'How's Xav getting on with his wonder job?'

'Still at it. They've got him assigned to devising new marketing concepts now.'

Francis Xavier was James's foster brother, son of his English guardians. He was a no-good no-account wastrel just like Sandy. His latest venture was unusually innocent: it involved selling some shady kind of vitamin supplements. Down in Hampshire Sandy had ridden a horse, eaten roast pheasant, been taken along a mediaeval haunted secret passage and attended a Christian midnight Mass (RC

8

rite). She was fascinated by this cornucopia. You never knew what might fall from it next. Maybe even a job, with lots of money and very little to do.

'Is there anything for me in it? Could he hire me to lick envelopes or something?'

'Oh, Sandy don't waste your time. The whole thing's barely legal, and probably about to go bankrupt.'

'I s'ppose you're right. A firm that would take on your brother must be well iffy.'

'Well indeed. Definitely unsafe. But I wish you'd stop working or stop claiming Benefit. You're bound to get caught sooner or later.'

Luci returned and squatted to burrow in more plastic carriers for the rest of the feast: a good pork pie with decent mustard, tomatoes, choclatinas, a buttered lardy cake. He glanced up quizzically, feeling the prickly field of James's gloom.

'What's eating my James? Spot of the mono no awares?'

James laughed. 'Oh, leave me alone both of you. It's *not* going to be the same.' He accepted a choclatina. 'But whatever Ottoline the all right does, is all right with me.'

'That's the attitude, my son. Have faith in yer political officer.'

They sat munching and drinking and smoking in the cold and dark, Luci occasionally running out to light another firework. He put up a good show. Somewhere near here was the Neolithic camp, home of the oldest inhabitants of Brighton. The four of them had come to search for it one memorable acid-tinged night: failed to find any Stone Age relics but discovered instead a fellow feeling that had made this spot sacred. They were the Nouveau Primitives, or *Nouprims*, as the movement would come to be known. It was a school of revolutionary thought which embraced radical socialist feminism, the desire to live on cake and chocolate ice cream, the desire to ride in the Grand National wearing silver *lamé* with a little mermaid train; and the knowing by heart of every single Gilbert and Sullivan chorus...

It was a tough life: struggling towards civilisation while the other apes, incomprehending in their tree houses, threw rotten fruit and organised moral majority legislation.

'The Nouprims will have to invent some colourful ritual to welcome the tribe's first offspring,' decided Luci. 'This is a start, but there'll have to be more. Could you fancy eating the navel cord, Sand? With chocolate fudge sauce, of course.'

'I thought it was one of the male sponsors that did that. Especially if he was an elective blond.'

The orange lights twinkled, the nearest of them blurred in places by persistent smoky flames.

'The cities of the plain,' murmured James. 'Sodom and Gomorrah. Did you know, cities were originally places of refuge for criminals? Normal people were nomadic. If you'd broken the social contract, say by murdering someone, you could escape society's vengeance only by staying put, in quarantine as it were. So when it says in the bible the whole population of Sodom was evil, it uses unorthodox sexuality to emphasise this point: but that's not what makes them so irredeemable.'

'Ah, I get it.' Luci chuckled. 'The fire and brimstone is reserved for those who live within the walls.'

'That's the idea.'

'And though not exempt from punishment, sexual inverts are in no special danger of having lava poured over them. Crucial bit of analysis, James. We like it.'

The sitting fireworks were finished, the feast consumed. Cloaked in shadow, the Nouprims gazed towards France, each lost in hazy private musing. If I could ever find a woman attractive, decided Luci, it would be Otter. A kind of busy, rangy amazon empress sort of creature. He glanced at Sandy's chilly little profile, dimly outlined by moonlight as she tipped up her can. Our queen chose well, he thought. A reliable type. Once Sandy had met him in a secluded part of Sussex campus, where by chance he happened to be in a fairly compromising position with Bobby the American exchange. She never turned a hair, good scout. Were there really people who would come upon a scene like that and cry *oh teehee does James know about this???* Maybe not, but she was still a good scout.

James knew, in general if not in particular. He did not stray himself. Didn't have to. James wasn't afraid of being swallowed by the karase, of losing his separate self. It would never occur to him that such a thing was possible. Too much ego, these actor-johnnies.

If I ever had some money, thought Sandy, I wouldn't buy a Triumph, much less a Stag. Bloody joke car. I'd buy a Cortina, an S or a V reg. It would have to be white. Bright white. I'd get it fixed up all in period, with visor-green OTTO and SANDY stickers on the windscreen, and I'd wash it every Sunday.

Sodom and Gomorrah I

One Ford Cortina
There's only one Ford Cortina
Oh! Ford Cortina!

She'd never stand for it. Poor Otter. I'm going to have to re-educate that woman.

James heard a car passing on the road, imaginary footsteps, and hoped he'd remembered to lock the Stag. Otto's child seemed unreal to him. It wasn't possible. Everything must go on the same. Friends, fireworks, midnight picnics: all very good things. But such dangers stalk outside the circle of the fire. Why invite trouble?

'I think it's time,' announced Luci. He stood up. 'How many hours old is it now Sand?'

She peered at her watch. Four fifty-two. 'Erm. Three hours and fifty minutes.'

What moment counted as birth? And who had noted it? Not Sandy, but a time was entered on the baby's little id card. She wiped her eyes again.

'Good enough. I think I shall pray to Otto now.'

He spread his bat cloak over the pinprick lights and dark sea and sky.

Hail, Holy Queen, Mother of Mercy
Hail our life, our sweetness and our hope
To thee do we cry, poor banished children of Eve,
Mourning and weeping in this vale of tears
O Clement, O loving, O sweet Virgin...'

' – She was a virgin, wasn't she Sand?'

Sandy raised her eyebrows. She had no idea.

'I expect so. Does it matter?'

'Take no notice of him Sandy. He's getting overexcited.'

'I should say I am. It is not every night I have a chance to preside over such a cosmic occasion. And now, I will light the blue touchpapers and retire.'

Luci ran, laughing and stumbling, from his sizzling bottles. The rockets lifted screaming into the dark. Stars burst all over the sky, and Sandy remembered Otter, pregnant and miserable: *I don't care. I want fireworks. She's going to be the best baby in the world...*

The stars winked out.

Δ

Otto Murray lay and watched the moonlit sky over her wide view of the sea.

One day when I was ten years old, she thought, it was polling day. I sat on a hard chair in the passage outside the infants classroom where people were casting their votes, and I asked for their cards as they came out so that we could see whether all our people had voted, and if not go and haul them in. I wonder if I was ten. Maybe I was thirteen, or both. Anyway, all of us election workers went to a hall somewhere and had corned beef hash and red cabbage for our lunch. It was only for us election workers. I used to love that. I loved being one of the people who was allowed through the door that was marked Private. I loved being busy and purposeful and, most important, in on things. Knowing what was going on.

She closed her eyes. Somewhere outside this place, her friends were celebrating an event in the course of a friendship. For Otto it was an event that changed the course of a life. Examination seemed forced on her, as if she was drowning.

When Jane Murray first arrived at university somebody misheard the family nickname, which she had acquired when they used to play The Wind in the Willows. She liked the sound of the mistake so after that she was Otto to everyone, but real friends called her Otter. In those days she believed it was okay, even politically sound to be predatory – non-monogamous – so she cut quite a swathe through the local scene. But her most constant personal connection was with James Esumare, and his long time boyfriend Luci (Gordon) Lytten, who was supposed to be a Cambridge student, but was always down in Brighton. The friendship was based on shared childhood memories, shared family habits, shared mythology. And then there was Sandy Brize, with her pale skin that looked so fragile you wanted to cover it up; and those remarkably cool, candid blue eyes. Otto Murray spent a long time wondering if Sand was a dyke as well as working class, or was that too good to be true. Time went by, other adventures. You managed to make a friend of Sandy, though she soon taught you you'd better not try and matronise: *cette animal est si méchante, quand'on attaque elle se défende.* Then it was finals year and you suddenly wondered – dear me, have I left that one too late?

Tears trickled under Otto's eyelids: after childbirth, the easy tears. People warned you about that.

She saw herself as a bandit leader, striding around campus in her carefully arranged tatters, hair a flying thicket of rusty dreadlocks. Dealing incisively with the pretensions of the male left (she had a head start there, her father was a Labour MP): and even respected in her women's group, that most unforgiving of political entities. She greatly admired the purity of her own views. She'd always wanted to have children, or at least a child, and this seemed like the right time. It was a necessary gesture of hope and faith.

Oh, woeful vanity.

The baby belonging to the young girl with tattoos on her arms stopped grizzling at last, and the ward grew very quiet. Otto climbed out of bed groggily. She wanted a cup of tea, which Luci's hamper would not provide. She knew where there was a coffee machine. She did not know the form: can they be left? Rather than summon a nurse and admit ignorance, she pushed the perspex crib on wheels ahead of her through the dusky and echoing hallway. The nurses' station was deserted, anyway.

Returning to the self-criticism.

In her first postgraduate year Otto acquired a kit, an obliging donor, and the support of the clandestine Radical Birth Network. She made several attempts to inseminate herself, to no avail. By this time she and Sandy had become lovers. Otto didn't know then that her bandit days were over, but she suspected something of the sort. She was concerned lest an important part of her life-plan should be put aside for the sake of romance. Tired of fiddling about with plastic syringes, got drunk one night and did it with Colin. The whole experience was an embarrassing joke. The next morning she was convinced she'd caught AIDS, and certain it was a terrible idea to have a baby. That's okay, can't possibly be pregnant. But she was. And of course she was too proud then even to think of an abortion.

She leaned on the coffee machine sipping hogwash, staring down at the crib. She'd covered the infant with her anarchist scarf, the one with the skulls and crossbones all over it, knitted for her by a former lover. One more credential, one more lapel button. She wasn't surprised that it was a boy: she'd got what she deserved. Poor little bugger. Mustn't take it out on him.

Hope, faith, and charity too.

But I'm in love with someone else, baby...

She ought to be longing to get home, away from the despised interventionist male medicine, but she could feel herself wanting to cling, to hide in here as long as possible. Was she already becoming institutionalised? Otto shivered. For the first time in her life she had had a taste of those social evils she was determined to destroy. She had been a pregnant woman in a public hospital and so had glimpsed the rest, the life of the unrespected. Hospitals, horrible places, the poor have always feared them. In this fag-end of the twentieth century, UK Ltd was doing rather well. Just be careful not to be poor, like the man said. If you have to be poor, take care not to get sick. Above all don't get old. We come full circle. What do we fear most ? – the straw death, the long drawn out misery of humiliation: *to die like a woman*. Obasuteyama, the mountain of throwing grannies away, it isn't such a bad idea after all. Take me out there and leave me, son. Please don't put me in a geriatric ward.

The registrar who had seen the baby born came past and found her.

'You ought to be in bed, Mrs Murray.'

The tone of voice aroused instant hostility. But the man's eyes were rimmed in purple, his hands were shaking as he tried to force money into the slot.

'So ought you. And it doesn't take fifty pence pieces, by the way.'

'Oh Christ!'

'How long have you been on shift?'

'About a week.'

'D'you want to talk about it? I've got nothing better to do.'

A short while later the registrar slept, head on his arms on a battered table covered with leaflets about fundraising. The baby in the crib slept, under his raggedy blue blanket and the anarchist scarf. Otto watched over them both.

She laid her face down by her plastic beaker. The jolly roger grinned at her cheerfully through perspex. I must not lose heart, she thought. This is a minor setback. La lutte continue. Nouprims forever! I will regroup. I will gather my people around me, and.... fell asleep.

△

'Well, what are we waiting for?'

'I don't know. The dawn, maybe.'

'It is November, James. Much as I love colourful ritual I do not intend to sit here for four hours, getting piles.'

Sandy was the last to leave the picnic spot. She stooped and picked up a fragment of flint pebble, possibly part of a Neolithic tool: a memory stone to be kept until she forgot why. Stood again, and briefly a puzzled frown crossed her face. That scrap of life in the hospital. She did not know how to feel about it, what it would be like to live with a child. And then, the exacting claims of Otto's revolution, the yawning gaps between her lover's culture and her own...The shiver of premonition passed. Safe, loved, hopeful, happy, she turned to follow her friends.

3
Sodom and Gomorrah II:
Outlaws

In Grosvenor Square quite a reasonable crowd had gathered. It was an illegal demonstration, but only because there was no other kind now. The police had been alerted by the demonstrators themselves, by the customary phone call about an hour after the fact. They arrived late and bored. The current stringent controls on public assembly were not directed against peaceniks. Until four in the afternoon Christian CTD and the Buddhists were holding the traditional front line without any barricades to lean against. The people sang: *We're here because we're here because we're here because we're here*, and *You can't kill the Spirit*. The people wrote on the insides of their wrists the legal support number. Young braves taunted the good natured constables, trying to get arrested. Older braves watched for the chinstraps to go on, for even a quiet meeting could be unpredictable; and told people to sit down. Tourists pointed their vcs and asked the police to explain who was who.

Candide sat in the road, next to a smear of desiccated dogshit: a nice looking ten-year-old boy with limp chestnut brown hair. His sexy white-lensed headband was any ten year old's trophy; but his shabby Greenish clothes declared his tribal identity as clearly as the number proudly scrawled on his arm. He couldn't see much except the legs of the disobedient majority, most of them bare and hideously goosepimpled. High up, if he squinted, he could glimpse a pair of wings and a windtorn flag.

'Why did Sandy go off like that?' he asked his mother.

'She had a crisis of conscience,' said Otto.

Candide made a derisive noise. He had known Sandy Brize for all of his ten years. He didn't believe she had any conscience at all, not deep down.

16

'She's not sure any more that the Americans are to blame.'

'Well they're not, are they. No more than us I mean.'

Otto sighed. It was hard to bring up a child. Teaching them to tell right from wrong was no effort. Only time would fill in the grades between.

'We protest about what the EU does too. But even though we have no special relationship with the USA any more, still on this occasion – '

He had lost interest.

'Anyway, that's not it. You're having a row.'

'Had,' she corrected. 'We had a row. It's over now.'

The child studied dogshit and looked at his mother from behind the white lenses with a faint embarrassed smile. He made no comment. He welcomed the reassurance. She might be right after all. Who can tell what adults know?

A little while later there was a baton charge on the other side of the square. A surge of banners and heads went down like flowers under hail, as people suddenly understood why they should not be on their feet. Otto Murray matter of factly exchanged names and addresses with her neighbours, even the young idiot who was blowing cheeky kisses at the roof-top surveillance. The folk hymns and the drone of the lotus sutra rose with greater confidence. BREAKTHRU reps stalked about in their ridiculous fancy dress, dispensing poisonous right-wing millenarian fantasy.

Candide persuaded his mother to get up and walk about. Otto scanned faces wistfully, unused to being alone in any crowd. Candide looked for Sandy too, but with less hope. He was fascinated by the sightseers: any collision with the alien world ouside his own was deeply interesting to him. Outside the Indonesian Embassy they bumped into James Esumare. Otto and he greeted each other jovially: old friends at the awkward stage, that may last a lifetime, of intimacy struggling to revert to acquaintanceship.

'Quelle chance!' she cried. 'I'm always meeting people I haven't seen for years on demos, but I never thought you'd turn up at one. Is Luci here too?'

'He's about somewhere.' James smiled nervously. 'Actually I was hoping to find Gerry.'

'Sandy couldn't make up her mind, so we nearly missed the coach, and now she's gone off somewhere. Gerry Howard, do you mean? What on earth would she be doing at an anti-war meeting?'

'BREAKTHRU.'

'Oh yes. I'd forgotten.'

The twins, Francis Xavier and Geraldine, were the children of James's English guardians. With an effort, Otto recalled that Xav had been involved in this idiotic new religion for years.

They sat on the edge of the kerb. 'I'm not against Islam,' she said. 'People assume we must be, because of the veil and clitoridectomy and so on. But Christianity was just as oppressive and just as murderous when it played the kind of role Islam plays today. I don't see any right or wrong sides in any war - '

James was inattentive. She noticed he was looking very twitchy. 'Is something wrong?'

'It's Gerry,' he groaned. 'She's done something that's going to get me in la merde profonde with Xav. How many times have I sworn never to go near those two again. They have this awful occult power to drag me into their affairs and then fuck me up – '

James had been two years old when his parents first deposited him with the Howards. They were young and rich and had no taste for childcare, but they didn't wish to leave a hostage with the strangling Esumare clan while they enjoyed their freedom. James had grown up more English than the English, as they say, and the tragic death of his young parents had estranged him even further. He had hardly spent a tenth of his life in Nigeria: the Howards were all the family he knew.

'What are they up to now?'

'Oh, Otto, you know what it's like – '

Once she had known, exactly. James had been Otto's best friend at university. They shared a past, a peculiarly English kind of extended childhood: childish alliances and tribal struggles played out in long vivid make believe games between boarding school terms – the expedition to the North Pole, the quest of the Cracks of Doom. The Murrays' imaginary landscape was coincident with a Borders farmhouse (the farmland all sold off) about forty miles north of Carlisle, and the whale-backed hills around it. The Hampshire version was New Forest manor house (financed by a small but good restaurant in its west wing): a young oakwood, a stream, a training stables next door. Otto's lover and James's lover, Luci and Sandy, had had to learn the rules of the game, the magic world. It included no one else, except the Howard twins: who were always amazingly evil, leaving other peoples' innocent and gentle rebellions

18

far behind. They were Catholics like James, which gave them a head start in devilry.

It was over. Otto had left the nursery behind and so had James, and without that tie they had very little in common. She heard of James and Luci mainly from her brothers, who were the kind of people who sent Christmas cards and generally kept their address books up to date. But now James's air of helpless anxiety vividly invoked the past. The twins had always had an unbreakable hold on him. The blood tie wasn't necessary, memory was enough: childhood cruelties, torture, certain key words.

'The thing is, Gerry wants to get out of BREAKTHRU. At least, that's what she said.'

'I thought she did. I thought she got married to that Italian chap.'

'Oh yes, she was married for a while. But he was in BREAK-THRU too, didn't you know? The company decided the relationship was too stable. She got an annulment…Pietro kept the children.'

Otto had never had much time for Gerry Howard. It was sexy to be helpless, fun to be raped and being a career woman is no problem, you just find a nanny who can use a hoover… that kind of woman.

She nodded wisely, feeling slightly embarrassed to discover how little she knew about all these people. Was it only two or three years ago that they had still been friends?

'She's taken something of Xav's, some kind of evidence of crime in the higher echelons, I think, and she means to use it to protect herself if they get vindictive. Like a fool, I let her leave her insurance with me and now she has disappeared from the face of the earth.'

'But that's stupid, James. These new religion types are always the same. They don't *care* if you show them that the reincarnated Jesus Christ is – um – growing vat fetuses for his neuron-shock drug empire, or whatever. They are *happy* for him. You can't "unmask" a thing like BREAKTHRU.'

'I know, I know. That's why – I mean, I didn't take it seriously. But why has she disappeared?'

The BREAKTHRU company had never been one of those gentle fin de siècle sects, hiring rooms in the Friends' Meeting House for ill-attended press conferences with God. It was the more aggressive kind, demanding large and regular donations and full-time commitment from its recruits. In return they were promised that when the end of the world came (soon) they would survive to become founders

19

of a superrace. The cult had a curious history, having started off as a marketing ploy devised by a failing British pharmaceutical company. The vitamin pills were gone. BREAKTHRU now had subsidiaries worldwide, preaching their simple credo: *the yes*. (Say YES! to health! Take Breakey's pure products daily!) Be positive. If things are falling apart, help them along. The new age will come all the sooner.

'I've tried the company dorm, which is where she's supposed to be living. They just tell me she's not available. I keep trying the Camden house. Pietro's still living there, with the kids. Not at home, not to me. I get the bloody machine every time.'

'And where's Xav?'

James grinned wryly. 'Ford.'

'Oh, really. I thought he'd turned into a respectable executive.'

'Yeah, well, as you say, BREAKTHRU isn't exactly a straight organisation. They were done for some major crook fundraising stunt last year – didn't you see it? It was on all the cable – and apparently it was part of Francis's job to be the guilty party. Elected to get sent down rather than take a tag. He was a social martyr, got a lot of cover, you must've seen it.'

'Didn't notice.'

James rubbed his forehead gloomily. 'They're holding his job for him anyway: in fact I'd expect a promotion if I was him. I suppose I'm safe until he's out again but you never know. He must be in touch with the firm, mustn't he.'

'But what makes you think Gerry's here?'

'It was just a chance.'

A BREAKTHRU rep crossed in front of them, dressed in a kilt made of strips of gilded leather. Her high-shouldered gold jacket was open to a moulded breastplate also gold. She wore calf boots with appliquéd wings and a cap to match, a dagger at her hip. The recruiters were always about at dissident gatherings. They even had some success. People took them for anti-authority figures: and incredible as it might seem the fancy dress itself attracted many.

'Slash hack burn,' murmured James. 'Like Fassebinder guardian angels.'

'Is that it? I thought they were supposed to be the god Mercury, or Aesculepios or something.'

20

'Same difference. I brought the stuff with me. I think it's a roll of film. I *really* want to be rid of it before Xav finds out what she has been up to.'

I might have known, she was thinking, there would be some ulterior motive. He hasn't the slightest idea what brings my kind of people to Grosvenor Square, to sit in the dirt feeling stupid for four cold weary hours. We won't be reported on the television news and that makes us absolutely nothing in James's estimation. The truth is, I hardly like this person any more.

'So - ' she recapped, with an air of having weighed all the options. 'You're afraid of being caught between Gerry and Xav...'

She had forgotten how well James used to know her. He was not deceived. 'It's okay, Otto. I didn't ask for a solution. I just like the sound of my own voice. I'm an African, you know. The oral tradition is very strong.'

Candide had vanished somewhere while they were talking. Otto didn't mind, he was safe enough in this company. Now he came running out of the crowd. 'I've seen the horses!' he shouted. 'They've got masses of police horses, in vans in Mount Row! And I found Luci - '

Behind Candide a slim muscular young man walked with a group of teenage anarchists. He had slick fair hair and startlingly bright green eyes. Otto observed that the sporty look was in vogue again, and it truly was okay for men to wear those crazy divided skirts.

To do Luci justice the athletic look was earned. She supposed he still rode point-to-point and did all those super-English prize-fighting dandy type things that the fashion plates pretended to do. Still her hackles rose. She had begun to hate Luci, before the foursome finally broke up. He was so completely the young male, and only more so for being gay. As far as she could tell he'd started to hate her too, at about the same time.

Not so young now, she thought meanly. He'd be heading for his first little chin-tuck soon.

'Good God,' he chirruped, in an affected neo-corinthian accent. 'If it isn't the leaderene of lesbian-bisexual-utopia. What a rare privilege!'

James decided abruptly that he had better go and interview the golden leafletter. They watched him attempting to break through company protocol, with dazzling smiles and honeyed body language.

21

Kairos

'Silly boy,' remarked Luci. 'I'm sure the little beast will turn up. That sort always does.'

Otto knew at once that James had not told his lover about the really silly part. She pitied them both, for such lack of trust.

'Don't you find you see everything yellow?'

'What? Oh, that was years ago, Otto. We have an intelligent colloid now, which adapts to the shape of the iris.'

'And you're into transvestism this season, I see.'

'No no, dear lady. I'm a Hungarian gypsy. Think Ivor Novello.'

'I'll try.'

He accepted a handout, sighed over it and stuffed it in his pocket. 'Pity about Istanbul. I don't suppose I'll ever see the inside of Santa Sophia now.'

'It seems unlikely. But didn't you two go to Turkey years ago, before things got bad?'

'Ah, but it wasn't worth it, with himself pacin' up and down outside feelin' betrayed. No one could get James inside a mosque, not for anything. He is a good hater, is our James: which is something few people know.'

James had told Otto once that Holy Wisdom, the third person of the Trinity, was female in Aramaic. She was supposed to be flattered, or maybe grateful. Did people like Luci and James really care more for the loss of a 'sacred building' than for all the dead?

The anarchists went to look for trouble, calling over their shoulders, 'Don't get arrested, Sir', 'See you, Sir'. Their pinched adolescent faces, dead white or grey urban black, were shining with happy innocence: the joy of being on the sexy side, the wild side. Oh, she remembered it...

Luci was smiling too. A moment of sympathy hovered between them, a brief flicker of the past.

'So what's the agenda today, Otto? What's the party line?'

'Don't you know why you're here?'

He grinned. 'I'm just picking up some cred. Makes my life easier in the non-academic classroom if I'm seen doin' something illegal now and then.'

Candide, who had wandered away again, came scooting back. 'Hey, Luci. Those girls over there've got their pockets full of marbles. They're going to use them. I just heard – '

The gentleman jockey sprang into life, and caught the child's eager hand. 'Have they, the devils!' He winked at Otto. 'Now

22

there's an issue two Englishmen can understand – Let's go and sort them out, kid.'

That was enough. Tactfully, she eased Candide away from an exciting confrontation with the horse-cripplers. She didn't blame him. He was young, he liked to see life: but she wasn't going to let Luci Lytten win a little skirmish of that kind.

It was hard to take any men in the anti-war movement seriously, she decided, even if they'd been born and brought up in the milieu Luci sneeringly described as 'lesbian-bisexual-utopia'. The best of them would eventually come up with a scheme for mass producing molotov cocktails to throw at the weapons traders. It was male nature: the battling spermatazoa.

The ordinary people stopped and stared at the cordons, lost interest and strolled away. Otto gazed at them unseeing. She was habituated to this process, no longer hammered on the glass demanding to be recognised: *I'm human too. I'm doing this for all of us.* But the encounter with James and Luci had saddened her, set her wondering whether the old alliance could ever be revived. It was something, after all, that they were on whichever grapevine had let them know about this event. It used to amuse Otto and Sandy to follow the boys' career: to discover what impractical antique sports car had replaced the old Stag, what bizarre sexual practices fear of AIDS had brought to Luci's little excursions. What did one listen to, and eat and wear in the smart world of turn of the century UK? The cable adverts pretended to know, but they were bound to be full of vulgar errors.

No doubt bulletins from the revolutionary front had amused James and Luci in much the same way. Essentially, the boys had become haves while Otto and Sandy had cast in their lot with the have-nots. Maybe they had their problems, maybe Luci would be a famous scientist and James a famous West End star if people didn't know they were gay: but their ghetto was a pretty comfortable affair. No, it was impossible. She couldn't blame James and Luci but she couldn't forgive them either. Nor could she expect them to forgive her for permanently monopolising the moral high ground. It was best if the two parties stayed away from each other.

Nothing so endless as a cold summer afternoon. The cavalry never emerged. At half past seven Otto was with the Brighton Peace Group and everyone wanted to go home. The square had been closed, people were beginning to filter into a police caravan and out into Brook Street. Otto joined the queue, absent-mindedly obedient to the chivvying police, who were now armed and in half-riot gear. She was used to them. Candide ran around to keep warm with a little girl called Vixen whose mother was Otto's lodger. Vix wore a fuchsia pink rara skirt over matching pants, with an emerald sweat shirt. She pawed the ground with her hands in front of her little belly, controlling the huge tower of muscle and bone which was herself. Her bare knees were chalky and goosepimpled, but centaurs don't feel the cold.

Otto watched the brilliant little figure, and all at once realised that Sandy was not going to relent. She had stayed away. The fact must be accepted, a lover's right to choose. But it was frightening. An afternoon alone had shown her how much she needed Sand. For ten years she had lived bathed in love, swimming in it like a fish, no trouble touching her without that mitigation. Today was the first time they had ever parted in anger, however much they fought. The thought made her shiver. I must find something challenging for her to do, she decided. There is so much. There is no reason for anyone to feel useless.

Suddenly James appeared again, brought to her side by the jostling lines.

'I thought you'd gone home.'

'Luci has, he was bored. What are we queuing for Otto?'

'To get searched.'

'*What?*'

She grinned. 'Ha. I suppose the extension of public order controls doesn't get much cover on your cable. They've been doing it for years. It's required by law. Check your id, check what you're carrying. Sometimes they do it both ends, but only when they've cordoned off the assembly area in advance...'

'Shit - ' he whispered.

'James, don't be absurd. It's no worse than any airport. It's a formality. They're not interested in us,' (she confessed, though she hated to admit it).

'You don't understand. It's that – whatever Gerry left with me. Suppose it isn't a roll of film. Suppose – '

He broke off. She could feel him stiffen and shudder. An armed squad constable had turned, and James had seen the assault rifle. He probably didn't recognise the stun batons which were carried

24

by all the Old Bill at events like this: thought Bobbies still used truncheons, as in *The Pirates of Penzance.*

'Well, don't drop anything,' she advised unkindly. 'There's some fairly useful equipment up on the roofs. They'd definitely spot you, and they don't like that sort of gesture.'

But the gunmetal steps were coming up. She looked at him and saw her duty was clear. All James's friends knew how much he hated uniforms: and the undeniable right he had to that phobia. He was in a cold sweat, he would arouse the most inattentive copper's suspicions. 'Oh, give it here.'

The police watched unmoved as Otto tucked James's burden into her daypack. It was a small black cannister, container for a roll of old fashioned 35mm film. The lid was sealed with tape, the plastic felt chill and clammy. Her bag went into a machine and out of it. She spread her arms and legs obligingly for the neutral hands of a policewoman. 'You had a nasty day for it.'

'Oh well, at least the snow held off.'

She was joking. But outside the sky had darkened. The air was suddenly filled with a furious cloud of mingled sleet and hail. She couldn't see James anywhere. Everybody wanted to get back to the coach. Let's go, let's go yelled Candide. So Otto gave up.

Sandy was on the chartered coach waiting for them. When they got home Otto rang James to tell him she had not been arrested.

'I'll come and pick it up,' he assured her apologetically. 'I'll be down for it tomorrow. I'll call you.'

Δ

They watched a Ralph Churchill before going to bed. Detective Superintendent Churchill was the main attraction on Channel 16, cheap commercial television in the modern meaning of the term. The old film taped around Ralph's six four-minute episodes was barely marginal. Everybody watched for the black high-ranking police officer with the public school voice. There was something very reassuring to the populace in that fantasy image. Ralph, a pensive frown on his attractive regular features, lifted a stylish rock crystal table lamp and admired it at some length. He was about to arrest the owner. Across the nation poor-but-creditworthy viewers reached for their plastic...

It had been a long day. The Peace Group held an impromptu meeting when it arrived back in Brighton, in Otto's living room of course. Always the same question: where do we draw the line? If we defy the law how can the public identify us as decent citizens? Is there anything left that we can do without defying the law? Otto longed to be alone with Sandy, but hadn't the heart to chase them away.

At last emptied of bodies, the room had subsided into a comfortable gloom. The only light was from the tube and a couple of studio lamps with their faces turned to the wall, which was singed just there from long practice of this habit. Over the threadbare carpet straggled cable from three vtrs, a spare tv, massive old speakers: a confusion of battered communications hardware. The walls were lined with books and tapes and discs: under a broad crowded noticeboard a jam jar of garden flowers stood on the big table, surrounded by more books, papers and the remains of supper. On the noticeboard were photographs, political handouts, shopping lists, postcards, cuttings, children's drawings. The hessian backing sagged under its freight of life and incident.

Otto lay on a scaly old leather chesterfield smoking a joint of last year's home grown and drinking homemade Thunderbird. Encapsulated in the grass and wine she felt vague pity for James. This certainly wasn't what he had wanted out of life, to become the jingle no one can get out of their head, a more or less pleasing pattern on a piece of furniture.

Another part of her was sighing, *wish I had a room that looked like that...*

She was hoping Peggy would go to bed. She had her own tv in the flat, but unfortunately she was unlikely to move now until the Ralph was over.

The door opened. Candide stood there in his trackies. He seemed a little uncertain of his welcome.

'Hallo. Er – there's someone in my room.'

He did not seem to be asleep, he did not look frightened. If he was playing a joke he was not trying very hard to convince. The three women raised their heads doubtfully.

'Cand – are you fooling?'

'No. I mean – I'm not sure.'

'I'll go,' said Sandy.

The living room was over the shop. Otto and Sandy's bedroom came next to it, and a room called the study, and a bathroom. The floor above was mainly Peggy's flat. Facing her front door, across a

narrow landing and up three steps was a slip of a room belonging to
Candide. He followed Sandy up the stairs, breathing rather hard.

Candide's Jack Russell terrier, Vera, sat on his pillow looking up
insolently. If she had heard Otto's footsteps she would have been
hiding. Vera had a crafty old lag's talent for gauging authority. 'You
know you're not supposed to have that creature in bed.'

Candide ignored this, safely.

The room was small, the window shut. The wardrobe door
stood open, revealing only a tangle of clothes and shoes. There was
a pungent smell of boy. The walls were decorated with old rock
posters and Candide's Animal Liberation collection. Some of the
handouts were very exciting: tales of daring and defiant virtue. All
were hideously gruesome. Candide loved the stuff, to his mother's
despair. Wherever bare paper showed its nursery pattern was almost
worn away. By the wardrobe there was a hole that Candide had
kicked in in a temper, knocked through to the lath and plaster.
Really must mend that some time – . The covers on Candide's bed
were faded cream, with a pink flower sprig pattern unkindly named
by Sandy I-don't-remember-eating-that. They had been a present
from Otto's mother long ago. Unfortunately for Candide the cotton
was very hard-wearing.

All this and nothing more, in the yellow light and slightly
unearthly stillness of two am.

'There,' said Candide. He hadn't moved from the doorway. His
expression was curious. He seemed to be fascinated by Sandy's
behaviour. He was pointing at the wall at the foot of his bed,
at the palm-sized hole where paper hung in tatters, crusted with
scabs of plaster.

'That's where you saw someone?'

'No – now. There now.'

Sandy frowned at him. 'Be serious.'

Candide sighed.

'Cand, I can't see a thing. Tell me what the person looks like.'

This request had a strange effect. The child seemed about to
speak. He looked at Sandy, looked at the wall: his mouth closed
firmly. It was uncannily as if he had exchanged glances with
someone, and accepted instruction or advice.

'Well?'

He shook his head. 'You wouldn't believe me.'

Sandy laughed.

He sighed again, shrugging his shoulders and mugging resignation like a cartoon character. He went to the bed and climbed in, pulling up the quilt in its sickly envelope. She was about to leave when the unpleasantness of Candide's situation struck her. Supposing, for whatever reason, he really could see something indescribable crouched by his wardrobe...

'D'you want to sleep in our room in your sleeping bag?'

'No.'

'Shall I leave the light on?'

'No, it's all right,' he answered stoically, and settled down to sleep. 'I've got Vera.'

Sandy crossed the landing to Peggy's flat. The door was unlocked as usual. She looked in on Vixen, but the little girl was sleeping soundly. There was no sign of disturbance. She went down to the shop, switched on its lights and peered around. The door and windows were blanked by heavy shutters, proof against their enemies. Bookstacks, display stands, till, counter. The cubby hole where lived the oldest microcomputer in the world, with extra bits of brain grossly protruding from its skull. Stacks of fanfold paper, posters, illegal vt copies of samizdat tv. She opened the door to the basement and looked down into Otto's secret lair. Switched on the light and descended halfway. There was nowhere to hide. Only books, more books, antique vinyl LPs in cardboard boxes and a miasma of old damp print. Arson? They had a smoke sniffer system, bought off the back of a lorry and installed by themselves. It worked all right, however. Their enemies had proved that once or twice.

The intruder was the spirit of two am: a cold, grey sinister emptiness. It had filled up the house, unsuspected, while they were watching Channel 16.

She went back to the others. 'It was nothing,' she said, 'A dream.'

4

The Eyes of That Dead
Gentleman

James and Luci had a flat on the city borders, a converted office suite in a small block of similar units. The ground floor had been breezeblocked and turned into a smart card lock-up garage for the residents: it was very secure. They went to a party that night and came home late, up from the river swinging arms and singing loudly *We've been together now for forty years, And it don't seem a day too long!* At the foot of St John's they stood embraced: You know what, said Luci. Ten years ago we couldn'ta done this. If we'd touched each other out in the street we'dve been bashed to bits.

Now you only have to be careful which street. You win some, you lose some.

When they got in, James sat for a long time gazing at a print of the Van Dyke portrait of Charles II seated in state, which hung incongruously on the wall of their minimalist-rococo living space.

The party had been in Blackfriars, in a basement of long low rooms full of concealed tech and sparsely scattered elaborate furniture. David Copperfield might have washed bottles there once. It was populated by elderly young men dressed in English worsted djellebas or Hungarian embroidery. There was some serious drinking, considerably more fooling around with semi-legal chemicals: the kind of thing where you put some drops in your eye and one part of your brain becomes temporarily overexcited, confused or disconnected from the rest. A specific neural inhibitor that would separate the cerebral hemispheres for a few minutes produced some hilarious amateur cabaret.

Their host had a new houseboy, a refugee from brave little Botswana. He insisted on introducing this acquisition to James: a tiny shrivelled stick insect of a man dressed in charity clothes.

His name was Ephraim, and he was an Episcopalian. He looked about forty-five.

James and Ephraim danced together, the Bushman with enormous energy and a drunken sexual frankness that was startling to discreet and inhibited Londoners.

'What tribe are you?' he demanded.

'I'm Nigerian.'

'But what people?'

'I'm Nigerian,' laughed James, making a joke of it.

'WHAT TRIBE ARE YOU!!!'

'Nigerian!'

'Pah! Communist!' For a moment a breath of hot life passed through the enervated, overcrowded room: heat from the vital conflict that at present enveloped about two-thirds of the human race.

In Blackfriars knowledge that the future of the world was being decided somewhere out there seemed to have gone underground, into the subconscious. The tradegoods crept in, and the odd attitudes and 'new' customs. In a generation or two these people were going to look around them like the rulers of the decadent gold empires a hundred odd years ago, and wonder how the devil that happened. How did we turn into slaves? Who took our magic away?

Meanwhile, barely six months after the brutal annexation of Botswana, Zimbabwe and the allies were contemplating an unholy pact with Israel and the Mad Zulus in Pretoria, as West Asia, the North Coast and the Sub-Sahara moved ominously closer together. The cult of that inhuman Unity was pulling the whole of Africa into war on a scale that not even Africa could swallow – much as it had absorbed in the last decades.

James smiled sadly at Charles. He had developed a passionate crush on the Merry Monarch at a very early age, long before he could possibly have understood the man's story. The romantic exile who knew too much: about the corruption that fuels a noble cause and the grisly self-inflicted wounds of the righteous. The restored monarch, who was in essence the puppet of his father's murderers and he knew it. The great sombre eyes looked down, full of amused and weary self-acceptance. If there's no hope and no justice on any side of any quarrel, one might as well be comfortable.

He supposed Otto Murray would want him to take offence at things like the term 'houseboy'. What nonsense. But then, it was almost incredible that an intelligent woman still considered it worthwhile to wave placards in Grosvenor Square. She should be pitifully grateful that the combatants still *needed* to buy some of their weapons from the White North. It probably cramped their style a little.

But all this was old news. Tonight, in spite of Otto and the nagging irritations she'd woken again, he was far more worried about Francis Xavier. It had never struck him before so forcefully how much Xav had to do with the BREAKTHRU phenomenon. Xav had openly abandoned his parents' religion about the time he learned to read but he'd always liked its imagery. A stylised golden angel had been the old drug firm's logo...but surely it was Xav who'd put the reps in fancy dress. And later changed those pitiful, sub-mid-Atlantic catchphrases into something altogether more sinister and more alluring. The healing pain, the refining fire; ecstatic purging.

Yes, Xav was well in. He'd practically invented the whole nasty show. James felt obscurely guilty, as if he should somehow have kept Francis under better control.

The flat was very quiet. Luci stood in the door.

'D'you want to tell me what's wrong James-bai?'

'Not really.'

'It's that Otto Murray isn't it. She's been poisoning your mind, with her martyrdom fixation and her poverty stigmata and her fragments of the one true fence...'

'Nothing to do with Otto.'

Luci did not understand why they had had to go to Grosvenor Square. A peacenik gathering seemed harmless enough: but any contact between James and the war made him nervous. He sometimes 'accidentally' wiped the less anodyne newscasts. (He could get away with this because James never watched anything unrecorded: he complained it was like reading a book where only the right hand pages turned.)

'Don't you *dare* let her bother you, James. She dunt know nuthen about nuthen.'

He went to bed. James sat on, uneasily but distinctly relieved to have parted company with that small package. He discovered, with a little internal shuffling, that he wouldn't have time to get to Brighton tomorrow...maybe not for a week or two. Maybe not until Gerry had resurfaced somewhere. After all, the thing wasn't going to do Otto any harm.

SECOND ANGEL

1

The Best of All Possible Worlds

Candide was nearly four months old. They went to Devon for the weekend, abandoning the horrible confusion of conveyancing, commercial property regulations, mortgage arrangements that surrounded the great plan. It had been an unpredictable winter: warm and rainy with spasms of incredible cold. It was not cold this February weekend, but long dark by the time they arrived. Midge went to bed early, she was very pregnant. Colin took them down to see the river, into the night cleft that opened under the cottage garden wall. The descent was over glistening stones through a plantation, trees pressing thick and jagged and black on either side. In the depths there was a sound of pent up water and suddenly it lay at their feet, a roaring stream much more wide and impressive than they had expected. From a ribbon of sky far overhead, the fierce glossy movement reflected starlight. They squatted on the bank like red indians, like wild animals. They stayed there for a long time, no one saying a word.

Up at the cottage again Colin fastened the wooden latch and turned to them, his eyes brimming with peace and vast content. 'Goodnight,' he whispered.

Sandy and Otto sat by the stove, Otto in Colin's chair, Sandy hunkered down close to the heat. They were exhausted. Their faces had the same look, hollow eyed and bewildered, as if they were both young mothers. Candide had his wonderful moments but he was not an easy baby. Neither of them dared even to glance at the door behind which he was (miraculously) sleeping.

'Would you like this?'

'In a weird way it's a temptation,' said Otto. 'Sex doesn't come into it: but then why would it after the honeymoon? I'd only be

33

like millions of other wives and mothers. But I know how it would be. I'm a big strong girl Sand, but I get my period. I get pregnant. Before you know it, the man is hewing the wood and drawing the water, driving the plough and hunting the food; and the woman is doing the cooking. I can breastfeed, he can't. So naturally I stay in the house, he deals with the world...'

'I didn't exactly mean you and Col, Otter. I meant us, doing this.'

Otto was unembarrassed. This was the first time she had been with her baby in the home of the child's father. It was reasonable enough that she should be thinking *why not?* Because of the child, she and Sandy had spent an unnatural proportion of their young relationship like this: together because they didn't want to be apart but not making love, not out having fun: stone cold sober or dazed from lack of sleep and talking, talking, talking. Very little was left unexamined.

'Oh, I don't know – '

Sandy waited, interested, insistent: like a coolly cerebral hearth-cat.

'All this - ' Otto waved her hand, encompassing the simple room where every artefact was beautiful and tenderly handmade. 'Even if it could survive without consumerism going on somewhere close, which I doubt – it is just damage limitation. It says we failed. We give up. No more fantastic medicine, no more silver birds up in the sky no more particle accelerators no more Mission to Mars no more satellite tv. Just births and deaths and seasons the way it always was and always will be amen. I can't accept that defeat. I want everything Sandy, that's my trouble. I am not prepared to give up any clever or frivolous or exciting thing human beings have devised, not even for the revolution. I refuse to take one step backwards.'

Faintly, from outside, Sandy could hear the river. She could still see and feel in her mind that cold, relentless, endless flowing under the stars: a pleasure that chimed strangely with Otto's passionate optimism.

She laughed.

'Okay, Otter. I'll buy that. When can you deliver?'

From Otto's manifesto, Wombega was born. She had been wondering since she was twenty-one what she ought to do with a modest legacy left to her by her grandmother. A sense of its power to effect change kept her from handing it over to some reputable charity, which would have been the simple solution. Some time in the middle of her pregnancy she had realised what that money was for. The doctorate she had embarked on no longer made sense. She did not want a high-flying academic-stroke-political career.

'What *do* you want then, Otto?' asked her supervisor, when she went to apologise. She was curious. This young woman, though not a brilliant student, had success (of a certain kind) written all over her.

Otto looked sheepish, touched her belly protectively (though who was protecting whom she wasn't sure).

'I want to run a secondhand bookshop.'

In the end, because Otto would not take up a government grant, buying the shop, fixing it up and financing the first year in business took the whole of the legacy, a bank mortgage and another loan from Otto's father. The name was proposed by Otto and Sandy's women's group. It was supposed to mean the great O of the womb, source of all beginnings and all endings. Of course, Wombega wasn't just any secondhand bookshop. In commendable late-capitalist style it neatly filled a gap in a shrinking but still active market. There were other outlets in the area serving various alternative interest groups, but no bookshop exclusively for women. However, Otto never advertised or described her shop as a feminist or in any way a politically motivated enterprise. She resisted pressure to have a women only coffee bar in the back, and filled up more than half her shelf space with all kinds of heterogenous subject matter.

Later, as those other outlets vanished one by one, she was to congratulate herself, grimly, on her prescience.

Otto's mother was dying of cancer by then. She kept it to herself until Candide appeared, and spent some of her last months helping the young couple to set up house. It was a situation she recognised easily though it infuriated Jane to have her say so. Otto's brothers helped with the decorating. Her sister came down once, was astonishingly rude to Sandy and vanished, never to be seen in Brighton again. Her father spoke philosophically of wild oats, meaning Sandy. He knew what Otto was up to, perhaps better than anyone. He advised his daughter to steer clear of the Communist Party. And never to do anything downright illegal without good reason.

Sandy's family didn't come into it. She had no contact with them now at all.

Wombega survived. Candide became a toddler and then an independent and friendly little boy. He was at home in most houses on the street, from the prosperous matriarchal clan of Rastafarian motor mechanics to the places with the cardboard windows; where he acquired nits, worms, a startling vocabulary and once, scarlet fever. He ran around backstage at politically sound rock and roll gigs, and at three and a half proudly told a door to door merchandiser that he didn't have any use for those toys. He never watched consumerish poison: *he* only watched samidativi.

Until her luck ran out Sandy was doing, even after servicing her debts, far better than the shop ever would: with her Benefit cheques and her endless succession of shifty part-time jobs. When her luck did run out the state took over the debts and added to them her fine, and the sum of all the wrongfully claimed Benefit. Sandy became a non-person, her economic value so hopelessly below zero she might as well be saddled with the whole deficit of the Americas. She was enrolled in The Force, and set to work on socially useful menial tasks for which she was paid – over the amount nominally withheld towards interest payments - a bonepared subsistence.

In practical terms the change made little difference to her life or maybe even improved it. Assigned to litter collection in the smart streets down by the sea she took Candide along with her and every day they visited a whole menagerie of beautiful cars: a forty-year-old Jensen Interceptor, the new wasp-tailed custom Fords and Nissans; a gorgeous scarlet Ferrari Meraviglia, the most exotic animal in their zoo. They salvaged dustbin copies of What Car and drooled over them, unable to understand Otto's total lack of interest. It was a pity Sandy had to wear her Force overalls, otherwise they might have collected some tips by doing little cleaning jobs for the beauties. 'Never mind,' said Sandy. 'Say more like true love this way.'

Small presses and distributors went out of business and Otto's credit suffered. There was always some new political scare to worry about. Sometimes they ate more date expired food than was good for them, and the one time Candide was really ill it was terrible. Still their life was relatively secure and more than relatively happy. As time went by and revolutionary optimism became rather a poor joke, Otto occasionally wished she had a shop called The Bookshop and a child called Boy. But it was in the nature of this life she had chosen that she had to live with all her old selves, and she was glad of it. Her past grew along with her: carelessly carved initials expanding on the bark of the spreading Otto tree.

One day Otto was surprised to see, through the glass of the shop door, two prosperous looking business men coming up the steps. It was winter. They were wearing camel hair coats, one more expensive than the other. The bigger man wore the cheaper coat.

'Can you get someone to look after the shop for a minute?'

'Not instantly,' she replied.

One of the men turned the CLOSED sign outward and slid the bolt across. The other took a matt finished steel box with a short lead out of his substantial attaché case, and began to run the sensor over the glossy remainders in her front stacks. The box clattered briskly.

'Just for a few minutes. Shall we go upstairs?'

Otto was completely taken in. She led them up to her living room, palms sweating.

'Dungeness is pretty close here, isn't it. And you're in a bad direction for the wind.'

'Say une right scandale, the state of that reactor. Shoulda been decommissioned forty years ago.' The men expanded in her shabby room. One sat down, the other walked around touching things.

'Now I want you to consider this proposition very carefully, Mrs Murray. A business person in your position can't afford to be undercovered. All sort of accidents can happen.'

'Wait a minute. Are we still talking about wind direction?'

'That and other things. This is an information centre for political extremists, isn't it.'

'It is nothing of the kind. I sell books – cheap remainders, anything I can get hold of. Would you mind telling me what department you are from?'

'Department? I'm not quite sure what you mean. We represent the New Age International Security Company.'

The big man tugged curiously at a nest of cable. He had black hair slicked back with a heavy dressing, he wore a formal scowl and carried his arms like weapons: Japanese design and parts, put together in England. The more expensive man opened his attache case and began to sell insurance. Otto stood paralysed by this dream-like sequence of events, still wondering if it was a real geiger counter. The shop door was bolted but the kitchen door down the alley must have been unlocked, for Mrs Eliot suddenly appeared. She was dressed in a filthy slip and some wrinkled stockings, she had a bedraggled shawl wrapped round her shoulders. 'I'm cold!'

she cried. 'I'm hungry!' She was only seventy, but lost in dementia. She lived with her granddaughter who had cleaning work. The granddaughter's husband – people still used this courtesy term in Otto's street - was probably in the pub. This reeling shell of a human being always managed to escape when she was left in the care of the children. Mrs Eliot staggered around the room, her raddled old dugs falling out of her underwear. The man selling insurance, unperturbed, made remarks of jovial menace. His companion plucked at Otto's noticeboard, trying the strength of its attachment to the wall.

'All sorts of things could happen - '

Otto suddenly erupted. 'Out,' she said, calmly and furiously. 'Get out.'

'Oh, come on,' chuckled Mr New Age. 'No need to work yourself up. We're all smiling here.'

'I'm not smiling. This is a snarl.'

She escorted them off the premises. Nothing got broken, this time. The men seemed merely amused.

Otto stood in the doorway of her shop and noted some things that would have to be upgraded: the night shutters and the tamperproof mailbox. Dirty children played by the kerbside, inadequately wrapped little parcels with skinny bare arms and ankles turning purple in the cold. Down the street Josh and Zep MacDonall were working on a car. Josh was singing the catch from a Collins Family song, one of the local rockstars' stirring alternative anthems.

> *And heaven is my destination*
> *And paradise my dwelling place*
> *I may not get there, get there with you*
> *But I have SEEN the promised land...*

She was wryly amused by the twinge of reassurance she felt at the sight of those two stalwart young men. The New Age executives were quite correct in their assumptions. The police and the law courts were not – in reason - available to members of the underclass. In that sense, as in many others, ex-imperial Great Britain had joined what used to be called the Third World.

Otto had become accustomed to seeing a kind of justice in this fate. The mills of God grind slow they do, but they grind exceeding small. Now, suddenly, standing there in the cold and dirty street, it came to her that she was thirty next year and this was life. No longer youth, no longer preparation, but the real thing and the only life she was going to have. She had been betrayed by an accident of time. Brought up in the last fading glow of a golden age, she had no choice but to consider certain conditions normal and struggle for their recovery. She was chasing a rainbow. This was normality: the few rich and the many poor, the helplessness of a woman on her own. This was the balance that would always reinstate itself.

Otto set her determined scots jaw, and firmly turned the shop sign back to OPEN. There it stood, the baled seed corn: communication, communication. There were more discs than when she'd started, less paper: basic hardware was so cheap now that even poverty stricken 'political extremists' routinely bought their mindfood in ROM. Otto had been told that language was a male preserve, but she knew better. The world of words was her natural environment: knowledge and argument, refuges of the powerless. It would be her life's work to keep this route open, to hold this pass, this secret gateway.

She went back upstairs, where she found Sandy had come in and taken charge. Mrs Eliot was wrapped in Otto's dressing gown rolling papers for the fire. She liked rolling papers. She came from up north like Sandy where people still do things like that. Otto went up to Sandy and hugged her, burying her face in the warm white hollow of her lover's throat, feeling the tensile strength of Sandy's arms closing across her shoulders.

'We'll get there,' she muttered. 'We may not live to see it, but the people will get back there, one day.'

△

The year that Otto was thirty the Channel tunnel finally opened. Wombega held a party to celebrate (ironically of course). Otto's brothers came down, minus their wives and children, and so did James and Luci and Xav and Gerry's husband, Pietro. (This was the last such invitation that the boys would accept, as it turned out.) The group made an extraordinary island in the sea of worn, old-fashioned clothing and unmade-up faces: Xav most extraordinary of all because he had come in full angelic regalia. Otto really thought she must have given the impression it was fancy dress and, drunkenly benign, even apologised to him. Xav told her that he was working tonight. He regarded her party as prime recruiting territory. This was Otto's first close encounter with the BREAKTHRU phenomenon. She laughed until she choked, delighted to get back at Xav for all the times he'd sneered and snickered at *her* beliefs.

△

On Candide's seventh birthday, something wonderful happened. Spacey Lacey the acid queen, who sometimes lived in a teepee on the slopes of Mount Caburn, came back to Brighton from one of her walkabouts. She arrived to pay her respects at Wombega: smelling of sweat and animals and woodsmoke, with the little Jackie squirming inside her coat. Lacey was one of the eccentrics of lesbian-bisexual-utopia. She was said to have impossibly exalted origins, to be twenty-fifth or so in line to the Throne. It might be: certainly she hadn't a political thought in her head. She consorted with mediaeval gamers and survivalists out in the wild, fell in love with ferocious travelling girls and beat them black and blue, until they ran off back to the Romany men who seemed lamblike in comparison. Boy ought to have dog, she explained shyly, rubbing the knees of her vile greasy denims. Train it, belt it, they respect that. One cussed little bitch more'll be no trouble. (She referred to Sandy, whose ice blue eyes she admired.) Otto was furious: the puppy yelping and peeing and shitting, another mouth to feed. But she could not bear to play the heavy parent: Vera stayed.

In Africa and Asia the various wars began to blur into one: cloud shapes breaking and reforming on a red sunset sky. A moderate Labour government that had swept away eighteen unbroken years of Conservative rule was narrowly beaten at the end of its first term, and the Tories regained command. The oil crisis, dollar crisis, the Japanese Rearmament: the first decade of the twenty-first century settled into its stride. Through the long summer evenings of childhood Candide lay on his bed watching the foliage shift, white to green, on the branches of the great pear tree that grew up out of the MacDonalls' back yard. He thought about James and Luci, whom he still counted as his friends, and, though he would not have expressed it so; of Sandy's growing unhappiness. He thought about his mother's reverses: he was a passionately loyal but not uncritical footsoldier in the army of utopia. In Maytime the pear tree was a fabulous tower of white blossom, in winter a black skeleton that seemed able to reach his window and scratch its way in. With Vera hugged in his arms Candide dreamed long dreams of heroic violence, his innocent eyes fixed on the horrible pictures which Otto kept trying to throw away. Every night when he finally got into bed he would tell her – go down to the kitchen, good dog. She obeyed as far as the floor, every night: depressed her stump of a tail and half lifted her white and tan ears: Please? Oh, all right, sighed Candide in long-suffering tones, and only then she scrambled up to his pillow. You take first watch, murmured the child.

Otto had had an older brother who died of leukemia, and now there was her mother too. She dosed her child with potassium iodate in wet weather, wheedled him into protecting his vulnerable blue eyes in high UVB: and hoped and prayed he was on the right end of the resistance scales. She couldn't afford the testing and didn't live near enough to that old monster at Dungeness (by the state's reckoning) to get it done at reduced rate. Fear for Candide's health was her customary way, it was all she had time for, of expressing her fierce, irrational love for the child. Loving Sandy was necessary to her: food, bread, the terms of her existence. Loving Candide was treasure: secret, unearned, unforeseen joy. They were her life and the meaning of it. She could not do without either. And thank God (or whatever), whatever happened to her cause she would always have these two.

One cold spring day she was cooking skirlie pudding and cabbage while Candide and Vera played under the kitchen table. Sandy and Otto had hoped they would get used to having a dog around. They had not. There was something fundamentally repellent about the little terrier, with her slavish regard for beatings, her periods of abject sexuality; her constant amoral measuring of every comer – do I show my belly or do I bite? But Candide loved her as tenderly and painfully as he would ever love in his life: and it was impossible not to be touched by his initiation into the heart's world.

The two of them were looking after Vixen today while her mother was out. Candide grumbled about the lodger's little girl, but in fact he enjoyed these excursions back into earlier childhood. Otto's thoughts ran on. Just exactly how am I different from my grandmother? I do the cooking and the cleaning. I don't go out to work. I carry dinners to senile old ladies and sit with poor women's sick children like something out of bloody Charlotte Yonge. He knows I don't run the world. Whatever I tell him this is what he'll remember. Woman – Mummy – at the old gas stove, cooking the food of the poor...

He was ten years old now, coming up to secondary school. And what to do about that? Her father had offered to pay. Which was out of the question, simply not an option. But the alternatives... Oh how horrible, how impossible life is when you have a child.

'Now,' said Candide firmly. 'You know what's happened. There's been a Nuclear War.'

'Okay.'

'And we're the only survivors.'

Two children and an idiot terrier bitch, surveying desolate Eden.

'We'll have to – '

The disembodied voice dropped to a whisper. Vixen snickered evilly. 'Candeed!'

Otto was wondering if she should intervene. Vixen was only four, was her son developing paedophilia? Probably all talk. Suddenly into the glum depression of that particular afternoon, fell the words 'Nuclear War'.

The dismantling had begun. The ghost of old Reagan's star wars sobbed around the corridors of the Capitol, fading like Tinkerbell without an audience. There were no more nuclear warheads on British soil, and Trident was as dead as the Blue Streak. The great armouries of West Germany and the Ukraine were being taken apart, bit by bit. The dumping process was the new target for protest: and the Campaign for Nuclear Disarmament had had to change its name.

For this historic victory Otto should have been supremely grateful. Unfortunately, she knew that was all it was: an amoral process of history. The 'great powers' of her youth were now backers not runners in the arms race, that was all. There were still the EU bases with their non-nuclear but sufficiently horrific stores, there was still the Islamic bomb and the Israeli bomb. Not to mention stockpiles in the hands of the no one knew how many loony US fundamentalists who'd turned up at the infamous 'garage sales' and just hauled the things away.

Nuclear War. The old terror shivered through her. It was irrational, she knew. This offshore island was well out of any likely 21st century scenario. But the mushroom cloud, the searing wind, the *destroyed world* had always been her nightmare: no other image of doom had such power.

There was a sortie from the bunker. Candide shot across the room, out and down the passage with Vera yelping behind. Vixen emerged

more cautiously holding her ears, taking shallow wary breaths and
treading the dog-eared vinyl as if it might give way under foot. She
was always the more imaginative of the pair. Then suddenly she
skipped away, calling 'Candeed! Candeed! You forgot your speshul
smog mask!'

War's annals will fade into night,
e'er their story die...

Otto's eyes were stinging, tears dropping into the savoury mess
of bacon fat and oatmeal. *I won't let it happen.* I swear to you,
Candide, I won't let the monster get you...

Δ

Sandy borrowed twenty pounds from the rainy day jar and went up
to London. The seminar was held in the barely adequate conference
rooms of an executive class hotel – executive having come to mean
what budget meant twenty years ago. The decor was dull yellow and
khaki, the ceilings too low. The seminar leader said she was going
to talk about sex. She made a circle of her finger and thumb and
poked it with the index finger of her other hand: the gesture repeated
enormously overhead and on the fuzzy little screen at every desk.

'Now that's what we mean by sex. The male penetrates the
female, the female swallows the male. And in case we have any
feminists here today I'd better point out that these views are
completely interchangeable and we at BREAKTHRU don't value
one any more than the other. What I want you to do is to pair
off with the person next to you and talk. Talk about whatever you
like – lifestories, what you saw on the cable last night, anything. But
mentally I want you to keep on thinking about this action: in out
in out in out. It'll continue on the screen, or you can use your own
hands if you like. And just in case we have any exhibitionists, I mean
this gesture only. I don't want anyone to start giving themselves a
quiet rub. We're not talking about pleasure today. We'll take care
of pleasure another time.'

Aha, thought Sandy. So this is the famous no-risk orgy. God-
dammit, I might have known.

Twenty pounds was a lot of money. She wondered if the organisation would really refund her bus fare, there was probably a catch
in that too. But she turned cheerfully enough to her left-hand
neighbour, a plump Asian girl, poked her finger in and out and
chatted. There were several subjects who refused to cooperate,

43

complained of the gross stupidity of the exercise or wanted to know why. They got what they were asking for: personal attention from the seminar leader. Sandy decided they were probably the ones who would join up.

She was alarmed to discover, about half-way through the third presentation (there was no lunch break), that she had become the only girl in class who had not in some way demanded to have her ego massaged.

'Isn't there anything you want to ask, Sandy?'

'Well, yes there is. D'you get anything to eat in with the twenty sovs?'

The leader, a middle aged man this time, grinned broadly. 'No, Sandy. I'm afraid you don't.'

General laughter. But on her screen his grin was complicit and inviting. Sandy alone had grasped the ko'an, passed the test.

Very sexy. Terminal! as Candide would say.

There was a catch. You had to sign away a portion of your next year's income there and then if you wanted your expenses back: which counted Sandy out. As she turned away from the desk in the foyer digesting this unwelcome information, Sandy was accosted by a voice she recognised.

'Is that Sandy Brize? My, my: does Otto know about this? Or have you two broken up by now?'

Xav was dressed in street clothes. His complexion was enhanced/protected by a slick of skin-sealed make-up, he was wearing besides an insufferably self-important smirk.

'I didn't know you'd be here,' she said crossly. 'I thought you'd be in conference in Tokyo or something.' She glanced, cuttingly, around the dingy entrance. 'Is this all there is of BREAKTHRU, then?'

Xav took no notice. 'Well, did you get the idea?'

She thought about it. 'Funnily enough, I think I did.'

Francis Xavier grinned, just like the man on the stage. 'So come back when you've got something to offer, such as money. We'll hold your place.'

She told Otto all about it. She had to because of the twenty pounds. Otto was confused, alarmed: there was no room for expensive whims in her life, in the life they shared. Examination followed. The deliberate senselessness of that no-risk orgy, the reductive process which, you saw at once, could be applied to any cosmic concept... Sandy had wanted to understand what BREAKTHRU was about.

'And now you do.' Relieved, Otto closed the subject. Perhaps that was the moment, one of the moments, when the end began.

△

That year Sandy was on the public tip. She wandered through the graveyard with her collecting pouch and tools, examining small computers, washing machines, microwaves, vtrs, disc players. When she found an undamaged control unit she took it apart and rescued a still functional chip or some other tasty giblet on her see-and-know chart. It was the kind of glancing contact with the twenty-first century she could expect: like the sensors in the sleeves of her overalls, which detected metal coins or the metal strip in a note and dissuaded her from 'begging'. Candide came to join her after school for old times' sake, to keep company and chat – but warily. You never knew now whether she would turn and bite.

Sometimes I hunt for haddocks' eyes, among the heather bright.

'Could you mend one and make it work again?'

Candide deeply envied the tools and took Sandy's rote learned speed for technical skill.

'Not I, mancub. Otto might, but you know what she'd say if we took anything home. Thou shalt not steal from the state.'

'But it's not *our* state.'

'Ah, but we have to act as though it is. That's magic.'

Over scoured acres of the downs rooks and seagulls screamed reproachfully. Land taken out of wheat production grew scrub grass and dockleaves while it waited for new housing development. Away, far away beyond the eastern horizon there was the Chunnel which had ended thirty thousand years or so of splendid isolation, but neither Candide nor Sandy had ever been to France. They sat on a heap of mouldy soft furniture and pored over a tattered handout about timeshares in a space habitat resort...which were going to be ready for occupation in just a year or two. 'If it was an EU habitat you could go, Sand.' Sandy wasn't able to apply for a passport for the simple and just reason that officially she had no money to pay for it and if she ever did have any money, she owed it to UK Ltd, debt collectors.

'Waster time in my opinion, Cand. It doesn't cost you half a million pounds a minute to get inside a shopping mall: and they have potted palms and dioramas and glass lifts'n all that just the same.'

The orange overalled Force personnel did not have the tip to themselves. Men in battered cars and small trucks came and picked over the pickings, and took the best away. The Force was supposed to stop this but of course they could do nothing. Candide was outraged. The men must be poor or they wouldn't be picking rubbish, but he knew they were not his kind. They clearly despised the government workers. Candide caught looks that made him feel dirty and helpless, for Sandy's sake.

'Why don't you do something?' he demanded. 'This is your patch. The Benefit office sent you here.'

Sandy laughed. 'Property is theft, mancub. Didn't your mama ever tell you?'

'Don't call me that. I hate it.'

'Say what you are. And I, Bagheera the panther, I foretell: one day you will leave us jungle folk...'

'Oh, get lost.' Candide stormed away, stamping over piled corpses to an eyrie of hedgecuttings and rotting blankets. He glared at the jackals, bruised to his soul by Sandy's accusation.

'I'm *not*. I won't. I'm *not* one.'

Sandy could see that he was crying. She didn't even care. She had always teased him over those old story books which were so alien to her own memories of childhood: but there had used to be affection in it. Wind In The Willows, Swallows and Amazons, The Elephant's Child, Mowgli... He'd got it all from James when he was very young. Otto claimed to despise those insanitary sweeties (racist, sexist, elitist), but secretly she adored them. Sandy knew.

It was very, very mean to hit at Otto through the child. Through Candide, who was her friend in his own right. She could not stop herself. To rise above the smell of rubbish and the promise of fifty years more of days like this, she had to give up a good deal. The person who had loved Otter and Cand was breaking up. Sandy was losing substance, becoming a thin scum over depths she no longer dared to visit.

After that day in August, the day of the anti-war meeting, Sandy stopped working. Otto still tried not to see. She persuaded her lover to make an appointment at the office and talk to her supervisor. The room was small and bare. 'Tell me, Miss Brize. What exactly are you complaining about?'

'Well, everything really.'

'Could you be more specific?'

A long pause.

'No.'

He was trying to raise her file on his terminal. Failing, he turned to a pile of dirty papers wrapped in a card folder, ten years of accumulated rubbish. Sandy watched the man's hands. She wished him ill. In a sensual, luxurious rush she wished him all the evil his life could hold. The sense of wrongdoing was so real and the pleasure was so intense that she knew for certain there was nothing – in her mind - between this and actual murder. She carried on. *I don't care if I do.*

The man looked up. For a moment she saw his bewildered panic. It was gone.

'There's no compulsion you know.'

'Yes there is. I'm in debt. I can't get a job, any kind of job except on The Force. D'you want me to go on the game? That'd be illegal wouldn't it, without a health cert. And I can't buy one.'

'Well, I can't help that. Do you want to be taken off the Benefit Related Workforce?'

'No, I need money. I mean – yes.'

It was her period. She had stopped using tampons years ago, they were too expensive. She felt the thick dirty seeping and knew she'd forgotten to replace the wad of paper waste in her pants. Getting up to leave she looked round furtively. To her disappointment the grimy plastic chair was unmarked.

Outside, she raged against Otto. She hated Otto as much as the supervisor, if not more. She pictured herself a beggar in front of Brighton station: not with fear but with longing for something forbidden. Oh, let me be down and out. Oh, let me go. She wanted to cry. But instead of tears came a strange sensation of displacement. All the passers-by seemed to turn to her as they walked. A myriad viewpoints: the wall of the Benefit Office, shop windows, worn out mossy grass in the churchyard across the road.

She found herself walking very fast down the hill. Blood was trickling on her thighs. She looked into the eyes of a boy coming towards her, and saw acknowledgement. But perhaps that was imagined. The multiple vision had faded and no one else seemed ready to admit anything had happened. Sandy pressed the heels of her hands to her eyes. *I don't want to go mad.*

47

Otto reorganised their finances and discovered how things could be managed. She tried hard to involve Sandy in this absorbing game of snip a little cut a little: longing inexpressibly for those hours of talking through sleepless nights, years ago when their love was new. Sandy said: don't worry. Non-persons don't get hungry. She said: It was your manifesto, Otto. I was only a fellow traveller. Surely that was always obvious.

Sandy started to spend all her time alone in the room called the study. It was the place where they kept old magazines and journals which might have some value as ephemera one day: popular science, politics, UFO sightings, Occult News, Organic Farming. The air that came in through the window rose from a minute yard where a honeysuckle vine struggled up one wall. It smelled of grit and cold in winter, traffic fumes and honey as the year wore on. Sandy read: *most things that can happen, have happened. The general view has been that all things, or an extraordinary number of things, are possible. This is not the case...* The article was about evolution. It sounded like her life. She thought of the golden angels working the crowds, preaching their mad contradictory creed. Embrace Anomie. Turn on to hopelessness.

It is not that I understand BREAKTHRU, Otto. The point is, it seems to understand me. Which is strange because BREAKTHRU appears to be a very ordinary sort of hustle, whereas I am getting very, very weird. I am decaying, I am dying, I am nearly all gone now.

2

Windhover

At the beginning of October, Bernie Howard and his foster son went to pay a last visit to Francis Xavier in prison. He was getting out in a day or two but he would be met by BREAKTHRU, he wanted no one else. His parents were hurt. They had never had a child in prison before. They wanted to put their arms round him, take him home and give him his favourite things to eat. A triumph, in this case, of instinct over experience. James stayed in the car park. He had come to provide moral support to Bernie, not to Xav.

Afterwards Bernie didn't want to talk. They drove away in the big ageing Volvo. A mile or two from the prison Bernie pulled up in a layby. The sky was hazy and warm and grey, the grass verge a tired dark green of autumn, littered with rubbish. Bernie wept into a cotton handkerchief. He never used a paper tissue. He had dozens of these archaic cotton squares, which he laundered himself. At length he blew his nose and wiped his eyes. He sat hunched with his elbows on his knees. His face, through the tears, retained the curiously childlike dignity of good old age.

Bernie was seventy-eight. He had been godfather to James's father long ago, great friend of James's grandfather. That youth and boyhood serving the British Empire in Yorubaland must seem incredibly distant.

'Xav was up to his usual form, I see.'

Bernie stuffed the handkerchief away and attempted, loyally, to make the best of things. 'He's a bit depressed, of course. Tries to hide it – good job you didn't come in, James. You might have upset him. I must say, I'm glad he didn't go into one of those private places. They can be very callous, no privacy at all. I wish Margot could have come.'

James was glad she hadn't.

'How's the Parkies?'

'It's tolerable. She's sleeping better on this new drug.'

Margot's disease had been diagnosed PTP, a kind of allergy. It was comforting in a way to know that a fetal graft wouldn't have helped, even if she could have accepted it on moral grounds.

'And how's life generally?'

'Oh, terribly busy. Since your grandmother died, you know, this Natural Death business has really snowballed. We hardly have time to run the restaurant. Did I tell you we've taken on the hospital monitoring network? Spreading the gospel, you know.' Bernie nodded cheerfully. 'The thing is you have to convince people technology isn't *bad*. Not everybody wants to die out of doors, or by running water. And after being with your granny, I wouldn't advise anyone to refuse drugs. She was *greatly* helped - '

'Umnh.'

Just a few more years, he thought. It was up to him, the twins were right out. He would not shirk his domestic responsibilities. He would settle down, as it were, and look after the children until they didn't need him any more.

Bernie's cheerfulness faded as his thought turned again to his son.

'They think a lot of him in the company, you know. This time last year, and this was when they already knew he was going to prison, the managing director took Margot and me out to lunch with Xav. Man in charge of the whole deal, no less. Terrible food, one of those hotel chain places on the Park – but that's by the way. Your son's a plumber, he said to me. Gets things done. No one else to touch him.'

That sinister term, repeated in innocence, made James pause a little. What did Mr Fixit fix? Better not to know.

'Gerry's back with them, you know. She's gone off to Birmingham on a refresher course.'

James started. 'Oh, has she? I wondered what had happened.'

Bernie pondered, chewing his lower lip. 'I've satisfied myself it isn't any kind of "phony" religion. Not that there can be such a thing, by the way. If there's anything of love, anything of grace in these silly cults, it goes to God and comes from God we can be sure of that...But I must admit I've yet to work out what BREAKTHRU actually *does* ...'

He glanced at James, and had difficulty for a moment. Eyes on the road, he seemed to retreat from some disclosure, some expression of new concern. Xav had made a coward of his father in the end.

By the roadside, above a stake and wire fence, a kestrel had appeared, pumping the air with its wings, its small head bowed intently between.

'James, would you mind saying the Windhover poem for me? You know the one.'

James saw the pain and understood the cowardice. He was ready to give whatever consolation he could provide.

'*I caught –* ' he began obediently, '*this morning morning's minion, Kingdom of Daylight's dauphin…*'

Bernie leaned back and closed his eyes, lost in the beauty of the boy's voice. He never went to the theatre or a cinema. He thought Ralph Churchill was marvellous, was not aware that James was a failure, immorally touting shoddy goods to the poor. At the end he sighed deeply.

'You know, that poem always means you to me James. Kingdom of daylight's dauphin…Don't groan like that. I'm your father not your boyfriend. I can say what I like.'

The little falcon tipped its wings and plunged, out of sight into the grass.

'Did you know,' said James. 'The kestrel used to be called the fucker bird, because of the way it bounces up and down on the spot like that. That's what the saxon word means, that motion.'

Bernard laughed heartily. They drove on back to Standards, where James would eat Xav's fatted calf for him. He was wary of this transparent substitution and only allowed it rarely. He knew Xav would find out somehow, and then there would be trouble.

3

A Night Visitor

Otto kept telling herself that things were getting back to normal. But the sudden dread of that moment outside the police caravan had turned into a pervasive undercurrent of panic which never left her in peace. Mysteriously, her enemies seemed to know all about it. They gathered hungrily around, able to break through her armour at last and prove to her the futility of resistance.

It was October, the weather was still very warm, the sky milky and dull with trapped heat. A party of street livers had been camping in the butterfly wilderness of Japanese knotweed and rampant buddleia that covered a derelict lot opposite Wombega. Candide and his friends played with the filthy skeletal kids and reported, scandalised and impressed: They shit in the bushes and they don't even bury it. Even the grown ups. When the dumper truck arrived guarded by police Candide naturally came for his mother, confident of her protective power.

'Their things are in the road! Their bedclothes!'

Otto went out, as she must. But she had no energy, she could not reach the sullen bailiffs. The police said 'Come on Mrs Murray, have sense. You don't want your little lad getting epidemic diarrhoea.'

She did not.

'You mean cholera,' she said coldly, and walked away.

The children of utopia stared at her retreat, defeat, in stunned amazement.

Mary Kathleen Collins came into the shop. Otto had not seen her for a while. She cringed behind the till, afraid of sympathy. She was sure that her friends were gossiping, had 'seen this coming'. Mary Kathleen, rock singer and composer, was the epitome of cool just the way Otto used to be: though if you were cool you called cool sexy now. She dressed in rags the colour of dust and ashes, wore a long spooklock over her left ear; A for Anarchy stencilled on the back of her stubbled head. Mary wasn't wearing her customary ghostdance paint. On her milky Irish skin, the freckles stood out angrily.

'O God, he's gone. Danny's gone.'

She burst into noisy laughter.

'He's gone to fight the infidel, Otto. He's after writing himself in with Don John of Austria and Jan Sobieski at the gates of Vienna. He's off to help the Russians holding back the hordes of Mohammet.'

'Mary, what are you talking about?'

'I was as near him as I am to you. That Englishwoman he lives with set it up. May the Heavenly Mother forgive her, I won't. I found out what she'd done, I went after and pleaded with him. I said Christ won't you talk to Otto first. I said violence is no solution. Begod you wouldn't have been a provo and what's the difference? He unpicked my fingers from him. And these two louts in union jack shirts holding me by the arms. They said scream if you like. But I couldn't. He's gone. He's off on the underground. I can't find him.'

That damned war, it was so alluring. Danny Collins wasn't the first loss. The young men of utopia were desperate to get over there to the steppes or down into Africa, and have the fun of shooting and killing in a good cause...No one in the shop was taking any notice. After her first outburst, Mary's story came out in a savage undertone. Only Otto could see the tears on her face. Otto leaned over her desk, speaking low. She couldn't afford to have this sort of stuff discussed openly on her premises: still she tried to summon her strength, flogging the tired horse.

'When was this? We'll find him. He can't be out of the country yet.'

Mary Kathleen shook her head. 'No.' She rubbed her arms, bare and cold: the unseasonable heat had just broken. 'No, it's no use Otto. That's not why I came. I came to say I'm taking JackJohn home. I can't bear to lose the both of them and the band's finished without Danny. We'll go back to granna's farm, she needs the help. Look, I'll be around in a day or two when we've fixed the date. Ye can give us a big send off. The Collins Family wake.'

Shaking her head, she backed away.

'I'm sorry, Otto. I'm sorry – '

She was gone. Otto was left staring at the door of the shop. There goes my rightful heir, she thought selfishly, abdicating before I'm even dead. She was too weary for anybody's grief but her own.

It was unlucky that the next customer should be wearing a complete veil. A cone of blackness interposed itself between the shopkeeper and her misery. Brilliantly skinsealed eyes looked out, one beringed hand escaped, proffering a volume of lesbian poetry. Otto went mad. She snatched the book, threw it down in a pile of lapel buttons.

'Get out of my shop!' she yelled. 'You whore, you stupid bitch!'

'Bitch yourself!' exclaimed the woman in the chador, astonished.

'Get out - '

'I want to buy that book.'

'It's not for sale.'

Otto rushed around the counter, bent on murder.

'Just because I don't choose to expose myself – '

'Get out, get out, you *damned* fool - '

Stumbling, still defending itself indignantly, the veil beat a retreat. Otto slammed the door behind, and then the fit left her. Three other customers, two men and a bare-headed woman, raised a ragged cheer from around the stacks. Otto looked at them with hatred. She felt sick.

It was very late. Otto and Sandy had been drinking wine and smoking a lot of grass. They were making love, for the first time in months. Otto was trying desperately hard. She was pinned as if by fever between the mattress and Sandy's flesh, her body starved and greedy for pleasure. But it wasn't good enough. She couldn't seem to make contact. Sandy bent over her white as a ghost, limbs without angles. She worked her fingers between Otto's thighs as she rode to and fro, rocking herself hard and steadily. Her eyes were open, thoughtfully fixed on the middle distance. *I love you*, cried Otto silently. *I love you so much..!*

'Sand - '

'Mmm?'

'Can we - ?'

'Shut...up...'

Otto pulled herself free, reclaimed her dildo hand. Sandy dropped onto the sheet.

'Fuck it,' she grumbled. 'I wanted to come. Couldn't you even let me come.'

She spread her fingers, admiring the whitish goo that pulled out into elastic threads between them. 'Look. Just like that android lubricant. You know, the stuff that always spills out of them in old sf films.'

Otto sat up. She pushed her hair out of her eyes, feeling the weight of the dreadlocks. *Must cut them off. I'm far too old. I look ridiculous.* She was trembling.

'Sandy, look, there's something wrong – '

The white thing laughed. 'Well, you've changed your tune. I thought you didn't want to know.'

Otto panicked. 'I mean just now - ' she cried. 'It seemed so mechanical. I mean, if you don't feel like sex we don't have to pretend.'

'Who's pretending? Not me. What you get is what there is.'

Someone knocked on the door. He was absolutely forbidden to come in here uninvited so the door waited patiently while Otto put her dressing gown on.

'There's someone in my room.'

Sandy was sitting up in bed with the quilt tucked under her arms. Her memory worked more quickly than Otto's.

'Ah, Cand, not that one again.'

Back in August, Candide had persisted in his new game until he'd tried his experiment on all of them: Otto, Peggy, Vixen. Then he'd seemed satisfied, and that was the end of it.

'No, no you don't understand.' Candide was jumping from foot to foot in urgent anxiety. 'This is different.'

'You mean this time there *is* someone in your room?' suggested his friend cynically.

'No – yes. It's different...'

He looked frantic.

'I'll come and see,' soothed Otto.

Her head was spinning. She was aware that she had just been teetering on the brink of utter disaster. Candide's nightmare had saved her: she grasped at it eagerly.

There was nothing to see. Only the wallpaper peeling away from the hole in the wall, the bedclothes with their nauseating little flower pattern. Yet the child's hand gripped convulsively. Sandy appeared beside them. She had dressed in jeans and a teeshirt. She and Otto exchanged a neutral, parenting look: but wasn't there something a little overbright and strange in Sandy's attention?

'Candide love, there's no one here.'

'Look!' he whispered fiercely. 'In the bed - '

'Good God.'

Across the bottom of Candide's bed, I-don't-remember-eating-that was raised in a long hummock. A foot dangled. The sole was calloused and dirty, the upper part so white it looked blue.

'I woke up,' breathed Candide. 'And I just put my toes down and felt her. She's not dead. She's warm.'

Something moved the quilt. Vera sneaked out from under her master's bed and crept to his feet, her ears pressed to her head.

Sandy brought Otto's big black and white border plaid from their room. They wrapped the body and carried it downstairs. Although a dead weight, the burden was pitifully slight. She was a young white woman, brown haired, a complete stranger. She was quite naked, wore no jewellery; was slender to emaciation. Her closed eyelids, pale around the lashes, lay in pits of bruised shadow. Otto looked for needle marks but found none. The stranger did not wake or stir as they arranged her on the chesterfield. Her breathing was lax and faint. Without a word Sandy left the room. She came back a few minutes later shaking her head.

'Not a sign. Vixen's okay. I wonder what happened to her clothes.'

'What?'

'They're not in Candide's room.'

Candide was standing away from the couch, twisting a corner of his trackie top. 'Something's gone wrong,' he explained. 'I thought they were real ones, like in religion. James used to have one, you know. I thought it would be good for us... But something's gone wrong.'

Vera whimpered. He picked her up, hugged her square bulk awkwardly, her legs splayed on his chest.

'Like in religion?' repeated Otto bemusedly.

Candide had hidden his face in Vera's neck. He didn't answer. The whole room felt dazed. It was blurred with grass and wine, the walls shimmered. What do you do with a naked dead body that materialises out of thin air? But at least the body wasn't dead.

'I'm going to call a doctor.'

'Why?'

Otto stared. 'Because she's sick. That sleep is not natural. What d'you think I should do, call the police?'

Sandy left the room again. She came back while Otto was waiting for Dr Mendis to answer, carrying some clothes. She began to dress the limp body.

'Why are you doing that?' asked Candide.

'I feel sorry for her. Say horrible to be naked.'

Neemi Mendis had known Otto for a long time, but she did not live in utopia and viewed its inhabitants with suspicion. She arrived carefully made up and dressed in a severe ladylike suit, obviously calculating that this incident would end up in the police station. She took one look at the mystery and diagnosed briskly.

'One of your friend Zappo's performers, I suppose. You should throw that girlfriend of his out.'

When Otto had first taken her in, Peggy had been on the run from Vixen's father. She was sixteen at the time with a two-year-old child, and could barely write her name. She had improved immensely, though the idea of her working in the shop in lieu of rent had never worked out. But it had transpired that Zappo was going to be a recurrent hazard. Inevitably, classically, two years later he was still around. He ran girls. He was a small time dealer in vile, polluted street heroin and crack. In theory, he wasn't allowed inside Wombega. In practice, Otto had recently had another very serious talk with Peggy...

At this moment, however, she was glad of any rational explanation. She laughed in relief. 'How stupid! That's it of course. Zap must've sneaked her into the flat to sleep something off and she got up and wandered.'

Dr Mendis knelt by the breathing corpse, felt its pulse, turned down its eyes and began to slap the white face.

'I don't see anything amusing, Otto. With that shop downstairs, and doped-out whores in the attic – '

'He gives them LHR,' piped up Candide. 'A kind of enzyme. Say an aphrodisiac.'

'LHR? Where would he get that kind of money? This looks like plain old smack to me – '

'Candide,' snapped Otto. 'Get to bed - '

Peggy arrived home. She bounced into the room garrulously apologetic for being so late. Mendis took the opportunity to deliver a few precise home truths. Peggy howled.

'That piece of shit! That piece of fucking shit! He swore he'd never use your house again – '

'*Again* – ?

'She is drunk,' remarked Neemi, curling her supercilious Aryan lip.

'Who the fuck are you calling drunk – '

'*Get to bed, Candide* – '

Sandy stayed by the body ignoring them all, watching the sick face with rapt attention. Neemi's eyes rested on her, in intervals of Peggy's tirade, with covert interest.

After the fracas Neemi and Otto were alone in the kitchen drinking tea. Neemi had refused to do anything. She didn't know what drugs were involved, it would be too risky. She wanted Otto to call the police. Or failing that put the girl in a taxi and despatch her to the nearest public casualty department. But no hospital would take her in with no money and no Benefit card either, so that was impossible.

'Will she die?'

'I expect not. She will simply wake up with a hangover, steal anything she can see and leave. Of course, she could vomit and choke on it. But she is not so deeply unconscious. It is more a trance than a coma.'

'She can stay here.'

Neemi sighed. 'Otto you are living in a dream world. You had better wake up before something really serious happens.'

Ever since Otto had known her, Neemi Mendis had been claiming that as soon as the troubles were over she would go back to Lanka, and have her family pick her out a wealthy husband. Why else does a woman collect qualifications?

Otto's vision was confused. Without her contact lenses the world looked very strange, half dissolved, like an oil painting blurred in close up: you could see the brush strokes. On the kitchen table lay a sheaf of letters, an invitation to her sister Betty's wedding engraved on creamy unrecycled card. It had been a bad day, the post not even sorted. She was filled with a sense of dread. Neemi's words suddenly made perfect sense. *She was dreaming.* That was what this meant, the body appearing out of the air. And the way Sandy had turned into a frightening stranger when they were making love. In the clairvoyance of her dream she knew why Neemi had been looking at Sand so oddly and why Sand pretended not to know the doctor was there.

A Night Visitor

Heartless Mendis, breaker up of happy homes. She used to be famous for it in the days when there was a scene. Now no more: what consenting adults do in private isn't against the law but that is where they have to do it, show it, be it. The arrangement suited some people so much better than freedom. Mendis sneaking up the backstairs, big-eyed alley cat.

'You've slept with her haven't you – ' she demanded abruptly.

Neemi raised her eyebrows. 'With whom?'

'Sandy.'

'Ah, I see. No Otto, I have not.' She paused. Her tone became more kindly. 'Is she also sleeping around then? I think you are right to be worried. Have her come to surgery if you can, and I'll try to help.' She raised her hand. 'No, don't bother to say you can't afford it Otto. We are still friends, I hope.'

The next morning Otto woke convinced the whole incident had been a nightmare. It might as well have been, for the visitor was gone. Nothing had been stolen except Sandy's clothes: the clothes the girl must have been wearing never turned up. Zappo denied everything but nobody believed him. Even when she knew it hadn't been a dream the sense of nightmare persisted, colouring Otto's day as she tried to think of how to approach Sandy and tell her: You're sick. Everybody sees it. You have to get help.

She went out to a meeting in town the next evening, and when she came back Sandy had gone.

A strange spook appeared the morning after to collect some of her things. It reported (it was of indeterminate gender) that Sandy would not be coming back. For the present she'd decided that she didn't want to see Otto. 'She wants to make a clean break,' said the spook. 'It will be better for both of you.'

Candide was waiting. The first time he'd seen the angel, he had refused to tell Sandy what it looked like for a very good reason. They both knew he'd seen BREAKTHRU reps at the anti-war meeting that same afternoon. His story would be discredited at once, according to adult reasoning. The angels, there were several of them taking turns, had told him no one else would be able to see and invited him to prove it: which he did. They couldn't be touched either. He had tried it, you felt wall. He was not afraid. Years ago, he had heard about guardian angels from James. There had been a

59

time when everyone was supposed to have one, or at least everyone who believed in religion like James. Candide was not a believer but he kept an open mind.

He didn't take the angel watch very seriously. He became used to it, as you might get used to a family ghost if such creatures existed. But then things went wrong. An angel decayed into human dimensions, like a computer graphic projection collapsing, and it was not replaced. To his surprise Candide found he was quite worried. The angels had never told him what they were guarding him against.

He didn't imagine Sandy's departure was the answer. He'd been expecting that for a long time. Besides, he reasoned, people often split up. They usually made friends again after a while, even if they didn't live together any more.

Candide lay awake in the warm autumn night. He heard his mother prowling downstairs. He heard her go into the study and shuffle things about as if she was looking for clues as to why Sandy had left. If he stayed awake long enough he would hear her go back to her own room, and then she would start crying. He shrugged his shoulders up against the pillow. There was nothing he could do. He wasn't the one she wanted. He turned over and reached out for Vera. 'You take first watch,' he mumbled sleepily.

She wasn't there.

He sat up, switched on his bedside light.

'Vera?'

Not yet anxious, he suddenly remembered he hadn't seen her since he came to bed. He got up, and padded all over the house. Gently, he opened the door of the flat and whistled into Peggy's hall. No rattle of claws, no cheerful yip! yip! With something tightening in his stomach, he tried to remember when he had last seen his dog.

Otto came down and caught him struggling with the bolts on the back door.

'What d'you think you're doing?'

'I can't find Vera. She must be outside!'

'Don't be stupid. If she's locked out she can stay out till morning.'

It was no use trying to argue with her in this mood. He lay awake for hours instead, imagining that he could hear a pathetic whimpering from the street and hating his mother.

But in the morning Vera wasn't there. She wasn't there when he came home from school either. He searched the streets and still there was no sign, not even a pitiful little crushed body chucked by the kerb. Vera would not wander. Someone had taken her.

Candide cried himself to sleep. There was no one he could turn to. Sandy was gone and Otto didn't care. Now he understood what the loss of the angel meant. It was so terrible he could hardly believe it was true. But something warned him, some lover's instinct, that there was worse to come.

4

Some Gentlemen Are
Not Ladies

Otto was late for her sister's wedding. She blundered into the little grey church, confused by doors and curtains. The Murrays were Presbyterian by ethnic origin, nothing in practice. She wondered why the faithful allowed this sort of charade on their premises. But probably nothing was ever worshipped here except the status quo, and Betty certainly believed in that. A pink faced man in black discovered her. He had a pink rosebud in his lapel. 'Friend of the bride or the groom?' 'Neither' snapped Otto before she could stop herself. George Washington's disease. He smirked. 'You must be Jane.'

He ushered her efficiently, the heel of his masculine palm securely connecting with the small of her back. For all her adult life Otto had not had to tolerate such gestures. But she was in cannibal country now.

She could see why he had smirked. It wasn't just her manners, her clothes branded her. This was the good suit: black and white houndstooth, shawl collared, narrow in the leg. It looked very fine in Brighton. Suddenly it was old, shabby, and she was the only woman wearing men's clothes. Otto had not meant to pose. She was supposed to be securely disguised as a respectable business woman. Morale plunged. Why had she come? Candide had refused to leave Brighton because of that damned dog. She had had to leave Peggy looking after both children on her own, which wasn't fair.

Betty wore rose pink in multitudinous pleats to the floor. She turned round when Otto came in to see what the noise was: and glared savagely.

The wedding service was appalling. Near the end of it, Otto noticed James Esumare and Francis Xavier in one of the benches

62

in front of her. O God, she thought. I can't bear it, a whole college reunion. Which was perverse of her because she'd come looking for exactly that.

She travelled to the reception with her father and Raushan in one of the white ribboned Mercedes, the unmarried child. The Hon. Andrew Murray MP and his second wife, the tiny dainty Bengali wrapped in rustling silk like a lovely little birthday present. Her father's face looked shockingly familiar: the squashed roman nose and long thin mouth that he had passed on faithfully to all of them except Betty. Blue eyes that he had given to no one, but the shape of the eyes she knew well.

'How's things at the House?'

'Oh, not so bad.'

She was a disappointment to him. She could see it in those eyes every time they met, and he made the inevitable joking reference to her dissident activities. Not because she was a rebel, oh, precisely not, but because she was such a passive, womanly rebel. He'd have thought a daughter of his would have more fire in her belly...Today she hated him for that disappointment. Did he want her to salvage his lost youth, lost ideals, lost integrity? Well, that's impossible *Daddy*. Office or clean hands is the choice and you took it, Mr Westminster Socialist.

'Sandy's not coming? Looking after Candide I suppose?'

'No. Why would Sandy want to come to a ghastly thing like this.'

No one was to know the truth.

'I see Xav Howard's chaperoning James still.'

'Oh *him*.' Otto sneered. 'I hardly recognised him without his angel suit.'

'James isn't part of this "BREAKTHRU" business by any chance?'

'Of course not, Daddy.' She laughed. 'What a joke, a millenarian religion still hanging on. The end of the world's a bit late, isn't it. You'd think people would be asking for their money back.'

Andrew Murray glanced at her.

'I'm surprised at you Otto. BREAKTHRU isn't a religion, it is a political organisation.' He smiled slyly. 'I'd have thought you'd've spotted them – after all, you're doing exactly the same thing yourself.'

'Oh,' said Otto.

She hated him.

'Well, I wonder what kind of politics that would be. Would it be just a tiny bit to the right of P.W.Botha? I suppose Betty invited him so she and the groom can join up. Hey, maybe I've struck lucky and we'll get one of those no-risk orgies - '

Raushan sighed. 'Otto, you know I don't like to interfere in my adopted family. But please don't make scenes today. Nobody is attacking you.'

The chauffeur could hear nothing through his security glass. His eyes in the mirror found time to assess Otto and dismiss her. Funny looking, ugly, practically middle aged.

The ballroom of the hotel had blue green walls, spindly gilt furniture and big white windows, outside which lawns swept down to a little loch. She remembered it well, the time-honoured venue for middle class festivities: the last time she'd been here was for Richard's wedding. The crowd displayed an awesome complacency. You would never guess from the looks of these people that they had lost in the last twenty years most of the personal freedoms secured for them by blood, sweat and tears through the previous nine hundred. It would take an expert in female fashion even to put a date on the gathering, the palimpsest of successful conservatism was so closely written. It could be any year of the bourgeois in the last half century.

Betty saw her sister and dived out of her stately progress to the high table. At twenty-eight, the beauty of a female executive is scarcely impaired, if at all. Yet she begins to be a little concerned. Married women have so much more freedom. They are less threatening, they can make better deals.

'Why did you have to come dressed like that?' hissed the rose pink vision.

'You invited me.'

'I wish I hadn't. Thanks for the *insult* by the way. I can't seriously call it a present. I'll put it with all the CTD propaganda. And *stop* that. Adrian and I don't want to be on your crummy mailing list. Making us look like freaks - '

Well, stuff you little sister.

The men and women separated quite naturally, the children staying with the womenfolk. The Murrays as naturally defied convention and Otto found herself standing by one of the damasked tables with her brothers eating wedding food, while the two wives sat at it with their children. Little Duncan, plump Mr Toad in a

64

silver grey-waistcoat, foraged for the three of them. The wine was muck – these teetotallers always get robbed - but he knew where there was a barrel of Robinsons. Duncan was born to his role: squat and compact and cheerful. He still had to look up at his big sister. He patted Otto kindly.

'Don't you worry about old Moley, Otter. All she ever thinks about these days is nylons and boyfriends.'

'We call it going bad inside,' intoned Richard. 'I like your haircut. It makes you look a lot younger.'

Otto couldn't remember the wives' names. She couldn't take her eyes off their dresses. And their shoes. Otto used to think shoes like that were going to wither away like the state.

James arrived, with Francis Xavier beside him. James was looking hunted. Francis Xavier was wearing a sugar candy striped tiger suit, with his hair newly stubbled and stencilled and only missing the spooklock. He appeared unhumbled by his stay in Ford. Otto saw that Xav was grinning broadly, his face alight with pleasurable malice -

'Otto, you look gorgeous - '

She found herself embraced, held off at arm's length, squeezed again.

'I love you in that suit. I love that louche bull dyke look. And the body odour. And the bit of tomato soup you forgot to wipe off a few years ago.'

His voice was always incongrously pleasant, soft and husky. She hadn't seen him for three years. She couldn't imagine what she'd done to deserve this... Keeping hold of her shoulder with one hand he thrust the other between her thighs: a gesture of such insolence Otto was too stunned to save herself.

He sucked his finger.

'At least, I *think* it's tomato soup – '

The wives giggled.

'Hit 'im Otter. Hit 'im,' crowed Duncan.

It must be instinctive, like a shark homing in on the smell of blood. How did Francis Xavier ever crawl into my life? By supplying drugs. By wearing clothes and listening to music in a way that fooled me when I was young. There was no adequate reaction except that suggested by Duncan so she made none: stood there fuming with her elbows pressed to her sides. She tried to glare at James...*if you're his keeper, take him away*... but after one helpless glance he wouldn't meet her eyes.

Xav was instantly at home. He sat down with the wives and soon had everybody relaxed and chatting. He took Duncan's little girl between his knees and held her captive, tickling and squeezing. The way he touched the child made Otto feel ill, but no one else seemed to see anything wrong. The filthy little worm.

Xav turned to her, and smiled sweetly.

'Say très weird to see perverts at a wedding,' he remarked, over the child's head. 'Look how quiet they've gone. They must feel so left out. Of course, old body odour's got nowhere to put her imaginary prick at the moment. And our James – what's that James, mimosa?'

'No.'

'James is having trouble with his lovely big black plonker. Pity they can't swap, really.'

He does know about Sandy, she thought. The bastard, how did he find out?

James laughed. 'Francis, Francis, you really ought to to be in television.'

'Like you, James?'

The speeches and the toasts were over. The bride and groom began to circulate and the frocks and suits and silk cravats began to rush away from Otto. She remembered what her father had said in the car: an instantly convincing shift in perspective. She must now see that filthy little worm as her rival. Her successful rival, because there he was accepted and cosy between Ratty's wife and Toad's while Otto's revolution was nowhere. Otto couldn't think of a word to say, to the people whose hearts and minds she had set out to win. Poor Jane Murray – just a pitiful freak. She got up from the table and fled.

She wandered in limbo. Her father discussing safety levels with a voter, 'We're getting there. I know and you know: the average housewife has to be convinced – ' A broad Cumbrian voice saying softly, elsewhere, 'What're ye doing with the non-viables now? Petfood?' 'Petfood, aye - '

An aunt in a flowered hat, grown suddenly old.

'Jane, how nice to see you. What a terrible long drive, you look exhausted.'

'I came by bus.'

Puzzled expression. 'Is that a convenient way to travel now?'

'Not particularly.'

A red-faced man, no longer young. The same age as herself.

'How's things Otter. Has your cadre claimed responsibility for blowing up Stonehenge yet?'

She bared her teeth. 'That was the CIA.'

Servants, the war, defitzitny, the extension of work-related benefits: a good thing for the yobs. Travel restrictions: one hardly notices, really. There are so few foreign places left that one would *want* to visit. A woman's voice archly protesting: '*but I can never understand why it's called the* Islamic *war. Aren't there Muslim countries on both sides?* Here was Betty pondering on the complete veil: 'Well, it is somehow dignified, isn't it - '

Conversation, that was all the world outside their cosy blinkered existence meant to them. Useful snippets to fill in the spaces between the eating and the dancing...She found a deserted sofa by the windows and cowered there. The ballroom was full of ghosts. There was Gerry Howard surely, in a white dress with stiff petticoats, a shining floss of red hair across her shoulders. Gerry the amoral waif, every man's dream woman, cutting up powder on the hotel's decent white napery. The girl turned round, a young unknown. If she still wore it natural Gerry's hair was probably weasel coloured now like Xav's. What a pity.

A nicely dressed woman came briskly through the throng: tall, with greying temples and deep-set bright brown eyes. Otto knew that questing look. The woman wanted a child, a daughter preferably. Her children were so badly behaved at social functions, always getting into a clique and ignoring everyone...Otto stood up. She could see, through the shadow, James and Francis Xavier. If she had been drinking enough for maudlin hallucinations she was in no condition to face Xav again. She slipped quickly and quietly out into the garden.

It was nearly dark. The pewter-coloured water lip-lapped on fine gravel. She found a little beach sheltered by a thornbush that was still in full leaf. *I want my mother,* Otto cried. She had left Candide in Brighton crying too. She'd done everything common sense allowed to find the dog, but you had to give up eventually. He was inconsolable, irrational: it was frightening. 'Look Cand,' she said, trying to reason with him. 'It's only an animal. It isn't right to grieve like this.' He was lying on his bed, he spent most of his time there when he wasn't out searching. He raised a tear-stained face, eyes glinting spitefully under swollen lids. 'Sandy's only a woman,' he choked. 'You're not supposed to love her. But you do.' Otto had to walk out of the room or she would have half killed him.

The sound of his thin little voice out in the streeet night after night, shouting Ve-ra, Ve-ra, Ve-ra. It was more than she could bear.

Xav said: 'Otto's looking a bit wobbly. Should we follow her? She might fall in the water.'

'She can swim.'

James watched his brother warily. He did not understand what was going on today. Until the moment Xav pounced on Otto he'd believed it was his own idea to come to the Murray wedding.

'Francis, this headlong pursuit is becoming unladylike. Tell me, do you usually find the technique successful? It seems a little rough cut.'

'I'll have her if I like. She is dying for it. I can always tell.'

'Why the sudden crush on Otto Murray anyway? You've never shown any interest before.'

James reflected that he was probably the only person in the world, besides Bernie and Margot, who knew Francis any more. Knew, for instance, that he was feeling sore and defiant on this first public appearence out of prison: and that the crude masculine argot was his way of covering up an abiding sense of sexual inadequacy. Perhaps the only person altogether because parents hardly counted as independent witnesses. He was not, however, liable to let ancient memories get in the way of caution. Xav liked to hurt people, that was all you really needed to remember. Forgive thy brother? James was always willing to try, in theory at any rate.

But only a fool forgets.

The little matter outstanding between them had not been mentioned. James was too cowardly to raise the subject: he was resigned to wait in silence until vengeance fell.

The old-fashioned yellow light from a ballroom chandelier glinted on Xav's stubby red gold lashes. The contracted pupils of his clear hazel eyes looked very black. He gazed up into James's face, as if he enjoyed reading the implacable dismissal there.

'This is one of my trials of the yes,' he said. 'Have you ever wondered, James, where our creed comes from? You probably think it sounds stupid and obvious, which it is meant to, but it is also very subtle. We take our inspiration from the works of James

Joyce. Joyce wanted the last word of Ulysses to be the most positive in language: Yes. The last word of Finnegans is the most negative, the most empty: the. These are the two concepts which we'd like to see united. Have you ever read Finnegans Wake James?'

'No.'

'You keep saying no to everything. You do, you know. You should listen to yourself. BREAKTHRU members read Finnegans Wake all the time. Did you know it is all about child molesting?'

'I never knew that.'

'Haha. Now you're trying to avoid it. You're so suggestible James. He had a daughter who went mad, remember. Wanted to fuck Samuel Beckett, of all things. Died in a loony bin. Well, that's a sure sign: remember Freud. He was diddling her in her cot, obviously. It is all in the book. The Wake is a casebook schizo confession, all wrapped up in dog's vomit the way loonies do. He wants to tell, for the fun of it, but he doesn't mean to get caught. Llarge by the smal, alp on earwig. O mind you poo tickly. Sall I puhim in momou. Mummm. Funny spot to have a fingy... Child molesting, see. Incest. The Yes is all about incest: that's how we're going to bring about our break through.'

Beth and Adrian had departed for their Highland hideaway. The floor was cleared. Everybody danced the reels and squares, grandmothers with grandchildren, uncles with nieces, up and down and round and round, breaking and reforming in the vital ancient patterns. Otto stalked the margin, nursing her glass. She had been drinking steadily and her mood had changed from resentment to sentimentality.

It wasn't even true that she didn't know the wives. She had sat with June and Duncan through the long hours, terrible nights and days, when little Deborah was so ill with typhoid...

It was good to be at this wedding. She looked on the dancers' flushed faces and linked bodies – marrying and giving in marriage, births and deaths and seasons for ever and ever amen - like a rejected but still loving suitorr. She had forgotten for a while what pressure groups are for. You don't win, you don't hope to win - but it's all fastened together. If you can manage to keep the 'lunatic fringe' well over, the whole of the social formation is hauled with it. She might never effect change but she would always be there, a counterweight against society's worse impulses. A samurai, a

69

guardian spirit keeping bad at bay. It was a momentary weakness to expect thanks or even recognition. Oh, the bright faces, so heartbreakingly complacent.

The dance went on.

Otto stood transfixed, appalled by a sudden conviction that came from nowhere. The idle conversations of this afternoon crystallised into a truth that couldn't be seen from utopia. This is doomsday. The bad time is coming, horror is coming, nothing can save us. It is too late. They wouldn't listen, and there is no more time.

She stared around wildly to see where this psychic knife thrust had come from, and saw Xav staring back at her across the whirling crowd.

Her impulse was to hide. She backed away from the dance floor, and found a refuge between the tables of less energetic revellers. She was immediately unsure of what she'd seen: Xav Howard with a funny look in his eyes, nothing more.

'Come on Otto,' whispered a voice in her ear. 'You know you're dying for it.'

An arm went round her waist from behind. Her street-proofed reflexes failed her: this was hardly a dark alley. Xav was kissing her on the mouth. There was a scuffle. Otto hauled off, without too much difficulty, and straight-armed him from the shoulder, their relative heights being such that her fist connected soundly with the angle of his jaw. Xav went over backwards, into a table. Its occupiers jumped up shouting, spilled drink flew everywhere. Otto stood wiping her mouth with a tissue while Richard and Duncan and James rushed to the trouble spot. Xav was lying on the floor in the beer and orange juice and broken glass, cackling.

'Oh Lord, he's well gone.'

'He's not drunk,' said James. 'He never touches the stuff. He's just pissing around.'

But Xav was obviously paralytic. Richard and Duncan helped him away and put him to bed in a hotel room. Everyone was very glad Betty had missed this scene, it would have ruined her big day.

THIRD ANGEL

1

Oberon

The housekeeper had left out a cold supper for about twenty. But Betty's friends had dispersed, all the relatives had somehow melted away and Duncan and his family were staying at Richard's farm in the next valley. Otto's father and Raushan had gone straight to bed, or at any rate disappeared. Her father was angry with her about the fisticuffs on the dance floor.

Otto picked at a dish of salmon mousse en croute and called:

'D'you still drink vodka?'

'Yes.'

'Sorry, there isn't any.'

She took a bottle of brandy and two glasses back to the study: handed James his drink and went to close the curtains. They were still dark red heavy velvet, as they had always been.

To step inside this house was like falling into deep water. It smelled of beeswax polish and damp, the way it did on the first day back. The rugs lying in the hall were not the ones of thirty years ago but the contours of the grey flags were the same: shores and promontories, shallow whorled hollows, seas of the moon. She had known those outlines since before she could speak. She leaned her forehead against the cold dark glass. Throughout her youth and young adulthood Underhill had remained the desired Eden. What riotous houseparties they had held here, Otto and Sandy, James and Luci and the rest of the Murrays and the Howards: full of adult pleasures yet with nothing lost from The Wind in the Willows days, like visits to an orgiastic apotheosis of childhood. And now the Murrays senior lived in Highbury, and Underhill stood empty between holiday lets.

She came back to the fire. James was stretched out in one of the armchairs that faced each other across the hearth, chin on one hand, staring broodily into his brandy glass. The material of the suit he

71

was wearing was dull purple with a slight nap to it: it glowed beside his dark skin and the dark rich colours of the room.

'What are you thinking?'

He sighed. 'Oh, Ur-scenarios.'

Otto laughed bitterly. 'O God, yes. Love and sex and the whole damned thing. Marriages are so earthy. I hate it. I don't know why I come back to these shindigs, they always make me feel ill. The Ideological Status Apparatus in m-more flowery hats than you could shake a stick at, the indestructible organism that conceives for itself no beginning and no end…and they've won, James. They've won. You and I are a couple of outrageous old relics, like Uncle Silas, like the bad baroness in Henry Esmond.'

He had been thinking of Francis Xavier.

'I didn't exactly mean that. I did wonder though, why your sister had decided to get married on the feast of the dead.'

'Is that what it is? I'm sure she has no idea. I think it was prep-school half term, for the pageboys.'

Otto was beginning to feel rather strange. The excess of alcohol, on top of that dire overnight bus journey and the exhaustion of her grief, it was all catching up with her. Her utter weariness had the effect of lowering all kinds of defences. She felt extraordinarily conscious of her own body, of the hollow between her breasts and the line of sweat under them, of her spine pressing against the skin of her back, of the warm faintly meaty smell of her cunt. She noticed that she had her hands tucked between her thighs as she knelt by the hearth, a common human gesture not allowed in public: she shifted quickly to a more guarded posture. More guarded because less frankly protective, the constant unreflecting deceit of body language.

'I wish I wasn't called Otto. I'd drop it and be Jane again but I think it's too late. What a dead give away: boy's name, tomboy, butch dyke.'

'I'm sorry about Xav.'

'Oh, don't worry. I probably asked for it, I always do. He brings out the worst in me. Oh, listen to that. James isn't it strange how instantly a gap of years can seal over. The moment we walked into Underhill together I felt as if – a sort of timewarp. You and me by the study fire discussing Xav: it could be ten years ago.'

'I'm sorry I had to bring him. There was no one else readily available, Luci's up to his eyes in work. I thought this would be my chance to see you – naturally as it were. He might have suspected something if I suddenly headed down to Brighton. He knows we don't meet any more.'

Otto stared at him.

'James, what are you talking about?'

'The package, Otto. The thing I left with you. We've got to try and get it back to Xav without him knowing that you had it. And I suspect he's having me watched.'

Otto struggled to identify 'the thing'.

'Oh, *that*!'

She burst out laughing. 'James, you are incredibly paranoid.'

'I am incredibly well acquainted with Francis Xavier.'

Otto scowled, tried to push her hands into her dreadlocks and remembered that she couldn't do that any more. 'Look, you can have it back anytime, but I'm afraid just at the moment I haven't the faintest idea where it is. All right, don't panic - ' James was visibly alarmed. 'It'll be somewhere. But the house is in a bit of a state - '

What's the point, she thought. I have to start telling people sometime. I may as well use this timewarp.

She was bothered more and more by the sense of her body's presence: nipples, belly, the skin between her thighs, all the soft points of contact. It was so miserable to have a body and no lover. Supposing nobody ever touches me again? She lay awake at nights and couldn't bear to masturbate because it made her feel so lonely, thinking with straightforward *anger* of the last time she'd been with Sandy. If she'd only waited a few more minutes before she started wailing. At least she could have had that last bit of pleasure.

'The truth is, James, Sandy's left me.'

'Oh,' he said stupidly. And then, 'What, seriously?'

Otto nodded glumly.

'Yes. Very seriously.'

She drew up her knees and wrapped her arms around them.

'And you see, she's not only left me – she's um, she's not well. It was coming on for a while but I tried not to see. She keeps coming back to the house when I'm not about and rearranging things. I mean like putting the beans on the rice shelf, putting the bills where the stamps ought to be. It's really rather scary in an inconsequential sort of way. I think she's trying to destroy...all the little signs of us, of the way we lived together.'

'Otter! That's horrible!'

James had dumped his glass. He looked really shocked. She had forgotten that (in the timewarp) he also knew Sandy Brize. Otto looked forward to all the repetitions of this moment as she started coming out as a deserted spouse. She would get tired, bored. She would start telling them – well, it's not the end of the world.

She began to laugh: choked, wiped her eyes.

'I'm sorry James, I shouldn't have sprung it on you like that. Look, I probably exaggerate: she leaves me and I say she's sick, say classique, non? I probably put the beans on the rice shelf myself.'

A tactical withdrawal: she could bear to break the news, but not to discuss it.

She poured two more glasses of brandy and a silence fell between them.

'Does Luci still have adventures?' she asked abruptly.

'Not all the time.'

'And don't you mind?'

James thought, she had been right about the timewarp. The shock of learning that Sandy Brize had left his life was real. He could feel the change: a small, self-possessed, angular fragment gone from his internal skyline. And how well he remembered Otter now: not at all the woman he'd met in Grosvenor Square a few months ago, and yet they merged into one. Her bluntness, her transparency, her habit of saying exactly what came into her head: an endearing weakness in an ideologue.

'Don't mind?' He shook his head. 'I wouldn't say that. It's something we row about – like money, you know.' He tried to convey the precise status of the problem. 'It doesn't *frighten* me.'

Otto chuckled.

'Say no more. Anything that doesn't frighten our James has to be a pretty benign phenomenon. Is he having one now?'

'None er your business, Otter.'

He recalled too late that that was what Sandy always used to say.

Otto stared at the blue and silver gas flames.

'D'you remember when we were cave people and cut up a great hunk of steak fillet and broiled the chunks over this fire? What a filthy mess we used to make, and we never cleared up either. I used to think my poor mother was *deranged* when she complained about it.'

She used to think James was like an exiled prince: which was more an exasperated comment than a compliment. His air of noble helplessness, which excused him from any kind of uncouth exertion. He looked very helpless now, stretched out there all relaxed and beautiful.

Otto was suddenly aware of what she was going to do. After all, it was ridiculous that she should crouch here hungry right next to that very fine body, merely on account of an accident of gender. It was patently ridiculous, now she came to think about it, that they'd known each other fifteen years and never even tried, just to see what would happen.

'James, are you happy? I mean, about what you do an'all?'

'Oh - ' He grinned ruefully. 'Maybe not completely beatific...But I believe I made some rather poor career decisions when I was young and foolish, and that sort of thing cannot be undone. Old Ralph pays the rent.'

'You mean like the Playboy feature?'

'I don't suppose you'll ever forgive me for that, will you.'

'Well – no.' George Washington's disease.

'Which is unfair, because it was your fault Otto. You were the one who taught me the principles of utopia. Did you never realise, displaying my beauty like that was the nearest I ever came to political activism?'

'No, I never did.'

She was watching him so steadily that their eyes must meet: and met. There. Yes, amazingly, she still remembered how. That is fair warning. Now make an excuse and go off to bed, James, saying you have a headache and a long drive in the morning.

James's eyes widened. He picked up the brandy bottle and surveyed its level with quizzical interest: and refilled their glasses.

'Ah, poor us. Such is the way of the world. Why do sinners' ways prosper - '

The room was getting cold. The central heating must have turned itself off hours ago.

'James,' she asked, 'what's the best thing you've ever done? In acting, I mean.'

'That I most enjoyed? Has to be Oberon. When we did The Dream outdoors at Sussex, end of second year.'

'Really? Oh, I remember that. *The isle is full of noises. Sounds and strange airs that give delight and hurt not...*'

'That's The Tempest, Otto.'

She started to laugh, apparently overcome by laughter turned and leaned against his chair, one arm across his thigh. 'I'm hopeless. You know, all that stuff sounds the same to me.'

Leaning, she reached up her hand and drew his shoulder down. Their lips just met. Smoothly, she transferred herself to the arm of the chair: part of her mind astonished, horrified, most of it excited and triumphant. His mouth was soft, his body as she took it in her arms not bulky at all. She would not have known it was a man, except that when she slipped her hand inside his jacket she found only bare curves of pectoral muscle through the silk, with nipples like hard little stars.

It was the brandy. The brandy and all that sex, sex, sex dressed up in flowered hats: weddings are so earthy.

She kissed his mouth open, searched it, invaded the clothes with her hands. It was smooth firm and yielding flesh, and what more did you need. He hadn't said a word. Neither had she, but feeling the need of some justification she slid her hand down over his belly, and laughed against his open mouth on finding the warm tension of an erection. She cupped the velvety bump in her palm like the breast she couldn't find. A hand came and closed over her wrist. She realised he was trying gently to dislodge her, but he'd left that far too late, she eluded his fingers and continued kissing, exploring, moving until she was certain that, no matter what gender, he was just as aroused as she.

'James, have you got some rubber?'

She pulled away. The room had grown horribly bright, James's face looked blurred. He didn't answer.

'No, don't bother. There'll be some in the bathroom. Come on, come to bed.'

The children's rooms were on the top floor in the farmhouse's attics: Duncan's room and Richard's and Betty's; and Otto's which was the biggest with a wonderful view across the whaleback hills. She stood in the little bathroom (horribly bright) and found the rubbers. Oh, Babylon, Babylon she giggled, unfurling the glaucous second skin over her hands. Sandy and she had lived so long in paradise she had almost forgotten the mechanics of donning this protection against a casual encounter with death. She used to do this all the time when she was on the scene because you never know.

James was sitting on her bed.

'Otto – we don't have to do this.' She was afraid he was right, but no: lust had survived the hiatus. There was no problem at all, fucking James was like fucking anyone else and better than many: body coolfired dark and crystal, mine to do with as I please.

In the middle of it all she noticed that she felt watched. Someone was looking on, with voyeuristic distaste. Well, too bad. She would come to terms with her conscience in the morning.

'James, this was all right? I mean, you wanted it too? James?'

The body beside her sighed. 'Hush, never mind, go to sleep.'

She burrowed into unconsciousness like a greedy animal well fed.

In the blue and silver morning Otto woke up alone. She had a nasty hangover lurking somewhere. She raised herself cautiously on one elbow. The attic was almost bare of mementoes by now, unless you counted the view. The bedclothes were crisp blue linen. She looked at the dent in the second pillow, with a puzzled frown. On the floor beside her, her indestructible old hard contacts lay in a saucer alongside a sordid handful of used paper tissue. She stared, in fascinated disbelief.

She took an armful of linen downstairs and stuffed it in the washing machine. There was a note for her on the kitchen table, under a jar of marmalade.

Dear Otto. Don't forget to *lock up* all doors and screens. Leave no perishable food. Switch over the alarms before you leave and give the keys to Mrs Ridley *in person*. P.S. Sorry we didn't see more of each other. And I'm sure he deserved it. Love from yr Father.

She smiled warmly. It was eleven by the kitchen clock. She would have to ring up Peggy, she thought, with a horrified chuckle: *I picked up this bloke see, and we were jagging all night so I missed the bus…*

There was no sign of James.

'Where'd he go Heinze? Out for a walk?'

The Underhill cat, a massive and venerable tabby, stretched and mewed silently at the window. She looked out and saw that James's pale blue TR7 had gone from the yard.

Otto ate a hearty breakfast, took two painkillers, unearthed her beloved old Treklites from her pack and went for a hike: a brisk ten mile stroll around the whalebacks.

It was a fine chilly afternoon, the bracken well turned but showing no sign of winter yet. She climbed to a cairn above Eskdale and sat there looking south and west towards the distant Cumbrian fells.

77

You couldn't coat yourself all over with rubber. It wasn't so bad. Eleven years ago people had been saying AIDS was going to run wild, like the Black Death. But that wasn't what happened. It became one of those things, one of the tolerable hazards of life. She supposed most people were carrying some kind of HIV. She supposed she was herself – testing was a middle class ritual. You just try not to get sick, because if you get sick you might well die. In a way it was healthy, the way death had become ordinary again. Everybody's got to go sometime.

She wished James hadn't done a runner. What shocking behaviour! She squirmed at the thought of her raggedy and extremely sensible underwear: hoped he hadn't been paying too much attention. A horrible memory came to her: groping around that strange, sealed jointure for the entrance she wanted she had thought of Candide – vividly, sensually recalled the intimacy of washing his baby body, changing nappies. Was that Candide, or a fragment of phyllogenetic memory crawling to the surface? In some sense all women regard men as their children...the Jocasta complex has not been sufficiently studied.

Otto shuddered.

It would have been better if he'd stayed. But since he was gone, she was glad. The more her memory surfaced from under the alcohol, the more appalled she became. And yet, and yet – since it was over and done why not admit it. She was feeling a little bit of furtive satisfaction. The whole fucking arrogant male world: that had broken Sandy's heart and ruined Otto's life. She'd *done it* to one of them at last.

Sorry, James. It was nothing personal.

Over the bleak and lovely hills and down into the green vale, to many-towered Camelot. The Murrays had been staunch partisans of the archaeological hypothesis that placed the Matter of Britain up here on their doorstep. And when Otto was growing up she had them all convinced that the Morte d'Arthur was littered with references to Bronze Age matriarchy. She dreamed of herself as a woman-warrior, travelling these hills with a squire/wench who had come to call her to her quest: one of those aloof, ambiguous young ladies so frequently met in Malory.

O Sandy, O Sandy!

Her back was against stone, all around her the uniquely reassuring, bleak beauty of home. Why do I feel so terrible physically today, she found herself wondering. Is this just a hangover or am I coming down with flu? And suddenly, without warning, she burst into tears.

Δ

That morning in Brighton Candide dressed quickly. He hurried down to the shop to wait for the post, which he must intercept before it went into the locked mail box. He waited in the grey shuttered dusk. His eyes were like cinders, his mouth puckered and old. The footsteps came. Candide's heart started to pound. He threw back the bolts in desperate haste.

'Packet for you this morning.'

He let the rest of the letters fall to the floor. The packet was a box about ten centimetres square, addressed to Master C. Murray. It was exactly like the others. It weighed practically nothing. His palms were wet. He opened the wrapping carefully and then the box. He lifted a layer of cotton wool, and stared, and stared.

The little boy whimpered.

Vixen came rattling down the kitchen passage singing Postie! Postie! Quickly he bundled up the brown paper. He shoved past her cradling his treasure. 'Candeed? What you got? - '

'Get away from me,' he snarled. 'Just get away from me.'

Another hour of that day, he was down in the basement. Surrounding him were walls of words, wrapped in calf and cloth and paper: all of them loved and guarded by his mother. They must be good for something, they were no good to Candide now. Carefully he pulled out a tattered row of miscellaneous novels and travel books. The Great White South, a book on the Crimean war. Part of a collected edition of Stevenson. Maud Diver. The Wide Wide World. A Campfire Girl's First Council Fire. From below, a block of Mrs Humphrey Ward, all of a piece in brown morocco binding. The door of the safe was behind. Candide did not fool himself. He was about to commit a crime. He had never done anything like this before. But he had no choice. As he keyed in the combination his mind was filled with bitterness against his mother. He knew what she would say about negotiating with terrorists. He was so helpless, helpless. It maddened him to know that whatever he did he would still once have been inside her. He was a part of her, a spare bit of flesh. Who could stand being that? When he tried to explain something and she looked at him with that smile:

remembering him small and squashy, having his nappy changed. It was so foul.

I'll kill her. It's the only solution.

He began to weep. The cold dark basement looked different. His mother's books even smelled different. They made him feel sick. Everything was like that now – sick, sick, fouled. It would be no use *even if Vera was saved*. He imagined what she would look like. He would still love her whatever happened but his stomach heaved. The only thing that would be any good would be if this filthiness turned out not to have happened. But it had. There was no way back.

2

Some Ladies Are
Not Gentlemen

A great fan of speaker cones blocked off the Clerkenwell Road. Banners and placards jogged up and down. A thousand people, several thousand, danced around: city borders residents, street livers, sharp-suited office workers of both sexes. Outside the church on the corner a grimy stone crucifix hung over the street, behind railings. A long time ago someone had sprayed a message over the roll of forgotten war dead beneath: NO MORE GODS NO MORE MASTERS. James had liked to see it there – a very Christian sentiment, and one that street-fighting Man would certainly endorse. A party of the saved were down on their knees, scrubbing it with paint remover.

'He's here to bring you comfort - ' the preacher shouted, enormously magnified. 'Anyone who's found Jesus will tell you, you don't need anything else. You don't need a JOB, you don't need a DEMONSTRATION. You don't need a UNION. You don't need your RIGHTS. You don't need to buck the boss, you don't need to moan at your husband. All you need is JESUS in your life.'

JE-SUS JE-SUS JE-SUS

There's a lot of simple human comfort to be had in clapping the hands and swaying the body to and fro. James walked by with his head down, wondering whether he was right to condemn.

'Hm. Jesus I know, and Paul I know. But who are you?'

Otto was outside the Smithfield Pavilion, just beyond the invisible walls of the ghetto. The day was grey and cold, featureless November weather. There were not many people about. Labour Force youths in their orange overalls trailed a rubbish cart, picking up the litter that scurried in a chilly wind and fouled the ankles of the passers-by. In spite of that wind the air seemed dead. She couldn't get inside the Pavilion. Her one and only piece of plastic was not the

81

right kind at all. She was shivering, acutely aware of her shabby inadequate clothes. The expensive restoration of these streets, a glowing William Morris mock-up of mediaeval London, made her choke with anger. In a country where the children of the poor are literally starving...Her eyes teared in the wind. It's a rich country, we made a successful transition to post-industrial wealth; we're doing well. What do a few poor children matter? Giltspur Street vanished. She was looking up a steep dingy boulevard, flanked by piles of massive granite. In the middle distance an unmistakable skyline, with the castle standing black against a red sky of reflected sunset. Otto blinked and the mirage was gone. She couldn't imagine why she should be thinking of Edinburgh at all.

The three pasty youths glanced at each other. The girl shrugged her shoulders: the others hurriedly looked away.

James was walking towards her. How exquisitely he dressed. Nothing too extravagant, nothing too boystown. The waisted jacket fitting like skin, high collar with the points turned down precisely. Lamartine. A black Lamartine, nervously surveying the barricades. She hated him, all the more because of that treacherous voice always whispering: *wish I could buy clothes like that...*

'Sorry I'm late.'

'James, is there something wrong with Luci?'

'Wrong?' repeated James, cautiously.

'I'm referring to the fact that he wouldn't let me talk to you on the phone, and clearly doesn't want me at your flat.'

'Well, I told him about – um, Betty's wedding. He wasn't very pleased. I'm sorry Otto.'

In strict justice he didn't know why he was apologising. He could remember the events of that night quite clearly. But he had come out prepared to be magnanimous. *We were both pissed, let's forget it,* was the line he'd chosen.

'But he fucks other people all the time, I thought.'

'Ah, but I don't, see. I'm naturally monogamous, have been from a child. That's the arrangement.'

'So you're his wife. Patriarchy in the improved, pure style. Congratulations.'

It appeared that the prepared speech was not going to be appropriate. Otto observed the change in his face with satisfaction.

Under the glass there was warmth and greenery and the sound of water. She felt her body responding insensately and gritted her teeth.

'I'm paying,' he said hurriedly, as they sat down in the Firenze. He could see that his crimes were mounting. He had named the first place that came into his head, flustered by Luci's sarcasm. He should have known better: people like Otto don't lunch. When she saw the prices here she would be ready to kill.

'I'm sorry – you are vegetarian, aren't you?'

'I was. I gave up expensive affectations of that kind a long time ago.'

Otto felt polluted. He had a brilliant little rainbow decal, spray-sealed into the skin just below his left shoulder-blade. She could see it now. She'd have liked to burn those hours out of her memory with a laser, and out of his. The fact that she had been the seducer had become totally irrelevant. The waitress proffered a bottle of Pouilly and began to pour rather rapidly into James's glass.

'Just a moment.'

He pointed to the label, not quite obscured by a napkin and her white gloved thumb.

'That's – ah, a figure three isn't it.'

'Uh – '

'Twos are different, you know. They're not so curly. It was number 19 we mentioned, I thought. The 02?'

'*James* – '

She glared at him savagely.

'Sorry, sorry. Stupid habit. What does it matter – '

Over the first course they did not speak. This artichoke's tinned, thought James, and was so nervous he almost said so. He could not make out how he was to blame but the righteous fury blazing in her eyes cowed him completely. She was always the politician: she'd managed to recapture the moral advantage somehow, obviously. (They'd done nothing in any way dangerous, he was certain of that.) I don't know this place well, he wanted to explain, as though good food would have placated her.

'You're not drinking?'

'Trying to lay off.'

'You weren't drinking too much, were you?'

'Yes I was.'

This could be taken as a reference to Betty's wedding night. It silenced them again.

'I saw a very odd thing just now-' He attempted an easy tone. 'A big revivalist meeting, all over the Clerkenwell Road – '

83

'James, I don't care if you saw the Four Horsemen of the Apocalypse coming down Oxford Street - '

Finally, she had watched him squirm for long enough. She hauled up her grubby daypack, delved inside it and put on the table in front of him a small cardboard box.

'Open that.'

He obeyed, warily. Inside he found some scraps of dingy white fur, smeared with what appeared to be dried blood.

'What's this?'

'Small pieces,' she told him distinctly, 'Of a Jack Russell terrier bitch belonging to my son. A paw, an ear and the end of a tail so far. The dog's name was Vera, maybe you remember it. It - she disappeared about three weeks ago. Candide was heartbroken. I don't know what you call the way he feels now.'

With her eyes on his face she removed something else from the bag and laid it down. It was the black film tub she had taken from him in August, the lid still sealed with tape.

James understood nothing: unless possibly Otto had suddenly gone crazy. Instinct told him to make an excuse and escape. He reached out for Gerry's 'evidence': he was still very anxious to deal with that problem.

'Not yet.' She moved the canister out of reach. 'I haven't finished. Do you remember, I told you someone was interfering with my belongings? That wasn't Sandy, as it turns out. Somebody has been blackmailing Candide. He had an anonymous phone call, and then the little presents started. Someone told him to recover a certain package which his mother had 'stolen'. And do it in secret, or else. Did you know, James, a certain ex-pharmaceutical company still runs labs, where vivisection is performed as a kind of libertarian ritual? Candide knows. He reads that Animal Rights stuff. And if he didn't know all the details before, he certainly does now.'

'Oh no - '

'Oh yes. Your fucking brother. This is exactly his idea of a joke, isn't it.'

'But he didn't know I gave the thing to you!'

'Apparently he did, James.'

Otto swallowed. To her fury, she felt her voice beginning to crack. 'It's so horrible to see him. It was his *birthday*, the day I found out, can you imagine what kind of fun that was. Christ, I know I'm not the perfect mother. But I've been telling him all his life the world *is* good. Kindness does win out, we just have to try harder. And now, if you could see his eyes...I wanted to ask you. When something terrible happens to a child, something that damns the world. Does he – does the child ever get over it?'

Nobody ever spoke to James about the fact that he had seen his parents killed. He saw that Otto didn't realise the enormity of her comparison. For her, at the moment, only Candide mattered.

'I don't know,' he said, after a short silence. 'I'm not the child. I don't know what the child was going to be like.'

It was one o'clock. Most of the locals, hard working boys and girls, had lunched and gone. The Firenze practised selective keying and did not open its doors to the average tourist, however well plasticed. Two businesswomen in black suits and needle heels whispered ominously behind a potted cypress, the little net veils on their identical small hats brushing. Their voices drifted around the restaurant's coffered cobalt walls, across the empty islands of terracotta damask.

Perhaps Otto was right. The scale of the event didn't matter. The skin came off the world, you saw what lay beneath. You can't reassure him Otto. Don't try and mend the fences, it is too late, you'll only discredit yourself. He'll have to conclude that you are either crazy or deliberately collaborating.

Or else a politician, which covers everything. The poor child. He had worried a lot about Candide in the time when he still felt connected: wondering how the little boy would cope with the yawning gap between his mother's statements and observable reality. Luckily, there was always Sandy.

He remembered a summer morning in the kitchen at Wombega. He had been visiting and was about to give Otto a lift to London, to some furtive feminist book trade conference. Candide, eighteen months old, had just realised his mother was going to disappear. He sat in his breakfast highchair and howled, holding out his arms rigid as if they were broken and splinted. 'Otter! Otter!' That note of utter desolation and outrage and betrayal. Otto rushed about collecting her belongings, occasionally casting a glance of helpless resentment at the screaming child. James tried to pretend he was deaf, or elsewhere. Sandy stepped up to the wet, red, mucus dripping flower that was Candide's face and stood examining it coldly. 'You'd better stop that crying,' she told it, completely unmoved. 'You're going to run out of tears before you're five if you're not careful. And I promise you Candide. *It gets much worse than this.*'

The baby stopped crying. Its face became human again. It gazed, its little mouth open, and wiped its nose with its fist.

'Otto, have you told Sandy about this? I know she moved out, but - '

Otto's eyes showed a bleak increase in satisfaction.

'I don't think that would be a good idea. Or necessary. I think she's been recruited into BREAKTHRU.'

At that word, for the first time, James understood what they were talking about. He forgot the child. He remembered Francis Xavier, and the whole sinister and amoral organisation he had at his command.

'I told you, didn't I, that she was behaving weirdly. She went to one of their recruiting "seminars" a while ago you know: I'd forgotten. Do you know how it is when someone has a secret life? How you get a clue eventually, and you look back and everything falls into place? Sandy's not been my lover for - for ages. I knew something was pulling her away, now I know what. So you see, there's no mystery as to how Xav found out who had the goods.'

She touched the canister. 'What do you suggest I do? Go to the police? BREAKTHRU isn't an ordinary hustle designed to remove money from the weak-minded. Xav's people are rightist activists, you could run into their support anywhere you turn. God knows what they're up to, what Gerry was trying expose. And now they think we know too.'

'Otto – we're in trouble.'

She showed her teeth. 'Thanks for the "we".'

It was probably too late already to hand the package back. How could they prove they had not investigated the contents? Libertarians can't take anything on trust, or accept apologies. It is against their religion. They can, however, administer punishment.

He made a sudden move, to quell his panic, reaching for the package again.

'Okay, give it to me. I'll get it back to Xav - '

'No!'

She pulled it away. 'Tell me again. What exactly did Gerry say was in here?'

'What does it matter?'

'Tell.'

He frowned. 'She said it was aljawar, that's Arabic, the real thing, the gear: modern slang, you know. She also mentioned - an odd word, I'm not sure I remember it: something to do with Cairo.'

'So you made up all that stuff about its being a roll of film, evidence of criminal practices?'

'Otto, you know the kind of gibberish they talk. One has to construct something.'

'Pick it up, James.'

She watched, with malign pleasure, as he did so.

'This is the same – ?'

'It turns out I'd put it in my safe, I can't imagine why. I have a tricky homemade lock. It's pointless really, anyone could torch the door out in ten seconds. But no. You can be fairly sure no one has touched that thing.'

'Otto, the weight has changed.'

'I wondered if you would notice.'

Their first course had been cleared. Otto stared with surprise at a plate of glistening white rice noodles, scattered with slivers of vegetable cut into whimsical shapes: little chairs and cars and aeroplanes. The waitress had come and gone. Otto's heart jumped. What had they been saying?

Oh, I can't live like this –

She drew a breath.

'James, Candide's pet is dead and nothing will bring her back. I don't give a shit what's in this tube. I know when I'm beaten.' (James could not see how he deserved the stare of burning hatred.) 'Whatever nastiness this reveals, I can't do anything about it. I am powerless. But I want to *know*. I'm not going to open the tub. Candide tells me it is boobytrapped somehow, and knowing your brother I think I'll take notice of that. But I've thought of a way.'

'Otter, what is the point? As you say, we are powerless. All we can do is try to get out from under, as quickly as possible – '

'Shut up and listen, will you. D'you remember a bloke named Barry Cunningham?'

'Who - ?'

'He was in our year at Sussex. We knew him quite well at one time, used to buy dope from him. He was in one of the science schools before they shut down: transferred to Media Technology. He's still in the same area, only nowadays he works for the MoD out in Berkshire. It's part of my stupid hobby to know as much as a powerless person can about what goes on in the military industrial complex, which is how I happened to spot his name, in one of the class lists we dissidents collect, and now it has come in useful. He'll help us. All we have to do is take the object to his works, which he thinks is less risky than him trying to take the necessary equipment home. By hand, of course. I'm not trusting whatever this is to the postal company.'

'Otter, that's crazy. You can't - '

She smiled. 'No, of course I can't, not with my record. He'll cooperate, but not that far. Not me – you.'

'But Otter, you know I can't do that.'

'Oh, James, don't be such a baby. You used to come to Wombega all the time a few years ago.'

'Otto, I *can't*.

The puling coward. She was going to make him pay for his pretty clothes, for her guilt at having coupled with the enemy (those jerking, grunting bodies on the blue sheets): most of all for this hideous shameful impotence...nothing, nothing she could do to protect her child.

'Otter - !' he wailed.

It was a small revenge but a good one. Let him try what it felt like, for once, to step outside the cosy ghetto.

When he left the Pavilion James was surprised to find it was still daylight. He felt exhausted. The thing Gerry had stolen weighed in his pocket making him as fragile as glass, afraid to brush against people on the pavement. He would do as he had been told. He knew he was being punished unjustly, but that knowledge had only fatally weakened his protests: making him sure before he started that she would not listen to reason. He was punished already. He carried the fear she had given him through the London streets, like an infection.

△

Otto arrived home in a murky, pinkish urban darkness. Every window in the house was bright except for the metalled shopfront. She felt sick. Waves of nausea pulsed through her, while hands inside struggled with the bolts and chains. Peggy was holding Vixen in her arms. There were snailtracks of dried tears on the little girl's round cheeks.

'Candide's gone,' said Otto.

'He didn't come home from school.'

Peggy followed her up to the living room: explaining, describing her growing anxiety – five o'clock, six, seven, and no Candide. Everything looked hollow. She had been afraid of this, afraid of this.

'Why didn't you go and fetch him?' she shouted.

Vix began to cry.

'Otto you never told me. I had to mind the shop. I didn't know – '

'He's out looking for that bloody dog. Have you tried getting hold of the MacDonall boys? They'll help us search.'

Peggy looked frightened. 'I been round to see Tirzah. She says, that you and me and Candide are in trouble with powerful people. "Ja don't decree my family should get involved." That's what she said. Otto, what's happening?'

Otto didn't answer. Abruptly, she turned away and went to the phone. In a moment she was talking to the desk sergeant at John Street.

'I want to report a missing person,' she said, not knowing how else to put it. 'My little boy.'

She explained the circumstances and the voice said soothingly that was hardly enough time to get worried and had she rung around her friends? Behind the words the tone was saying...dead. Little children who don't come home are always...dead. It doesn't take twenty minutes to rape and kill an eleven year old. She knew it wasn't that so she told him about BREAKTHRU, and that she'd been 'being harassed' – her fear overleaping her discretion and then pulling her back before she went into details.

There was a long pause at the other end. At last the police voice returned.

'Look Mrs Murray, as you know there's very little we can do in these cases. Just keep calm. I'm sure he'll turn up safe and sound.'

The phone ticked, whined and beeped to itself for a few seconds. It was tapped of course. She had never let that worry her: claimed, wryly, she'd shut up shop if they ever stopped bothering.

But who is listening now?

She put down the phone with a dry mouth, and stood staring at the familiar litter of her noticeboard. She decided not to call James. She knew she'd only get the bloody machine, anyway.

She walked the cold unlit alleys with a torch calling over and over again. Candide! Candide!

Otto had a recurrent fantasy: a strange one, she had shared it with
no one. It came to her sometimes when she was in the kitchen or
in the shop working, and for some reason she was alone for an
hour or so. Her body occupied, her mind wandered. And then
it seemed that a stranger came into the room. More often it was
the shop. The bell didn't ring but a customer entered and waited
silently for her attention. She knew at once that this was death. She
was not shocked or frightened. In death's presence she thought of
everything that would be left undone. Her life's work put down so
soon, all the unfinished projects and half fought battles: not an end
in sight anywhere. But her hands and eyes kept on with what they
were doing, unhurried and calm. Will I have time to say goodbye
to Sandy and Candide, she asked. Oh yes, said the figure she could
never describe to herself. There will be time. This is only a warning.

But now death had come and there was no serenity only unrelent-
ing mind-crushing terror. She had been surprised and pleased that
she could parley with the monster even in a dream. She had never
dreamed of rehearsing how she would feel if it took her child.

The house where Sandy was living was a squat, dilapidated Victorian
terraced house near Dyke Road. Otto had been to look at it before
but she hadn't had the courage to defy Sandy's decision, and got
no further than the end of the street. She had not noticed then
how sinister the place looked. A big Victorian house was always
saleable. Why did the owners let it stand empty? Why did they
tolerate squatters?

The door was opened by a gaunt spook with blackened teeth.
She was held off while consultation went on: she was allowed
inside. The hallway stank of damp and urine, there was a yellow
paper with no discernible pattern hanging in strips from the walls.
This was rather far from the public image of BREAKTHRU. Otto
wondered at the elaborate deception. This must be a calculated
infiltration of the opposing territory.

'Keep going up,' the spook told her, smiling elegantly like a
Heian court lady.

Sandy's room was a garret. The ceiling came down to floor level
in the corners. Some of it was ripped away revealing guts of lath
and plaster, darkness and specks of light between the slates above.
There was a gaping hole in the floor mended by two planks and a
piece of decayed vinyl. The smell here was of very old cat shit. Beside

a ruined chest of drawers stood a red plastic bucket. It was very cold.

Sandy was sitting in a rumpled pile of bedclothes, on a mattress under the one small window. She wore a seedy grey track suit visibly stained at the crotch. Her hair was unbrushed, her face unwashed, her eyes wandered. Her deterioration was evident and shocking: and Otto at once gave up what she had thought was her worst fear – that Sand was actively involved in whatever had happened to Candide. For some strange reason her horrified reaction came out first as diffidence.

'I know you said you wanted a clean break,' she apologised. 'But Candide's disappeared.'

Through the story, Sandy didn't say a word. Occasionally she turned her head and squinted up at the pale sky which was all she could see through her four panes of grimy glass, as if she was watching a clock up there. It was impossible not to get the impression that she'd heard it all before.

At the end, she almost yawned.

'Well, what d'you want *me* to do?'

And then as anger.

I will kill her, thought Otto. She had found so much aggression in herself these last few days she thought They must be right. She had been polluted with testosterone in her mother's womb. The filthy room leered at her, its statement an impossible barrier.

'What's the point in this?' she cried. 'Why d'you have to live in squalor, weren't we poor enough?'

Sandy laughed. 'Who are you calling squalid? We have a working toilet, thank you.' She glanced at the bucket and grinned without embarrassment. 'Mind you, it is a long way downstairs.'

Otto wrapped her arms around her body and shuddered. She had not slept for forty-eight hours. 'I don't understand. There's plenty of work to do in the world. What does it matter if you don't get paid? Only shits get rich, you know that. We could live, we were happy. What is it that you want?'

'Otto, you know perfectly well what I want. Rights without responsibilities, claims without duties, pleasure without cost.'

Sandy looked around the attic with such complacency you wondered what she saw.

'D'you remember how you used to say you wanted everything? Well, I tried that. Now I've decided to want nothing. It's a short cut to the same end: complete satisfaction.'

'You're destroying yourself - '

Sandy nodded. 'At least, I'm finding out if it can be done.'

Beside the mattress was a milk bottle with two scrawny dead chrysanthemums standing in it. Sandy always wanted to buy flowers. She used to cry real tears because Otto insisted food had to come first. She had the kind of blue eyes that turn grey in winter or under a cold light. They were the colour of dirty water now: depthless, closed. Otto wanted to weep. She was the one who had done this, not BREAKTHRU. She had pushed her darling too far, pressed her too hard, driven her into the arms of the seductive rival.

'You've joined BREAKTHRU, haven't you – '

The dirty water eyes remained completely passive. 'In a way,' remarked Sandy after a moment. 'In a way, I suppose I have.'

Otto swallowed. It was confirmed then.

'Can you tell me anything?'

The mad woman considered. 'You mean from that seminar? It was an awfully long time ago Otto. The most negative word, the most positive word. Words are the symptoms of consciousness which is the disease of mankind.' Sandy pulled the covers up over her knees. The patient was tired, and would soon be sending this demanding stranger away. Otto looked down at the hands knotted round her knees, surprised that they still looked solid.

'Fundraising tech. Doorstep tech. Dissolving things by draining out the meaning. Biological radiation.'

'Biological radiation – what's that?'

Sandy chuckled, pulling the covers up higher. 'Extracting sunshine from cucumbers, I expect.'

When Otto reached the door a hard little voice called her back.

'Hey, Otter, have you any money? I'm skint.'

The 'Otter' was a nasty touch.

'Oh – sure. Take what you like.'

She handed over her wallet and took it back without looking round, for pity was giving way to horror again. Like an animal in the face of some natural disaster, an earthquake or a flood, she wanted to get away. Her own sanity would not survive much more of this creature's company.

Sandy sat looking at the door until she was sure that her lover was well out of the house. At last she sighed and got up. She padded barefoot to the hole in the floor and pulled aside the vinyl and the planks. Candide wriggled out of the crawlspace, covered in dank grime and cobwebs.

'You little monster,' she said. 'How could you listen to all that, and not come out?'

'Well, how could you and not tell her.'

'That's different. I'd promised.'

Candide also looked at the open door, guiltily.

'She wouldn't let me do it, Sand. You know she wouldn't.'

He pulled up his bulky rucksack. 'Anyway, I don't owe her anything.' His eyes narrowed, brooding on ancient wrongs. 'She threw away my pram toy.'

Sandy retired to her nest and sat watching the child with the same shallow, affectless regard that had terrified her lover.

'Okay Cand, explain to me again about those angels.'

3

Who Is This
Who Is Coming

The minister, James's uncle, knew that trouble was coming. He
told Christopher and Elizabeth to leave the country for a while and
gave similar advice to other idle members of his family: they made
him nervous. So James's parents came with him to the airport,
that September when he was eleven years old, and their servant,
a woman who had formerly been James's nursemaid. The car was
recognised and stopped by a group of soldiers in uniform. They
were northerners, which meant at that time anti-elitists, besides
the religious and tribal significance. Catherine, the servant, was a
woman from the Plateau. She managed to convince them somehow
that James was her son and the boy was not harmed. James's mother
kept up a furious tirade (as she had been taught to do, should
these circumstances arise). Have you no mothers? Have you no
sisters? Aren't you ashamed? James's father preserved a dignified
but cooperative attitude, the best tactic for a man. The driver had
been shot as he pulled up, he was dead. The man and woman were
both cut down with repeated machete blows. The soldiers had
submachine guns but did not use them for the execution. They
'gave' the car to Catherine as proof of their good faith and set her
on her way with her son, begging her to take care and not to stop
for anyone. Go with God, they cried. Live like human beings. We
are giving our souls for you.

It had taken fifty-seven cuts to subdue James's mother. So his
Esumare grandfather told him later. The old man almost worshipped
physical vitality, he was immensely proud of his daughter-in-law.

Ironically, years later when James told them he was gay, everybody assumed the tragedy was to blame. Since in Nigeria at least
a scapegoat seemed to be required, James was content that they

94

had found one. When his uncle accused him of 'opting out of the human race - ' he answered – what if I am? Can you honestly blame me? The irony was that the lesson James had learned was quite different. There was no moral superiority in it. Even at eleven, James was well aware that his parents were not 'innocent'. They were happy, charming, feckless thieves and liars. But nor were the soldiers justified. They didn't even feel so, you could see that in their eyes. The only rule, then, was don't let it happen to you. James therefore resolved to keep his head down for life, no matter what the provocation. Coming out was the one occasion that forced him into the open: and even then it was by no means his own idea, it was a case of the lesser evil. If he didn't go public, Luci would not love him any more.

As he drove to Berkshire to find Barry Cunningham he was thinking of how much undeserved admiration he had attracted over the years – except from Otto. Even the Esumares respected him: *it takes guts you know*, they would say *to be open about these things*. But the strategy of minimum resistance could become a liability. As he drove, he frequently reached a hand and touched the car's documentation lying on the seat beside him. And his passport in his jacket pocket. It was a condition of his permission to reside in the UK, that he should leave his area of domicile only accompanied by a British citizen and to visit one of the addresses he had registered at his nearest police office.

James was well aware that out here in the hinterland his passport didn't matter much: any unfamiliar black face would be in trouble. He just hoped to God that if he *did* get stopped the country bobbies would understand the distinction, and not treat him like one of their own unwanted.

He found he remembered Barry Cunningham quite well: another loangranter like Sandy Brize, but a much harder case. Barry had always been cheerfully on the make, with a glib and irreverent grasp of the relationship between rebel aristocrats and the educated poor. James had disliked him. The chemistry between them was bad. Barry was a working-class black. He called himself a 'token escapologist'. He called James Uncle Jim; and 'Mr Spook', before the term had acquired its creditable street-meaning.

Ironic. James had asked Otto how she'd persuaded Barry to do her this favour. She grinned brutally. 'I said I'd come visiting, start writing to him – revive the old friendship you know.' A token escapologist has to bear in mind that his value is never, finally, other than aesthetic. He has to take care of his appearence, in every detail.

The MoD plant was set in green fields on the edge of a trim modern village. James sat in the TR7 sweating, staring at the fence.

He was taken from the gates into a kind of concrete burrow. A sullen middle-aged white man in olive green fatigues sat and stared at twenty monitor screens of fence and grass. Each time his eyes had checked every one he swivelled round again, nursing the elaborate weapon in his lap, and stared at James. Something had gone wrong, and James had no explanation, no defence... He found himself growing horribly conscious of the object in his pocket, the idea of being caught with that guilty thing more fearful even than the presence of the soldier.

The guard watched him like a dog watching a biscuit.

Suddenly the massive door of the burrow flew open and Barry Cunningham breezed in. He had not changed at all: the same spongy bouffant hairstyle, the same sallow coffee skin marked with old acne scars.

'Hiya James. Got your pass yet?'

He crossed to the desk under the monitors and began rifling through a pile of plastic blanks. 'What d'you fancy? Treasury, DOE. Entertainment and Culture haha - ' – and affected to notice James's expression of panic for the first time.

'Oh, don't worry about Darren here, Jimbo. He's a mate of mine. We're in business together.'

The man leaned forward, groping in his tunic pocket.

'Are you really Ralph Churchill? Can I have your autograph? It's not for me, mind – '

The plant was an ominous block of black glass, but indoors there was a somewhat reassuring atmosphere of brightly lit functional shabbiness.

'Lost our address, did you.'

'I – '

'Thought so. I never got the Christmas cards. How's the old bourgeois-radical princess then? Still pushing everybody around, I see.'

'What's your business with the security guards. Barry?'

'Oh, the usual. One out the front, ten out the back. Cosi fan tutte, as they say.'

They walked the corridors, Barry frowning sadly as he approached each camera and grinning broadly under it. People in white coats passed. James was acutely aware of his nonsense badge with the tacky but recognisable instant portrait.

'At the moment we've got a contract with a porno mail order firm. To the army it's an inert laser penetrative surveillance device, to the honest punters it's a peekaboo binocular. See right through yer neighbour's bedroom wall. The perfect Xmas present.'

He grinned, virtuously. 'You was scared back there, wasn't you? Thought I was going to turn you in? You misjudged me, Uncle James. Just because I work in a place like this doesn't mean I've gone soft in the head.'

Barry unlocked an empty lab with his thumbprint and a combination. He moved coffee cups, print out, papers, from a bench, sat down and folded his arms in a leisurely way.

'Is this room monitored?'

'Course it is. Son et lumiere tout completly. Don't worry, Darren's boss is my partner. Machine surveillance is the same as any other machine init. It's the operator you worry about. Come on then, let's have a geek at the mystery object.'

He took the tub and looked it over thoughtfully, at length. 'Hope we've got power today. Some of Otto's comrades took out the local substation last week. Did the emergency generator kick in? It did not. Us and half the nerve centre of the British Armed Forces, totally paralysed. Good job nobody declared war, eh...What d'you reckon James? Is it really coming up this time, the Big One? The Third World War?'

Now he wanted the thing back. He was mad to have accepted Otto's mission. He should have taken the tub straight to Xav as soon as he left the Firenze: or if that was too fearfully direct given it to Bernie, have him hand it over. James controlled himself.

'That's been going on for a long time.'

'How right you are. North of the Trent and South of Gibraltar, but we've escaped so far, you and me. Young, gifted and black.' He laughed morosely, and gazed up into the service lines. 'Are you married James? I suppose not. Well, I am. Got two kids. Macaroons they are, or one of those things. Wife's white. Want to see their pictures? Ah, fuck it.'

He had noticed his guest's extreme unease. He eyed James with malicious interest, rolling the little tub between his palms.

'And you, you ought to be out there at this moment, am I right. Are you still a vegetarian, I mean pacifist? What'll you do if they actually come for you though? Actually come and get hold of you and stick you in a uniform?'

'Could you get on with it, Barry?'

'Ho hum. If you like. I'm not to open this?'

'No.'

Barry raised his eyebrows. His malicious smile was beginning to fade.

'You ought to be more careful Jimbo, with a passport like yours to look after. Just what am I getting into here? If there's money in it do I get a percentage?'

But he handled the aljawar more gingerly than before. 'No - ' he said, after a moment. 'On second thoughts you and Otto can keep it all to yourself. What the fuck *is* this James?'

'We don't know. That's what Otto wants to find out.'

'Oh well, I suppose it can't bite. Let's take a look.'

It was extraordinary, thought James, how what Xav had done to Candide's pet had informed that object with meaning: changing the nervous caution he had felt before to palpable disgust and dread. Otto had infected him and he passed the message on. Now this whole lab, with its corral of massive instruments and web of cables dangling listlessly from the ceiling, seemed wary and ill at ease.

Barry rubbed his finger along the tape, held the tub up and peered at it, weighed it in his hand. He got up and dropped it with a casual air onto the band of a machine much like the one that it had passed through in Grosvenor Square.

'This ain't exactly the cutting edge of penetrative surveillance you know, James. You could have found out this much by taking it through anywhere where there's a security check. All you had to do was put it in your handbag and go to Harrods. Didn't you think of that?'

I didn't think at all, and Otto wanted to punish me more than she wanted to find out anything.

'We suspect it is just what it looks like, a roll of old 35mm film, exposed. If it was, could you recover anything of the pictures?'

'Mmm, possibly.'

He donned a 3D visor and handed one to James.

James didn't want to see. He imagined bloodstained scraps of some unidentifiable small creature. It didn't make sense, but that was his image.

Barry laughed.

'What is it?'

'Come and have a look.'

The blurred object visible on the viewplate cleared and contracted. James could see through the plastic shell, he could make out a section of grey convex cylinder within the cylinder, packed around with a yellowish white material that was covered in small black scratchings. He made no sense of it.

A deadpan boffin voice remarked over his shoulder. 'Of course, only extensive testing will prove my hypothesis, but off the top of my head, Jimbo: what you have there is a little bit of antique pipe...lead, I'd say, by the weight. Accompanied by what we scientists call old newspaper.'

'The weight had changed.'

'D'you really want me to investigate further? I mean, is that dead clever camouflage, or has somebody been pulling your leg - ?'

At the wedding in Roxburghshire Francis Xavier had displayed a strange interest in Otto Murray. When asked to explain it he had told his brother openly that it was BREAKTHRU business. And that BREAKTHRU business involved, above all else, the abuse and grotesque torture of small children. James fell into the anger laid in his past like a booby trap, at the same instant as he understood the substitution.

'Give it to me. I've got to get back – '

Barry was laughing, complaining delightedly that James and Otto had wasted government time, wanting to know what James – the pacifist - planned to do to the joker.

'They had you scared shitless, didn't they. Whoever they are - '

There was a definite note of relief in the crowing, another effect of Xav's successful projection. James ignored it all. He hardly noticed Barry's cavalier manner with the plant security. His mind was on the child, who might be trying at this moment to make a deal with Francis Xavier.

He was at his car beyond the barriers when he realised he must contact Otto at once. He had no phone in the car, he hated those things. He saw to his immense relief a public call box on the verge down by the first houses of the village. He began to walk towards it rapidly, feeling in his pocket for plastic. Suddenly there was someone walking beside him. She must have come from the plant. There was no other building near, no vehicle but his own. She was dressed in gold: a skirt of gilded leather and a shining moulded breastplate, a dagger at her hip and wings on her cap and heels.

James

She did not touch him but put herself in his path.

Things were getting worse. BREAKTHRU must have had him followed. Or maybe had been contacted by their people in this establishment: the guard who wanted Ralph's autograph, Barry. She was young, no more than nineteen or twenty but there were purple shadows under her eyes, a greyness in the fair English complexion. He recognised that it was fear that made her look so ill.

James trust me

'Why should I,' he demanded indignantly, without waiting to know what else she was going to ask. 'Get out of my way. I have to make a phone call.'

All right but don't use plastic. There's a trace on your numbers.

That stopped him. He put his hands in his pockets. 'I haven't any cash. I'll have to take the risk.'

You know who has hold of the Kairos?

James was angry. He glared at the golden angel, noticing that there was an eye-confusing shimmer of body paint over her exposed skin. She was simply glowing, except where the mask of fear overcame all cosmetics.

'Yes I know,' he snapped. 'And so does your boss I'm sure. It is a simple enough deduction.'

She recoiled and put up her hands dramatically. Don't tell me anything! It isn't safe!

Off to their right across the grass a figure appeared out of the ground. A stout woman in a pink overall climbed up from the subway under the fence and followed a path that lead towards the village. She carried a shopping bag that seemed to be heavy. She might be a cleaner taking home her perks, taking out whatever was marketable in Ministry of Defence supplies. She waved to the couple standing on the verge. James's angel responded distractedly with an automatic smile and called: Hello Liane - The woman turned and looked back twice, either at the fancy dress or at the strange black man.

'What is this Kairos? Tell me?'

It is a reality changing drug.

'Something like acid?'

The angel shivered at his innocence. Her face crumpled. No. That's not what I said.

She whispered, as if the road was not empty but full of listening enemies.

Take me back to London with you. I'll try to explain.

Coming up to the Reading junction on the M4, they joined a long tailback that indicated either an accident or some other kind of trouble ahead. She insisted that they should leave the motorway. James thought she was right, although he certainly didn't trust her. He was bringing her back because it made sense to keep this angel in sight: a contact with BREAKTHRU. She must know plenty that he and Otto didn't, whereas there was nothing new she could learn from them.

'Do you always go about dressed like that? Don't you find it a little chilly at this time of year?'

She did not answer. She was huddled low in the seat, as if trying to make herself invisible. The degree of fear she showed was ominous, but it was in her favour. It was a convincing performance – though James, professionally sceptical, wouldn't bet on it's being genuine.

Real or not, it was infectious. James found he was no longer thinking of Candide. He was afraid for himself. All his unease at having left the compound came back. He didn't want to be out here but since he was he wanted to drive faster: which was impractical as the TR was currently negotiating the chaotic streets of Reading town centre. He was lost, he felt appallingly exposed. He would have asked the angel for help but she was obviously beyond speech: her knuckles and her mouth white with panic. When the sirens started up behind he put on speed automatically. The little car scuttled frantically through disorganised waves of traffic.

'What's going on?' he snapped. 'Are you in trouble?'

He only heard a desperate whimpering. *Don't stop, don't stop* –

But up ahead the road was blocked. He had driven himself into the mouth of a pedestrian precinct. Wailing, two white Rovettes passed him. On the precinct a rabble of spooks were providing some street cabaret, scattering the shoppers. James read a news vendor's placard: IS THE WEEKEND DEAD? as it was overturned.

Straggling letters sprayed on plate glass. THE MEN IN GREY
SHUT THEIR FREEDOM AWAY WE MUST MAKE AND
HELP THEM FIND –

James had forgotten his angel. Men in uniform got out of their
cars. He could not remember why he had been behaving so stupidly.
He was fighting with a kind of déjà vu, which he couldn't quite
recognise. He must forget it, must concentrate on this moment and
get these next lines exactly right. The situation was not irretrievable.
This is England, after all –

A police officer tapped on the window. James opened it. The
uniform leaned down to him confidingly.

'You left the motorway to avoid a roadblock, Sir. Now why was
that?'

He assumed they had ways of knowing, helicopter watch perhaps.
He apologised humbly but without becoming too fullsome. His
manner and facial gesture worked on blurring the question of ethnic
origin – not without some success, he judged. The officer asked to
see James's licence and passport and the car's log book: but politely.
He didn't seem to recognise Ralph Churchill.

'A long way from home, aren't you, Sir. Well, we won't say
anything more this time. But you know its really better for people
of your persuasion if you stick to your own patch. Makes our job
of protecting you a lot easier - '

James remained relaxed. He pictured himself driving away,
having paid his fine and perhaps a little more. A normal citizen,
chastened but unharmed. He concentrated on that image, and
wished he was carrying cash. His documents came back like a
blessing out of heaven.

'Okay, Sir. On your way.'

And only now he realised how frightened he had been, for the
girl sitting beside him had disappeared. She had left, or been taken,
through the passenger door and he hadn't noticed a thing.

James got out into the road. The traffic police were ignoring the
rioting spooks. There was no sign of the frightened girl. His palms
were wet. He had forgotten BREAKTHRU. Something else had
taken over. This was why James could never leave the compound,
it was nothing to do with the entries on his passport. This was what
was waiting for him outside: the uncompleted thing.

You might call it a second chance.

'Anything the matter Sir?'

'I'd like to know what happened to my passenger.'

James would swear for a moment this affable officer thought of saying 'What passenger?'. The tactic flickered in his eyes and was dismissed. He was middle aged. He had a serene, weighty pink face, not without character. There was a little bright silvery stubble lurking in the creases round his jaw.

'You didn't know her Sir, did you. You must be aware that it is illegal to pick up hitchhikers.'

'I don't know her,' James agreed placatingly. 'I don't want to interfere. I just want to know why – '

The officer hit him hard, without warning, in the stomach. James doubled over, grunting. As he tried to straighten up, the same fist connected again. In a corner of his mind he resisted, jabbering: *Oh, what is this? A middle-class black gets beaten up by the police, for no reason, and is astonished. This is nothing special, nothing very significant. Hold on, hold on* – But pain was the final catalyst. He was gone. The shouting of the spooks faded, the street blurred. He could not stay with this present, time had dissolved. He took the repeated blows as if he owned them, had possessed them all his life. Don't want to escape, don't want to survive. The cold pavement struck his cheek and disappeared. He saw red laeterite earth, and a field of spindly little cassavas under a grey and purple sky. *Don't stop for them, don't stop, don't stop...* The world was always made of this. Now at last he opened his mouth and swallowed it, let it become himself. The salt dark filled his lungs. He was safe, he was safe: home at last.

FOURTH ANGEL

1

Umbriel

He woke with the worst hangover he had ever had in his life. But his mind was clear. He knew precisely what had been going on before he lost consciousness for the last time. He remembered Otto's angry eyes, blazing at him across the restaurant table, and no, it was not injustice. Anyone who lived in comfort in this world deserved her fury. Ah, but poor Otto she knew, too. She had always known that this was what must win in the end, for all the marching and standing up to be counted. He lay bathed in the truth, a red-shot blackness. You couldn't call these things pain and fear, once you knew there was nothing else. It was just the world, the normal everyday world... Slowly his eyes opened and he turned his head. The cell door was open and Luci stood there, in the clothes he wore when he had to face the governors' committee. Beside him was a dark blue uniform – James avoided looking at the face attached.

Luci's expression was wary and reserved.

'Was it about a bicycle?' he asked.

'That's not funny.'

James closed his eyes, smiling weakly.

'I thought I was on the road to the airport.'

'I'll bet you did. Can you stand up?'

'Oh, yes.'

But when he tried he fell, grabbing at the side of the bunk. He noticed with surprise that he was naked except for his underpants. So that was why it was so cold.

Luci left the doorway. He put his arms around James, kissing his bruised throat and shoulder.

'Oh, my rainbow warrior. James, my little lamb. How many times have I told you? – *never* cheek a policeman.'

The uniform watched impassively as they got James dressed: Luci keeping up all the while a soft, light commentary. 'Now James just

105

sign anything you're told to sign and speak when you are spoken to. Not at all if possible. Lose any teeth? No? Jolly good. I must recommend Reading bobbies for the discreet damage award. Does it hurt to breathe? Not much? Okay. Let's see your eyes. Not bad. Now here we go. Don't do anything. Don't smile don't frown. And if you feel surprised – at any point – don't show it. Withdraw your presence from this James. Be elsewhere. You're good enough at that when you want to be...'

In this way they walked out to the front desk. James did not understand. He assumed he would find himself in another cell eventually and Luci would not be allowed to stay for long. He saw that someone was already standing by the counter, and noticed vaguely the gold BREAKTHRU costume under a very well cut grey overcoat. He only thought: that's strange. They arrested the other one. Still dumbly obedient he followed Luci outside through the tall concrete riot baffles, out of the police compound. It seemed to be mid afternoon, grey and chill. Suddenly James baulked, hugging the plastic envelope he had acquired.

'What day is this?'

'I think it's probably tomorrow James.'

The street was unfamiliar. This was Reading, he remembered.

'Where's my car?'

Luci sighed. 'Car? What car? 'Fraid you had an accident my boy. One of those things you signed was a report on the subject. It looked a bit terminal. I'm shocked, frankly. Naturally no honest provincial bobby likes to see an ethnic person of your description driving a pretty little thing like that. But why take it out on the poor dumb machine?'

James's eyes filled with tears.

'You mean the TR's dead too?'

'Sorry, love. I should have broken it more gently. Come on. Let's move before they change their minds.'

The car they got into was Otto's ancient Renault. James did not question that. Apparently they were giving someone a lift. The figure in the grey overcoat had followed them out of the police station. He coolly opened a back door and cleared himself a place in the morass of rubbish. At this James looked at Luci doubtfully, but Luci affected not to notice. Perhaps I should know this person, thought James. Perhaps I have amnesia. In his mind clouds drifted, covering and revealing. The actual events of the last few days had receded. Their significance loomed larger. He had grasped an enormously important concept. It was written in the street, in passing faces, in the sky.

The town centre was jammed solid with traffic, perhaps the motorway was still blocked. Cars edged around potholes and jostled slowly across faded one way markings. Children ran out whenever things came to a complete standstill, trying to sell newspapers and cheap sweets. But all the drivers sat motionless: their eyes set, stunned, despairing. James saw endless reflections of himself. He emptied the envelope into his lap and discovered that all his possessions seemed to be intact except for one gold and turquoise ear stud. He hid the passport quickly before anyone could take it away again, and held in his hand the heavy little black canister.

'What did I do?'

'You breached the peace, James. But don't worry. You accepted a formal caution just now. And since you had a good character reference we may hear no more about it.'

Small palms batted at the windows.

The first necessity was to get away. James was grateful that Luci seemed to understand this and drove in silence. He said nothing about his ferocious headache. Eventually they pulled up in a layby before a petrol station on the outskirts of town. Luci left the car and returned with a plastic cup of water and a packet of painkillers.

The water was cold and bitter, it hurt his throat to swallow: but James began to feel a little more normal. He looked at Luci, who ran a hand through his slick bleached hair and stared ahead, bleakly.

'How did you know where I was? Did the police call you?'

Luci turned. James saw that his silence had not been forbearance. He had been keeping quiet because he was absolutely furious and trying not to show it.

'Candide's disappeared, James. Ah, I see that does not astonish you.' His eyes snapped. 'Everybody knows what's goin' on except me. Otto turned up at the flat this morning, caught me on my way out to school. I was surprised. I'd assumed you were with her, you naughty stop-out – '

'Luci, it was one freak – '

'Hush. Not in company, please. Anyway, there was Otto, gibbering. As I was trying to make sense of her garbled tale, there comes another buzz on the doorphone. Who should be standin' on the front mat but my very own guardian angel, come to tell me that my boyfriend is at Reading police station and possibly a little the worse for wear. Why Reading? says I, amazed. Because I know James doesn't wander into the sticks, he's a good child.' Luci's mouth turned down at the corners in a moue of exasperation. 'Well, as if there isn't enough trouble in the world, my angel then launches into another extraordinary story – *most of which is quite familiar to Otto Murray.* I mean gosh, James, what did a boy do wrong? Are we not best friends any more? Is it right, is it kind to go off and have all these adventures...'

James turned around carefully, minding his bruises: and stared at the angel. The back of his head felt Luci's anger like a shower of bright insubstantial needles. This childish jealousy of Otto didn't worry him. It was endearing even: nothing to be afraid of. But the angel, though...It was a boy this time, equally young but instead of English fairness had the rich colour of a mediterranean or maybe a subcontinental type: dark curling hair and long lashed full dark eyes. He sat with his coat spread around him, all gilded leather and shining nakedness within. He looked like a mildly erotic advertisement for something. The body paint glowed as if with its own light. Presumably it *was* just paint.

'How did you know where I was? Did they let the girl go?'

'*What fucking girl??*' demanded Luci, outraged.

'Everything one of us knows,' said the angel, 'we all know now.'

On the way back to London the traffic never diminished. It oozed with miserable slowness in both directions. 'Like a summer birdcage in a garden,' murmured Luci. 'The ones who are out want to be in. The ones who are in want to be out.' The only music they could find was an old Nigerian bootleg, which Luci played over and over. Once James tried to switch it off and turn on the radio but Luci slapped his hand away.

'None of that, thank you. Let's concentrate on our own problems while we can.'

Otto met them at the door of the flat. She stared at James solemnly, almost with reverence. He understood that she recognised him as an initiate, and was glad he didn't have to explain. A moment later he realised that the blurred purplish mass he had glimpsed in the hall mirror was his own face. I've lost my job, he thought. I'm not going to look very reassuring for the punters, not for a long time.

After one shocked glance at James, Otto's eyes moved unwillingly to the angel. It was real, it had not disappeared.

It was late, it had taken them hours to cover the thirty miles from Reading. Luci was embracing a large greasy newspaper parcel. 'Us girls will dish up,' he announced. 'You two go and make yourselves at home.'

Otto followed Luci and stood with arms folded, mutinous, while he darted around the elegant fitments of the boys' kitchen. Sometimes she could tolerate this elaborate pastiche of the career housewife (lies, all lies, the musclebound little poser), but not tonight. What the devil did he think he was doing? She glared at him, radiating contempt, while he laid out fish and chips on stylish assymetric china: put the plates to keep warm, assembled napkins, fingerbowls, bottles, jars; freshly squeezed lemon juice, mayonnaise, buffalo milk yoghurt.

A life of pleasurable details...sweet comfort.

Apple vinegar, a little salad from the coolbox...'Now what shall we drink? Some ignorant persons would say white, in fact one wants a fairly robust red with fish and chips, nothing heavy, let us try a nice Côte du Rhone... But we have to think of the angel, mmm, caviar to the sound of trumpets: rather unsophisticated in the food line, we'd better provide him with an Italian white, not too dry... Glasses please Otto. No, not those, the larger goblets...'

Luci let his forehead rest against a cupboard door.

'Now let me think – '.

He could not think. What has happened to me? he was crying. He had never imagined that he would fall apart like this. He would have collapsed on Otto's neck and howled – even Otto – if she had offered the least encouragement. There must be some mistake. Sensationalism, exaggerated reports. It would all blow over.

'By the way Otto, I forgot to thank you.'

'Huh?'

'For the marriage guidance. The therapy sessions.'

His eyes were unenhanced tonight, shining dully like riverwashed pebbles. She recoiled, affronted.

'There was only one.'

The newspaper in which the fish and chips had been wrapped was spread over the kitchen counter. More pastiche, expensive newsprint wrapping luxury food: the poor might as well hope to feast on oysters. Otto did not read newspapers. She couldn't afford to, and anyway they were all as corrupt as state tv. But she noticed the banner headline, translucent in grease. EEC ISRAEL PACT SIGNED. 'Oh, that's come off, has it?' she remarked automatically.

'Making it impossible,' said Luci, 'for the UK to continue the accommodation they have been providing for draft-dodging citizens of the late lamented Commonwealth, because a pact with Israel is alliance with non-Islamic Africa.'

She saw that she was supposed to learn something of vital significance from this speech, but Otto wasn't in the mood for the meaningless complexities of that idiot tomcat war. She had no attention to spare for Luci's pain. All her resources were used up in defence, no funds left for charity.

Next door James took the canister from his pocket. The angel said, making no move to touch it, 'Where's the real one?'

'I don't know.'

'Do you know who has it?'

'I can only guess.'

'That's right, James, be careful. We *can* lie to each other, But the consequences are likely to be very weird.'

He walked over to the music library, shimmering. 'Have you any more January Boys? I liked them.'

The living space in the flat was a vast area, divided by hanging screens. In an alcove was Luci's work station, surrounded by shelves of books and paper. The accent piece was a Madrid school coffee table, they sat around it on mock Roman couches with elaborate scrolled backs. West African masks looked down from the screens, their blank eyes echoing oddly the sardonic gaze of King Charles. A giant rock crystal floor lamp stood like a menhir, like a heathen idol. Otto was thinking how much she hated the boys. Luci had refused to take her to Reading. She had been stuck in this gross temple of consumerism all day, clinging to the telephone, getting no answers from anywhere. There were no lines, she hadn't even been able to contact Candide's father. She had been forced to sit and wait for the men to come back and inject her with information, and now that they had returned she was convinced it was useless. Xav's emissary was only here to make sure that she was suffering enough. All the furniture was rimmed in black. The air smelled of ozone, as if literally charged with foreboding.

James was amazed, briefly, at the fish and chips banquet. He

cast a startled glance at his lover, but Luci was playing crime and
punishment and was not going to acknowledge James's existence
until they were alone. No one else seemed to notice anything
unusual.

'So what's going on?' demanded Otto. 'Where is my son?'

The angel was naked under his kilt, except for a gold mesh pouch
that cupped his genitals. His breastplate seemed to be made of a
supple plastic rather than metal or leather. Every detail was moulded
into it, including exaggerated erect nipples. He leaned forward and
started to eat from one of the plates. Suddenly Otto saw the black
canister. She grabbed it and thrust it at him.

'Look, here it is. This is what you want. You can have it back
as soon as I have Candide, alive and unharmed.'

She knew as she spoke that she was talking nonsense. The
angel had his mouth full, but he grinned and shook his head so the
glistening dark curls trembled on his shoulders.

He swallowed. 'Show them what Barry showed you, James.'

He was the one in control here. They had no weapons against
him and no surprises to offer, his manner made that clear.

James unsealed the tape and shook out the contents of the tube
into the archipelago of Luci's picnic.

'I'm sorry Otto.'

'Candide picked your lock,' explained the angel. 'No one kidnapped him. He has run away with some valuable and dangerous
property belonging to BREAKTHRU, and that's why I'm with
you now.'

Otto stared, trying to control and hide a blinding rush of relief:
but the relief quickly passed. Xav's angel watched her, smiling all
the while.

She gritted her teeth. 'No, I don't understand. If you haven't got
Candide, what is there to talk about? Just go away. I'll find him.
And as soon as I do you can have this whatever-it-is back. There's
no need to threaten me. Or have anyone else beaten up.'

'But we don't think you will find him, Otto. Not without our
help.'

The angel licked his fingers. 'This is very good food. I can
help you recover your son, Otto. I don't ask you to trust me
or anyone who sent me. I am simply all you've got. And I
promise you, if we don't find him soon you will never see him
again. At least, not in any shape you will recognise...No, that's

not a threat. Nobody knows, nobody knows what will happen, if Kairos stays in the hands of a child, who cannot possibly understand...'

He paused and waited for their response, as if everything had been made clear.

She could not imagine where Candide would have gone, or why he would run away.

'Who are you anyway? One of Xav's minions? Do you even have a name?'

The angel picked up a piece of fish and ate some of it, with relish, before he answered. 'You can call me – Umbriel.'

'All right Umbriel. What do you want from us?'

She was ready to play whatever game the little beast wanted to play, she had no choice. But James at this stirred from his dazed silence: his familiar voice sounding very odd coming out of the mess that they'd made of his face.

'Otto, wait,' he said. 'Umbriel, when I was at Barry's plant I met another angel. She seemed to want to help us too. But the police took her away, and beat me up when I tried to find out why. Whereas you and those particular officers seemed to get on very well. Could you explain that?'

'What did she call herself, James? Since names are clearly chosen to suit the occasion.'

'I don't know. We didn't get that far.'

Umbriel, angel of the shadows, moon of the ruler of change, shook his head sadly at them both. 'Otto, if she said she belonged to the light it wouldn't help you. Light and dark doesn't mean wrong and right, does it. And I warn you, don't set too high a value on our apparent divisions. We are all one now. Whether we like it or not.'

Luci was lying propped on one elbow on the rug. He had filled a tumbler half and half with vodka and white wine, and as he drank he began to feel a little better. He noticed that the angel was not only enjoying his power, he was also very excited in a way that Luci recognised fondly: the shining eyes, the big nervous grin, the uncontrollable shivering. There were no horses around and nothing big and bonebreaking that had to be jumped over at speed, but angel boy was about to do something that scared him very much indeed – and loving the sensation. He wondered if he ought to warn the others that they were dealing with an adrenalin junkie who could see a big fix just ahead. But the scene seemed far away and none of his concern.

(Grief, grief, grief. It's over, it's over... Why can't you just piss off, leaderene, and take your trouble with you.)

Otto saw Luci watching the angel intently, and felt disgusted. He probably fancies the creep she thought viciously. I bet if we weren't here they'd slip into the toilet and have a quick fuck. She was in a mood to be brutal about someone who couldn't harm her: Luci would do.

Umbriel picked up the piece of lead pipe and examined it as if for inspiration.

'Okay, so we'll rerun the story so far. The container that has gone astray holds an enormous quantity, relatively speaking, of a very new and potentially very dangerous drug. A while ago the container was given to James who gave it to Otto. We've been trying to get the stuff back. The method used so far might seem to you grotesque, but there was a reason for it – '

Otto stared with cold distaste: the angel was unruffled by her opinion.

'This drug operates in a way that won't be familiar to you. With the concentration that is packed in that little tube, there is no need to ingest it. It affects any contacts like a kind of radiation. Touch isn't necessary, even: intention is enough. The reason you kept it for so long without feeling any effects Otto, is that you were – well, you were protected but in the circumstances it is hard to tell whether that was effective. It might be better to say you were safe until you started thinking about it: all of you.'

Somewhere outside in the city a night devil began to shriek. Police, ambulance? The unearthly cadence blocked speech, it went on for far too long.

'They're testing the sirens,' said Umbriel. He seemed overtaken by a fit of secret laughter, looking down at his own golden hands; a joke he could not share.

'We in BREAKTHRU have habituated ourselves with incredibly minute doses. We're safe enough – '

Drug. He had said that before sometime – this morning: Kairos was a drug, not a roll of film after all. Most of the fantastic by-products of modern medicine were more or less legal – because the poor didn't use them – and therefore unexciting financially. What could it be that packed so small and yet was new and interesting to villains?

'What kind of a drug?'

'What kind of a drug? Oh – listen.' Umbriel's voice changed.

It was a different persona now, one he thought might suit them better: tricks of the doorstep religionist. 'You know what the acid breakthrough was, sixty years ago? This is bigger still. This is totally different from anything that's gone before. You know how the neural inhibitors work? Mind crackers? This is infinitely infinitely better than that. You see, mind crackers work on the like DNA and dendrites and the basic chemical agents, but the Kairos works not even actually on the atoms that make up the cells of your brain but deeper than that on the you know, quarks and kaons and so on. It gets right back to the um, sub-particulate interface between mind and matter. It is operating under Planck's constant, down where everything turns into everything else. It's like, *you can really play around with things.*'

His eyes glistened. 'You know what it means to spike someone? Well, with Kairos it's like you do that, but the drug experience is yours. D'you see what I mean? It gives a completely new significance to the expression 'consciousness expanding'. Your consciousness expands over whoever's around you. Because when you get down there, there's no difference, and with the Kairos they just run together, like to like. I mean, any scientist would tell you it's possible. Things happen in the mind – of such colour, such charm, such strangeness. You know what I mean – time runs backwards, things appear out of nothing.'

Umbriel giggled. He looked around to see if anyone was sharing the joke.

Luci gazed into his momentarily empty tumbler, keeping a straight face.

'It came from a bio-chemical plant originally, in Saudi or somewhere around that area. The Islamics called it "Al'jawar", the real thing. We call it Kairos, that's greek, it means opportunity. The Americans at the lab, expats, called it Ego Dominus Tuus.'

Luci allowed himself to chuckle now. 'Is that supposed to be Latin? American Latin, maybe.'

James was lying back in a corner of the couch being elsewhere, as Luci had told him to be at the police desk. He felt a little worried about the way Luci was drinking. But he was only half in this place. Half of him was on the road to the airport watching truth: making up for twenty years of lies and evasion. He opened his half shut eyes, briefly.

'A late dialect, Lu. It is what Love said to Dante, at the start of his Vita Nuova.'

Luci began to laugh.

'Oh ho,' he chuckled. 'Oh, Umbriel, is that who you're dealing with? No wonder you are scared shitless.'

The angel gave him a long thoughtful look.

'Anyway – ' he said to Otto and James, 'the thing is, when you get near to someone who's in Al'jawar – which is what we say, rather than its in them – you've got *no idea* what's going to happen next... And that's at our doses. With this amount...'

Umbriel grinned, and shook his head, and shuddered.

A crazy suspicion came into Otto's mind then, from nowhere. It was like the sting of an insect: making her start and flash a look of sudden anger at James.

'But let's stop playing quiz games.'

The angel had changed gear again, becoming suddenly serious and analytical.

'You're feeling upset and confused, I know that. Maybe it would help if I explained what is happening here in BREAKTHRU terms, in terms of our relationship with The Yes. You see you two, James and Otto, probably think of yourselves as outsiders, dissenters. That isn't true at all. In fact you epitomise the present state of the world, especially in this country and the others like it: white consumerism. A man-living woman and a woman-living man, wanking off with your backs to each other. You're very comfortable in your separate ways but deep down it's all based on denial. You really hate this world, both of you.'

Luci snorted under his breath. Umbriel turned on him with a sweet smile. 'And your name's Gordon, isn't it Dr Lytten – but you make everyone call you Luci. And you work in a slum school when you could be doing high prestige research. There's more denial.'

Luci felt ridiculously put out to learn that the angel had rumbled him. Put out? No, positively chilled. Though why it should be dangerous that this idiot chemical-head knew there was someone in the room unlikely to be bemused by a load of old psychic-physics ...he didn't know. He was too drunk to make any sense of it.

'You three don't think much of the company, do you? You think we're harmless cranks like yourselves. But you know, most changes in the world have been brought about by a mere handful of men, a visionary elite: we see ourselves as part of that great tradition. I'm sorry Otto. I would say 'people', but the fact is cela n'arrive jamais. We didn't engineer sex differences, it's natural...You see us as a little enclave here, a little group in the States, another in France and so on. But we know anything is possible. We're not afraid to grasp the irrational, the impossible deed. It can be done. We can achieve our aims. And you are exactly the right sort of people to help us.'

Otto stirred angrily. 'Do we have to listen to this fascist drivel? Even you must realise you're not going to pick up any recruits tonight. Get to the point.'

'But I am there.'

'Sorry, you've lost me.'

'I know.' His lips stretched wide: he tucked the grin away carefully and arranged his features in a serious frown.

'We want the Kairos. We know that at least one of you has to be aware of the child's location...I'm here to help you reach that knowledge.'

Luci stretched himself beside his glass. (Dangerous, dangerous. We had better not cross this bastard. James is well out of it, but doesn't Otto see?)

'Ah, now we come to cases. Unto the middle of the bridge and further there were none.' He smiled up at the angel, teasing gently. 'The blip has gone from your screen, has it? But how can that be, we ask ourselves. What about quantum inseparability, Umbriel, my son? And speaking of implausibilities, isn't this user-used dichotomy a bit of a canard to start with – ?'

'Oh, shut up Luci.' Otto steeled herself. 'I have no idea where Candide is. But if I did know, of course I wouldn't tell you. So come on. What's the real story?'

The angel turned to her in a golden glitter of movement. 'I know you don't have access to the information, Otto. But I can help you. The real story goes like this. Somebody here agrees to join me in a sexual experience of The Yes, and that way we bring unconscious knowledge to the surface. You have to fuck with me. It means communicate, doesn't it?'

He smiled into her suddenly stony face.

'And if none of you wants to fuck with BREAKTHRU, then I will have to go back to my boss, Mr Howard, and tell him that you're not being very cooperative.'

Silence. The angel watched Otto swallow this nasty little mouthful.

'Is that why you came dressed up?' she demanded abruptly. 'Is that costume supposed to turn me on? I'd rather eat shit.'

Which was exactly what Xav wanted to see her do.

'Sex is death, Otto. And death is sex. You're right, our costume is meant to be sexy. But it's not for fun. Sex is information passed on: and everybody knows if there were no such process, we'd be immortal. BREAKTHRU wants to smash this world and make way for the next, so you see we have to be very interested in sex in all its forms: even though, of course, we have to smash it too.'

Luci burst into a shout of appreciative laughter.

'What, right here on the rug?'

'Francis Xavier,' declared James, raising his eyes and addressing the empty air. 'You surpass yourself.'

The angel looked from one to the other. 'Well?'

Otto wanted to weep. Umbriel was lying. Xav had Candide and whatever was in that original container too: obviously. What was happening was simply revenge. She had to find a place to stand, couldn't let herself be dragged any further. It must be here then: we don't cooperate with terrorists. If she ate this there would be more, and more, and more. It's only Xav, she thought. He can't do anything terrible, not to Candide. She knew he could. He would do it anyway.

'I'm a lesbian. Find me a little girl-angel.'

'Yeah, but I hear you make exceptions.'

The insect stung again, but she ignored it. Luci was cackling foolishly. How I hate him, thought Otto. He'd love to see me humiliated too, well he shall not.

'James?'

'Sorry, I'm too worn out after the policemen's ball.'

'Luci - '

Strips of leather slipped from Umbriel's golden thighs. The sexual invitation of his costume was suddenly strongly apparent: although a moment ago it had seemed only bizarre. Otto felt herself totally unmoved, and yet aware of the change. What was Umbriel doing? Had he secretly broken a concealed phial of pheromones, part of the sales kit of every BREAKTHRU rep? She was not surprised at all to see Luci sitting up cheerfully.

'Shit – why not? What harm can it do?'

Why not indeed, though he wasn't sure just now whether he was humouring the dangerous angel or doing this to spite the leaderene. Her face – when the wicked male suggested sex on the rug. What a joke! And James in his dream, refusing nicely as if someone had offered him a biscuit: the blotted, ruined ghost of James's lovely smile.

(his heart crumpled into everlasting darkness...)

Luci and the angel knelt facing each other on the grey rug in front of the coffee table. The angel began very seriously to poke the index finger of his right hand through the circled finger and thumb of the other, while Luci did the same and they gazed into each other's eyes. She was called James Dominic Esumare, thought James. She was myself. I don't think she was arrested, I don't think she was ever there...He was drawn back from his inner vision, by the change of alignment in the room. Luci and his guardian angel absorbed in their private no-risk orgy: it was like a parody of the old days when Luci used to try to force him, by some fairly exhibitionist behaviour, to play around as well. But that time was over long ago...

Otto looked at James, signalling *I don't like this...* Was Luci just pissed or was he actually drugged in some way? It was extraordinary how *empty* this Umbriel creature was. From moment to moment there was no continuity in him...The horrible suspicion, the stinging insect, attacked her again: she was guessing at something outrageous. The sudden terrifying notion that perhaps this wasn't a practical joke at all.

When she glanced back to the rug, she found Luci and the angel locked in a close embrace. As she watched they moved together, the angel's plump gold pouch kneading into Luci's crotch.

Luci drew back from the shining musculature. He stripped off his shirt and trousers. Like the angel, he was visibly aroused. 'Isn't this a riot?' he laughed. Suddenly he seemed very drunk indeed.

'Come on, James, let's have some fun. Put Otto out in the hall,' – he was becoming incoherent – ' – s'nothing to do with Candy. Poor little bugger's done for like the rest of us. Come on James, last chance, don't be a spoilsport – '

He grappled with the angel mumbling as he kissed, his tanned body catching gleams of Umbriel's light.

Otto was paralysed, amazed, wished she had a bucket of water. She glared indignantly at James – *What does your boyfriend think he's doing?* But James only motioned with one lax hand, for her to keep quiet.

This tableau vivant arranged by Xav did not impress him at all. Only Luci had seemed to look at him soberly once, out of the angel's embrace. Luci's eyes said he knew the truth too.

That must be why he had been drinking so hard. It must be telepathy...

James noticed then how far he was taking it for granted that the angel was, in some practical way, Francis himself. Did that mean he believed in the properties of this drug, Kairos? He had hardly been listening to the story Umbriel told. He hoped it was true that Candide was still safe (as far as anyone was ever safe). Wherever he might be...

Watch out. Mustn't think about Candide now.

James sat up. Adrenalin flooded him before he knew why. Only then he saw the angel had pulled his gilded dagger out of its sheath. It was not a toy. James leapt to his feet. He propelled himself across the space between, screaming in terror. He grabbed the angel by the shoulders and hauled backwards. His hand closed on solid flesh but somehow ineffectively. He fell away, warm liquid splashed on his chest. He pulled, he tugged, but the arm had uncanny strength and it went on thrusting in out, in out, in a hideous mockery of copulation. He could hear Otto screaming Luci! Luci!

Umbriel was backed off, crouched against the table sobbing, whimpering like a dog. There was blood all over the place. Luci lay on his back with his legs doubled under him. Otto was trying to breathe into his mouth. James grabbed something (a shirt). Wadding it, he lunged forward. Get me some more cloth! he shouted, but nothing came to his hand.

Wad was working. No. The blood and air had stopped pumping, from those frothing open splits in the ribcage. There was blood on Luci's mouth. His eyes were open, his head laid back by Otto's knees. How do you revive someone with wounds like that?

James stared at Otto, over the body. He was trying to say *get a doctor* but could not make the words.

They went on kneeling like that, until Umbriel crept forward and stood looking down, huddling himself in his bloody arms.

'Don't call the police,' he whispered. 'Don't call the police. You might get the wrong person. I've got a number, let me call my number. Let me call the Bin Men. We have a contract. It's, you know, necessary sometimes...'

Eventually James heard Otto say: 'I think we'd better let him send for these people.'

Umbriel fumbled with the phone: snivelling, his teeth chattering. He seemed a different person. He looked smaller, and the body paint had lost its glow.

'O God,' he mumbled. 'I didn't mean to do it. Fucking is so like stabbing blood's information, isn't it. I'm on drugs, I'm not responsible...'

'Yes. It's a "big job".'

'Yes.'

'There's a lot of blood, that's all – '

The Bin Men arrived, from the kind of refuse collection firm that asks no questions except the strictly practical kind. They came well equipped. They moved Luci into a large plastic sack, along with his clothes and the guardian angel dagger. They checked the flat over, then cleaned the whole problem area with dry foam, and did not forget to polish the phone. They ignored the two non-clients entirely.

Otto heard one of the men say to Umbriel. 'This place is being followed.' 'Yes, I know,' he answered in a low voice. The team left. Umbriel went with them, wrapped in a dark blue blanket over the bloodstained fantasy dress.

Δ

Otto rebuilt an array of bolts and switches. When she turned round she was facing one of the Playboy pictures, blown up to poster size. James in a clinging muscle T swimsuit reclined on sunbaked rock by some African seashore: really very chaste. *Brilliant young actor James Esumare gets our wow reviews. James has a first class honours degree in European History. His best sport is dancing, particularly in private with that special partner. He is also an ace silver-service waiter!*

The hallway held one sombre rococo armchair, a pink and yellow rag rug and a row of coathooks. On another wall there was more framed memorabilia: a screen print of a photo of Luci's noticeboard from his room in Cambridge long ago. The childish scribbles and treasured arcane phrases looked so pitiful, enshrined like that.

Special Relativity Is Much Easier Than The Ordinary Kind

The Magic Word Is A Duck

On the armchair lay Luci's black briefcase, embossed in silver: Impossible Mission Force.

'Why?' she said aloud – and her voice cracked. 'Why kill him? It doesn't make sense.'

But in secret she was thinking, singlemindedly – I've lost my only chance. Umbriel was my only chance to reach Candide.

The hanging panels in the big room had become a strange blank maze. James was where she had left him, sitting like Rameses with his forearms along his thighs.

She picked up the cable control, thumbed the screen on and found herself watching the evening news. The whole room was ringing, ringing. Something peculiar had happened to the news. She waited in vain for an item on the EU–Israel pact. In fact, this must be a faction-drama. She tried a few other channels. Nothing but testcards and bad prints of aged films anywhere, continental or domestic. What time is it? And still the nightmare rang in her head. She became uneasy and tried to return to her newscast. The screen dissolved into jumping pixels: she had dropped the control. She picked it up and switched off. What do you do when someone has died by violence? Maybe it is wrong to watch tv.

'James, you're covered in blood. You'd better wash and change.'

'So are you.'

But she felt she was the competent one. She took Rameses by the arm and eased him to his feet. They moved two steps, he stopped.

'Blood.'

He pulled his shirt over his head and clutched the stained bundle frantically.

'That will come out,' she reassured him. 'Soak it in cold salt water.'

James stared, incredulous.

'Sorry,' she muttered. 'I'm sorry.'

He took his chance and broke away. He made for the bedroom, it was empty. The flat smelled of cleaning foam.

'Why did you let them take Luci away?' he shouted. 'Why didn't we call the police? I'm going to call the police – '

'The police are not our friends James. You agreed – '

'I don't remember that.'

He shied and bolted back to the Madrid table, where the phoneset lay among shattered fragments of Luci's icons of protection. But she was there before him and pulled out the jack.

'James you mustn't. Don't.'

She could see he wouldn't give up. She wrapped the cable round her hand and tugged savagely: it came out of the handset.

She knew there was only one other phone in the flat, a cordless. She had seen it lying on Luci's workstation. She ran for it before he could remember, brought it back.

'I want to call the police.'

She was breathing hard. Her mind was catching up with her desperate body, she could explain.

'James, this is serious. We can't trust the police. Didn't you hear what that maniac said? BREAKTHRU is plotting something, some mad act involving this stuff Kairos. Why he told us, I don't know. Just to show off – But if we report Luci's murder, the least we'll be is witnesses. We'll be helpless, and no one else knows. Maybe that's why he killed Luci – Oh, no, no. I get it. He killed Luci because Lu *knows* about stuff like this – '

He wouldn't try to overpower her, not James. He sat collapsed on a couch still hugging his bloody shirt, staring at her with animal eyes, waiting for her to be off her guard. She licked her lips. It was hopeless, she wasn't getting through.

'Listen James, it's Candide. I can't be trapped. I've got to find him before BREAKTHRU does. If you call the police, will you swear not to tell them I was here? It can't make any difference to Luci.'

But he couldn't be trusted. He wouldn't remember to lie. Even if he tried, they would catch him out. Even if she killed this phone too, he would go out and find a callbox. He was out of his mind with shock. And not only that, she remembered, His brain – mind – was full of Kairos, the protean substance converted into terror. It was pouring out of him, infecting Otto, giving her nightmare ideas (such as: there's only one way to be sure he keeps quiet...).

She had a startling glimpse of herself, infected by James, raving and clutching a telephone as if it was a club. She recalled the newscast that was like hair-raising fiction.

Her eyes widened, and widened, and widened.

She's going to faint, he thought. Then I'll get it.

Otto dropped the phone. She put her hands up to her temples. James dived – but she had her foot on the plastic body.

'*James.*'

She grabbed the little machine again, holding him off with the extraordinary expression in her eyes. She began to talk, rapidly. 'Listen, listen James. I want to tell you about Candide. I was thinking of killing you just now – *no, listen.* It's about the day he was born. I did good in labour you know. I've got a wide pelvis and everything worked. There was no pain. Of course there was pain, but only that of the most unbelievable, blinding physical effort. And Sandy was with me. We were doing it together, climbing K2 maybe. But the baby itself – it was a political decision you know, to have it. And now had no meaning at all. That was how I felt when they gave me Candide. I wasn't at all interested. I don't know when it happened James. One day in those first weeks it was suddenly – you and me against the world, baby. How can I describe to you? I felt like an animal. No, no. The apotheosis of an animal. I was doing something I was designed to do, by all the pressures and counter pressures of thousands of millions of years. But consciously. Willing it. I was making the dumb chemistry into *me*, *Otto*...Oh, sometimes I really hate him. But do you understand?'

He only watched, alert and mutely intransigent as a sick cat.

She shook her head, and winced. The ringing still went on.

'James, am I right. You were stopped at a roadblock out in Reading. There were men in uniform, they attacked you. I'm sorry James, but would I be right in saying that hit a pretty deep trauma of yours? And now Luci. James, would you say that you and I are in the process of living out our worst fears – ?'

At last, a glimmer of intelligence. 'What are you saying?'

'I'm saying this isn't just happening, this is being done to us. You know how it is with any psychotropic. The mood you're in when you take the stuff defines your experience. We've been given a massive dose of Kairos, and then systematically frightened out of our minds. We are being used by the BREAKTHRU company. For an – oh, I can't make you see it. For an act of surreal terrorism.'

The room had become enormous. Its shuttered windows were like dead eyes. Grotesque faces peered at her, hanging in the air. Otto's throat hurt, she had been screaming and shouting for too long. She felt her mind struggling to pin together the scraps of this monstrous plot, in some way that would convince. She couldn't do it. Her knees had begun to shake. She saw Luci's workstation. If she had a password to the nets ... But she didn't. That world was too expensive, and too well-policed for the likes of Otto. But if it were true, who could she tell? No one on the networks. *There was no one she could tell...*

James had lost the dumb animal look.

'Listen – Don't you remember what the boy said. Xav uses this stuff. He used it on us, at Betty's wedding I know he did. I felt him watching. I mean, I felt someone...'

James moved carefully, his eyes gentle. 'No one gave us a dose of anything, Otto. The angel was talking nonsense from start to finish. And whatever is in that tub, Gerry stole it.'

She sneered. 'That was a plant, stupid.'

He was on his feet and moving towards her.

'Otter, I know how you feel. You want there to be a meaning, any meaning – '

She retreated, holding the phone in front of her. She had forgotten its function, it had become simply a hostage.

'It might be true,' she whispered, stunned. 'What I said. It might be true.' She was trying to reach for her jacket which was hanging on the back of a couch.

'James it's no use. I can't stay with you. We can't trust each other. I mean, at all. I don't even know if you're here.'

The jacket was in her hand. James looked terrible. His face was grey, puffy with bruises, his bare torso smeared with Luci's blood. She felt a spasm of revulsion, for the fucking that was so like stabbing, for chemical heads and orgiastic violence. This was the place for it. This is boystown, they have nights like this all the time.

'I'm leaving. I have to find Candide.'

She threw the phone back into the hall, yanked the outer grille across and ran.

After a few moments James followed as far as the front door. Mechanically he fastened it all up. He went back and sat down, his head in his hands. He ought to go after Otto. She was in such a state, she shouldn't be alone. He was trying to make himself move when he saw a corner of brown paper under the table. He crouched and groped. The two envelopes had both been opened. They were spattered and crumpled, they must have been in Luci's pocket. One was stamped all over, forwarded via the Nigerian Embassy. The other was from the Immigration Office. His resident's permit had been cancelled. The first thing was his call up papers.

So that was what made Luci drink vodka splits: that was what made him so vulnerable that he fell for Xav's trick angel.

They had always said they would not be parted. They would go bush and live in the Forest like outlaws, if the dreaded day ever came. The papers fell from his hand. He rolled over on his side and began to cry, rocking the bloody shirt in his arms.

2

The Island Where Dreams Come True

It was dark, the grey darkness of a winter morning without streetlight. She stepped around humpy archipelagoes of bus station transients, and the yellow glimmer of their lights and bucket-braziers. The big dolphin fountain in the Steine gardens had been seriously vandalised, the whole stone dish was on its side: it looked like the aftermath of an earthquake. She walked, because she couldn't remember where she had left the car, skirting an enormous hole that had appeared outside the derelict old polytechnic buildings. Was that there yesterday? More sewers must have fallen in. Eventually she recalled that she had driven it to London and forgotten to drive it back. This satisfied her for a while and she didn't ask her memory what had happened up there. There was no traffic on the roads at all. She passed a petrol station where the pump blocks had been torn out and lay with their roots in the air like extracted teeth. Strangely, there was no smell of petrol.

Now a brutal weight descended on her. On foot or driving it would always be the same. She would never approach this street without remembering the house of lights. The same sick foreboding would fill her: coming home was ruined. We'll have to move. We'll have to start up afresh in another town, nothing less will do. Then she remembered there was no more 'we'. Someone – euphemism, almost certainly not a woman – had smashed up Wombega's front window. Peggy must have forgotten to put the shutters up. Inside, her shop was grey with dust. The pages of the books scattered on the floor were yellow and dimpled with moisture.

There were people now, out in the street. They stood in groups in the murk in oddly assorted garments, as if there had been a fire in the middle of the night. A noise came from them, compound of crying and muttering and the occasional loud angry wail of a frightened infant. But none of the faces seemed to move.

'What's happened?' asked Otto.

The man passing by stared at her and she couldn't tell what he saw. As she looked into his eyes the solid stone beneath her feet gave way. It seemed to melt into nothingness. She clutched the doorposts for support.

Mrs Eliot ran up, a transmuted Mrs Eliot, hugging a ragged crochet shawl over her nightie. She was no longer improperly dressed.

'Oh, she's gone away Mrs Murray,' she cried. 'She's gone and took the children. She left me the address, look I'll write it down.'

'The *children*!' shouted Otto.

'When I think, it was only the little piccaninny. Such a lovely little girl, always smiling – '

Otto knew she was talking to a ghost. She knew a walking corpse: the woman who spoke out of its face now had been dead and rotten for years. Her skin crawled.

'Mrs Eliot – what was it?'

Skinny shoulders lifted and fell. The old lady peered at her silent neighbours.

'I hope it's not going to be like the last one, with cards and evacuations. They took me away from my Mum, I was only a little girl but I've never forgotten it. I thought with modern war it was all over very quick.'

The door of the squat off Dyke Road was standing open. The toilet had been concreted already. Burst plastics lay about, scattering pathetic trails of spook regalia. Up in Sandy's garret she found a slashed and twisted mattress, a hole in the floor and very little else.

She walked along Western Road in the alien land of big chain stores. There was another place where the road had fallen in, a hollow black ragged rectangle. Some of the shops had been looted, others were untouched. The silence was uncanny. Nothing moved, not even a breeze to blow the litter. She was shivering and repeating under her breath the word revolution. Revolution, revolution, revolution. Western Road, which had always been approximately level, developed a steep incline, so steep it made her breathe hard to climb it. She was appalled, filled with terror: a hideous, formless, unlimited sense of betrayal.

The next thing she knew she was lying in bed with her eyes open, in the spare room of her father and stepmother's Highbury maisonette. Raushan's blue and white batik blinds were drawn at the window. The loss and betrayal of the dream had inverted itelf in her waking, producing an almost unbearable sense that she was the one who had done something wrong, badly wrong. She sat up. She was fully dressed, sticky and dirty. Her watch had stopped.

She remembered arriving here last night or in the early morning: and being passionately grateful at finding the place empty. It shouldn't be. This wasn't a weekend and the House was in session. But she had slept like the dead and the weight of that dream was still heaped on her mind. It was not easy to decide even what day of the week this was.

The anodyne tasteful room was familiar enough to be soothing. She sat at the dressing table and saw in the mirror that Luci's blood was still around her mouth.

Oh, Christ.

Doubled over, fists clenched between her knees, she tried to think coherently. Candide was lost and Luci was dead. The thought of James struck a nerve. Of course he had not believed her, after the Bin Men left. She had been raving. When the time for it came it was going to be difficult to explain that smashed phone, and the way she'd run off from the scene of the crime like a mad woman.

She wondered now if she believed the mad woman herself.

The signs were that Raushan and her father had not been gone for long. The kitchen was stocked even to perishables. There was the impression of a suitcase in the plumped up quilt on their bed. But there wasn't a functioning timepiece in the flat. Eating bread and butter and marmalade standing (she was ravenous) she dialled the talking clock. The line just hummed: must be a fault.

An act of surreal terrorism.

Xav had been in prison, but not out of circulation, when Gerry 'stole' the Kairos. He had picked out his brother as the ideal subject – she could believe that. Planted the device weeks in advance in classic style, sat back and waited for his moment. He couldn't have picked out Otto or planned the dog-blackmail, he couldn't have known how things were going to work. But Xav was nothing if not an opportunist.

Why would BREAKTHRU want to do such a thing? Because to certain minds abject paranoia seems like an ideal working environment. They believed they would not be affected, having innoculated themselves. They set the contaminant loose through James and Otto, like dropping something in the water supply. By the time people start coming back to their senses, there is a revolutionary government. It happens everywhere, why not here. We have a right wing coup, neutron style with all the buildings left standing.

She flashed on Western Road. My God, is that what they want? But it was hard to understand why a sloping pavement should awake such a feeling of horror.

There were problems with this plot. She could see it going badly, badly wrong. Which didn't make it any less likely that she had guessed the truth. You don't have to be clever, you don't have to be able to think something through, to be a psychopath.

With what sadistic glee he had laid his fuses. He had choreographed that attack of lust after Betty's wedding, she was sure of it: a test of his power, of course.

But what was Xav's moment? Otto sat in the capsule kitchen (how grey the sky was, didn't seem to be any daylight) her hands knotted around a mug of tea. She was trying to remember what was happening in the world. What was going on out there? The last few days, what was it, forty-eight hours? No, count back to when she found out about the blackmail...it had been nothing but Candide, Candide. War news. The Sunday Closing act that someone was trying to get through, a vain attempt to resurrect the weekend. Money markets quiet. A stop the news raid on the cable that she'd meant to take part in...which involved cutting in on the state tv to protest about transfer of political prisoners to private jails. (Overeducated criminals, that is: everyone knows there are no pps in this country.) Where they'd probably be better off actually...

She chewed her lip, feeling panic battering and fluttering inside her ribcage and belly. How long was it since Otto knew *what was going on*, besides her little dissident concerns ? She'd given all that up.

She needed her father. In utopia the BREAKTHRU company was a bad joke: those more directly threatened must have some idea of these wild ambitions, must have been noticing ominous signs.

The switchboard at the House of Commons was either deserted or terminally jammed with calls. On the private number Mr Andrew Murray's secretary was temporarily unavailable. He would deal with urgent messages as soon as possible. Tone. She tried the constituency office, on the off chance; but there were no lines to the North.

Otto ate more bread and marmalade, drank a lot of tea and went to the bathroom to clean up. Unfortunately she couldn't change her clothes. She never could handle a sari unaided, and Raushan's tiny western clothes wouldn't go near her.

She arrived at the river, her tube journey a blank. It had been performed on autopilot while she tried to rehearse what she would say. The river buses were not running but it wasn't far to walk. And here she was, coming up to that array of shabby-picturesque little buildings, clustered beside the square as if it was a village green. This next part was not going to be easy, with the record she carried on her id card and no official business. She had tried to get to her father without a prior appointment before, and once spent hours in what seemed to be a real mediaeval dungeon. He said he couldn't help it. They couldn't have just anyone wandering about in the House of Commons. Otto grinned ruefully. This place was a democracy once, for a few days about three hundred and fifty years ago...She had recovered enough to be amused at her situation. She was a strayed sheep returning to the fold, to announce to the wolves in there that some other wolves of an even more rapacious breed were up to even worse mischief.

There was a police cordon across Westminster Bridge. She could see why the buses weren't running. The river was cordoned off too. A restless little crowd hovered against the wall of New Scotland Yard. It came to her, like a temporarily misplaced memory, that the old queen had died. But the crowd wasn't half big enough for that: looked like something fairly minor.

Sorry, no further Miss.

'Why, what's going on?' demanded Otto, slipping into another, more comfortable role. Always ask questions. Use or lose those eroded civil rights.

'The emergency debate.'

'All this for a debate? Well, pardon me for breathing. No – please tell me. I missed the news.'

A squaddie behind the cordon nervously raised his rifle. Otto caught the movement out of the corner of her eye but was not alarmed. That was normal.

'There isn't any news,' said the policeman. 'Not since the attack.'

129

He started to tremble. His hands fumbled over his tunic, searching for a weapon or else trying to hide themselves.

'Just get away from here. Get away from me – '

She looked into his eyes and she couldn't tell what he saw. The solid stone beneath her feet gave way, she felt that hideous, limitless betrayal....

'No – ' she cried. 'Don't be afraid. I know – '

But she saw the rifle move again and knew she had to run.

Otto sat on a bench in the Embankment gardens. The knees of her black wool leggings were tacky and stiff in patches. She tried to pick out the dried stain with her fingernails, forgetting where it had come from. How dark it was, the sky so ominous it looked ready for a summer thunderstorm. But she was cold, and very hungry again. She turned up the collar of her jacket, matted old sheepskin curls comforting her cheeks.

The faction drama she had found on Luci and James's cable in the early hours of this morning had been envisaging a sudden, terrible speeding up and expanding of the Islamic war. EU–Israel pact signed...(no, that was real). In a night, in hours, the EU had changed from a spectator to a battlefield. My God, they must have got through the Russians. Must have been through Germany, that stupid buffer-state arrangement. Or did both parties agree to re-arm the Rhine last year? *I can't remember...* But she remembered now what she had forgotten last night: James and Luci never watched anything in realtime. I watched it after Luci died, but it had been recorded hours before, before the Kairos effect. We are at war. It is here. This is Xav's moment.

It must be true. That police cordon was not imaginery. Or the extraordinary silence everywhere. You live for years in a dangerous, violent world. Merely because for two generations nothing has directly affected your little patch, you start to think you have some special arrangement with the fates. Let the rest of them choke on poison gas: we are going to worry about whether the seven day week is inhumane.

She screwed her eyes shut, shook her head, laughed nervously.

It was impossible.

She remembered then that there was only one thing to do. Find Candide. She took out her wallet, to see how much money she had. Not much. She found herself looking at a small shrivelled bud of a pink chrysanthemum. How did that get there? In Sandy's garret, there had been a milk bottle full of dead flowers. Poor Sandy, this must be meant for some kind of IOU. Though she didn't seem to have taken any money.

Between them, for one to give the other a single flower had always meant *I love you*. It ended quarrels, cut through misunderstandings; reassured.

Her eyes filled with tears. Now she knew what it was, that hideous sense of betrayal. It was Sandy turned into a stranger, the centre of life just vanished: unstable earth, unbreathable air...Wiping her eyes, she put the wallet away. There was something else in her pocket. It was a scrap of paper torn from the flyleaf of a book. The paper looked as if it had been lying in a puddle. One one side was a fragmentary title. THE DIALECTICS OF S. Subtitled, The Case For A Feminist Revolut. On the other side was an address in Crawley, shakily written in an old lady's spider handwriting.

Otto stared. She jumped up, threw the flower and the paper away, and ran out of the gardens.

The great cavernous hangar of Victoria Coach Station was packed with bodies. The poor, like the rich, wanted to get out of the city. They wanted to be with people they loved or to find some place of safety, or were simply forced by instinct to make the motions of escape. Everyone guessed there would be no freedom of movement at all soon. The pa system cried out over the din and waves of the crowd rushed to and fro trying to follow its cryptic instructions.

Otto had decided not to try to find her car. It might be in Clerkenwell and it might be in Highbury: it would be very stupid to go back to either of those addresses. She shuffled and elbowed in an undisciplined queue. She was going to Devon, she was certain that Candide was with his father. She knew that according to the thriller plot of last night she should be doing almost anything but this. If Candide was safe his mother ought to stay well away, she might be leading Xav straight to him. But that didn't make sense any more. Let BREAKTHRU take over the damned country, good luck to them. Let them track her child down, what could they do to him that would be worse than what was going to happen anyway.

Damned, damned. She was trying to keep her eyes to herself, with some idea this would limit the spread of the infection. But how could these people, she kept thinking, be made more afraid

than by the threat of the Holocaust that was rushing over them...
Her hand touched another on the metal dividing rail. The woman
ahead wore a tweed coat over a cheap ugly yellow and green sari. Her
bare chalky heels slipped in and out of a pair of worn down plastic
shoes. She turned and looked at Otto. An unremarkable dark face.
A pair of eyes: where was the mind behind them? What did it see,
what did it touch? Otto wrenched herself out of that, just in time.
She wasn't going to let herself go crazy.

She reached the desk and asked for a ticket to Taunton. The
clerk refused cash. She gave up her credit card and immediately
realised that this was a ploy to get round the business of illegal
wholesale identity checks. He ran her bit of plastic down a print
out list on a clip board. Bodies pressed on all sides. She couldn't
even try to run.

Two police officers came to fetch her. This time if they were
suffering from irrational panic they were able to control it. Otto
was taken to a bus company office that had become some kind of
operations centre. Her mind had cleared. She grabbed the front of
the desk and shouted at the man behind it.

'This isn't really happening! You're the victims of a surreal act
of terrorism!'

The young women wore a mixture of street clothes and uniform.
They were wheeling in and setting up their terminals, uncoiling
ropes of fibreoptic cable. Already, they looked sleepless and desperately competent. Already, the women were coming back, the
young men were needed elsewhere. They looked around at Otto
with black, staring animal eyes.

'You don't have to tell me that,' he said. 'We're getting clear
indications that certain people are prepared to use even this hideous
situation for some imaginary pseudo-political advantage. Which is
why you and your kind are going behind wire, now, at once and
for the duration.'

Come on now Mrs Murray, come quietly. You always knew it
might end up like this. You made your choices long ago.

The sergeant brought her a cup of tea, to a commandeered
ladies' waiting room where an ancient electric heater rattled out
stale warm air. He was fifty, he couldn't remember the last lot:
only what your parents told you. This is not the same, he explained.
They've got the bombs you know, those Islamics, and they're
already using them. That's the truth. They say there's nothing, no

communication at all, come out of the Americas for twenty-four hours. They've gone. They're not there any more. They say the stock market and every computer in Europe crashed last night. It was the electromagnetic surge.

He borrowed all her coins that would fit, to use in the machine that dispensed ready pasted disposable toothbrushes. Anything rather than money, he said. It'll soon enough get down to barter, we've seen that on our models....His hands were shaking slightly.

His whole figure began to shake and dissolve, and the dirty scribbled walls. Otto was crying helplessly from shock and confusion and lack of sleep. This is my fear, my fear. It's a kind of hallucination. If I can make myself believe that, Candide will be safe and all this will just vanish. A whole world war will vanish, with all its dead and all – . Now she understood why Umbriel had told the truth. He knew that when she needed it the truth would do her no good. She could not use it. Resistance was impossible. The nightmare closed over her, seamless reality.

FIFTH ANGEL

1

The Shit Coloured
Rolls-Royce

On the day that James drove to Berkshire, Candide was poring over roadmaps in the attic that smelled of cat shit. The maps were ten years out of date but they were the best he had. He had taken the book from his mother's car.

'She won't notice. It's such a tip in there.'

Otto's native untidiness struggled for expression elsewhere, but in the interior of her car it flowered freely. Sandy and Candide viewed the results with disgust.

He was studying the route to Isobel Porter House, the old original pill factory that was headquarters of BREAKTHRU UK. The company kept up some of the old pharmeceutical research and production plant, at defunct usines renamed in this witty pseudo-intellectual style. Recruits, and any reps in need of 'redemolition', would be sent to Isobel Porter or one of two or three similar centres; and be put to work for a while as semi-skilled lab technicians.

Sandy had heard all about it at the seminar. Yesterday's effective work, they said, is today's meaningless ritual. That's the way the process goes: and meaningless ritual exactly serves our purpose. BREAKTHRU isn't a religion. But BREAKTHRU is what religion is.

'It's right up in the West Midlands Conurbation...' he breathed, impressed. Candide had been to London often; and to Underhill and to Devon. The world outside those three destinations might as well be intergalactic space for all he knew of it.

'Stop saying "The West Midlands",' said Sandy. 'People don't like being lumped under points of the compass, not when they are otherwise disadvantaged as well. It causes riots.'

He rolled over and peered under his fringe.

'You come from there, don't you.'

'Near enough. A long time ago.'

'Good. I need a native guide. What should I say then?'

'Up there, between Birmingham and Wolverhampton, you're in the Black Country.'

Candide made noises of disbelief. '*The Black Country* ' he intoned ominously. '*Where the ultimate evil dwells* – This isn't a game, Sand. Stop messing around.'

'It's true, honest.'

He laughed. But to Candide, she thought, the distinction between game and life was a protection. He was in pain now, real pain. He was also enjoying the planning of his rescue expedition very much. It was a state of mind she could understand, close to her own.

'How do you know that Vera is at their head office? I'm sure the blackmailer didn't tell you.'

The child sighed weightily. 'Three reasons. First, that's where the biggest labs are. In fact, it might be the only place where they still keep animals. They're very secretive about it, but AL thinks they're scaling down. And he definitely told me 'she'll be in the torture labs, with all the other lost pets', He *said* that. I think he was telling the truth: it was a slip.' He nodded, in satisfaction. 'Second, he would want to get her away from my friends, somewhere remote and well guarded. That points to Isobel Porter. And third – '

Candide scowled. He chased after third and lost it, and the protection began to fail.

'I just know – I just know.'

'Say an intuition?'

He looked her in the eye and nodded fractionally, with a hard little smile.

'We've got to start somewhere,' he muttered, returning to his maps.

In her warm unclean nest of bedclothes Sandy leaned her chin on her knees and contemplated. Candide was like his father in colouring, with that limp chestnut hair and dark blue eyes. Perhaps it was because Sandy had never known Colin well that the child seemed otherwise entirely Otto – her gesture, her expressions, her voice, her moods. Having him around had been like having the whole of her lover; all the years she had missed being slowly filled in.

Watching him, she looked back fondly into the distant past. In those days Otto had seemed the same sort of earnest child:

magically oblivious of the real facts of life. And if Sandy Brize at eighteen had been corruptly attracted by status and privilege, she had also been touched and fascinated to discover someone of her own age who knew without thinking about it what phase the moon was in, knew most birds by their calls; knew trees by their leaves or the shape of their growth in winter...

She could bear to remember things like that, since she'd left Wombega. There was no need any more to dismiss everything they'd had so violently.

In a way it seemed as if an interlude was over. Sandra Brize had not been in the least interested in politics. She couldn't believe, still didn't believe that there was anything special about passing exams, getting a scholarship. It was a trick that anyone could learn, only most people of her kind just didn't want to escape. Anyway, she hadn't got out by being clever in the end, she'd done it by cheating and lying. Business Studies, how absurd. But they wouldn't give you a loan-grant, would they, if you said you wanted the money so you could have a good time.

That was what she had always wanted – pleasure. That was the quest to which she had returned, at last, and most unexpectedly.

She was on the scrap heap, and Otto's positive attitude had become torture. So she gave up being positive. That was the starting point, and there was half the pain gone at a stroke, before she even knew where she was heading. She began to seek for other contradictions, and deliberately to let them go. Slowly, she was getting the hang of it, steadily approaching her goal: indestructible pleasure: an unlimited, *unlimitable* supply of chocolate ice cream. And all because she was no longer happy or sad on any predetermined plan. She let herself move like a root towards water...

...and she was sorry the effect had disturbed Otto so, but it was amazing how small a part the thing they call consciousness wanted to play, when stripped of all the scars and grafts and accretions. Perhaps it would vanish altogether or perhaps it would at last find a new base line. That remained to be seen. In the meantime, she was strangely, completely, content. Some people claimed to reach this pleasant state by fasting, orgies, magic rituals in far Tibet: good luck to them. Sandy's way was through long-term unemployment, it seemed to have worked just as well.

'It's like the feeling you might get, Cand, lying awake in the night. Or staring at the sky, or running water. You know, when you feel you could simply let go, dissolve, and you would actually, literally, die or disappear. It usually only lasts about three seconds. But if you practice, if you dare, you can go on for longer and longer. It's like holding your breath, only as far as I've discovered there is no limit – '

Candide nodded inattentively.

'By now I can do it most of the time. Now, while I talk to you, the blank is there behind. I look at this creature talking and the world she lives in, and it's like a game. Not that I don't care any more, it's just that finally I don't *rate* my caring...or not caring, about anything.'

'Is that why you didn't want to come to Grosvenor Square?'

'I suppose so. I was beginning then, though I didn't know what.'

Candide worked with a pencil and a ruler and a piece of string. The mileage chart had gone from the back of the book. He entered figures on his calculator. He didn't want to use any organised transport. He was convinced BREAKTHRU was watching the exits from Brighton. They would be safest on foot, or maybe hitch-hiking if there were no police about. He believed they could cover easily twenty-five miles a day. Soon enough they would be devant l'usine. In his rucksack, along with other vital supplies, he had his mother's boltcutters, from the old days of fence cutting activism in another cause.

Candide tolerated the occasional bulletin from Sandy's voyage into inner space. He was too preoccupied to pay much attention. But he noticed in the end that she wasn't responding to any of his explanation of their plans. He studied her with sudden uneasiness.

'Have you really got no money at all Sand? What do you do for food? Do you beg, or do you shoplift?'

'Neither. I can't be bothered.'

'Are you hungry now?'

She was touched that he would break into his supplies.

'No thanks. I don't want to rob the expedition.'

He put the tin of baked beans away, relieved. 'Sand – do you believe Vera is still alive?'

'I believe you about the angels,' she answered thoughtfully. 'I saw one myself once, and I didn't tell anyone for just the same reason as you. About Vera – what I honestly believe Cand, is that what you love in her – '

Sandy had detested Vera. But it was Candide here, not the dog.

138

'What you love: the way she trots about, the way she looks at you, is dog. The dogness of dog – and that doesn't die when she does. If she lived to be old and then died you'd get another puppy one day. And love dog again. D'you see?'

Candide scowled.

'But she is being hurt. Even if Vera's – even if she doesn't really exist, it still hurts her when someone – ' His mouth (Otto's mouth) began to quiver. 'Look. If you don't want to come, don't worry.'

'All right,' said Sandy quickly. 'All right, you've got a point.' She climbed out of her nest and offered her hand.

'Okay Cand. This gun's for hire. I'll come with you, and I'll do whatever I can to help. But don't keep asking me what I believe: it gets on my nerves. Will you shake on that?'

Formally, they sealed the contract.

Poor Otto. As a disinterested observer Sandy could see that what she was doing was unfair. She didn't have to imagine her lover's grief and terror, she had seen it. But it was no use. This was the way the root wanted to move. Candide asked something defined and manageable, whereas when Otto came into the room all the different things she was and wanted buzzed like flies, it was difficult even to look at her. That interview had indeed been Sandy's first warning that it might be no longer possible for her to behave 'normally'. Probably it was not normal to join in Candide's game this way...

The contract had just been sealed when Sandy's garret started to move. It shifted like the head of a large animal, as if the house beneath them were lumbering to its feet. Kneeling on the edge of her mattress, Sandy relaxed. She lifted her face and let the tremor pass through her. This was the complement to what she was doing with her will, to her mind. This, and occasions like that time outside the Benefit Office when all the people turned to her, a myriad viewpoints poured into one. She wasn't sure why such effects should come: she supposed it was something a part of her fragmenting self had devised, to express the idea of letting go. But she felt distinctly the great intaken breath pulling on bricks and mortar, moving through the streets below. Inward from outside she traced the vibration through air, through cloud, through atmosphere: into the black, the star-knotted plasma. Still found that pulse. Where did it originate? The vastness deafened and blinded her. It comes from here, me, no place...

And the walls were still.

'It's that Mohole,' remarked Candide.

'Huh?'

'The earth-tremor,' he explained. 'You must've felt it. You know, it's that Mohole they're boring near Horsham.'

Sandy shook her head uncertainly. 'You don't get earth tremors in Sussex. There are no fault lines under our chalk.'

'There weren't – ' he corrected, with gloomy relish.

For a moment Sandy considered the idea that she might be simply mistaken. What she'd taken for a recurrent hallucination, if that was the word, might be something reported on the news. But she became fascinated by another possibility. Did Candide really say that? Or was his confirmation, like the tremor itself, an event within Sandy?

She was trying to frame the question which eludes philosophy, when a car drew up very quietly in the street outside.

Instantly, they both jumped to the window. Sandy looked at the boy and grinned.

'Let's be existentialists, mancub. And see how we get on.'

He pulled a hideous face at the hated word, and they looked down eagerly.

Perhaps they had heard the car, though it was so quiet and three storeys below, because they were both in love with the soft purr of that engine. Their view, passing peeling bay windows and an overgrown laurel hedge, was into a side street. The car pulled up along the kerb was a Rolls Challis. Not too vulgarly new: two years old, they judged. The body and trim was all in that pale shit colour the rich consider so elegant. There were no shiny old fashioned touches of chrome, the two connoisseurs thought this a pity. But nothing could dim the beauty of it as it lay there, long and sleek as a sleeping puma in the dull November afternoon.

Candide let out his breath in a soft moan. He could be in the West Midlands in about half an hour if he had that Roller.

They retired to the edge of the mattress, and now they were both frowning. Something was happening in the house. It wasn't possible to hear what was going on at the front door from Sandy's room. But a disturbance travelled upwards: a general shutting of doors and going to earth. They listened, with the stilled attention of all small hunted things.

'Cand, I think you'd better get back under the floor.'

She put the bedclothes on top of the rucksack.

However black their teeth or ghoulish their skinseals, the guardians of Sandy's retreat were no match for the driver of a Roller. Francis Xavier came lightly into the attic, bringing with him a whiff of exclusive masculine fragrance and a hint of silk and leather. He wore a classic flying jacket over his Solyut coveralls, and baseball boots with discreet little gilded wings stamped on the ankles. His expression as he entered was urgent and virtuously anxious.

'I've tracked you down at last Sandy. Have you seen Otto?'

He paused to take in his surroundings, and Sandy and the way she was.

He smiled, letting some of the virtue and anxiety slip.

She did not know what to do. This came as a shock. She had thought she would never be helpless again. But now her invulnerable inner blankness offered absolutely no suggestions. This was Candide's enemy, she knew that. It was necessary to lie – but she could not lie, not in this state.

'I've seen Otto lots of times – '

Xav sat himself down tailor fashion, facing her. He leaned forward seriously.

'It's about Candide. You see, he's disappeared.' She saw that in his mind's eye he was removing the grubby tracksuit top and a vest he found under it. Sandy had round white breasts, rather small but not fallen much yet, with soft little pink nipples. Not a bad pair of titties –

'Piss off – '

'It is serious I'm afraid. Otto's been quite hysterical, if you'll pardon the term. She's convinced that you're the enemy. I've come here – ' he shook his head ruefully, 'to take him away from you, that's the idea.'

'You're not lying, are you Xav.'

The mental undressing stopped. She saw him momentarily startled, and then recovering: telling himself that only *sounded* like a perceptive comment.

Francis Xavier Howard. Her memory was behaving oddly, it flashed on the first night she had ever met him: an awful restaurant meal, food she didn't know how to eat. There were things floating in the water jug (slices of lime). She couldn't drink water with things floating in it and nobody was ordering alcohol because it was not, at that time, sexy to do so. She sat between Xav and Gerry Howard, and felt real class hatred while they talked as if she wasn't there.

Later, he would call her Otto's working class squeeze: but that was aimed at Otto, Sandy still wasn't there.

She had not seen him since that seminar. *Come back when you've got something to offer*. He had forgotten. Sandy had forgotten too, until this moment. She had decided eventually that BREAKTHRU's appearance of understanding was an illusion. They hadn't the slightest serious interest in galloping entropy, the abysses of non-being. They used these icons as bait and decor for the punters, same as some other cult might use 'brotherly love'. Those in the know, the important people, were well aware that BREAKTHRU's real business was something *much more important*...

(Falling in the abyss, Sandy laughed.)

Sandy paused in thought, for she had suddenly realised the significance of Otto's odd questions. She constructed: Otto thinks I helped Xav/BREAKTHRU to steal and torture Vera and then kidnap Candide... She was not offended. How could she be, for it seemed to have come true. Here was Xav and she did have something to offer: it was exactly as if she'd sent for him to take Candide away.

(She was very puzzled by this coincidence. Maybe that was what was happening – how could she tell?)

When she first knew them both Sandy used to confuse Xav with Luci in her mind, because they were both connected with James and similar in physical type, slight and lean and lightish coloured. She was doing it again now. There were two figures in front of her: one was Xav and one was Luci, only the clothes were the same which seemed unlikely – Luci considered Xav's taste utterly appalling. Two figures? No, there were more. In the darkening room there was James too, and Otto, all four of them sitting crosslegged and staring at her intently. Sandy kept her head. She leaned forward and picked up one of her battered trainers, then the other, thus discovering that the one that could be touched was Xav. But wait a moment. What does that prove?

She was breathing as if she'd been running.

The extra figures vanished, or she managed to edit them out.

Why isn't he lying? She had worked out why she herself could not lie. After all her deletions, she now believed that her mind was close to being completely reconciled with reality. Therefore, if she said Candide was not – where he was – there seemed a real risk that he would not be there.

Was it possible that Francis Xavier was in the same state as herself? She stared. Was it possible BREAKTHRU was sincere after all?

Xav laughed. He snapped his fingers in front of Sandy's eyes. She blinked, and was aware that she'd been silent far too long.

'You don't know what's going on, do you our Sandra. Whatever have you been eating? D'you think it's ergot of rye in the Welfare Blue sliced?'

Slowly, holding her eyes, he reached out and picked up something from the floor. It was a compass in a plastic case, a little boy's treasure.

'Running away from home?'

He stood up, cast a glance around and stepped across to the mend in the floor.

'This is very silly.'

He hauled Candide out into the light.

The child's face was white, his fists were flailing. If he hadn't made the connection before, he had obviously guessed who the blackmailer was now.

He screamed, 'Sandy! Sandy! – '

But she didn't move. She made no attempt to help him.

Candide stopped struggling, and gave Xav a wide-eyed stare of contempt.

'Fancy upsetting your mother like this, you bad boy. Let's go down to the car.'

Sandy stood up. She unearthed the rucksack, handed it to Candide and put on her coat.

'Are you coming with us?' asked Xav lightly. 'Well, suit yourself.'

He was not heading for Wombega.

Candide shouted from the back seat: 'Where are you taking us?'

Francis Xavier hummed a little tune. He touched a button and the sound was cut off by a security plate. Candide hammered impotently, and yanked at the locked doors.

'Otto isn't at home. We'll go and sit in the local office for a while.'

He grinned like an animal, white shiny teeth opening up his narrow face.

Sandy was trying to concentrate on chances of escape, but it was difficult. The great car moved so gently, with such grace. She had never travelled in a Roller before. It was lovely. In a kind of meditation her eyes rested on the icons and the lights, the dashboard

143

image in the air, the little bright screen for in-transit entertainment, the computer readouts, the fingerpads in the wheelrim. Otto's old rust bucket gave you no idea. A car like this might take you anywhere. It was a magic carpet.

I am falling apart, she thought. Poor Cand, he's only got me and I am going mad. She almost panicked then, naming her progress as other people would name it. Dirty, unkempt, incapable, unable to concentrate, inappropriate responses. Insane, I am going insane.

The car turned into the gates of a small office block on the London Road. The courtyard was bordered by well kept trees and shrubs. Piles of golden elm leaves were neatly swept into the corners. There was a discreet brass plate at the Georgian doorway: BREAKTHRU.

'First the dog, now the child. You're going to give Otto the same treatment that you gave Candide, aren't you.'

Xav leaned over and pressed her thigh. He was in high spirits.

'What are you, Sandra, clairvoyant or something? I'm the bloke who knows what's in room 101, that's who I am. I can show you too, if I like.'

His fingers squeezed knowingly. He released the locks. 'Don't!' shouted Sandy, in time to stop Candide from making a dash for freedom.

'Very wise.'

She did not know what she was going to do. She only felt –

Xav raised his eyebrows. 'What are we waiting for?'

'For you to act like a gentleman,' she snapped. 'Get out and open the fucking door for me.'

He cackled in delight. Secure on his own territory, he gave his prisoner a mock bow from the waist and got out of the car.

Sandy, moving with superhuman speed, flung herself into the driver's seat, locked the doors, started the Rolls and turned it on its beautiful heels. The spikes in the gateway were still down, the gates open. Somewhere indoors they must be able to override commands from one of their own cars. But not quickly enough.

Candide shrieked. He hardly waited until she had put the plate down before he pitched over the seat head first. He righted himself, whooping.

'Sand! You can't drive!'

'I can drive, I just haven't taken a test.'

'They'll chase us!'

144

'I suppose they will.'

The Rolls stood in splendour in the forecourt of a service garage. Candide had found a hoard of cash and plastic in the glove compartment so they could afford to fill the tank. It was sheer luxury to sit inside, while attendants caressed the windscreen and performed all the other small services such a great car elicits and deserves. It was nearly dark and Sandy had shadowed the glass. She put on a pair of expensive driving gloves they had found with the hoard: the garage attendants saw nothing but a suitably clad hand, proffering notes and waving away the change. It was eccentric to use cash, but not too weird.

'Shall I go and buy some sweets?'

'Don't get out, you don't look right and besides BREAKTHRU people might turn up at any moment. Candide, you know he might have already killed Vera. Blackmailers do that sometimes.'

'No. She's safe.'

He grubbed in the pocket of his anorak and produced a small black canister.

'Because I've got what they want.'

Sandy stared. She recalled Otto's story perfectly now, with every unpleasant inference.

'So that's why you were so sure they'd have the aufgangs guarded. I thought Otto had it.'

'She only thinks so.' Candide set his jaw. 'I took it out of the safe. I knew I couldn't trust her. She'd hand it over to the police or something. But if it's a case of Vera's life I don't care who I do a deal with. I'll trade. The condition is I want to see her first. They can have it when she's over the bridge, you know what I mean?'

He spoke and behaved so much like a reasonable person, it was only occasionally that Candide reminded you he was a child, and crazy like a child.

Seeing her expression, he held out the cannister.

'I think you'd better keep it now.'

He was taking a risk, she was an adult. But his eyes were full of confidence. Unlike the angels, this guardian had proved herself.

They set off again quietly.

'I suppose,' remarked Candide, 'we ought to be trying to stop BREAKTHRU. I'm sure they're up to something evil. But after all there's Otto and James and Luci. We can leave them to tackle Xav's gang, while we concentrate on saving Vera.'

She glanced at him and nodded. She would not insult him again. Candide knew perfectly well what had happened to his dog. And he was dealing with the situation, in his own way.

The crazy child relaxed, for the moment without a care in the world.

Sandy laughed. She began to sing, because she was crazy too.

> Se vuol ballare, Signor Contino
> Se vuol ballare, Signor Contino –

And Candide joined in, making dog-noises to her Italian; but he seemed to have got the general idea...

'You want to dance, my Lord? Well, for once we're calling the tune.'

All the small childish defiances of the underclass. Though every one of them must come to nothing, they were always fun at the start.

2

Home Sweet Home

At the tolls, the great car had already picked up the roadside signal and prompted Sandy to an account-holders channel. It glided through with assurance. Candide found a disc in the dashboard route library and selected West Midlands Urban Margin, which was as far as electronic signposting extended on the way to their destination. Thereafter Sandy was prompted smoothly at every lane change. Candide could have taken a turn himself, practically all the driver had to do was keep hold of the wheel.

Sandy resisted a distinct temptation to try the car's paces. She slotted into the midstream and away they floated. It was like a miracle. They had jumped from the mediaeval peasantry of utopia into the space age where the rich people live. They wouldn't be able to stop anywhere, because the contrast between a glossy Rolls and themselves was bound to lead to trouble, but that didn't matter. Their two week journey had turned into a matter of two or three hours.

Somewhere in the spangled dark between Brighton and the M1, they hit the traffic jam. 'Switch on the news. Let's find out how bad it is.'

'No!'

'Why not?'

'I'm maintaining radio silence.'

Sandy giggled. 'I could try and escape and take the non-toll roads?'

'No. We're safe in this lot. It'd be much easier for BREAKTHRU to run us aground out there.'

faire échouer: he meant kill. All these scraps of European-speak, borrowings and muddlings. Maybe it would have become a new language eventually. She noticed with curiosity the tense she had used... But he might be right.

The midstream crawled and grunted at a bare walking pace. They looked at each other, laughed, and settled resignedly to sit it out.

Candide woke to find that excitement had deserted him. Motorway land slipped by, grey-green and featureless: like the in between place in faster than light travel when you were actually in a time warp. The view was too boring to hold his attention. Vera, Vera, Vera...He knew for a fact that if you imagine something in any detail it never comes true: as if the imagined thing exists then in some other world and therefore can't get into this one. So he squashed his hope, deliberately filling his mind with pictures of Vera dead, describing to himself in detail how she must look even if she was alive. In a cage, shaved, with tubes pushed into her and one leg ending in a bloody stump. He destroyed the brilliant moment when Sandy had grabbed the Rolls. It was bugged, Xav was tracking them, there would be a reception committee at the other end of this route. The whole attempt was stupid. And too late anyway: she's dead, dead.

He didn't have to try very hard. The pain inside filled him from the throat down whenever he wasn't distracted. It was as if he'd swallowed an empty metal box and it was crushing his insides to mush.

A light flashed, the car sang out a warning tone. Sandy shook herself and steadied her grip on the wheel, dead man's handle. Waking, she caught the tail of Candide's thought: *in a cage, shaved, with tubes pushed into her*. It seemed a good description of the English countryside, viewed from this slowly moving band. I blame you, she thought, considering the grey turf and the spindly trees, the water and the metal and the stone. Collaborators *tous*. You didn't have to play. If you'd had the courage to refuse – satyagraha – there would be no motorways. If iron had refused to be a party to what the humans wanted to do, and just gone away and died like the snow leopards, it would have saved us all a lot of grief.

She moved her eyes through the traffic, into the coloured shells with their ephemeral labels. She noticed absently that the block had eased, though they were still a considerable margin away from light-speed. The lanes were filled and seething, but in Sandy's plane of motion there was a great impression of stillness and silence. She was looking in on the driver of a big Ford, level with the Rolls. He was at her elbow. It was another modern car, he wasn't driving. He was doing a puzzle in a comic book, not even keeping a finger on the wheel (that's illegal). He scratched his nose with the end of his pen. She could see coloured sections of naked women, interspersed with simple puzzles. The split open parts had a pallid, boneless Japanese look. The quiz was not pornographic. He had to find the names of cable characters in a word square. Sandy watched. It was almost an intimate relationship. If the driver knew that she was watching would he be embarrassed? He would blame the inquisitive girl, not himself. Most likely he would see no cause for offence at all, not if you explained it to him in a year of evening classes. You'd only make him resentful, and he would go out and buy a puzzle book where the female organs were ripped out alive, gnawed by rats, roasted over slow fires.

The man's face was turning grey. He looked very tired. Where a moment ago his cheekbone had been cushioned in ruddy flesh it was now clearly visible: an arrowhead under the skin. He had white circles round his eyes. The ligaments attaching muscle to the bony part of his nose were outlined as if on an anatomical drawing. He is dying, she thought. The eye that she could see closed: the lid sank inward.

On the car's bright fascia blue green paint had begun to blister. The blisters puckered and spread and drew away from naked areas of rust. Rust spread out from around the rims of dials and clawed towards the plastic body shell. Clear perspex rounds and lozenges fell with a tinkling sound. There was nothing left but a waste of dark friable rotten metal, many layered. Plastic knobs stood up like bones out of a burned carcase.

But there is no such thing as iron, thought Sandy. It is a state of being, not a...not anything separate of itself. One cannot single it out for blame.

She found that she was staring at a section of the Roll's wheelrim with preternatural attention: the kind of attention a good film-maker can make you give to the flowers in the vase on the table in the room where the lovers are having their final quarrel. She ran her tongue over her unbrushed teeth, catching at shreds of a vanished existence: Otto will be frantic. We ought to go home, find someone to look after us. She was very much aware that the car was stolen, and undoubtedly had been crying out to its owners all this time like the giant's purse in the story. Her palms were wet and her mouth was dry. Fear tingled in her buttocks and between her thighs, climbed

149

the column of her spine. She did not know why she should suddenly panic. Perhaps this was the return of sanity.

But against the fear, pushing through it and equally insistent, was the impulse that had taken her away from Wombega. Thinking: She didn't accuse the driver of the big Ford of anything, that was for Otto. She didn't ask or expect him to change his ways. She just ... No. Wouldn't have him. His whole structure, right down to the pornographic puzzle books, interferes with my enjoyment of life. Therefore with all my will, with all my power: I wish him not. (I know I have no power and my will is meaningless. But in terms of personal, internal satisfaction, that doesn't matter.)

She was afraid, intensely, intensely afraid. But what could she do? The very things that made her most frightened, all the weird special effects, were also signs of success, little triumphs of the pleasure principle: I can do just what I like...

Another of those tremors was coming. She could feel it building, from the centre of the universe.

She looked up with a gasp, and saw the pale November sun burst into an arc. A multiple arc of white suns spanned the sky. Everyone in all the cars shouted in terror and amazement.

Sandy shouted Oh!

It's come, she thought, astonished by the turmoil. I have gone over the edge. I am mad.

The Rolls drifted gently to a halt on the hard shoulder. It switched itself off. Candide woke up, he'd been staring out of the window lost in his imagining.

'Did the car do that or was it you?' he asked. 'Is this the end of the route?'

Sandy stared up at the exploded sun. She put her hands over her ears.

'Is this really happening?' she cried. 'Or am I imagining it?'

Candide looked at her in exasperation. He was only eleven, but he knew an infinite loop when he hit one.

'Stop messing about, Sand. You know I can't answer that.'

She got out and began to walk. She had an idea that she had to do this because she was no longer fit to drive, though really in a car like that her state of mind was irrelevant. Candide looked around and saw that they had indeed come to an edge of the route-marking grid. Ahead of them was a black and white sign planted in the verge, they were about to enter Coventry.

'Right. We dump the Rolls and go on foot from now on. Better not hang around. If they're tracing the car they'll soon be here.'

The city rose up with strange immediacy. Two red spires lifted out of a helix of flyovers.

'Are we in the Black Country now?'

'Not yet.'

He wanted to know what the two spires were. She told him about the shell of the dead cathedral. She had been there once on a school trip, and seen the peace altar. It was bombed to bits in the second world war, she explained. So they turned it into a shrine.

'What was it like here then? Was it like Istanbul?'

'I don't remember.'

Suddenly, she stopped dead.

'What time is it?'

'I don't know. My watch stopped somewhere on the motorway.' Then he saw it too. 'Hey! It's daylight! Wow!' He laughed excitedly. 'We must've been in that traffic jam a whole night, and I never noticed!'

Sandy went on walking.

Mysteriously, the spires disappeared. They trudged and trudged beside cleared ground, beside battered blocks of flats corralled behind white rails; between rows of houses, shabby small shops and derelict factories. Candide consulted the town plans at the back of his book of road maps, but found no help there. It was bad luck, he complained, that Xav had taken the compass. He could only hope they were heading north west.

'Actually, it's better if we're lost for the moment, so that anyone who was tracking the Rolls will lose the scent.'

But Coventry seemed an ugly place, and it was getting dark again already.

'You know,' remarked Candide, in a subdued voice. 'I hope Mum's all right. She seemed pretty upset back in your attic.'

Sandy had been planning to tell him, but not at once in case he thought it counted as a breach of trust. 'It's okay, Cand. I cheated. I managed to slip her a kind of message. She'll know when she finds it, that things aren't as bad as they look.'

That cheered him up for a while, then he began to sigh again.

'What's the matter now?'

'Fish and chips...'

'What about them?'

151

'I smelled some.'

Sandy had been walking in a dream, absorbed by a dim and muted uproar: the imaginary sound effects of her disintegration. She did not like being woken up and told that she was cold and hungry and had nowhere to sleep. But once awake she was compelled to take note of their surroundings, and she did not care for what she saw.

Her feet dragged, her head turned. 'Well, I don't think you're going to get any, Cand.'

They appeared to have wandered into the wake of a small tornado. The roadway was scattered with crushed cans, fragments of food, torn handouts. There was a sporadic trail of odd shoes, and once a teeshirt in the middle of the pavement with one sleeve ripped out and smeared rusty stains. And yet no one was in sight.

Candide recognised the signs.

'There's been a demo – I mean a public meeting. That's funny. I didn't know there were people like us up here.'

'If you mean people who'd like to be somewhere different from where they are, there's no shortage.'

'What d'you think it was about? The war?'

'Oh, take your choice. The Force, deurbanisation, food prices, curfews, powercuts, cable breakdowns. There's always an excuse for a street party.'

They were surrounded by an invisible crowd, haunted by the wail of sirens, rushing riot police; the sound of running feet. It must have been a sizeable disturbance. Perhaps even a substation taken out, because surely streetlights should be on by now. The police seemed to have cleared the area. Sandy realised that this haunted silence was the vague roaring that she had been listening to: and also, more practically, she understood why the streets were so totally empty. She was surprised that Candide hadn't commented on it before: maybe he thought the West Midlands was naturally like this.

'Cand, I don't think we ought to go any farther. The police might come by and haul us in. It looks as if there's a curfew on.'

He heaved a sigh. 'Okay.'

He'd have preferred to keep on walking until they hit a road junction big enough to have numbered signs, so he could find their place on the map. But this was what he had hired her for: to make the awkward decisions.

They had passed an empty house, emptiness advertised by a front door fallen in on one remaining hinge. It had looked more or less intact, with net curtains still at the windows.

'I think I know where we can shelter.'

Sandy had only caught a glimpse of the 'living space', her mind provided the rest: the three-piece suite bought on credit that would be rubbish long before it was paid for, the 'hologram images' of weepy kittens and puppies, the magnificent chrome finished video rack with all its flashing lights. They would eat shit before they parted with that video rack: which was costing them twenty times its list price, in cynically calculated instalments. They ate shit anyway, disguised by one cursory passage through a bacteria farm. It was their staple diet, that and a good dollop of sugar.

They squeezed inside the broken door. Candide tried to prop it closed, then cunningly decided to leave well alone. Better have no sign of disturbance. His torch showed an intact light fitting, but either the bulb had failed or there was no power. The remains of a mangy fitted carpet was shredding off its rubber backing. He didn't notice anything odd yet, but explored to the end of the hall and opened the door there.

'Hey – Sand – '

She was still by the front door, she seemed to be listening, or maybe smelling the air.

'There's something weird. Come and look.'

He took matches and candles out of his rucksack, lit three and stood them on the kitchen table. There were pans in the sink, an open packet of cereal, a dish that held a little heap of desiccated blue flakes. Everything, to the picture on the cereal packet, looked as if it could have been bought yesterday. But the rubber seal on the fridge door had perished. It was slumped open, revealing the fossilised corpses of food on which even the mould had long ago rotted and died. The pans had fallen into rust. They had begun to look like something crushed in an ancient volcanic eruption, only to be deciphered by experts. Candide was fascinated. He prowled about, making spooky soundtrack noises to illustrate his finds. Sandy had followed him as far as the door.

It had not been a poverty stricken place, by its own standards. There was no sign of desperation. But even hurrying death did not yet conceal how mean and helpless everything had been. That pathetic breakfast cereal: she remembered Xav's jeering comment. You have to be pretty low to eat blue food when you're not even on The Force. But these people didn't know any different. They believed the advertising – enriched with Japanese seaweed. 'How long would you say they'd been gone?'

'About fifteen years.'

He animated scorn of her poor observation.

'You'd be wrong.' He shone his torch on a plastic digital calendar, which was incorporated into a hologram picture of a purple kitten in a cute basket.

'This year, this month, today. This house has been hit by a time ray.'

'Death.'

'All right, a death ray. D'you think it'll get us and turn us into old wrinkled wrecks?'

There were rumpled sheets and desiccated cheap quilts rotting on the beds, clothes hung rotting in the chipboard wardrobe, the floor of the children's room was still littered with toys. They found no sign of squatters, dossers, mice or cockroaches. Only everywhere piles of thick dust and the mysterious speeded up decay. The people had walked out: half an hour and/or fifteen years ago. Or else, Candide suggested hopefully, they were even more speeded up, and were lying about in the form of those heaps of dust.

There were no books. There was no music, aside from the sound-tracks on a small collection of videos over which Candide pretended to vomit. In the lounge where they found the tv there was another hologram picture, more lavish than the kitten, showing a slowly turning woman's torso: pink glass spattered with red bullet holes. Something told you it had been hung with pride, had represented scrimping, saving, and the dizzy height of sophistication. Candide retched over that too.

This was the place which was supposed to be a source of pride. But Sandy perversely lived in fear in case her radical friends ever offered to visit. She had never felt any sympathy for her parents. Still, now, she hated to picture their stupid ignorant faces. The mother, the father, the older brother who moved with his wife and children into the second bedroom so that Sandy had to sleep on the couch down here for the last few years. The mother was a cleaner. The men worked 'on call' at a local motor parts plant. They had bleepers that summoned them whenever unskilled meatmachines were needed any hour of the day or night: sometimes this was horribly often sometimes not at all, they had no control over the arrangements whatsoever. Men and women both hated child-molesters, coloureds, women's libbers, trade unions, rioters, socialists: they respected intensely the government, money, and anything that moved on state tv.

What can you do for people like that? Otto finds excuses but you can't, you're too proud. Don't matronise, leaderene of utopia. These people choose to be the way they are. There's nothing to be done for them. Nothing, only wipe them out. Just say no. I wish you not.

She followed Candide around whimpering in horror: the little boy didn't notice.

'I did this,' she whispered, over and over again. 'I destroyed them.'

Once she laughed. 'Room 101,' she said.

Candide had been going through the kitchen cupboards. He came to the front room with an armful of tins. Sandy was huddled up against the wall with her arms round her knees. He thought she looked cold.

'I wonder if this stuff's edible. D'you think we should risk it?'

'This is my house where I used to live, Cand. It's like this because I hated it. I should never have come back here.'

He opened a tin with his can opener and sniffed the contents.

'This muck's all made of dog dirt anyway. Why don't the poor eat lentils and things like we do. It'd be cheaper.'

He considered what she'd said.

'Is this really where you used to live?'

Sandy pulled herself back to his world (though she knew which was the real).

'No, not exactly. It's just very like.'

She shivered, rubbing the strange dust from her hands.

'Cand, do you know what? That motorway jam didn't last all night, not really. We were in a timewarp then. You know what happens to things if you speed them up?'

'What?'

'They die sooner. That's why I did it.'

'I wish you'd eat something,' he complained. 'You're beginning to sound like you're on drugs.'

Since his minder appeared to be off duty for the moment, Candide took charge. He decided it was time for bed. There was no water coming out of the taps or in the toilet, so he found a dustpan that would do for a spade and organised a latrine in the back yard. Sandy pulled herself together and dragged down the dining space curtains for bedclothes. They were made of some hardy synthetic that did not rot; she gave the larger share to Candide: she had her coat. They settled, Candide on the couch, Sandy on the two chairs.

He was soon asleep. Sandy lay examining the wreckage of her beautiful dream. She supposed this was being mad but now she was through that door it held no horrors. The horror was in the miserable form her madness had taken. Value-empty experience, what a stupid fantasy. It was easy enough in Brighton, in that garret where poverty was an elegant pose. But here in the first world the truth was waiting. Delusions don't lie. She was as much a slave as ever, the proof of it was all over this house. Not free at all but still terrified, disgusted, hitting out in panic...

She was afraid to close her eyes, in case she woke up in that back bedroom upstairs turned into her brother's wife. With the kids to feed and the man to placate and only half a packet of fags to last till pay day.

But if that's not the way out, what is?

Later, they both woke up. She knew Candide was awake because she saw, in the obscurity, his hand creeping out from between curtain folds like a little grey mouse. It touched the torch, candle and matches safely within reach, and retreated. It did that several times then stayed undercover.

The thing which had woken them came into the house. Sandy listened intently. Finally she realised that she had heard nothing. There was no sound of an intruder, only a presence. But she was afraid. She had slept, and for the moment her mind was quiet. This fear was different from what had gone before. It felt external.

Candide whispered hoarsely, 'Sand – '

'Yes, I know.'

His tousled head came up. He scooped torch, curtain, and the candle and matches from the floor; and shot across to join her.

'Oh, wow. What is it?'

It passed the door, it went upstairs. Sandy found that she could breathe once more.

'Trust us,' whispered Candide, through chattering teeth, 'to pick a haunted house.'

They crouched together listening – no, something other than listening, to the presence as it moved about overhead.

'Candide, I don't believe in ghosts.'

'No?' He produced a cracked bubble of laughter and held up their clasped hands. She managed with an effort to relax her white-nailed grip.

'It's our imagination. We're in a derelict house and we've been scaring ourselves, imagining things. This is the result, that's all there is to it.'

Sandy hated ghosts, ghosts, magic, psychic powers: all those mysteries traditionally awarded to the most helpless, women and the dead. Like the blue shit flakes it was another bright box of rubbish, something to make the underclass believe they weren't deprived after all. She knew that she had allowed herself a good deal of latitude while exploring inner space. She had been telepathic, she had felt the core of the universe moving. But after what she had found in this house, the new manifestation made her simply angry. The ghost of whom? Her mother maybe, sobbing at the door.

The thing had stopped moving, or else retreated to never never land. Sandy pushed away the curtain.

'Let's go and check it out. You'll sleep better when we've done that.'

There was no black darkness in the house. It was urban night, greyed-out and edgeless. They picked their way hand in hand to the foot of the stairs and climbed. Sandy pushed open the bathroom door. The room was eerie and empty, its spectres abandoned, shrivelled human possessions. The small window was open at the bottom. A cold musty breeze lifted the tattered hem of a net curtain. It had knocked a plastic bottle into the bath. Sandy started to laugh when she saw that.

Candide wailed.

'Nooo – Sand. Don't laugh!'

It was behind them in the children's bedroom. It was coming out.

When Candide had been guarded by angels, he had understood very well that those angels were people like himself doing a technical trick. However, he did not dismiss religion completely the way his mother did. He would have prayed now. But he didn't dare. As they taught you in street proofing: a weapon is worse than useless if you don't know how to use it. It will be snatched at once and turned against you.

The torch beam wavered frantically. Sandy stood facing the world invisible: no wistful fancy but a terror that forced itself imperiously through her blood and bones. And foremost in her mind was an intense curiosity. Instead of flight, what would it be like to move towards something that makes you feel like this?

If I want to do it, I should do it. That's the rule.

In another moment they broke and ran. Pelted down the stairs, slammed the door of the front room, fled to the couch and crouched there staring.

Nothing happened.

Sandy saw Candide's torch, dropped and kicked out of reach. It had gone out. She loosened his icy fingers from her arm and pointed, tried to reach it by leaning out but couldn't. She had to crawl out onto the floor. They were caught like that, separated, when it came through the closed door.

There was nothing to see but it was clearly delineated: a moving cone of about half human height. Sandy watched it glide across the wall, sliding in and out of furniture, encompassing the cheap video rack. She could hear Candide breathing short and fast. She could not imagine what it was going to do to them. Perhaps only frighten them to death, as the old stories said. But her bowels had turned to water. She would shit, piss, vomit. She would be very glad to do all these things, void herself: *get away*. It occurred to her that if this was really supernatural being frightened to death wouldn't necessarily be the end of it.

It occurred to her, last of all, that the ghost was real to her. Whereas she was quite certain that until earlier today, the world she inhabited – internal or external – had allowed no such possibility.

'You wanted something different?' it said, in silent intolerable progress towards her and the child. 'Well, here I am. How do you like me?'

Sandy stood up. She forgot about Candide. She forgot that she was afraid, though her body was still howling that this was worse than death. Since she had given up Otto's activism, she had penetrated a few layers of self-deceit, that was all. She was no better off in disillusion than she'd been waving banners and marching. She only saw more clearly how she was trapped: up against the wall of the world. It's nothing circumstantial that's making me suffer, it is *things as they are*. What I want is what is not. And this, as I told myself a little while ago, is one of those. And here it comes.

She did not abandon the rational position she had just described to Candide. Let this be a dream or a delusion: that made no difference whatsoever to its significance, to its meaning in the world of

Sandy. Or to the meaning of what Sandy chose to do on being confronted with her heart's desire.

'Welcome,' she said. 'Do what you like to me, I don't care. I am glad you are here.'

All the powers of darkness...

'It's gone,' whispered Candide.

The room was empty but for themselves. Sandy was surprised to find that she was still on her knees. She got to her feet and walked about a bit, through the space where the thing had been, to convince herself there was nothing there.

'What did you say, Sandy? Your voice went strange.'

She disliked the way he was staring.

'Candide, excuse me but did you wet your pants just now?'

That cooled him off.

'Yes, I did,' he admitted humbly.

'I don't blame you, I nearly did myself. Take them off and put your jeans back on without. We'll wash them when we find some water.'

She retrieved the torch and looked around for any stray possessions. 'What time is it? Is it nearly morning?'

'You asked me that before. My watch stopped ages ago. I was going to put it right when we saw a clock but we never did.'

He shivered. 'Sand, you know that demonstration. I don't think it was a demonstration. I think the people were running away from – from *that*.'

Sandy looked at him thoughtfully: a grey blur of a face with a tremulous mouth and enormous eyes.

'Do you want to go home?'

'Oh no.'

The sky seemed to be lighter outside. They decided to move on anyway, in case the thing came back.

3

The Black Country

They found an unlocked laundromat. Candide washed his under-pants without soap as the soap dispenser was broken. By the time they were banging about alone in a dryer he and Sandy were both dead asleep stretched out along a row of battered chairs. The encounter with the ghost had been exhausting.

It was going to be a long walk. In spite of his curiosity about the ghost and its effects, Candide was determined to keep right away from people. He didn't trust his mother. She had probably given his photo to the police, and his face had been flashed up on tv screens all over the country. They followed canal towpaths, and the tired scrubby derelict land beside railway lines. They made sorties to empty stretches of road, off the toll grid and scarcely maintained but still numbered on the outdated maps: they would fix their line by some distant landmark and then retreat out of sight of any stray traffic. Candide had a child's intuitive grasp of this kind of terrain. He slipped adroitly from one scrap of semi-urban wilderness to another, never straying into the adult-infested streets.

The loneliness of course made them easier prey. Candide soon noticed that he was seeing angels everywhere: flickers of gold on the edge of sight wherever you looked. He discovered that Sandy was being plagued in the same way, when once she clutched him and cried, 'Don't you see them? All in gold, walking on either side of us?' Bearing in mind the angels in his room which had been invisible to everyone else, he had to take these flickers seriously. But nothing happened, so maybe they were really imaginary angels this time.

The sky stayed deep grey: a slight persistent fog blurred the city towers that loomed always in the distance. They stopped to eat once or twice. Candide thought they were making good progress, maybe three miles an hour, but without a watch it was difficult to keep track.

'I've always hated being a woman,' said Sandy. 'Menstruation babies weak body inferior mind. Always hated it. That's why I left Otto you know. The effort of keeping up a positive feminist front was driving me crazy.'

They were lost in a wood. The plantation seemed to go on forever. It was not featured on Candide's ten year old map. The trees were larches. They had a very manmade look, their slender girlish bodies laid out ready for processing while still upright. Their boughs swept down as smoothly as combed hair along the rows. Errant branches had been aborted when they collided with the pattern, the flowing locks concealed bruises. And yet the effect was extremely beautiful: red gold on red gold, falling in endless sheaves. It seemed to be late afternoon. They had not yet seen a clock so time of day was still approximate. The band of sky above the ride was cold and blank and silent.

'But I wouldn't like to be a man either. Shaving every day and walking around with that horrible jelly pouch wobbling between your legs all the time, and the shit-smears on their underpants – yes, including yours Cand. Girls never do that.'

The excuse for Sandy's diatribe was that she'd begun to bleed. She wasn't sure whether she was due for this treat or not but here it was: the heaviness in her lower belly and the thick helpless drip drip drip. It was another reminder of how far she still had to go, another corpse of her past. She thought of Vera on heat.

Candide trailed a stick through the slithery carpet of needles. He wanted to get on. If it was two nights since they left Brighton…He closed his eyes and counted. One.. Two… You reached a point in tiredness when you carried on like a machine. He had vague, vague memories from when he was about two of time being like this: when you couldn't tell the difference between a day and a week. He was sure at least that his stomach was sickeningly empty and there was no food left in the pack. They had a bottle of water filled from a tap in a garage forecourt, but it was probably teeming with cholera. When he thought of Vera dead, Candide wanted to rush over and kill Sandy, smash her up with his stick. He *couldn't* make her move when she started talking like this.

But she had stolen the Rolls and vanquished a ghost, which meant she had earned the right to have most of her own way.

He was beginning to think she could do anything, if she felt like it.

'I mean to say, what's the point in fighting it? You want to live in a matriarchy? We're *living* in a matriarchy. You ask any normal woman and she'll tell you – women rule the world *underneath, inside, in all the important ways*. And men are our dear little wilful children. That isn't the way it was in bronze age Anatolia, that's the way it is was and always will be. Don't kid yourself, Candide, this set up in its entirety is designed and maintained by women exactly as much as by men. Dip dip my blue ship you have the blame I'll have the pain. I don't mean it works out even, any fool can see it doesn't work out even. But the responsibility for the way things are works out even. That's magic.'

'It's just like the old class war. Being shat upon doesn't mean you're a nicer person. Well I'm done with them both, I mean all. But that doesn't mean I've changed sides. If someone came to me here and now and said: you don't have to go through this, hand over Candide and you can wallow in chocolate ice cream for life, I'd laugh in his face. In theory I should take the money and run but I couldn't go back to that world, the way of accumulation. It is so – inelegant – Dismantling things is a much neater solution. I told Otto that.'

Candide had found an anthill. He counted the large woodants running on its surface, his mouth compressed in a thin line of resentful endurance.

'It is lucky normal criminal human nature takes over so quickly. If revolutionaries ever followed things through, where would it end? First you unmask your enemies. Then you unmask your friends, then you unmask yourself. You think you've got the world naked, free of bias, and then you see a little rough edge somewhere and you start picking at it. That's what happened to me. Scritch, scratch, another mask comes off. It hurts worse than anything. But it is such fun to see the stuff coming away. You start off with politics: sex and money, because that's what life with Otto was about. Before you know it you're right through to your skin. Unmask the street unmask the trees.'

She pressed the heels of her hands into her eyes.

'Oh, Cand, it is all coming apart. Do you realise how much goes, when you say to yourself – well, I'll simply get rid of everything that makes me unhappy? But I'm not going to stop. It's addictive just because it is so hard. You keep trying over and over again to do something and it is like those morning dreams, you know when you hear the alarm and dream you got up; find yourself still in bed and then it happens over again.'

She felt a drop of rich soil leaving her. On a sudden inspiration she made it stand for that resentment, la resentissement du pauvre, which she had found enshrined, thinly disguised as its own reverse image – (hatred) in the house of the ghost. It fascinated her to think of giving up something so fundamental, the contemptuous envy of the poor for the rich. The first shall be last and the last shall be first, sweetest promise...Go, little thing. I don't need you any more. Go out of this world.

'I wonder if I am doing anything at all really. Suppose I am literally changing my mind, wouldn't that be extraordinary. Do you think it would be measurable in my brain chemistry?'

The trees moved. They lifted into the air on a surge of energy, and reformed with all their rows broken. The larches stood in random grace, dishevelling all the golden autumn vistas.

Candide looked around, and then helplessly at Sandy.

'We have to find the M5. It must be in here somewhere... Sand, what did you do just then?'

'I'm destroying the world, that's all.'

He looked so horrified she got up and tried to put her arm round him. Candide backed away.

'Don't worry, kid. I mean the one inside me. I told you before. I've gone mad. I'm breaking up inside and I perceive – this is classic – that I'm breaking up the outside too. I thought I'd put the blight on that empty house, and I invented a ghost and I'm afraid I'm getting worse.'

'If that's true, why do I see all the strange things?'

'You don't, Cand. I just hear you telling me you do.'

She shouldered the pack.

'My turn.'

At the third larch she looked back.

'It's all right, mancub. I'm still capable of functioning in a fairly normal way. And I haven't forgotten Vera.'

Candide couldn't be sure but he thought the trees had not just shifted. There were fewer than before. He bit his lip. He had never heard of madness having such an effect on real life, but it might be a rare kind. He'd been thinking that they wouldn't have to trade with the villains at all, Sandy was so effective. But maybe he'd better think of an excuse to get his hostage back from her in case she went completely out of control.

Before they had gone much further there was light ahead. They could see how the ground fell away beyond the last curtain of larches into a shallow valley, and on the other bank a dark line where the plantation began again.

'The M5.' Candide hugged his map book in relief. 'I knew we weren't lost.'

Sandy could not hear any traffic. She thought she had never in her life been out of reach of that sound, before this journey. Every night at Wombega the cheap freight rumbled by, on its way to Newhaven and avoiding the bypass tolls. Even on the quietest day in a park, or in the country, there was always that faint subliminal sighing.

It is gone. They are gone. I am alone.

She walked more slowly. The winter sky had an eerie dull glow of lost sunlight. Beneath it the great grey river flowed endlessly between dark trees. She didn't like that image, it was sentimental. Why did I do that, she wondered. Surely she had no deep secret yearning to get back to nature, not seriously. There was nothing natural about Sandy Brize. She was as manmade as one of those larch trees, down to her polluted nuclear-age chromosomes.

No, it was all right. No tameless river of the neo-wilderness ever came painted with white stripes, or decorated in a tracery of tiny green and red and amber stars.

Sandy yelled. She ran out down the embankment, stumbling, waving her arms wildly, over the brink and out. She thought she could hear in the uncanny silence the echoes of brakes squealing and horns hooting. But that was in another world. She pranced around making the skirts of her coat whirl... To be mad. To die of it, under this coldly gleaming sky. How glorious.

The little boy stood on the edge of the embankment frowning. Then he yelled too, and pitched himself at the slope. They danced like dervishes, laughing wildly at each other: until Sandy screamed, 'Candide!' – grabbed him by the arm and dragged him across the southbound carriageway. They ran into the shelter of the trees.

'You lunatic. You might have got yourself killed.'

'But Sand – '

It was exasperating, trying to follow the rules of her game.

Sandy was looking at something behind him.

'Hush. Let's get on.'

On the other side of a ribbon of further plantation there were suburban fields, scattered with ditches and bushes and shacks for little girls' ponies. In the distance houses and a church tower rose out of blurred trees. Sandy kept glancing over her shoulder: she was imagining things again.

'What is it Sand? What is it?'

'Ssh.'

This time he saw it too, the glint of alien light.

They made for the cover of the buildings. It was a genuine village, only half swallowed by the outer Urban Area. They followed a cinder track between tall garden hedges until it became a metalled road. And now, when they'd have been glad to see some human activity, there was no one about.

'It was someone with binoculars – ' hissed Candide.

'No, not binoculars.'

'I knew they'd have a trace on the Rolls,' he wailed. 'We've been trailed all along, they've been playing cat and mouse. Shall we knock on someone's door?'

They ducked inside an open garden gate and crouched under the hedge to catch their breath. Nothing stirred in the house, its windows were blank. Sandy thought of what she had seen and Candide had not. The responsibilities of this venture might become too much for a mad woman. *I'm busy* – she thought. I can't cope with this.

'This one doesn't look very hopeful. Besides – think what we look like. The angel might be more plausible than us.'

They hurried on. Treacherously, the houses abandoned them. Sandy and Candide burst out, almost before they could stop themselves, onto the brink of a vast expanse of ploughland. It was naked as the moon, there wasn't a hedge in sight. Far away a thin purple fuzz of woodland rimmed the horizon. She grabbed the little boy's hand. They ran, the raw earth clogging their feet. The pursuer had been left behind, with luck it would take him some time to check over the village. There was a sound, a brief high pitched sound. It was the first noise of any kind that they had heard since they left the Rolls, that wasn't made by themselves.

Sandy stopped running to consider this.

She put her hand up and touched her cheek, curiously.

There was a figure standing in front of the last houses, holding a rifle. It was taking aim again. The sighting lens glittered.

Candide screamed, 'Get down – ' and threw himself on his face. The ploughed furrows were scarcely a hand high. Sandy didn't move. Candide was in the shelter of her body, but that meant nothing to a bullet from a high powered rifle. The angel, small and distant, shifted a little. She knew it pulled the trigger. She put up her hand in an absurd, futile gesture.

'Candide, look – '

She bent down beside him in the furrow, and uncurled her fingers: showing him as if it was a captured butterfly the slender bright object on her palm.

'It feels cool.'

The little boy stared at her blankly.

'Chance in a billion,' murmured Sandy. Although she knew the odds were somewhat worse than that.

She laughed. What had happened was so ridiculous that she couldn't resist the temptation to complete the joke. With a flick of her wrist, she sent the bullet flying back towards their pursuer.

After a minute or two Candide got up and knocked off the worst of the sticky dirt. The angel was no longer visible.

'What shall we do now?'

He sounded nervous.

She didn't answer, only started walking back.

On the edge of the moon there were rows of tired ex-council houses, an ancient primary school with boarded windows, a few swings in a concrete yard. Beyond the playground they were in what passed for a shopping centre. There was no one in sight except for a figure like a sleeping tramp, huddled in the doorway of the small supermarket.

Sandy and Candide approached it cautiously.

She looked down. The man was dressed in a good coat, though it showed signs of one or two rough nights. He must be new to the road, or else he'd been lucky at some charity handout. He had a pack on his back. He had not yet descended to the level of the bulging carrier bags, one inside the other, where the valuable and useful contents change by imperceptible degrees into dirt, dust, kitchen leavings...Before Candide appeared with his mission this was the end Sandy had imagined for herself. How often she had silently greeted the trolley drivers and bin searchers of the streets of Brighton, in those last weeks. Saying to them: I'm coming, I'm on my way.

She did not know why she should think of him as a derelict, on the run like herself from life, ideology and utopia. He was not that. He was wearing new walking boots and corduroy breeches. But where the coat had fallen aside you could see his angel corslet, and the gold sheened skin. In one gloved hand he was still clutching his rifle.

'Hey, mister – '

She bent over him, wondering if she should take the weapon.

'Hey mister – are you all right?'

The body rolled over as she touched it. The man's face was revealed. It was eyeless, and the lower jaw had fallen into the swathes of a gold mesh muffler. White grubs wriggled frantically inside the dark cavity of the mouth, desperate to escape the sudden light.

'Yuck!' shrieked Candide, bounding backwards. 'Dis-*gusting*!'

Sandy knelt back on her heels. She pressed her hand to her mouth, remembered what it had touched and wiped it violently on her coat.

'Oh, shut up. You'll look like that yourself one day. It's nothing to make a stupid fuss about.'

'But how Sandy, but how? It takes weeks for bodies to get like that – '

'I don't know. Shut up. And help me get his pack off him.'

'Eurgh! Why?'

Sometimes the child seemed incredibly stupid. Didn't he learn anything from the angel's costume and equipment?

'Well, don't bother if you're not hungry.'

It was an unpleasant job. The smell of rotting flesh, which they had not noticed at first, came off the body in waves as they pulled it about. They had to take the bag well up wind before they could raid it, like jackals dragging their private share away from a trove of carrion.

'D'you think we should tell the police?'

Incredibly stupid.

'You tell them if you can find them. I'm not keen. I killed him, remember.'

He was silenced, and voluntarily kept watch then while she packed away the loot. But nothing stirred in the empty street, not so much as a twitching curtain.

Δ

Candide had built a fire. It crouched in a hollow on a piece of ground that was something between a tip and a fragment of woodland. The trees were sycamore, rank growing suburban weeds. Their meagre stems glowed olive in the firelight. The miscellaneous rubbish under them was drifted with their leaves – damp papery hands of grey and yellow and blotched brown. Flames rummaged in the air around Candide's laths and bits of plank and sizzling branches. It was a November bonfire in a back garden, except that the night was silent, no bright rocket showers starred the low sky.

'You open the tins first,' muttered Candide wisely. 'Then you dig a hole in a hot place... We're having beans followed by tinned chicken followed by rice pudding. I've worked out a way – I'm going to bang one of our forks out of shape, but it's for getting tins out of the fire so it's worth it.'

Sandy watched him from their bedroom, an abandoned vehicle that had lost its wheels but miraculously kept its upholstery intact. It was a small plasticy Nissan, not more than three years old (the number plates had gone). Neither of them would have been seen dead in such a vulgar mass-marketer if it was moving, but there are times when even car snobbery must be put aside.

'Thus the male mind. Always tinker, tinker, tinker. That was *your* fork, you realise.'

She hadn't known how hungry she was until the tins were opened. The smell of food assaulted her.

'Okay, we'll trade. You can share my hot-tin-handling device, if I can share your eating device. That's fair.'

'Ah – but I would have been quite happy to eat the stuff cold.'

Their second ghost came on them quietly, without any terror. It slipped out from among the trees and approached the fire in wary little starts. It was a woman. She was wearing a green wool coat, a tidy unadventurous garment of neutral date. She could have been younger than Sandy (different tribes age at different rates), or in her fifties. But now she was dressed like a very little girl, with buttons in the wrong buttonholes and her hair all on end. She was wearing one shoe and carrying the other. She had walked the foot out of her tights: the thin brown stuff was riding up her leg as if she had been skinned from the ankle.

'Hallo,' said Candide gently. 'Are you hungry?'

He had his mother's trick of automatically taking in hand any passing human problem: natural born officer material, Sandy called it.

He made a place for the ghost on a pile of old fertiliser sacks and showed her how to hold the tin with his device. She took Sandy's fork, eagerly. But when she tried to lift the beans to her mouth something went wrong. They dripped back into the glistening orange matrix.

'Are you real – '

It was the ghost of a voice.

'What a question,' murmured Sandy.

'Yes, we're real as far as we know. What happened to you? Can you tell?'

But the woman ignored Candide and seemed to expect no answer to her own inquiry. She huddled, nursing her bruised foot in the warmth of the flames, then suddenly started up and ran away.

Candide ate his beans in silence. He passed the half empty tin to Sandy and bent over the chicken. It had begun to bubble tastily.

'Something's happened, hasn't it,' he remarked pensively. 'I've been wondering, and now I'm sure. You're not mad Sandy. All the weirdness is real. There's been a nuclear war, I think. We'd be pretty sick by now if we were going to die, so I expect we'll be all right unless we get cancer later.'

Sandy said nothing, only watched his face while she ate.

'And that's why BREAKTHRU hasn't managed to stop us yet. They've all been thrown into chaos too. I hope it doesn't mean they've killed Vera. But that angel was equipped for the post-holocaust and he was still chasing us. Therefore whatever it is in the tube is still important and that should mean they still value their hostage. I've decided we have to go on.' He sighed heavily. 'I hope Otto survived,' he added as an afterthought. 'Are you ready for some chicken? You can have first turn at this course.'

When the meal was over Candide went on feeding his fire with placid abandon. A tribe of him in a year would have deforested the vale of Arden over again. Sandy kept quiet, taking comfort in the feeling of warmth and a full stomach and trying not to think of anything else.

'I've seen people getting eaten by worms in videos, but I never realised it was true. Do bodies under the ground get eaten like that? Do earthworms eat meat? I thought they were vegetarian.'

Sandy swallowed. 'It's bacteria that do the first eating, Cand. When they've broken up the tissue, insect larvae and worms can get at the organic matter.'

'Oh, I see.'

Resting his chin on one hand, Candide turned a softly rounded profile to the fireglow. His skin was translucent rose.

'Bacteria, mmm. D'you remember when Otter made us eat the bacon with maggots?'

'Not actual maggots, Cand.'

'Well, it was pretty green.' He chuckled, poking the dirty tins further into a red cavern: produced a comic exaggeration of his mother's faint border accent. 'It's pairfectly all-reecht if ye scraipit the wee marks awa'.'

Sandy gave Candide the front seats with the gap. She buried him in fertiliser sacks: he should be warm enough. In the back she had more legroom, but there was a broken window and she was cold every time she moved. When she turned her face into the shelter of her coat collar she could smell decomposing flesh.

Outside the night was opaque charcoal. And she tried to count, like Candide, how many nights there had been.

She did not wonder that Candide could take his 'nuclear war' so calmly. All children played holocaust survivors. It was a game, a simple way of wiping out the adult world. It meant no more than making believe to be castaways on a tropic island. Sometime, if it was true, he would realise that his mother was actually dead – and all the rest of it. And she would have to cope with that. But Sandy could not take the idea seriously. She lifted her hand, she caught the rifle bullet and threw it back...Candide had apparently forgotten that incident. Or maybe he surmised that a massive dose of radiation had transformed her into a superbeing, in classic comicbook style.

I am destroying the world.

And as I destroy, all the rules go wild.

I am hallucinating, it started long ago. Nothing strange is going on, except in my mind.

Which?

She tried to think it through. Her brain seemed to heave and squirm inside her skull, like the grubs in the dead man's mouth.

Sandy kicked open the broken hatchback and rolled into darkness. Stumbling, blundering, her mouth running with saliva, she managed to reach the sycamores. She fell on all fours, retching.

Kneeling there, she groped in her pocket and brought out the small canister Candide had given to her when they left Brighton. This was what the man with the rifle wanted. What could it be?

And what would she do if there were more angels – commit more impossible murders? Is physical impossibility of method a defence in a court of law? Certainly not in a court of the mind. This is my world, she told herself. I can do what I like in it. Maybe she shouldn't be surprised that it turned out so nasty: the poor have very limited imaginations. She remembered with the pain she had missed before that Otto thought she was a traitor. She thought of Candide's pain too, always beside her. That must be the explanation. Candide's grief on account of that miserable dog was invading her madness, colouring her dream.

Ah yes, they were looking for the dog. That was something to hold on to.

And since I promised him I'd be able to function normally, I'd better lay off the undecidables.

It was cold. She put the tube back in her pocket. The rubbish under the trees was both slimy and jagged to kneel on. She crouched back on her heels, shuddering. Oh well, I always knew I would be like that, if ever I let myself out. Some lucky people cannot kill, I shouldn't think Otter could do it. I can. It would not be so bad, but there were more tins, and nothing else to eat. She hoped she wasn't going to vomit every time.

Back at the car she found Candide's rucksack by touch and rinsed her mouth with a little of the cholera water. She tried to move carefully but she needn't have bothered. The peaceful breathing continued without a hitch. Doubled up in her place she glared at the back of the front seats with deep hatred. It's true what people say: children have no morals. Insensitive little brute.

SIXTH ANGEL

1

Through the Door
Marked Private

Otto made friends with her squaddie. She saw only his eyes through the oblong spyhole. It was an odd reversal, he might have been in purdah. He, of course, saw all the cell as he peered between his veils. At first she wasn't sure but she became convinced that it was always the same man. Long lashed, very dark oval eyes and the slightly flattened bridge of a nose. His skin tone was burnt umber, smooth and bright; his voice was pure South London. He had been specifically instructed not to reveal his name, his regiment or even his trade. He didn't say so, Otto found it out. She kept up a barrage of questions like a three-year-old child. Where am I? What is this place? Why am I in solitary? Why can't I have my own clothes? Who's your commanding officer, what's your regiment? What's going on outside – When she complained about the bucket, challenging his acknowlegement of their common humanity, she knew by the lift of his eyes that he smiled. He was not the reachable kind. He had been warned about this tactic and was pleased with himself for recognising it when it came. She thought he watched when she used the thing, but never gave him the satisfaction of looking in that direction.

It was unpleasant to have to go on trying, fully aware that she was simply providing the young man with a free cabaret to relieve his boredom. But this was the work. It must be continued, with hope or without.

When she slept she dreamed, the most vivid and disturbing dreams. She was revenged on herself then, for her hours of meaningless toil under the gaze of those glossy and impenetrable male eyes. She walked along a corridor that seemed both walled and floored in grey rubber. There was an armed escort, but she soon realised she was not the prisoner. The prisoner was waiting for her in a bare room with a hospital atmosphere and smell. It was James. She strapped him to an iron bed. The escort waited outside the door. Sometimes he struggled but she was always stronger. Sometimes she just hit him, sometimes she beat him with a thick leather belt: as the sessions went on she gained courage and used the electrical equipment too. There was no pretence of an interrogation. She wanted to hear him scream, see his body twist about unsuccessfully trying to evade her hands, see him foul himself in terror. She felt a knot of sexual excitement tightening as he cried and sweated, although she never touched him except in the most clinical way, to humiliate. Often she woke as it burst in orgasm.

At first Otto, even dreaming, was horrified. But James was the one who had given her the Kairos. It was because of his stupidity and cowardice that she had lost Candide. No wonder she wanted to equal the score. And he was a man. It was inevitable, in this terrible situation, that he should become *man* to her: standing in for the jeering squaddie, for his brother Xav, and all the countless others; the whole great voluptuous paranoia machine of maleness.

She suffered the effects of solitary confinement. She was always very cold: her clothes and her one skimpy blanket totally, no doubt deliberately inadequate. Blurred vision upset her. She couldn't get used to being without her lenses, but the squaddie didn't know what had become of them. Broken, probably, and when would she ever get another pair? Her recent memory was confused, she thought she might have been sedated for a while after her arrest. Once she suddenly wondered if she had been keeping a tally of days. She searched the cell hoping to find one. But there were no marks on the tiled walls or the floor or her metal framed cot, not even fingernail tears in her blanket or hidden under the mattress. She lost hope: there was no point in starting now.

She did not know where she was or how long she could expect to be held. Her people had always understood that the effect of a full scale war would be disastrous – they weren't anarchists or back-to-the-woods gamers. The government was crazy when it classified active dissidents as a menace in this kind of crisis. She could have argued her case well. But it seemed she wasn't going to get the chance.

At her most dazed moments she thought she was living her life over again in its distilled essence. Her open eyes looked on marches and meetings and every small resolute practice of unpopular and unrewarded virtue. It was the same. Waking she must keep the faith and guard the pass, though she knew the battle was lost. Sleeping she had her self-indulgent dreams: an accessible enemy, and the vengeance that she would never allow herself in reality, even if she ever got the chance to 'equal the score'. She noticed now when she was too tired to dissemble, how her every image of resistance and revolution was begged, borrowed or stolen from the male discourse: noble combat and thankless glory. *Go, tell the Spartans...* Her task had always been hopeless. The contradictions went too deep, the weave was too close.

They moved her while she was asleep. Otto woke to rich sensations of warmth and comfort. At once some critical faculty that had been knocked out of action in solitary, awoke. She was on her guard.

She was lying on a capacious leather sofa, wrapped in a big soft plaid rug. She sat up, remembering to do so slowly, as if confused. On the floor there was a worn but handsome turkey carpet in shades of gold, rust and deep red. Deep red velvet curtains covered the wide bay window. Above a wainscotting of dark wood were bookcases filled with uneven rows of heterogenous, well-thumbed volumes. Firelight glowed and moved in every polished surface. There were two fat comfortable chairs drawn up on either side of the hearthrug, facing the flames. Otto let the rug fall. She looked at that pleasant hearth, broodingly.

What was happening? Why had they done this?

She even recognised some of the books, not by their titles but as individual objects; familiar as old friends.

But there was something wrong. Nothing in this well-known room seemed solid. She felt as if her hand would sink through the furniture at a touch: when she stood, the floor seemed about to give way. She was dizzy, sick, she felt drugged. Or maybe she had been drugged all along, and this feeling was the effect of withdrawal.

The door opened and someone came in. He sat down at the desk.

She saw the tall gaunt figure of a man in late middle age, dressed in a decent dark suit that looked a little rumpled, as always. He had a long bony jaw and broad high brow – a distinguished head on a man, not so good for a woman.

'Well, Otto.'

'What's going on?' she cried. 'Is it really war? What kind of war? Or was that just a scam to get us into the prison hulks?'

'Oh, the war is as real as you are,' he said. 'As to what's going on, I can't tell you. You may assume you've been released into my custody: the rest is classified.'

He leaned forward hiding his mouth behind peaked fingers, the classic sign of lying.

'But never mind about that, the most important thing is for us to find Candide. The country's in chaos. There are armed gangs running wild, and the child's out there on his own...'

'You bastard,' she shouted. 'You don't know me at all! I love Candide more than my life but he's *one child*. The most important thing is to stop the fighting. Or failing that alleviate the pain as best we can. For God's sake there must be *something* I can do to help – '

One of the books on the shelf behind him was a late Victorian single volume edition of Keats. The pages were edged in worn gilt and delicate and hard to handle as floss silk. When she was a little girl she used to sneak in here, take down that Keats and lift the tissue paper from its engravings. Feast her eyes on Queen Mab's exquisite naked bosom. And Lamia, and Isabella. Those dainties made to still an infant's cries...She remembered shouting at her father once in this very room. *Of course I fucking well get turned on by women's bodies. Doesn't everyone? Isn't that the basis of world consumersism? It certainly seems to be –*

But that cloth Keats died long ago. Loved to death, its spine split, it was sent to a jumble sale.

And yet this was not an actor. It was her father, as surely as it had been James in the torture dreams. Maybe it *was* her father, she didn't know all his secrets. The dizziness increased – if this was a puppet her enemies had set up to trick her, what else was the real man? My Daddy, my guru: scratch his opposition and you find the status quo, scratch mine and you find Daddy. She chanted at him, striding up and down.

> I could not dig I dared not rob
> And so I lied to please the mob –

Didn't know what she was doing. Didn't have to act confusion, it came naturally.

She was left alone. The synthetic firelight danced with the same blue and silver gilt as on the night of Betty's wedding. She wondered where the camera was. She was not afraid at all now. The stupidity of this charade elated her. It had achieved the very opposite of what was intended. She wondered on what authority she had been taken from the police – and guessed perhaps she had never been in their hands at all.

BREAKTHRU.

Were they still obsessed with their damned drug in the middle of a nuclear war, or was the war another stage set? She would find out soon enough once she got out of here. They wouldn't care if the war was real. It was what they preached. Knock the world down, we can always knock up another one...exactly the same. Riverruntheriverruntheriverrun. She had always detested Finnegan's Wake, deciphered enough of it to be sure (it was her business to find out these things) that it was both everything that was claimed for it, the pinnacle of a civilisation; and a load of old garbage. What she hated was the puerile delight in the allfalldown build up again: allfalldown build up again. The timeless world of patriarchy, the endless cycle. No progress, never, nothing new under the sun...*meaningless*...

She went and looked behind the dark red curtains. Instead of the border hills she found a door in an unwainscotted, undisguised blank wall. On reflection, she thought the father figure might have come in and left this way. The door was not locked. She followed him, without a plan: only knowing that she must take any chance to learn more about her circumstances if she was ever to escape. When stopped, she would fall back on the disorientation so as not to alarm them. It wouldn't be hard. She had been pumped full of something obviously, probably been under for days. Only the enduring effect of a misspent youth gave her the capacity to walk upright in this wavering, fearfully uncertain world. Born and bred, she muttered to herself grimly. Born and bred in this briar patch...A short distance beyond the door she turned out of habit into a corridor at right angles to the first. The walls were painted grey, the floor covering was some industrial grade grey stuff that suggested hospitals. She walked into a room rather larger than her old cell. It contained an iron bedstead and little else. The chair, the straps, the electrical gear had all been taken away. The smell was the same.

Otto began to shake all over.

It couldn't be true.

It was not James, at least it was not James. It was a dummy, an actor. She had been subject to disgusting, humiliating disorientation technique – but no one was hurt, surely no one was hurt.

She tried to shore them up but the walls fell down. She knew this room was a place inside her mind. Even to be able to walk into it was appalling, appalling: a violent, incestuous reversal – the world inside the brain, bursting the tiny ball of tissue with its vastness. This can happen now. The barriers are gone. She screamed. *I didn't want this*! She never meant to tear down the walls, only to shift them a little. Bad things, bad things come running out, when the old house falls down...

The room disintegrated. Her flailing arms hit something that gave way explosively, a red splash appeared on the sleeve of her prison smock. She had broken a pane in a half glassed door which had no handle on the inside. She thrust her hand through, wrenched something and the door flew open. Surfaces leapt at her, her vision so distorted she could not distinguish walls from floor, saw no perspective, no colour, no form. Almost blind but not in darkness she knew *window*, could articulate the word though shape, contrast, texture were all lost. There was another explosion, another fall. Otto clambered to her feet and ran.

There was a jangling of the air that might have been shouting voices, or an alarm going off. Not blind, not deaf but *senseless*, she expected to reach some final, defeating, obstacle which she would know only in that it ended her progress; but she didn't.

Some time later, she couldn't tell how long, she was sitting by the side of a narrow country lane, on wet grass with a ragged November hedge behind her. She was nursing her cut arm. By the thunderous battering of her heart and the harshness in her throat she had been running for quite a while. It was half dark: an evening twilight, she thought, not morning. There was no sign anywhere of her prison, or any pursuers.

Otto walked into a pub. A quiet village pub in the early evening was one of her favourite places on earth. She checked herself in the bar mirror as she'd already checked as well as she was able before she came in. But the glass cuts weren't bleeding any more and were hidden by her sleeves. There was surprisingly little evidence of what she'd just been through. The barman held her fiver up to the light, that helpless gesture of mistrust which was so much a feature of modern cash use. He decided it was good enough, as dubious little bits of paper go; and even gave her a sour but not unfriendly smile. She was the only customer. She took her pint into a corner, leaned back on a determinedly uncomfortable cushioned settle, and relaxed.

The brewery's disco lights played silently over the brewery's hunting prints. The tobacco coloured wallpaper had a pattern of peculiar looking little red fruits. She noted quietly (she had seen this outside of course) that all the windows were painted out with whitewash, and taped to restrict the damage should they shatter. The barman seemed calm, however. He polished a glass. There was a big screen over his head. Perhaps he would put some news on when a few more people had gathered, and she would find things out without asking suspiciously ignorant questions.

'D'you get a lot of BREAKTHRU people in here?'

He shrugged.

'I mean to say, with that place of theirs nearby – '

'What place?'

Otto beat a hasty retreat. 'Sorry, my mistake.'

She would have to be careful.

She still felt drugged. That unpleasant insubstantial effect returned whenever she brought her attention to bear on any solid object. She half closed her eyes.

The trick was to keep thoughts practical. This drug, this Kairos. It operated on a scale more minute and pervasive than anything biological, so the angel had said. Contiguous...in a sense there is nothing between one particular set of brain chemistry – one mind – and another, same as there's nothing between one cell in your toe and another in your eye, so long as the invader is small enough. Eventually, though, the damage must reach biological proportions, mustn't it? This Kairos stuff must be doing physical things, *maybe irreversible physical things*, to the neural pathways. What is this pervasive sense of disintegration that I feel? What am I experiencing? On the night before my period starts I often dream of blood. The 'body' can communicate with the 'mind' and not only by means of pain and so on. It can use mind's language sometimes...

She dredged up from the distant past Otto Murray, Social Psychology student. She had dipped then, dilettante, into the neurological material. (Lucky Cand never knew about that connection. He'd go beserk, picturing his mother sewing up kittens' eyelids.) The suppression of Raphe cell activity, highly excitable state in the

179

visual cortex... She told herself she mustn't be afraid of her own ignorance, fumbling with these obsolete scraps. Remember the old punk philosophy – don't care how and don't care why. It works any way I can make it work. She had taught herself to doctor the Wombega computer and run a sami video service on those terms: she must get the better of this too.

Back to the soft science: which I can handle. All seeing is perception. The world, effectively, is what we decide it is. Terribly frightening things happen to me and James. Everyone around us gets frightened, because of this contiguity effect: and since one can't just 'be afraid' in a vacuum, quite soon a new consensus-reality develops, based on whatever large scale fears are floating about. If James and I are still significant, the answer might be for us to get unfrightened. But how are we to do that? Luci is dead, and I don't believe I'll see Candide alive again. And anyway we are now surrounded by people who are reinfecting us all the time...

Given that this mass hallucination starts, on such a level, what worries me is that I don't see, logically, how it stops.

Marching up to the Houses of Parliament had been an absurd idea: the thought of that revealing impulse embarrassed her. She must go to her own kind, together they would find a way to outmanoeuvre the drug. She began a mental review of trustworthy characters and it struck her, with a shiver, that she was doing what BREAKTHRU had meant to do: preparing to form a revolutionary government. And why not? Supposing I am right in my guess, and the fascist angels find their explosion isn't so easily controlled: this might be it. This might be our chance instead of theirs.

The taste of bitter beer contained so much. A quiet life, a small life, le petit bonheur de tous les jours. She had chosen that: to cultivate her garden. Candide had been her shortcut across the world's stage. Making bread with bad flour and hustling publishers for miserable little sums of money. For entertainment the allowance of one half pint per week. Or a walk around an expensive supermarket where the three of them could only afford to admire. Recycling paper, jollying Candide along to drink the awful Brighton water...this is starship water Cand, like real space colonists drink. Boiling the stuff for fifteen minutes without fail and always turning off the tap, turning off the light...refusing packaging, blowing your nose and sopping up menstrual blood on dingy rag-paper: all that stuff, the obsessive Hasidic practices, rituals of optimism when all the time you knew it was too little too late the world was dying, dying...

No! That's the drug talking!

Suddenly she remembered a room, a dirty little cell on Sussex university campus. Sandy was reading poetry, a new experience for her as she didn't mind admitting. She read out to them 'for being taken with a man, Who has the worst of all bad names...' She found this vagueness irritating. What *is* the worst of all bad names, she complained. Corrupter of the innocent, said James and Luci, in chorus, without even glancing at each other. Sandy was disgusted. You Christians, you've got it all worked out for you. How nice...

What Xav had done to her child. Candide's cinder eyes and the set of his mouth. How could she ever make him believe now? He had seen the thing that she had been trying to hide, to will out of existence: the truth.

Oh no! That's the drug talking! I have to *stop* thinking like that. But I can't. It seems so real. It seems like all there ever was.

In the grubby little campus room Sandy was laughing. Otto felt so lost, so desperately lonely that she began to cry. She tried to stop herself, painfully gulping back the tears.

She raised her glass in an attempt to pass for normal. She saw her jacket sleeve of worn brown sheepskin: was transfixed. In that mock-up of the study at Underhill, she had been wearing a blue prison smock and trousers of some kind of cheap synthetic.

Amnesia patches. Try and remember. You found your own clothes in a cupboard, didn't you. On the way out. She noticed for the first time that she had also, apparently, recovered her contact lenses. The glass shook so badly she had to put it down. She had been mistaken. A person can *be afraid*, with no focus and no limit.

Otto stood up. The room began to shake. There was dust everywhere and the dishevelled barman, still polishing that same glass, was crouched against shelves of broken bottles grinning like a gargoyle. In his cinder eyes she saw reflected a terrible, inescapable, limitless isolation. Yet there was more to come. There was worse. Like a child she started pinching her own arm, and yelped at the unexpected pain. She ran to the door and saw a street bathed in livid stage twilight. There were some men walking towards her wearing gas masks. Others were getting out of a car. Tiled walls began to rise, closing off her vision: but they were no more certain, had no greater power.

You can't have wanted this she screamed. No one can live like this.

And ran blindly, deeper still, into the shattered, falling labyrinth of her mind.

2

Abîme des Oiseaux

At last Sandy and Candide approached Isobel Porter House. They were very tired and dirty at the end of the long walk. They had given up trying to distinguish day from night. Neither of them could say how long it was since Sandy killed the angel and the ghost visited their campfire. The former pill factory was set in its own grounds, at the back there was a private wood. When it was built it had been flanked by model housing estates for the new model working class but the city had changed shape since then. A few weary, half derelict fields away the giant Urban Area began but you would not have known it here. They walked under the bright gold canopy of the beeches. It was very quiet. They stayed on paths made by guards or keepers, keeping a look out for man traps. Sandy had begun to hear a steady rhythmical sound, a kind of heavy clapping noise. It seemed like the leaves of a great stone door opening and closing: slam slam slam.

Candide kept saying that they were heading north west, but more and more Sandy had felt that they were moving south. South, and down: those were the only directions possible, and soon they would have travelled as far as there was to go.

The wall was about four metres high, built of large square yellowish blocks. They climbed it with ease, mortar had crumbled out from between the courses leaving good holds for fingers and toes. Once astride the coping they saw a formidable obstacle: a massive plastic skinned mesh fence with posts of bedded concrete. The top half metre was angled outwards, with a thick lacing of razor wire. Candide pointed to a sign that was displayed prominently at intervals along the mesh. It indicated graphically that the fence was live, it carried enough current to kill you.

'D'you think that's just for show?'

'No I don't. You be careful what you touch,'

The banging of the stone doors went on, never any nearer, never any farther.

'Candide,' she said. 'What's happening is much worse than a Nuclear War. I think we're coming to the end of the world.'

Candide nodded gravely.

'I know. I always knew, really.'

He took the pack from his back and produced his mother's bolt cutters. He gave them to Sandy and they clambered down. The space between wall and fence had been stripped of vegetation and laid with white chippings. Candide began to sort through the patch around him, collecting.

'What's that for?'

'To make a trail so we can find our way back.'

Sandy cut wire economically. She was not afraid. Her body and her mind had changed so much that the presence of an electrical current meant nothing to her: or should she say the rules of the disintegrating world had changed. It was both, the two entities functionally indistinguishable. All forms and properties had become insubstantial as thought. She paused every so often. The tremors were coming closer together now.

'Hurry up – hurry up!'

'Don't rush me Candide. Keep calm. I won't let you down.'

She opened a large low flap and tucked the severed mesh out of the way. After they'd crawled through she pressed it back into place and they marked the spot with white stones. The steady banging of the doors where the world ended told her there was no need to take such precautions, but she did it anyway.

'Just think,' whispered Candide. 'Gerry Howard might be inside here, having a refresher course. Do you think we'll see her?'

In the tremors now everything vanished but for a profound shaking darkness. This made their progress disjointed: through a shrubbery, over some damp lawns. The building was a big yellow monster in the modernist-classical style of the thirties, with a massive arched window of countless small panes as the centre piece on the first floor of the facade. It still looked very like a factory, though the old Breakey's name had been removed and replaced everywhere by 'BREAKTHRU' and the revamped angel logos. On either side of the main block were wings of more recent development, and prefabs and concreted yards. A dark blue van, a newish Daihatsu, stood alone next to a loading bay. The whole place had a dull, discouraging air, like an old-fashioned boarding school deserted for the holidays.

Sandy broke a window. She took off her coat to cover the broken glass and pulled out dangerous shards carefully, while Candide danced and whimpered – Come on, come on. Inside Isobel Porter the silence was unbroken, except for that distant clapping of stone on stone. This was an empty shell. The angels had abandoned it, had dispersed already before the mysterious plague that was tearing Sandy's world apart. Candide said nothing but his eyes and mouth showed it all. He looked a hundred years old. They followed signs to the animal laboratories.

In the labs it was gloomy to the point of darkness. The glass in the big naked windows had been left switched against incoming light, what there was of it. They walked between desktop terminals and measuring machines set up to give precise doses of this and that to their living components. The apparatus looked neither innocent nor guilty now, that was all over. Finally they reached the cages of dead and dying animals. Candide saw everything he had imagined when he used to lie dreaming. This was the shape in which he had taught himself the lesson for life: that pain is, cruelty is. But he had planned then that he would win, one day.

Sandy followed behind. She experienced a revelation: or rather became finally certain of something she had suspected for some time. She was not the one to whom this event (the end of the world) was happening. It was Candide, the mancub. From the moment he had come to her she had done no more than officiate, not even at an execution but at a death bed. When something dies of being what it is there is no blame: and yet she noted remorselessly that there had always been an orgiastic and participatory element in his fixation with the horror stories. Candide did this: a crying, guilty child. Always, forever. And she, always, forever, was his judge and comforter and also (since this was Sandy's world to which this was happening) the thing that died.

'Do you want us to let them out?'

'No.' He sighed wearily. 'It's too late for that.'

He found Vera as he had pictured her. She lay on the floor of her cage, a tube inserted in her anus, another strapped to a shaved place on her upward flank. When she saw him the crusted stump of her tail began to jump. She tried to get up, she couldn't but her mouth opened in the old three cornered pink and white grin.

185

'Look Sand, she was expecting me. She knew I wouldn't give up.'

Sandy cut the wire around the lock on the cage door. With a convulsive jerk the mutilated creature pulled free of one tube. She writhed and yapped thinly, a wasted shred of her old self. Candide began to work at the strapping on her side.

'Hey, Cand – that drip might be keeping her alive.'

He gave her a bleak look and went on gently tugging. Vera howled piercingly and she was free, in his arms. Candide buried his face in the rough white coat.

And Sandy looked on. She wanted to congratulate him, to tell him that at least there was this moment, which he should always remember; that he had not been wholly defeated. But she could not speak.

They left the way they had come, except that they failed to find Candide's white trail and had to walk up and down the fence for a while before spotting the marked place. Sandy was self-conscious, chivvying the boy with his precious burden and staring around warily. But it was a nervous act, a kind of reflexive pretence that there was still reason to fear and to hope: she was rather ashamed of it. Just before they went through the hole Candide said suddenly: Oh, Vera's pissed herself. He was holding the dog inside his anorak cradled in both arms. A vile smell rose.

'Shit herself too,' apologised Candide. 'It's all over me.'

He looked frightened. Vera was very quiet now.

'She's ill,' Sandy reassured him. 'It isn't her fault.'

Candide climbed the wall with one hand, he wouldn't accept help. Outside in the wood there was a bird singing in the grey gloom. As they walked another joined it and another: tentative but clear.

'Have you noticed,' said Sandy, 'if you are out late in the dark and walking under trees there is often a bird singing, even in winter. I wonder what they are. They can't be nightingales in November.'

Candide cleaned himself and the dog off as best he could, and then nursed Vera while Sandy built a fire of fallen branches. Candide's male genius had contrived them some cooking pots out of empty tins: she used one to warm up a little jellied milk from the angel's stores. The dog managed to lap a little but showed no great interest.

'We need brandy to put in it.'

But there was no brandy.

Time passed very slowly. At last Sandy went away, she told herself it was to look for water. In this twilight the beech canopy was the colour of dried blood. The stone doors slammed on. She stood quietly listening to the birds, in that place where absolute grief and peace run together and become one. When she came back, without any water, Candide was asleep and the dog was gone from his lap. Sandy looked about. Vera had crawled into a hollow under a small tree by the fence. She was lying on her side. A thin trail of blackish excrement had oozed out along the leaves. The dirty white pelt rose and fell with a pitiful effort. She looked up at Sandy, her yellow eyes still containing whatever simulacrum of personality animal nature may have. She was not about to beg for mercy. She was one of the collaborators after all. She was only getting what she had asked for.

Sandy wondered if it was more decent to leave the dog alone. She decided otherwise. But lifting the body and feeling its lax coldness, the last vestige of uncertainty left her.

△

The red fire made a darkness for itself, obscuring the formless gloom that lay outside. Candide took off his anorak and wrapped it round Vera while he held her close to the fire, trying to make her warm.

'Look, she's trying to curl herself up. Maybe she feels better.'

A few minutes later, he suddenly cried out: 'She's dead!'

Sandy listened. She could no longer hear the stone doors.

'I can't leave her! I can't leave her!' he sobbed, rocking to and fro.

There was nothing for Sandy to do or say. They had both known from the start that this was how it would end. Pain is, cruelty is. A time comes when a decision has to be made and the flawed thing abandoned. Sandy Brize, not Xav or BREAKTHRU, had willed Vera's death. Willed it? Anybody would have done the same. She acted out what the world was, which was dying and glad to be dying. But tears ran down her face.

'You did rescue her Cand, we did try. We didn't lose too badly.'

They decided to bury her in the place she had chosen for herself. The soil was soft, there was no reason to dig deep: it didn't take very long to make a grave. Candide lined the scrape with leaves and laid Vera down, curled on her good side so she looked quite normal. He seemed to be playing the game of his pet's funeral quite happily then, but when it came to covering her over he began to cry in earnest.

'I'll never see you again. I'll never see you again.'

Sandy left him alone. She couldn't bear it. Let me not see the death of the child…For it was Candide's death too. He was not going to recover.

Candide came back to the fire, slowly.

'It all stops now,' he whispered. 'Is it because Vera died, or was that just the signal?'

'In my world that I made, there's no difference, Cand.'

The birds that sing in the dark were singing again. In a little while the two of them would fall asleep. They'd have liked to try and get home to Otto before the very end but there wasn't much time left, and little chance of that now.

3

Tilley Pool

Some endless waste of hours after Luci was killed James roused himself and tried to call the police. The remaining phone had suffered internal injury, none of their neighbours responded. He dressed and went out into the street to find a callbox. He walked down as far as Smithfield where he had met Otto that day. Around him bodies occupied the pavements, he assumed: an insubstantial crowd of ghosts with empty eyes. In Little Britain he tried to stop a passer-by to ask for change but could not make himself understood. The face was made of paper, crumpled up to suggest a mask of fear. The sky over London looked eerie and sullen, as if a great storm was coming or had just passed. There was a roaring in his ears. He stood on the brink of an endless torrent, rushing away, rushing away.

Standing, James put his hands over his face. This is all I have left of Luci, he thought. It will fade – shock, a few days a few hours. The sky will come right again, strangers' faces will not be haunted. He will still be gone. He might have sobbed aloud, he didn't know. No one stopped to see what was wrong, no one touched his shoulder or broke the hollow of silence. Why should they? In London or any city in the world.

As he was walking up St John's again, he remembered the conscription papers. He kept on going – suddenly in spite of himself forced to think. It was obvious to him that the call up was a hoax. He would not have learned about it this way. Oba Minister no go for dump his spineless unreliable relative on the army without warning him not to kick and scream. If it had to be done, if his existence out of uniform had become impossible for the Esumares, he would be well rehearsed. This was a trick like the arrest in Reading, organised by BREAKTHRU. Of course Luci couldn't have guessed. He had not understood even to the end how much trouble James and Otto were in.

But better not have any illusions. No doubt the company could somehow make it stick, really take his passport away. Perhaps even get him press ganged...... Within yards of the entrance to the building where he and Luci had lived, he turned and walked the other way.

He knew. In case of fire do not stop to dress, do not collect any belongings. In case of figures in uniform by the roadside never let yourself be flagged down. When you are in danger believe it: instantly, completely. That is the way to survive. There was nothing in that building he needed anyway. His car was dead, and the rest he never wanted to see again. It was like tearing off an arm, nevertheless. He told himself: Luci isn't there. They took him away in a bag, remember. Tears ran salt into his mouth, he wiped them hurriedly, afraid he was becoming conspicuous. The first bank automat was empty, cleaned out. So was the next: and this was a practical problem. He had hardly any cash on him. He dared to use plastic here where it would give nothing away, but he remembered the advice of his first angel – that number is an electronic marker. Third machine, still no money. Turning, he noticed out of the corner of his eye a piece of paper lying by the kerb; subliminally recognised it. He bent and picked up a fifty note. Someone must have dropped it as they left the automat. A fifty was better than nothing. There was a trail of notes, leading away along the gutter. James picked up three, his eyes followed. He noticed then that the streets were very silent today, even outside his grief. He walked on, thrusting the money into his pocket. Strange things happen in the little patchwork ghettos of London, strange little protests. It's best to ignore them. He did not consider or even remember Otto's theory of the Kairos effect.

He kept on. His mind fled back to childhood: Francis Xavier is in BAD trouble this time. He'll be along soon, demanding an escape route. But James had given up the human shield routine a long, long time ago...Even to a six-year-old child it was obvious that there was no future and no reward in trying to look out for Xav. The towers of the City reared up their beautiful and terrible heads all round him in a fantastic bestiary of glass and steel and stone. They seemed to lean down watching the tiny figure that stumbled between their feet. The sky behind them was a sea of grey ice. And no one spoke, no wheels turned: no brakes, no gears, not a murmur on the shore.

He walked into the aftermath of a serious traffic snarl up. There was no explanation, no placards announcing that the road ahead had fallen into its sewers overnight. But the wide metal was littered with abandoned vehicles: some nose to tail, some at odd angles as if the drivers had attempted to escape before giving up in disgust. Exasperation with a long defeated traffic system sometimes reaches the point where people will risk wheel clamps, summonses, vandalism, any reprisal on offer: for the brief pleasure of simply getting out and walking away. James stepped off the pavement, taking on a cloak of invisibility as he moved. In two steps he had become a citizen returning warily to the scene, keeping an eye out for the feds. A sixth sense, a fugitive's opportunism, had told him what to look for and he found it. Keys in the ignition. The citizen (black, but we can't help that: at least he's well dressed) – mugged rueful amusement. As a human animal will, for the audience that is always watching when you make a fool of yourself. He tried the driver's door: unlocked. (Laughing to himself – that's bloody lucky because I can't find my spare keys.) Citizen, grinning ruefully for unseen cameras, manouevred out of the line and drove off down the wrong side of the road.

He carried with him the image of a few lost figures wandering like ghosts: and the buildings cut out so sharply that they seemed a two-dimensional backdrop. He did not guess that there was anything amiss with London. It was Luci's death he saw, scrawled all over the world. He expected nothing else.

The strange car responded very sluggishly after his poor TR, but he had no serious difficulties with the mechanics of driving. He knew where he was going. Perhaps it would have been more sensible to find a hiding place in the Smoke. But there was no one, literally no one he could turn to. They were all vulnerable, and/or any one of them might have a secret angel-suit stowed away. He wouldn't go home either, he wouldn't take this trouble to Bernie and Margot. After all, Xav was their son too. He would go to the Forest. They had always promised each other that would be the place. If it all falls down. If we can't fool the public any more. When the straights finally come a-lynching.

Avoiding the tolls, where police and other eyes were so often watching, he took the low roads as Bernie called them.

It was lucky he knew this route blindfold for in spite of his real terror, his conviction that all-powerful BREAKTHRU was close behind, he could not keep his mind alert. Twice before he was out of London he found the car at a standstill: himself staring blankly over the wheel, the immediate past non-existent. Perhaps it was for the best. Conscious, he would have been sending out loud uncontrolled signals of terror. He would never have got by the most casual of police check points.

Outside Farnham he stopped at a farmshop and garage. Filled the tank and paid at the machine till before he knew what he was doing. That frightened him wide awake: but it was too late to retrieve the information flying away, undoubtedly winging straight to Xav. James was here! To the hour and minute. He consoled himself by trying to imagine the size of the operation required to trace a fugitive by credit card transactions. But all he achieved was to remind himself of BREAKTHRU's almost supernatural powers.

Not only was the forecourt deserted, which was normal enough: the door of the shop had been broken in. James had acquired a whole new set of responses. Seeing there was no one about he stepped inside and began to collect supplies. Between the washing powders and the petfoods he came upon the body of a middle aged woman, She was lying in the aisle, her legs frozen in the act of running, her head a bloody mess.

He dumped his loot in the back seat and drove away. At least she had looked definitely dead. At least there had been no question of helping her. In a layby screened by trees he turned on the car's radio. He found a news bulletin without difficulty. There didn't seem to be much else on the air. He listened. After a while he switched it off and sat staring ahead, amazed. It seemed a great deal had happened in the last forty-eight hours. It seemed his call up papers were probably the real thing, and probably Robert Esumare was in no position to influence anything. But how? But by what devastating twist of events – ? The African part of the report had been hideously incomplete. Senile, self-obsessed little island...He leapt forward in the seat, ready to turn the car and head back for London: find out the truth, find out if any of his family were still alive.

But then, supposing it was a trap. Supposing this car itself which he thought he had stolen at random, was a card forced on him by the conjurors of BREAKTHRU. It might be set up to play him disorienting information. His hands on the wheel broke out in sweat. For some moments then he lost control entirely. He attacked the radio, attacked the dashboard and speakers, scrabbled madly under the seats. He found nothing, only succeeded in silencing the sound system permanently.

There had been casual mention in the news of stringent State of Emergency arrangements, affecting several classes of political or social outcasts. James was on the run three times over, and he couldn't imagine why that still mattered. He had no reason to care.

He began to cry. Somewhere in the rapid fire of grief and shock he had lost that deathly calm he had found in the police station at Reading. Or rather it was still there but it didn't help. It was crazy, it was so banal. It was like watching the most ludicrous shock horror on the cable late at night: you know exactly what is being done to you and it is so banal, so meaningless... but still it is done. Your buttons are pushed, you twitch and jerk, you can't turn off the reaction.

The summer that Luci and James were fourteen, they took food and camping gear from Standards and lived out in the woods at Tilley Pool, in a ruined keeper's cottage that belonged to one of the Verderers but had long stood derelict. In reality the escape had lasted about ten days: James had to fly to Lagos and his family, since the country was quiet again for a while. Luci had to spend some time with his parents, who were doing so much for him: practically starving to give him a decent education. But in memory there lived a whole magical summer. It was hard to be friends with Luci in those days. He hated his parents so much. He camped it up so relentlessly to keep school at bay – making James feel hopelessly inadequate. But everything fell away when they were alone. So safe with each other. There was no sex that summer. Luci much later used to avow he had been crippled with lust the whole time, sick to death of having to sneak off and wank in private to save James's feelings. Liar. That time was perfect, not a substitute for anything. You were tired of being a fourteen-year-old sex bomb.

At Tilley Pool the ruined cottage was still there, wrapped in a shroud of brambles. The green nettles in the old privy were turning ragged in November, damp dead leaves choked the earth floors. James stared, trying to see the Peran-Wisa as it had been that long ago July. The walls rose up in small red brick. There was a roof and a smoking chimney, a gable over the door and a neat little garden.

Having charge of every green leaf or plant having green leaves that may serve as cover for deer. Having the power to cut green trees or wood, and to cull the deer in season ...I would like to have charge of every green leaf. You can do the shooting though.

Of course, James.

Red walls crumpled, a hundred years went by in an instant. The Forest was under another dispensation, a shrinking enclave invaded by oil donkeys and sitka spruce. Had been so even when James and Luci were young.

He went up to the pool on its patch of heath. Clumps of reed stood sadly. A skewbald mare and her foal watched him from the other side of the water. She looked lean and weary, not fit to face the coming winter. He sat on a log that lay on the shore: elbows on his knees, face between his hands. Come to me now. We're all alone. If you would only come to me...

But no one came, neither a bloodied corpse nor a glittering fourteen-year-old rebel child. It was time for James to wake up at last and find some way to meet this wildly altered world. He was dazed by the scope of the changes that had been flung at him. It was as if he had left the room briefly (on Otto's crazy errand): he'd come back and everyone was playing a different game. No one would tell him the rules, he would have to find them out by trial and error. He started to think about the army. His pacifism was built on a lie, wasn't it: it was cowardice not principle. Therefore he had better turn up somewhere and put on a uniform. Or else declare himself a conscientious objector and accept whatever fate Nigeria had prepared for such nuisances.

He tried to plan, understanding that acceptance was crucial. So much had happened he was in real danger of fugue, of complete breakdown. That business of being arrested: convinced he was discovering some great truth about the world in the impact of a policeman's fist. He might fall into that state again and never get out. He could feel himself falling now, the reedy ground giving way. Someone came and sat down next to him. James turned gladly – in any form, even dead and bleeding. For a horrible moment he thought he saw gold...But there was only an old countryman with a seamed, weathered gypsy face. He wore corduroy trousers tied at the knee with string, a red neck cloth and a baggy leather waistcoat over a checked shirt. The colours of his clothes were faded by years of outdoor life and hard washing. He smiled easily.

'Funny old day it's bin.'

'Yes – '

'Take some baccy?'

He had a plug of chewing tobacco, which he cut against his palm with a pocket knife.

'No thank you.'

'You on the roads too, are you?'

So that was it. He had become a vagrant.

'I suppose I am.'

'No need to be ashamed. I s'ppose we all are, after today. All of us out of work.'

The man laughed shortly. His bright glance took in the starved mare, and a marching line of bitter blue behind her.

'Always changing and always for the worst. I seen it begin. I wished and prayed then I might see it end. Vengeance is mine, sayeth the Lord. I will repay...I uster think those words was the most comforting in the Book. Shows what fools we are.'

'Oh, Lord – '

He looked James dead in the eye, turning his neck at a very unnatural angle to do so. In the old eyes opened lonely terror without definition, without end.

James looked away. The reflection was so exact it did not concern or startle him at all. On the surface of Tilley Pool a little light glimmered, caught from an almost lightless sky. He realised that he did not know what time of day it was. He had left his watch behind. If this was twilight, how had he managed to spend so many hours driving from London? Surely it had been early in the morning when he set out. He rubbed his eyes.

'Can you tell me,' he asked. 'exactly what's been going on. I just caught some of the news – '

There was no one sitting beside him. The old gypsy or keeper had vanished.

James stayed for a while longer, watching the steel coloured water. He was calmer. He was prepared to admit what he had meant by coming to Tilley Pool in the hope of joining Luci. But that wasn't possible somehow. He could not die.

At last he went back to the stolen car. He drove on for a while and then pulled it well off the road and piled leaves and branches over the light coloured shell.

The sky had turned no darker. He walked into the trees, a lost king: a tall, black man above two yards high. When Charles was a fugitive here after the battle of Worcester the Forest took him in and sheltered him. In the magic Forest a man can lose himself, find the ruined chapel and keep vigil before a drawn sword. Retreat, refuge...James shuddered. How could he believe in the death of Africa? It was too much. No one ever says Africa dies. *The superpowers wipe each other out.* It sounds so harmless, so benign: and always did, even when it might be true. But how can we go on if the birthland is gone, cradle of life, the Garden. That's it, that's the end. Something was moving under the half-naked trees. He peered. The movement was animal, but enormously bigger than pony or deer. James's scalp crawled, his mouth dried. He walked further, then stood and watched. The creatures, two of them, were emerging into a clearing of rust red bracken. Their great heads broke branches and nodded carefully across the sky, glittering. Thick lizard limbs carried them with a massive primordial smoothness, smashing bracken stems and bramble to a pulp.

He withdrew, leaving the monsters in possession. It was unlikely that they were looking for him specifically.

He was very tired now. He huddled down in the back seat of the car under a coat that smelled faintly, distastefully, of a stranger. He could not die, the time for dying was over. And anyway there was something he had to do: he would be able to remember what it was if he was allowed a short space of oblivion.

Instead of oblivion he fell at once into a dream. He was in the flat again with Luci and Otto and the angel. Aha, said Luci. So that's who we're dealing with. Umbriel picked up the little black tube and held it in the air. Out of it sprang tongues of fire, they lighted on the heads of each person in the room. A sound came from heaven like a strong wind blowing and filled the whole house where they were sitting. The angel began to sing. *Veni Creator Spiritus, mentes tuorum visita. Imple superna gratia, quae tu creasti pectora...*

Send forth thy spirit and they shall be created. And thou shalt BREAK THROUGH the face of the earth. James woke, sweating, filled with limitless, awesome dread, and it was as if the sun had risen and covered the whole sky so that there was no other word but darkness for that terrible light. He knew, *he knew*, beyond any doubt, what was happening to this world.

Fall on us and hide us from the face of him who is seated on the throne and from the wrath of the Lamb, for the great day of wrath has come and who can stand before it?

SEVENTH ANGEL

1

Queen of the Night

A crashing, rhythmical sound penetrated Sandy's sleep. She sat up with dead leaves cascading round her, waking into reassurance that something, which was already losing definition, had only been a bad dream.

The world flickered black and yellow and roared with a confusion of sound. She saw a huge man chopping down a tree. But Sandy knew the kind of tricks her new state of being could play. In another few strokes the job would be done. Undeterred by the transformation she leapt at the tree feller, the sound of whose axe was the sound of the gates of the end of the world.

'No!' she shouted. 'Don't! Don't!'

It was like jumping onto a moving bus. She kept on yelling but it had no effect. Clinging to his greasy leather collar she was being shaken to and fro by his swinging blows: she let go with one hand, grabbed an earlobe and twisted it. The giant's head jerked violently. He grunted in surprise. A massive unshaven jowl scraped Sandy's cheek, a tiny dark eye rolled backwards at her.

'Drop it! Drop it!'

'Hey – leave him alone, you – '

Sandy dropped. She secured the axe, abandoned by her victim, and stared around in confusion. The wood had changed dramatically. It was full of flaring light and black shadows and sound. She could hear people shouting and crashing about, and the grind and rumble of struggling motors. Candide was beside her, clutching the rucksack. Oh yes, she constructed, they had arrived at last. When? Must have been 'last night', and they had camped before the final assault. The giant peered down from his lumbering height, condensed into a large but not unnatural leather clad male with unkempt greasy hair. He looked nervous and apologetic, like a toddler in trouble and unable to work out why. Sandy gave him

197

his axe back. The dream had left her, she no longer knew why she had had to attack him.

'What's the matter with you?' demanded the voice that had stopped her.

'We need the tree to short the fence. Henry's going to pull it over the wall – '

A ring of much smaller figures had formed around the giant. They were all women, most of them carrying flares or torches. The light showed shaved heads, spooklocks, layered dirty clothing. The one who had first spoken came up too close and glared at Sandy. Her pale cheeks were scored over with the ritual scars favoured by certain separatist tribes.

'Are you one of those wimmin that talks to the trees?'

'A fucking essentialist – '

Sandy shook her head.

'I don't know why I jumped him. It was in a dream.'

'Oh, sorry.'

The scarred woman seemed to think she had made some commonplace social faux pas. Her tone became more friendly.

'All right, but you lay off Henry. He's our manscot.'

'But who are you? What are you all doing here-?'

Noise and light still crashed away, moving off down the wall.

'Same as you I suppose. Breaking into the factory.'

Candide gasped.

'But why?'

'Because BREAKTHRU have something we want, everybody knows that. The BREAKers've built themselves psychic barriers against the plague.' She grinned, glanced at her companions. 'Not that *we're* looking for safety, far fucking from it. But we have to get in there...'

A thin woman with a short tuft of purple hair above her left ear touched Sandy's arm. 'Be careful of Henry,' she advised gently. 'He's harmless but he cuts out when the tremors come. Well, we all do. But his head's higher up so more of the rays can get to him. And because he's so big, its dangerous when you don't know what he's seeing.'

Suddenly Candide shouted. 'They're not to attack BREAK-THRU!' His voice sounded thin and weak now that the adults had reappeared. 'They mustn't do that.'

'It's already started kid.'

'But Francis Xavier's side will kill their prisoners!'

Before Sandy could react he was gone, racing away into the dark towards the blurred uproar.

'Let him go,' said the purple tufted one, holding Sandy's sleeve. 'You'll find him inside.'

Sandy had been alone with Candide in a derelict landscape without reference, without even recognisable day or night, for she did not know how long. She had given up all attempt to distinguish a commonsense version of events: she was walking in her own mind and somehow carrying Candide with her. Surrounded by light and dark, noise and silence none of which she was conscious of having invented, she demanded in astonished surmise:

'When did it happen?' she asked. 'For you, I mean – '

'We don't remember. No one can answer that. But don't kid yourself. Nothing's happened yet. The big event is still on its way.'

The women drew closer. Henry stood swinging his axe at the air hopefully. But they seemed to have forgotten their plan for the tree. Everyone was staring at Sandy.

'We're de-rads,' said the woman with the scars. 'Womyn's radical resistance to the deurbanisation programme. We're the ones who've been running the occupation of Sarehole Estate, and holding off the dozers for eighteen months. But I don't suppose you hear about that on the southern media. Who are you?'

'Sandy.'

'No – I mean who *are* you?'

'Just Sandy. I haven't had an identity since I left Wombega.'

'You left Omega – ' The woman looked sarcastic, but restrained herself from further comment. 'I'm Tiamat.'

The rest of the derads were silent.

'There's something very strange here,' said the one with the purple tuft at last. 'I've never seen an aura like that before.'

She moved in even closer, 'I'm Maire – ': and took Sandy's hand carefully in both her own. Immediately she shuddered and dropped it.

'Oh, wow – . That's incredible.'

Sandy was fascinated. 'And you don't know why you have to get in there, but you know you must?'

Tiamat had had her front teeth filed into mean points. 'Oh, we know why, sister Omega. We're just not telling.'

The noise off to their left rose to a crescendo of heavy machinery in travail and what sounded like falling masonry.

'They're through the gates!' shouted a derad. 'Come on! Someone look out for Henry – '

All the women began to run, dodging round the tree boles, carrying Sandy with them.

Candide ran to the main gates, where the road from the city became a drive lined with shrubs and winter flowerbeds. There was a crowd of people waving flamy petrol stinking torches, swinging camping lanterns and big heavy flashlights. Four large off-roaders were ramming the gates – screeching back and slamming forward again. Candide screamed, 'Stop it! Stop it!' but no one heard him. In all the hubbub the strange thing was no two people were shouting together. Bodies stumbled over each other and jostled blindly like a nest of maggots, like a litter of blind sucking puppies. He put his head down and burrowed to the front, elbowing and kicking ruthlessly. By the time he'd fought his way through, the off-roaders had been joined by a giant yellow earthmover. It was grazing on the stone pillars with its great gap-toothed jaws, rumbling to and fro and masticating the verges into glistening soup.

'Don't! Let me in first! It's important!'

The pillars crumbled, the gates fell in. The off-roaders roared over the debris, each driven by a woman with a man riding armed beside her: the only people besides the derads who seemed free of maggot-fever. Once through the gates the men leapt out. They were wearing camouflage jackets and black balaclavas: they raced off along the front of the building two one way and two the other, doubled up commando style with their weapons held in front of them. Candide heard Sandy shouting to him.

'Candide! Candide! Wait for me!'

She came running up with the derads, through the broken gates and into BREAKTHRU headquarters. She saw Candide in the forefront of the crowd, but at the same moment her attention was caught by a blink of whiteness like a small hole in the dark. Sandy stooped, crouched: she picked up a white pebble. A little further off in the darkness another little white hole winked at her.

She remembered the dream. 'Candide...' she whispered. But by the time she stood up he had vanished. The bodies surged over her, broke around her: all of them unwashed, half dressed, with eyes like ashes and cinders, all of them alone and desperate. She had already guessed what was happening, but the explosion still overwhelmed her: she shouted frantically at every passing face, 'Did I do this? Did I do this?' Nobody gave her an answer.

BREAKTHRU headquarters was deserted. It seemed the company personnel didn't trust their own psychic barriers and had found somewhere safer to hide. Sandy wandered through a fragmented interior landscape. She discovered eventually that she was continuing her journey south and down, but with more company than she had had before. She felt Candide still with her, she could identify him among the marching figures. She was aware, however that somebody had been lost. She couldn't remember whether or not it mattered: surely in such a major expedition a single casualty was nothing to be ashamed of.

The derads settled around her. They had Sandy placed: they recognised her faded accent, her unpoliticised 'pretty' face, the education that branded her. She was a miserable renegade: not merely a man-woman consumerist Southerner but one who ought to know better. If it wasn't for her brilliant aura they would have thrown her to the maggots. As it was, they had decided to keep her as a secondary totem. They told her of the scale of their disaster, which as far as they were concerned encompassed the whole of the West Midlands and probably the world. One of the derads, crazy Andrea, believed that the Bomb had been dropped. She was the one who went around with a woollen cap pulled down over her face as protection against radiation burns. The others thought this was very funny.

'Has your hair fallen out yet, Andrea?'

'Well, I can't tell. I didn't have much.'

'Have you started being sick?'

'No – but, you see, I haven't had anything to eat.'

Andrea crept up close to each of her sisters in turn whispering pathetically, convinced everyone else knew the answers.

'What is a nuclear war? What does it mean? What is an atom, why do they make your hair fall out?'

All that could be seen of her face was a small sad trusting mouth like a soft beak, and the bottom halves of two moon cheeks.

Sandy walked through all this, onward and onward: sometimes returning to the superficial work of demolition, sometimes visiting the end of that work...She was concerned about the welfare of the rest of the expedition. She had been able to cater for Candide but she couldn't feed and shelter all these others who had been dragged into her quest, into the process and journey of her unravelling world. However, she herself had no consciousness of eating or sleeping or shitting, and yet felt no ill effects. She no longer *did* these things: maybe they'd become autonomic for everyone, like peristalsis or breathing, in exchange for other areas now taken over by consciousness. So she hoped, at any rate it was impossible to ask any of them how they felt. The derads spoke coherently but did not make sense. The others could not answer at all.

Some were even worse off. She paused in her snowblind journey at a turn of the pill-factory stairs, and felt a breath of mysterious absence. She reached out to touch the arm of the passing figure, and her hand went through empty air. She wondered was this a dead part of herself, or was it another manifestation of the stranger she had welcomed into the house where she was born. Tiamat was watching, she shuddered and grimaced uneasily.

'Is that your first time? We think they're dead or something.'

Sometimes she felt sorry for her companions, mostly their distress seemed to her an irritating puzzle. *It's true what's happening is terrible. But it's more wonderful than fearful, it is what I was looking for. Therefore it must be what they were looking for too...So why all the fuss?*

She drew in the dust of the old factory floor: a planetary system of nucleus and electron shells. She knew precious little about nuclear fission herself, but she was touched by Andrea's humble faith in the withheld information. She talked about the binding forces of the very small, the sleights that language uses to divide the indivisible. She had to insist all the time on the difference between her words and the flux, the caught points of vibration...because of the danger of her fusion with reality. But on the other hand that's all there is, Andrea. Behind the words there's nothing. It's a case of more intricate and more intricate maps of the barrier.

But what happens on the other side?

She looked up and found an angel sitting crosslegged opposite her. 'Well...if you insist...anything that doesn't here. But that's playing with words. I mean, the thing is, when you get down to this level of distinction what you're really studying is how human perception operates. I worked that out all by myself, Mister Smartie. You don't scare me with your old physics and your multidimensional particles...'

In principio erat Verbum, said the angel. The word giveth and the word taketh away. Blessed be the name of the word...hahaha...and she realised that she had already recognised him. It was Luci: how strange, she hadn't seen Luci for ages. She noticed that for some extraordinary reason he was seeing her as a donkey, a donkey with a yellow shaggy bundle draped over its shoulders.

'I didn't know you were one of them.'

She presumed he'd appeared because she was trying to educate Andrea. Luci had always been the one who made sure the Nouprims knew whatever was fashionable.

There isn't any them, Sandy. It doesn't work, that distinction: I told them so but they wouldn't listen. We're all in the same *galère*.

She got up and walked with him, onward. He talked about strings and superstrings and the clogged and viscous rate at which popular science slides into the public imagination. Up at the forward edge the old particle zoo has been about completely *subsumed*...so that we now think on an unbelievably 'smaller' scale that can never, never be experienced: a theory of reality that can never be experimentally driven...and at just about the same 'time' it becomes sexy to say the newest cocktail-drug has quarks in it. Is that a fact, she grinned. I bought some shampoo that had DNA in it once.

His face was ash grey under the gold, his eyes sunken and closed. He would have been in tears except that Luci never cried. She had recognised that stoicism in him from the start – like Otter and James, they shared a childhood.

Grief roared and crackled round him like cold flames.

Can you see me Sandy? Do I seem real?

'Yes, I can see you.'

Can you see through me?

He must know he was a ghost. He was asking had she acquired the power to read minds. No, she had not. The body beside her was transparent and deathlike but the presence of Luci was exactly as it had always been: as individual, as secret. It was odd to think of confusing him with Xav, of confusing him with anyone.

'You're just the same as ever.'

He was shivering hard and rubbing his gleaming naked arms. His fingernails were rimmed with dirty brown flakes.

You're my only hope Sandy, little donkey in the lion's skin. I'm trying to tell you what's really going on so you'll stop it. But you're not a *tame* donkey, are you Sand. And besides, a thing like the Kairos, the drug itself, if it exists it can't be a cause it must be an effect...I suspect this is the way we're perceiving something that's happening, some very large scale event. Do you see?

'I don't see why you're calling me a donkey. I haven't any delusions of grandeur. It's only *my* experience that I'm messing with, and I don't see why I shouldn't.'

So it can't be stopped. This is it. The end.

The drawings began to spread. Andrea brought charred sticks and little pieces of white chipping that made a mark like chalk. The tiny systems were scrawled everywhere, some of them bursting apart and flying in fragments, shooting through everything that came in their way. (That's what happens to your insides Andrea. That's what makes you sick.) She tried to make the diagrams three dimensional: four dimensional, carried out of her ignorance: so convinced that she agreed with reality that she felt her representation must try to be complete as her own coincidence.

'An atom is very small,' murmured Andrea reverently.

'O, I see it, Andrea. This is what it is, it's a mind flying apart. If someone tries to dismantle their mind, there comes a level of incredible resistance. And then the sun bursts open – I remember that! Flying apart, flying apart. And I said "I want what is not – ". I stepped out of the middle dimensions into the other world: and carried everything I touched with me, into myself.'

She held up her hands, grubby and grey with the white skin showing blue veins through the grime.

'Look, look. These aren't hands any more. They are words now...And soon, and soon...!'

The dead angel had vanished, there was only Andrea crouched with her fledgling beak a little open; listening intently. Where had Luci gone? Sandy shrugged and went on covering the old factory floor with exploding universes: trees and dreams and chairs and memories – all breaking, all spinning, all returning through the channel of her mind to the unnameable, the undivided...

Candide had stayed long enough in the forecourt to see there would be no battle. There was no sign of BREAKer security forces, no response at all. He would not let himself despair. He set his jaw and plunged on, while the mob came pouring in behind. He thought the labs, the modern part, would be round the back. It's always right to try your first guess first – that was what Luci said. It was scientific method.

Away from the torches it was hardly darker than it had been at any time on the long walk. He was back in a late afternoon of November, under the kind of sky that could mean coming morning, coming rain or coming night. He ran up against a wall. He was about to try to climb it when the brickwork suddenly melted against his hands. It was one of Sandy's tremors. Candide couldn't afford to be frightened. He closed his eyes and counted ten. It passed. At least he was on the other side of the wall. He checked doors and windows around a big yard. There was a blue van by a loading bay. Its tyres were all flat, it must have been there for a while. A door stood open: he rushed inside. These were the labs all right. But they were empty, stripped bare. He ran from room to room, finding cages torn apart and grisly looking apparatus smashed and strewn on the floor.

Scorched earth.

'Where is she?' he shouted. 'I've come to get you, Francis Xavier!' His voice sounded tiny, puny and defeated.

He decided he would search the whole building, systematically. It was the only thing left to do except give up. And I can do that anytime, said Candide to himself, stamping along a thick carpeted corridor. His inner voice captured exactly Otto's wry intonation. 'Give up? Well, there's no hurry. That's one option that's always available.' He disturbed the maggot people in various strange poses and activities, and was sometimes disturbed himself. Once he came across one of the off roader men having sex with a woman. The woman was naked, the man dressed and still holding his gun. Candide edged round them. He couldn't tell if it was rape or not. Both jerking bodies seemed empty: their eyes were blank as if they were puppets, or dead.

There were mad people everywhere, but some were more organised in their madness than the others. A man called Commander Zero had taken over the underground garages. He waited there with his people, tense and vigilant, sleeping in snatches on the cold oily concrete. One of his soldiers gave Candide a mug of soup, and made him promise never to go near the restaurant which was the nerve centre of all evil. She gave him a red and black badge to stick on his jacket. 'This is the last battle,' she said. 'La lutte finale, it has come at last. Are you for or against us? We have a very high standard of literacy and though some are barefoot everyone has enough to eat.'

'Have you seen my dog? She's a Jack Russell terrier bitch with one brown ear. She's called Vera, there's an id tube on her collar with her name and address in it...'

When he described Vera, he noticed guiltily, he never mentioned the mutilations. He couldn't bear to say those things.

'No, I'm afraid I haven't.'

All the soldiers promised to look out.

Candide, naturally, headed straight for the nerve centre of all evil. He crawled to the doors of the big dining hall on his belly, heart in his mouth: and stood up, disgusted. There were no BREAKTHRU angels in there, only the men from the off-roaders. There were several women with them, all of them pretty and wearing the kind of outdoor clothes that are not meant to get wet or dirty. Some of the women were bringing out supplies from the big kitchens behind and piling them up. One of the jeep drivers was taking dictation. She had beautiful red hair and wore tight marsonaut coveralls and high heeled cowboy boots.

'Wait a minute –'

The leader of the gang went over and opened the front of her spacesuit so he could see most of her breasts while she worked.

'That's better. It may be the end of the world, but we can still be civilised..'

Everyone laughed approvingly.

'Looting is now under control. The troublemakers – Animal Lib, Women's Lib, Spooks, will be dealt with. Next we will turn our attention to our friends in the basement. But since we control all essential supplies none of these problems poses any great challenge. Our survival in comfort is assured. Until, as and when, we achieve our objective here...whatever it may be...and the catastrophe out there returns to normal.'

He grinned, boyishly. 'And I don't know about the rest of you, but I for one rather hope that doesn't happen –'

Fool, thought Candide. I bet you don't look so cheerful when a tremor comes.

'The animal lovers have departed, Sir, with a few of the company's experimental animals. And a little judicious encouragement I may say –'

'Now then, no need to call me Sir. I'm just Andrew, remember, same as I was this time last week.'

'Yes, Sir.'

Beside the tins there was an awesome pile of weapons. BREAK-THRU must have been stocked for an army.

Candide knew it would be safer to have nothing to do with these people. He doubted if even Sandy could deal with them. But he walked in, drawing a deep breath.

'Did you find any dogs?'

'How many children are there?' asked Andrew of the red-haired woman.

'We've spotted four, Sir. That is, kids apparently under thirteen. All attached to parents or parent figures. This one's new.'

Now they were all looking at him. Candide backed away. Smartly, one of the junior men darted across with his sub-machine-gun, getting between Candide and the doors. 'Come on, sonny,' smiled Andrew, approaching. 'Time to surrender. If you're going to live in our house you'll have to start learning the rules. That's fair, isn't it.'

'Be careful, Sir. Some of them are tough little customers.'

Andrew's face was pink and plump. His smile was the smile of someone who knows the other person is helpless and always will be.

'You remind me of Xav!' yelled Candide.

He gripped the edge of the laden table that stood between them. He had a hopeless idea of turning it over and dashing off in the confusion. It was far too heavy. But then something happened to the room. It went out, completely. When it came back a murkiness stayed in the air, which smelled of old bonfires. The red-haired woman had a blanket wrapped round her shoulders and her hair was greasy and tangled. She was pushing her fingers into the tabletop: they disappeared as if into black water. Andrew stood between undiminished piles of dusty tins.

'Stop that!' he shouted.

'Andrew, you know you're not the boss any more. Henry is.'

The speaker was a blonde woman who was lounging with her arms folded, against the wall. Behind her you could see supply lists and orders pinned up, the writing dimmed under layers of smoke and grime.

He shot her. The body fell. Andrew put down his gun smiling: and at once looked uneasy and tried to pick it up. His hand went through the stock. He began to whimper, and to cry like a baby. He was losing his grip.

Candide laughed exultantly.

Now the red-haired woman was down on her hands and knees moving cartons of fruit juice. She was crying. She looked dirty, though not in such a bad way as she had been a moment ago. There was a bonfire on the tiled floor, without a fireplace or a chimney: and some of the furniture had gone. Candide saw, then felt, that his hands were still gripping the tabletop. Andrew was still big and armed but he was no longer frightening.

'You don't scare me!' shouted Candide. 'I know what you are. You're hallucinations, every one of you: you're just things in Sandy's mind.'

He was sure it was true, but still so much fear in an adult face almost panicked the little boy. Then he remembered something he had heard. There must have been some gaps in time, it must have taken longer than it felt like for him to get from the gates to the labs...Could a hallucination tell the truth? Well, they just must be able to. Hardly faltering, Candide's childish and absurd hope cut through the bewildering knot of contradictions. He pitched himself away from the table and ran, battering past the man at the door.

He wished he knew how much more time had 'really' gone by while he was in the restaurant. But he was beginning to learn not to think like that any more. Anything that happened had its own private measure. It wasn't easy to keep track, but it wasn't scary so long as you didn't keep trying to arrange it all in one line. There could be years between one thought and another after all, or no space at all. He had noticed that long ago.

The derads had moved into the room with the big window. This whole floor had been BREAKTHRU's main conference hall: decorated in period with wooden chairs, now heaped up madly against a wall, and a few carefully restored old machines. Its function and the high industrial decor both appealed to the womyn. And no one else wanted the place, especially after Henry had broken panes and pulled out framework to make a door in the bottom of the great arc of glass. The derads could climb out through this hole onto a flat roof and thence down the classical-modernist pillars to the ground. The new exit proved especially useful after they had to barricade the other doors against Andrew's people. They had a fire too, built on a glass oven door that was stolen in a raid on the kitchens. The glossy parquet floor around it became pitted and scored with black: when Andrew's people managed to break in they always made a point of kicking fire all over the women's possessions.

Sandy was at first irritated by the derads' sluttish behaviour. They made no attempt to organise their camp or protect their belongings: the barricades could have been much stronger but no one bothered about it. Then she saw that it was right, it fitted in. They were letting all order go, including the order of resistance and opposition.

It was usually raining now. Everything was wet and cold.

The derads shifted around beside their hearth, moving in a broken rhythm. Other figures came and went, fresh from the gates and still carrying lights or dirty and cinder-eyed in the gloom. Sandy sat out by the great window wrapped in her old black coat, the collar turned up around her ears. The rain that she now imagined gusted into the room, occasionally a fine cold spray reached her face. She never moved. She was thinking about time.

She had been mistaken in the larchwood. Whatever it was she lost there it was not blood. And still no blood came. She was fairly sure that her period had been due within one or two days, when she and Candide left Brighton. And if I bleed again, thought Sandy, will I then have a measure of the time that has gone by? Is that connection something that can't be disrupted? But unlike the woman in the cave who was first struck by this world-changing notion, she could not count the nights or the phases of the moon. A prisoner deliberately disoriented might well guess that the biological clock doesn't shift very easily: might rediscover night and day by sensing internal changes. But that kind of periodicity became gibberish if you didn't sleep and didn't get hungry.

Outside the leaves burned from the trees, their branches turned to fractal patterns of black and maroon on the grey. In *the world outside* was it still November? In Sandy's world perhaps it would always be. A figurative November, an empty season of dying light and growing shadows. Sometimes she imagined that the everlasting dull sky cleared and she saw stars like silver lines on tissue paper, or an infinitely phasing disc that might be the moon or the sun or both merged into one.

She contemplated the dizzying nature of existence without the forward arrow, and all that could not be if there should be no more time. The derads watched her from a respectful distance and coped pretty well, since they were not trying to *do* anything, only to undo. In the rest of Sandy's world, confusion reigned absolute.

'Sandy – '

She was moving to and fro up and down the line, counting heads. Quite definitely there was someone missing...It was so sad, so very sad, seemed to call the whole project into question. *There must be a way to solve this*, thought Sandy. But she knew, althought the details eluded her, that there was not...

Tiamat wore one long thin green spooklock. She had tied a muffler over her shorn head to keep it warm, the green tail strayed out wispily down the front of her coat. She blew on her red knuckles and rubbed her hands. 'It's time we started.'

Moonfaced Andrea nestled as close as she dared. Her purple and green woollen cap was pulled down tight. 'Admiration,' she whispered, touching the hem of Sandy's coat. 'Wanting to be like the person. Wishing I was educated, and knew all the lovely things – '

'Oh no,' The simplicity and humble trust of this aspect of her self touched Sandy to the heart: humility long suppressed in the name of self-preservation. 'No, that's not for me. You're thinking about Otter – '

Maire came up through the broken window, tramped over and tossed a bit of dirty paper into the fire. The derads were clean living animals, it was their last concession to all that they rejected. With a few of the others she began clearing heaps of sodden bedding. It was extraordinary how things piled up, as if they'd been here for months.

Sometimes they had. And sometimes hours, and sometimes years.

'No one knows,' said Tiamat, 'what started it off. I think there was something about a nerve gas attack on the news. But I don't know if anyone saw those broadcasts, or if it was a rumour that got into the air later and then we decided to stick it in our memories. You know how easy it is to mess about with the past. Some people think it was BREAKTHRU, that they ought to "claim responsibility". It hardly matters. Maybe they did start something, but they didn't know what they were doing. *We know.*'

Her filed teeth gleamed. 'The maggots don't understand. They bring us food (this had happened sometimes) because they think we're resisting Andrew, and they haven't got the nerve but they think someone should. If they knew what we really want – ' She shuddered violently. 'They wouldn't be so supportive. Listen, did I tell you we came to the factory because the BREAKers had built up psychic barriers against the big event? That was a lie, even if there could be such a thing as a barrier against this. We came because it's the centre of all that BREAKTHRU stood for. We're going to say THE YES for them, and according to the laws of magic it should work better here...'

It was funny that a de-rad should refer to the unnamed people as maggots: when actually they were the parts with some kind of autonomy...Sandy knew Tiamat through and through, she had no idea what some of those others were up to.

Someone in the back of the hall said, 'Where's Henry? Put him out, this is womyn only.'

The child giant in his greasy leathers was led to the window and shooed down the wall, despite tearful protests that it was so cold, and it was raining...Maire stood looking after him sadly.

'So what about it Sandy? I think you must know what we want. We want an *end* to this shitty world. BREAKTHRU claimed they wanted to end it all. They didn't know what they were talking about but *in magic* that doesn't mean they weren't saying it. Name things in magic, and they become what you say they are. We've been told these rituals and spells only work because the object of the ceremony believes: it's the power of suggestion. We're told things only happen after magic arts have been used if they were going to happen anyway. I say the yes to that, and the yes to that. The world believes, now. And we aren't asking for anything we're not going to get. This isn't work, it's a celebration.'

'Are you ready Sandy? Let's do it.'

The derads had started to take their clothes off. Maire, already undressed, went round anointing them with a dark oily paste out of a jar. Andrea had kept her cap on, and her boots because her feet were so cold. In this costume she looked more sinister and somehow more sincere that the rest. Tiamat fixed her eyes on Sandy and opened her coat. She was naked underneath. There was a pattern drawn in dark brown over her breasts and belly. The pattern was as real and horrible as the ghost in the empty house. It had meaning in a language that had never been spoken, since the beginning of the world.

The women waited, hands clasped in a broken circle.

Sandy got to her feet, surprised to find that she could still move easily. Though she had given up the arrow she had no other image

but time/distance to cover the scale of what she was doing. And
in that imagery surely she'd been kneeling here in the rain on the
pitted parquet floor for years.

Would she join them? This was what it meant to be a woman,
raised to the highest power: the final solution patiently waiting, the
black hole at the centre of all things. She had declared that she
was finished with patriarchy and its silent partner both: and her
irritation was still strong. Didn't the derads notice that they were
capable of nothing but *reaction*, never action, that they were joined
at every limit to what they said they hated? But the old partnership
wasn't so easily dismissed, it seemed. For here she was, and she had
already let them wipe out some of her exploding universes to make
room for the magic patterns. The only aspect she would question
– and here she halted, puzzled – was that she was only interested
in dismantling herself, and the derads were talking about *the world*.
Was there a difference?

The old annoying question...

The barricade in front of the hall doors was moving. It jerked a
little more and Candide's face appeared. He wriggled and scrambled
over the chairs and the decorative antique pill machines.

'Sandy! I've been looking for you everywhere!'

He ran up, his eyes bright.

'We're winning Sandy. You're going great. Andrew's a gibbering
wreck and no one cares if he's got all the food any more. It's the
final battle isn't it – you and me and Commander Zero, and we're
going to win – '

'What?'

'The final battle!'

'Oh that.'

She looked, in exasperation, from him to the painted wom-
en.

'I thought I explained it to you. I'm trying to dump all of it, the
winning and the losing. I'm not on anybody's side. Anyway, Cand,
you know perfectly well you're only seeing jumbled up bits of my
myths and legends.'

Candide grimaced horribly. He detested her when she made him
feel like a child.

'Oh well – what's more important is I've traced Vera! She was
here. The AL went through the labs, and took all the victims away
to safety – '

Tiamat scowled at Candide, noting his gender with disgust.

'Come on, Sandy, make up your mind.'

'What do they want you to do, Sand?'

'To join the circle.'

'Oh, but you can't, not now. You've got to help me find Vera. You *promised* – '

'Oh yes.' Sandy turned back to Tiamat. 'I'm sorry. I can't join in. I'm busy.'

The scarred derad sneered contemptuously, turning away.

'Suit yourself, sister Omega. If you don't want to admit what you're doing, we'll celebrate without you.'

'Have you still got Xav's little black tube?' demanded Candide.

Sandy checked her pocket. 'Yes.'

'Good. I've been thinking. It might be something incredibly valuable. We'd better hang on to it for barter. I don't think people are going to be using money any more.'

Sandy shook her head pityingly – but Candide had noticed the witches' strange behaviour.

'What are they doing?'

'Ssh. It's ceremonial magic. We'd better keep quiet.'

△

Afterwards, the derads were finished with BREAKTHRU. They wanted to be away from this place when their ritual took effect. Candide and Sandy left with them: Maire had said that she could take them to the Animal Liberation cell's flat at Sarehole. Sandy found herself walking down a gravel drive in a trail of tired and drained derads, the little boy trudging beside her. She had no memory of leaving the hall with the broken window; and that was not a lapse of attention. The lapse of attention was this – she felt a momentary clutch of nausea-: the gravel under foot, feet walking. Her mind was conjuring shadows of the layers that had been stripped away. While all along this mind and its world moved closer to a state where the pure events...the pure events are nameless, neither mind nor matter...

She saw the little trail of white stones crossing the gravel and disappearing into a shrubbery. She saw Candide looking down. He looked up, their eyes met – the child's face crumpled, he grimaced furiously and ran ahead: quickly, quickly to get to the city and rescue his darling.

Some of the witches carried plunder. Tiamat had a bulging primrose silk pillowcase over her shoulder. Two other women guided a hostess trolley on which they had loaded the oven door hearthstone and some damp blankets. Candide still kept his rucksack on his back. It wouldn't be an expedition if you didn't have any provisions. Crossing the gates: a tangle of rusted wrought iron and dead leaves. A lonely monster stooped in the grey haze, a gaunt yellow vulture brooding over the carcase. Blind Andrea wandered over to the earthmover and stood patting it, with a baby's love for the big bright helpless thing. Tiamat dropped back to drag her away. When Sandy saw them rejoin the others Andrea was crying pitifully.

'What's the matter, did it bite you?'

Andrea whimpered and held up her right hand. Three of the fingers had fused into a lump of yellow painted metal, the flesh pulling away from the intrusion in pink curled back petals.

Tiamat had the same look in her eyes as Andrew's squatters did as they huddled round their pathetic heaps of food. She was miserably afraid, afraid as any despised survivalist. She glared at Sandy and marched on.

Reaching the city. Sarehole estate was in the middle of the deurbanisation: a great tract of land, unsullied by nitrates and inerradicable pesticides, that was being cleared for modern organic farming. The inhabitants were to be rehoused elsewhere on poisoned acres: it was a pity that such a rational and enlightened policy aroused bitter opposition. A small family of tower blocks stood up defiantly in the new born fields. Walking towards them was like approaching a mediaeval stronghold. RESIST said giant painted letters down the towers. WE SHALL NOT BE MOVED. Beyond them a backdrop of distant untouched streets and houses and spires stretched along the horizon like a rack of cloud.

In the shopping mall of the estate there were plenty of people about. They stepped over broken glass, walked up to each other on the pavement and drew back shuddering. Some of them wore smog filters, others full gas masks. Figures slipped in and out of the opened shop fronts, but the looting phase was long over. A big white jeep was parked at the end of the mall. There were four noddy suits sitting inside. The derads looked in and laughed.

'Hey, coppers, what'you doing?'

'Shooting looters – '

'Searching for survivors – '

'Want to take my name and address?'

'Officer, could you tell me the correct time?'

The noddy suits did not stir. They were empty casing from which the imago had departed, had been lifted up. The State had undergone a metamorphosis and left its shell behind.

'It was the Rapture,' explained Maire, grinning. 'They were all swept away, to that big copper station in the sky.'

Sandy peered through strengthened glass into round blackness. She thought, with curiosity, of those little universes that had been wiped away. Perhaps, in a world where existence had ceased to be an autonomic function, the police officers had simply forgotten themselves for a moment.

The entrance to the Community Centre was flanked by two faded murals – one of whales and waves, the other of children playing in a city street. The inner doors and walls were plastered with fly sheets, handouts, handwritten posters, postcards, messages scribbled on torn jotter sheets and long out of date...Candide ran inside and began to study the tattered histories eagerly. Every few minutes there was a pulse running through things: the floor would seem to give way and everything would vanish. He braced himself and they passed but it was getting harder to hold on.

'Sand! Sand!'

She frowned at him, trying to concentrate. How much more unmasking could there be?

'You go ahead,' she told him. 'I'll be with the derads.'

'Okay, pod leader.'

He stuck his elbows out for fins, jumped up to swallow air and vanished into the interior.

At one end of the community centre lounge four old ladies sat together on battered armchairs covered in orange sacking. It was stifling hot. They were dressed in careless abandon: skirts unfastened, blouses loose, tights wrinkled. They had a guest, a man at least twenty years their junior; in his mid sixties. He was meticulously tidy in a brand new dark suit. The four were all drinking tea and eating biscuits with the placid solemnity of little girls playing house, but their guest had no cup. One of the women playfully offered him a biscuit. As Sandy watched, the old lady sitting next to the man frowned reprovingly and tried to take his hand. She failed. There was no body there. The stiff waxy face of the dead man moved awkwardly into a rueful smile. They were not yet *reunited*, as it says on the stones. Not quite yet.

Tiamat emptied her pillowcase and rifled through its contents.

'Has it started yet?' asked Andrea, nursing her changed hand. 'How will we know?'

Maire had switched on the community centre's tv and was searching from channel to channel. Finding no transmission, she looked warily at the stranger, sitting there in her shabby oversized black coat.

'It's all gone, Sandy.'

The process of disentanglement was nearly complete. There was just one knot, one value that refused to cancel: but it was very obstinate and it seemed to go all the way through. How could she claim to have wiped away everything, everything, everything, if grief and fear remained? And they clearly did. Maybe they would go last of all, because they were the most essential things: maybe that was the solution. Andrea began to snivel again.

Tiamat's hands shook as she examined her loot. She had robbed the company's surveillance archives. She unplugged the community centre's ancient vr and tried to replace it with the modern player she had stolen with her discs. After some hammering, the male end of its coax fitted into the port in the back of the tube.

'We've got power,' she said. 'It's random isn't it. The stations keep running, only nobody's doing any maintenance. So some places you get lights'n cable and some you don't. Electricity's pretty basic – ' She glanced at Sandy, annoyed at herself for doing so. 'You know all about that stuff, don't you. Which goes first, then? Us or the electrons?'

No answer. Tiamat grinned, twisting the purple scars on her thin white cheeks. She held out a sheaf of discs.

'The company will provide in-crash entertainment, up to the moment of impact. Choose, Sandy.'

Some of the derads had dispersed. Or else, it was possible, they had vanished like the wearers of those noddy suits. Sandy took a disc and Tiamat loaded it. In silence everybody stared at the fizzing screen: each wondering if the others could see and hear something intelligible.

'Shit, it doesn't work.'

'They never do. The hardware is never compatible. That's the first principle.'

'I'll make it work.'

Tiamat sat crosslegged. She settled herself, rotated her shoulders, drew a long hissing breath and jived the tube with stiff fingers.

'Zzoing!'

A picture appeared. The derads began to laugh.

'I saw it! I saw the electrons coming out of Tiamat's fingers! They were like little pink spidery things – '

'Don't be daft, Andrea. You can't see anything with that hat over your eyes.'

'Whose private life is this?'

'Fuck knows, except it should have something to do with Sandy.'

An interior. In a room out of an upmarket commercial four people were engaged in a thriller style conversation about blackmail and drugs. One of them was dressed as a BREAKer. The camera passed over three haunted faces, and slipped away to admire some tasteful decor. 'Hey – it's a Ralph Churchill!'

'That's a nice set. Much fancier than usual-'

The derads started to guess what Ralph was supposed to be selling. Was it the luxury heavy duty window blinds or the lopsided table? Voices were raised. The old ladies peered down the room crossly.

Sandy heard Otto's voice.

She saw her lover on the screen. Otter, called up like a spirit at a seance. She saw that she was looking into James and Luci's flat. She recognised the furniture, she had been in that room. The scene played on. Sandy picked up the story easily: part of it she already knew. She wanted to shout, as if Otto could hear her: *It's all right, don't be fooled. Cand is with me* – . She heard the angel use the same word that Luci had used when he came to her as a ghost: Kairos. The derads went on laughing and guessing. Sandy groped in her pocket. She brought out a small black cylinder, the lid sealed with tape. She stared at it, with an expression of intense speculation, and around her the drab and battered room shifted abruptly, like a dog shaking itself; and settled at a subtly altered level. Things happen in the mind – of such colour, such charm, such strangeness...

Is this real or am I imagining it? Deep as she had searched, she had never found her way to this interface the angel described, between her mind and the world. So how could she decide which of the two was falling into nothingness? If this video was not a part of her madness but the explanation of it, how would that distinction manifest itself, if the drug Kairos functioned as described? It would not.

Catching at shreds of a vanished existence, she stood on a brink of appalling vertigo: the derads in their magic circle, not aspects of Sandy's psyche but real women saying, Let's do it Sandy. What had she nearly done? Something totally outrageous...GRIEF. Luci was a ghost because Luci was dead. FEAR...no, there was no place for this relief, because she remembered the white stones. She recognised the missing member of the expedition, the one whose absence had worried her. The little dog-world is dead, poor miserable flawed creation, it is dead already and we are all ghosts now.

Holding the Kairos, Sandy was in the haunted house – I have achieved nothing, it was all illusion. She was in the dark wood with the lonely sound of a bird singing, enjoying the sweetness of never ending sorrow. She was in St Pauls staring at the door in the wall, wishing for annihilation. She wanted to say that that at least was before the Kairos and proved that this experience was her own, nothing to do with Xav and his drug. But logic forbade her: there was no before, not now. There was no one of these myriad, myriad moments ordered before or after any other. All were equally available, all equally tainted: everything that was wrong summed up in a single image.

There was no doubt about it. The dog was dead and buried, poor Candide. She could not understand then why they were still here, but yes she could: GRIEF, FEAR. Which all must feel, even Sandy who was so nearly at one with the world dying and glad to be dying. Maybe this dragging of the feet was essential, integral and death another unlimitedly intricate boundary. The little dog would recede and recede mysteriously, hope would recur and recur in an ever more shadowy and reduced environment...

It was no use, she could not hold on to the separation offered to her by the message on the screen. Am I object, or subject? What does it mean to say there is no difference between those two?

Candide rushed into the room.

'Sandy – come quickly!'

'Cand, do you know what this thing is, that you were going to use for barter? It's a bomb. A mind bomb, stuffed full of biological radiation – '

'Don't go weird on me – ' he wailed. 'This is serious. The AL are going to kill all their animals. They've decided it isn't fair to leave pets alive after we all die of the rays. I found them having a meeting – Oh, *please.*'

She put the Kairos back in her pocket, studying the grey faced, weary little boy with an acute, intent intellectual curiosity.

Candide groaned. He knew that look. It was Sandy having an amazing idea: he'd lost her, it was hopeless.

'Sandy!'

'Okay mancub, lead on. I'll do what I can.'

219

2

The Phoenix and
the Dragon

The prisoner had escaped. It could not remember how. That might have been in one of the pieces of time which had disappeared: or perhaps there was a worse reason. It had made itself forget because of something it had done to get out, some awful betrayal. The creature was in the nothing now. It was living in the nightmare that has no duration, no extension, no defined limits at all. It remembered dimly that once long ago it had struggled all life long trying to remodel the world according to its personal design. It had never begun to understand what it would be like to try and live there. This world had been the world of the creature: not its public dreams but its most rotten, secret, ones. It had found it preferred nothing. No dark, no light, no air no earth no past no future no present. She – didn't want to be called she anymore for reasons best concealed. It, then, knew it had visited the fringes of this state once, to admire a play of pretty colours over the abyss. Death of the mind fireworks.

Creature blubbered, stumbled, in a half-lit land of giants. They held up their arms in pain. The fountain of life rushing through their great bodies was stopped. Rushing from light to darkness forever and ever, rushing from built to falling. Creature had believed that what was happening to it was dissolution and it had been very afraid. Now, it was opposite. And worse. The flow was turning round, backed up. It was appalling. The giants screamed in agony. They were bursting cell by cell, overcharged with celf: a hundred thousand giants packed into each body. Time pouring backwards into itself, reversing the ever rolling displacement that lets things die and lets things live. We cannot hold this surfeit. We are breaking, breaking: exploded celf, exploded world no space left to separate them. If people only understood how precious is that illusion of separate they would pay any price to maintain it. They would never call it bad names – decay, death entropy...

But we know, we do know, said the creature. From celf and not-celf we build all the walls. We would rather be slave owners and slaves, torturers and victims for ever and ever, than try to live in the real world. It perceived how its own life had been dedicated to this purpose. It knew the price that it had been prepared to pay (secretly, if ever it got the chance). Creature's teeth began to jammer in horror, its mind was almost gone, into the final fugue, no thought ever again.

But it had seen a light. It was close to the thing that held the light – bigger than any giant but not in the same way alive. It failed to carry the information from one granular instant to the next, was astonished to find itself *in* something: surrounded on three sides by presence (multiple, multiple, as close packed as the giants and crying dimly), that seemed stuck all over with pictures cut out of magazines. Recognised some of them like a child at nursery school, and laboured to make the names.

There's someone else. It – I, have reached some one else.

Bang bang bang.

The door opened. A man stood there holding a shotgun.

'Is that loaded?'

The man smiled apologetically and broke the gun. It was not.

She gaped at him, arms wrapped around her great gaunt body, feeling the cloth of her prison clothes like a raucous sound. The eyes of that other prisoner in the hospital room looked at her with unbearable pity.

'Please – ' she sobbed. 'Eyes – '

The naked man condensed and changed into someone different: clothed, and his eyes clothed too. She felt safer.

'You are Otto,' he said quickly, gently.

'Porch,' she answered. 'Door boots doormat. Is that right?'

'Come inside.'

'Don't touch me,' she whispered. 'I'm made of plutonium.'

She entered Underhill again, falling into the dark water, into the scents of damp stone and beeswax. The waxy texture of uneven old polished boards, the slipperiness of worn down silk pile. From moment to moment the person beside her grew sketchy and turned solid: sometimes insisted on walking her through walls. Surreal images assaulted her: a disembowelled tv tube, clocks with their faces turned to the wall, a smashed telephone. That last almost made her vomit. The house was dark. The images seemed to leap because the man was lighting them with his lamp.

'Are these stairs?'

She touched the newel post and at once became absorbed in following with her fingers its carving of the green man and his wreath of green leaves. A shoot coming out of his mouth. A fertility symbol, vegetation god. When his season is over, kill him. This green man was black as old oak.

She began to cry.

'How long have you been here?'

'About fifteen billion years,' said the carved face.

'Don't think about how to do it,' suggested James kindly. 'Just head for the top. You'll find you get there.'

In another place, he said, 'Shall I run you a bath. Does that appeal?'

She was sitting on something white and cold and narrow. He was kneeling, holding one of her feet up by the ankle. It hardly looked like a foot at all. It looked like a big black and red dead frog.

She took off her clothes and kicked them aside, examined herself in the mirror above the handbasin.

'Pupils fixed and dilated. I'm dead. Well, that's about what I thought.'

Despite this fluency, he had to help her into the water and show her how to use the soap. 'Are you all right now?'

She nodded, frightened but not daring to ask him to stay.

'I won't be far, I'll be in the kitchen. Okay?'

Under the bright water lay a scarred and filthy human torso, a pair of gnarled distorted limbs like tree roots. The bath was deep and long and white. There was a green rug beside it, a handbasin a towel rail an airing cupboard a lavatory pan white as the bath with a black seat and lid. It's an old-fashioned room, she thought: and in train of that came a whole world, an assumed world into which she could dip, skim. This felt miraculously good. Under the basin she could see a lump of stiff dried rag, tucked rather sordidly between the pipes. On the floor below there was a battered plastic pack of scouring powder. Otto stared hungrily, forgetting to wash until the water began to get cold.

Her bruised feet ached on stone, blessed a soft textured carpet. Slipping in and out of her recovery she walked into a long room where tables stood in shrouded rows. Place settings still gleamed, as if the restaurant was ready for guests. Through french doors she looked onto a sunken terrace of yellowed paving. Three steps up to the narrow rectangular pool, flanked by straight rose beds. At the end an overweight toddler in marble, smirking down complacently at the belly that overhung his tiny prick. She knew these things, they were familiar to her. She touched the stuff of her dressing gown with curiosity. She had found it hanging behind the bathroom door. And a pair of pyjamas in the airing cupboard. But from moment to moment still her contact with the *she* who used names and placings without effort was broken. She kept on wakening astonished into this confidence, this animal unthinking trust.

It was twilight out there at the end of November. It would rain before long, the wind would get up and tear down wet dark leaves, spatter them against the glass. Her view was blurred as if by tears. Why am I crying? Tears would make wet cheeks, it wasn't tears. She was seeing the world without correcting lenses. And that realisation came as another astonishing blessing: she didn't know why.

However, there is plenty to cry about, she told herself. The country has been taken over by a gang of murderous crypto-fascists. I have been brainwashed and I'm on the run, and *they've got Candide...*

James came out of the restaurant kitchen still holding his empty shotgun. She realised why he had had to leave her in the bathroom. Otto had imagined, in whatever part of her that clung to sanity, that if she could find someone, anyone, who was in this same state and knew it, she would be saved. That had been a mistake, a bad mistake.

'This isn't Underhill is it.'

'No, you're in Hampshire.'

'Where are Margot and Bernie?'

'In Southampton, I suppose. It was an ancient tradition. If World War Three breaks out, head for the nearest first strike target. Do your best to get right under one, leaving the house unlocked and as it stands for the benefit of any poor buggers unlucky enough to survive. Which is what I found. There aren't any lines to Southampton, so I can't be sure.'

She swallowed. 'Is that what you think? D'you think this World War Three scenario is real?'

'It's one of the things I think,' he answered evenly. She looked at the empty shotgun. What was in James's mind, what did he see? She avoided his eyes.

'What about your neighbours, what do they think's going on?'

'There aren't many. Herman the German, who is writing a thesis or something in an old cabin about a mile away. He's been writing it for years. I think he's around, but he's harmless. Just down the road there's the Maguires' stables. I've a feeling their house is occupied, but we've been keeping ourselves to ourselves.'

'I wasn't joking about the plutonium, James. I'm dangerous. Those gangsters think I know something, they've tried all kinds of ways to get me to tell. I managed to escape somehow. I really don't know how I found my way here. Is their headquarters nearby?'

'No. That's the animal labs place, up near Birmingham. There's no BREAKTHRU centre in Hampshire that I know of. The nearest would be the Gerty MacDowell Interspace Zone.'

She choked. 'Are they all like that? Is there a Molly Bloom Alternative Orifice? How far is it?'

'About sixty miles. It's outside Guildford.'

She looked at her dead frog feet. 'My God. I think I ran all the way... Oh, James, if they come and get me they'll get you too.'

She tasted warm salt. James grew larger, larger still and something touched her mouth. He gave her the handkerchief, with her own blood making a red blot.

'Don't worry about it.'

He went back to the kitchen. She followed as if pulled by a string, dependent as a baby. In the restaurant there had been twilight. Here the shutters were tight closed and a lamp stood on one counter glowing brightly.

'The electric's off, but I haven't run out of oil yet. Are you hungry?'

She watched as he managed deftly, one handed: the other never leaving hold of the gun. Reserved, obstinate, timid human creature. There was no one like him. James's advice to Otto on the subject of rape, long ago. 'If it ever happens don't resist for God's sake, Otto,' (she had declared she would kill). 'Men are *dangerous*.' Never questioning but that it must be so. Or seeing the irony. She used to tell him. 'You're living on inherited wealth my lad. And you don't fucking want to think about where it comes from – '

James looked up, as if she had spoken aloud. Otto began to dissolve. 'Will you carry this?' he asked quickly, and gave her a tray.

The Phoenix and the Dragon

They passed through the cold dark house. It was always shabbier, more lived-in than Underhill. All its formality was concentrated in the restaurant. Xav and Gerry and James used to hate that place. They were outraged when people sometimes wandered curiously – imagining the house was open to the public. Later everybody waited on (for pocket money): became incredibly good at it; even learned to cook. Once Sandy, Otto and Luci kept the whole thing going *alone* from a Friday to a Monday. Xav only was never reconciled. Poor Xav, life was always so much beneath his dignity.

James walked warily, persecuted by shadows. Otto could almost see them herself.

His room had not changed in fifteen years. She remembered it so well: the cosy Victoria-red wallpaper, the odd mixture of prints and pictures; a few rather good ones and a lot of beloved rubbish. The armchairs and the spread of ribbed gold Chinese silk across his bed. A splendid manchu robe lay casually across a camphorwood chest at the bed's foot: repro of course, the original should be in a museum. On campus James favoured basic black, with black candles, taped down black out blinds and classic ANC posters. Otto had laughed aloud when she first walked into this sumptuous boys-own lair. Such a fraud! The curtains, dark red like those in the study at Underhill, were firmly closed. There was a fire in the hearth, a basket of logs a bucket of coal and a fuel can. The room smelled of paraffin. She was still naming the names: it grew easier.

Strangely, there was no sign that this room had belonged to two people. Otto grimaced. Continuity was returning, painfully as restored circulation.

'What a beautiful robe – ' she said, touching the sea green and luxuriant folds.

'Is it not. Luci gave it to me last Christmas. I have to keep it down here, it's far too gorgeous for the flat: wouldn't go with our town ambience at all.'

The embroidery was a pearly maelstrom of scales and feathers, a phoenix and a dragon locked together: chaos serpent and the bird that remakes itself.

'What are they doing? Fighting?'

'Fucking, we decided.' He smiled sadly.

James and Luci's private life.

'We often used to to this – ' he said, taking the tray and setting it down. 'When I was working on a Ralph. We'd drive down late

225

at night, raid the restaurant freezer like kids and sneak up here to midnight feast. Now what have we got? Eel and cranberry terrine, a ragout of hare – '

'James – '

'Sorry, I wasn't thinking vegetarian somehow. Broccoli with hollandaise, chestnut and chocolate cake. And a Cote de Nuits, Bevy. You may find that too light – '

'James I'm so sorry, so sorry. It was appalling, how could I run out like that-'

Eyes lowered, he held her off. 'To be honest, Otter, I didn't miss you. I was better off alone I think. Let's eat before it gets cold.'

She didn't want this food. She wanted, if anything, bread and cheese, hard biscuits: emergency rations. But as soon as she tasted, she was overwhelmed. Every mouthful, every texture. And the wine, so clear and bright: true ruby like the jewel. She wanted to cry, it was so beautiful. She ate as if she had been starved for weeks, she wanted never to stop because the act of eating seemed to hold her down. The creature, nightmare sufferer, still lived under the skin in its nameless world: but no doubt that effect would fade, along with the mysteriously nauseating sense that nothing was substantial. At least the woman whose son had been kidnapped, whose world was shattered, had found a refuge.

'Now we're together there must be something we can do. But the country's in such a mess: State of Emergency Rules, and implemented by paranoid schizophrenics, can you imagine? Did you try to find out – I mean, what's really happening?'

'I tried. I gave up after a while.'

His tone was reticent. She thought of the surreal images of destruction, flashed on dark rooms.

James watched the flames quietly. The empty shotgun lay across his lap.

'Is that your security blanket?'

He laughed. 'Did you know, after Charles escaped from Worcester he picked up a billet of wood somewhere, and became so attached to it his minders couldn't get it away from him, day or night.'

'You and your Merry Monarch. What did that represent? A spare penis?'

'Just a friend, Otto. You and me against the world, little stick. There was no one, no one human he could cling to, and he needed a friend.'

She poured herself another glass of wine.

'We'll have to plan. They want the Kairos back and they must not have it. The worst thing is, I don't know what's *happened* and what hasn't. If I had something, any confirmation from outside ourselves, from the real world, something objective.'

'What about Peggy's address. The piece of paper that Mrs Elliot wrote it on – ?'

She nodded eagerly. 'Yes, that's exactly what I mean. But it's no good, I threw it away.'

'Sandy's flower?'

'No, that's gone too. I suppose there's – ' She stared at him. 'When did I tell you all that?'

His surprise looked genuine. 'All what? Why – just now, didn't you?'

Otto shivered. She touched the sleeve of her dressing gown, sipped her wine. They looked away from each other.

'I was very stupid after I left you, James. I won't tell you some of it, I'm embarrassed. I found out about this World War business and I tried to get the bus to Devon, hoping Candide was with his father. I was picked up. For a long time I thought I was in government detention, on my way to one of those hulks on the Severn. But it was BREAKTHRU. They were brainwashing me, James. It wasn't funny at all. I was in an awful state, couldn't tell a chair from yellow, you know?'

'I know.'

She fixed her attention determinedly on the ash logs. There were strands of ivy still twined around the green wood, the leaves crisping and blackening.

'What about you, James?'

'I've been conscripted,' he said. 'But I don't think it matters since the allies got blown away. When I woke up, or whatever, after they took Luci, I found my call up papers and ran away from London. That's when I found out things had been moving very fast. I saw ASVs prowling in the Forest. I thought I was in hiding then, but since I recognised the signs I can't say I'm really worried about BREAKTHRU any more, or anyone else. I came here: I've been waiting. That's about all.'

His face was so quiet. Little prickles of alarm ran up and down Otto's spine.

'What's an ASV?'

'Articulated Suspension Vehicle. Those new tanks on legs, you know.'

'Oh yeah, dinosaurs. The army. My God, d'you think this war's real? That's one horror that crossed my mind, suppose our business is just a coincidence – '

'It could be. The day I went out to Berkshire Barry Cunningham was muttering something about he thought the Big One might be coming...and he's in the business, he would know. But then, it depends what you mean by a coincidence.'

His sombre profile, the carven stone lips. The prickles of unease turned to nausea. Something was happening to Otto's refuge. The room *shifted*, she fought to hold it in place. He's not as solid as he looks, she thought: I'm afraid he's gone a bit crazy.

'James? James, what are these "signs" that you recognised?'

He looked into the flames. 'That the world is ending, Otter. We are dying, you and I and everything. This is what they call the Apocalypse. It is happening now, I mean now, to both of us. You know it is Otter, why pretend.'

Otto panicked. The room *shifted* again and she was falling down a lift shaft, she knew everything, the outrageous truth. She half jumped to her feet staring wildly round for something – some incontrovertible evidence.

'*No* – . James, no it isn't real. Don't you remember? A week ago – Oh, I don't know how many days. Something happened to us, you and me. You must remember. The drug, Xav's drug! But the awful thing is, if we don't stop this epidemic soon all the bad could really happen. The trouble with biological weapons is they don't know where to stop. That's why nobody would use them except loonies like your brother and his mad fascists.'

He glanced over her shoulder and remarked irrelevantly: 'Did you know this house is haunted?'

'*James!*' she screamed. 'It's the drug! It's the drug!'

She grabbed him by his shoulders, meaning to shake some sense into him...MISTAKE! BAD MISTAKE! She fell down the lift shaft, the skin broke. It was the drug that BREAKTHRU had given her. It wasn't wearing off after all. She must never forget as long as she lived that whatever seemed to be happening there was always a chance she was still in that cell being brainwashed. She must not relax, never think of Candide. The tiled walls rose up, turned grey...

James looked up at her, she saw her hands tightening the thick leather straps that restrained him. As they plunged locked together into the horror they shared, the sickening pleasures, Otto glimpsed another reality: the bright terrible vision James had tried to invoke by that (to her) tired and cheapened term *Apocalypse*... It was gone.

Torturer and victim, one flesh. Torn from each other, made of each other, he welcomed the pain: it was what he'd always envied, he wanted pain and blood to prove he wasn't her flesh any more There was no drug, never had been a drug: that was a mask it used. This hideous embrace exactly as real and as present as any other of the myriad aspects...don't be stupid of course James's room has changed in fifteen years...The only escape to choose to be elsewhere, and from now on never not know that it is only choice, there is nothing else to fall back on, no place to stand.

Choose, then.

Is this what they call free will?

Slowly the red walls reasserted themselves, a thin film of comfort. *The other place did not go away. It never would.* They were kneeling in the firelight: each quickly dropped the other's hands.

Otto huddled herself together, wrapped her arms around her knees and turned her face: remnants of an obsolete language.

'That's why – ' muttered the huddled thing. 'That's why I came to Standards: I mean why I am here. I made you 'man'. I couldn't help it James, you're the only one I know.'

She had tried to tell herself what it meant to be without the walls. She had fled from the knowledge: rather be mad than live like that. But the option wasn't available. In Kairos you can be mad and sane at once.

In Kairos, what is willed, happens.

'James,' she whispered. 'I killed Luci didn't I. I was hating him that night, for various abysmal reasons.'

James sighed. 'No, Otter. That one's mine. It's such an effort you see, keeping hold of something precious. You're so much safer if you have nothing to lose.'

After a while, a charred log fell. And in spite of what they knew they were still together in the red walled room.

Otto drew a long, shuddering breath.

'I've always been afraid of sex. I'm very strong willed, I can make myself do things so I was able to play the bandit. But I was always on guard: except with Sandy right at the beginning...'

'So have I. Of other men and what they might do to me, but more afraid of women. The only reason I was ever friends with you was that you didn't seem to be one...though I never dared to tell you that.'

He laughed nervously. They crouched in a silence that might have lasted forever.

'Shall we go to bed?'

She felt inexpressibly weary now. This business of disintegration was such hard work: something told her that the tiredness was a dreadful warning from the collapsing mind-brain, but she was too exhausted to care.

It was warm and safe under the yellow quilt. She was glad to feel another body near though it wasn't the right one. I want Sandy, she cried: but Luci was dead. As soon as she closed her eyes she was lost again in the impossible multiplicity: integration packed on integration, the implosion of time. She believed she was watching the death of her own brain tissue, all those tiny frost flowers bursting and spreading the deadly, world dismantling spores. Meanwhile, she supposed James went on fighting his own demons, equally alone.

She sat up. James stirred, propped himself on one elbow beside her.

Sex is death, the angel said. Once you've passed on your information you're finished: therefore sex is the root of all fear. But he didn't go far enough. What do James and I have to do with reproduction? The terror of being invaded, of being consumed, is so much older than that modern invention. Down in the mitochondria, eukaryotes and prokaryotes. So deep, so deep in the past began the constant bartering between fear and survival: only with Kairos in me can I reach so far. But it lives in each cell, each symbiotic unit. And the self remembers because cell is the self, none other and *they were there*. I am my cells now, and all the information in them. That's what Kairos does...that's what we have to reverse: making the dumb chemistry me, Otto. And now she was in the study at Underhill again. No, in the attic bedroom. She was playing the part of a man, she was acting it out, and by whatever mysterious means, the terror in the cells had reached its expression in the long bitter war. But she was conscious this time that she was taking part in a healing process. I am you, you are me: that's what we must suffer, in order to know it. Let terror out of the world then, by the same route that it came in. Invade, be consumed. This must be the way.

It began like that, very seriously. But soon they had both forgotten the drug and the demons. They were neither woman nor man, female or male but simply flesh suffused with pleasure, riding air together like the little hawk of the roadsides.

James woke up in the dark and found that Otto had vanished. The cold of the room struck him fiercely. To his immeasurable relief he made out a standing shadow by the window. He went to join her, collecting the embroidered robe: and wrapped it around them both. She had opened the curtain. The sky was brighter than twilight, featureless but apparently without a cloud. Beyond the livid garden great naked trees were scattered over an expanse of turf. The giants throbbed and ached in overplus of being.

'It's still there,' she said. 'I thought we'd done something magic.'

'You ought to be glad, Otto. It seems to me, Francis may have stumbled on the cure for civilisation as we know it. We could be experiencing the fall of patriarchy: isn't that what you always wanted?'

'Not like this.'

Tears started in her eyes, she recalled her absurd flight to that little gothic monstrosity. 'How can one rejoice at the death of any man? It's a poor way of getting rid of an enemy. A fair, good discussion that turns him out is well, but death – no!'

'Who's that?'

'Charles James Fox. Another Charles. I'm as bad as you, James, riddled with heroes. And most of them are male.'

She sighed.

'Why is the house called Standards? I don't believe I've ever known. High standards of cuisine?'

'Oh no, it's the trees. We are outside the Forest here and the woods have always been coppiced except for our trees.'

'James, you loony, you pretend to be English with such naive pride, it is enough to turn an honest Scottish stomach.'

The giants flung up their arms and cried. They were breaking up inside. Soon even the shells, which from moment to moment preserved an illusory integrity, would be gone forever.

'No,' said Otto, 'I only wish you were right James. But there is more to this Kairos business than a changing of the guard. If it cannot be stopped, it is the end. Let's try to sleep. Perhaps that will make the magic work.'

3

The Chestnut Mare

She woke up knowing. She had always known.

In what they called morning the room looked unromantic, with curtains half open to shed the dull light of Kairos over a frowsty vagrants' den. James walked into it wearing the phoenix and dragon robe, bringing coffee; and saw that Otto had shed a hundred years overnight. Her cropped hair had dried into soft red tinged corkscrews that made a nimbus round her head.

'What do you feel?' he cried. 'Do you think it's over?'

She wrapped bony fingers round the coffee mug.

'I don't know. But I know who has the Kairos.'

'Well – yes.'

'Sssh. Don't say it. I know where they are, too. James, we can't do it. Luci can't do it, he's dead. But if there was ever anybody in the world who could simply refuse to accept a whole, seamless ginormous time-space continuum: it might be Sandy Brize.'

A car engine crooned, turning from the distant road into Standards' drive.

Otto's eyes went black, dilating instantly. She left the bed and darted across the chill glimmering room, pallid and horrible as a long, skinned rabbit. James followed. He snatched his wool shirt from the night before and dropped it over her shoulders. His room overlooked the restaurant entrance with its white pillared portico. A big black car came up. In the loss of texture and perspective it grew rather than moved, growling for no reason like a bad tempered animal. It pulled up on the sweep. Two men emerged.

'I told you – ' breathed Otto. 'I told you I was dangerous.'

She thrust her arms into the shirt, turned away and began to scavenge clothes from the floor: when she ran out of garments she started pulling drawers and opening wardrobes, ruthlessly.

'What are they doing?'

'Talking to a phone and looking in through the windows.'

'Is there any id on the car?'

'Not that I can see. Normal plates.'

She was dressed, in a jacket and trousers and short boots all belonging to Luci. 'Have you any money? In case I can use it-'

'Take my wallet.'

Guilty and desperate, she faced him.

'James, I know where Candide is. Candide and Sandy, they're together. I have to reach them, tell Sandy what it is the two of them are holding, are doing. *It's our only chance.* James, I'm going to run out on you again. I'm going to throw you to those wolves out there, to cover my escape.'

'So where are they?'

Otto licked dry lips, glanced at the bed. 'I'm not going to tell you.'

James said thoughtfully. 'I see, nothing's changed. That's a pity.'

She ran at him, grabbed him ferociously.

'James, James I love you, I trust you. But – even now, I don't know this is you I'm talking to.'

Dangerous! Don't question this version! Don't break the skin-

He recovered hurriedly.

'All right, sorry. Point taken. What do you want me to do?'

'Go down to the door. I'll watch from here. Maybe it's not BREAKTHRU after all. They'll pretend not but I think you will know. Do something that will tell me, and keep them occupied as long as you can. That's all.'

James laughed. He touched her face, following the long flat angles from brow to stubborn jaw. 'Otto, you're not the most convenient friend for a coward. But I couldn't do without you. Take care.'

The door closed behind him. She was alone again, in Kairos.

She watched through the window as he reappeared below. The conversation seemed civil enough. He's telling them I'm here. I was mad to trust him. Thoughts like that couldn't be prevented. She might still be in the detention cell being brainwashed...No, I'm afraid we're not serving lunch today. Morning coffee? James looked extraordinary in the dragon robe, his skin deep rosewood glowing against the heavy silk. This apparition smiled benignly on the two strangers, and slowly, carefully, lifted its right foot and began to examine the sole. The sea green folds slipped apart. Somehow James managed to make his pose at once archly innocent, unequivocally pornographic: Marilyn Monroe over the grating. How *did* he do that? Otto choked on scandalised laughter, turned and fled.

She ran between rows of leeks and cabbages in the shelter of Standards' glasshouses and cursed herself because she could not make any coherence at all of what had happened just before this interlude. The time spent with James, however measured, had given her back her senses and a way – perhaps – of holding on to them. But before it there was nothing. Only pursuit – perhaps simply by my own demons? What can two men in a car do? She scrambled up the kitchen garden wall: and instantly pitched herself backwards. There were men in the wood. Backed up against the mellow bricks, shaking: she climbed again and peered over. Yes, figures there in blurry close fitting-clothes. They were walking in between the trees. One of them was talking into a headset receiver close against his mouth.

And I can't even see properly.

Doggedly she got up and began to run back towards the house. Out of the kitchen garden gate and down the lane, trusting James to hold back the two in the car. She seemed to have taken her battered feet by surprise at first, but they had started to hurt horribly. In a few minutes she reached the entrance to the Maguires' stable yard. She slowed, afraid to cross the open gateway. Most likely people were shooting strangers on sight by now without any need for BREAKTHRU to intervene. Her situation was truly hopeless. The line of beaters didn't matter, she couldn't run on these feet. In the fugue state, maybe; but then she wouldn't know what she was doing. She would have to steal a car...

There was someone standing at the Maguires' gate, beckoning to her.

It looked like Paddy Maguire, the daughter. They had met quite often years ago. Otto made a desperate decision. Trust, optimism: these had to drive her because if things didn't go according to that plan she was finished anyway. She hurried up to the gate and ducked through. Someone closed it behind her. She looked, but Paddy wasn't there. A blurred face and a beckoning arm showed at the door of a long low white building, the white broken up by dark open half doors. Kairos was interrupting her continuity. Otto stood still. Whose face was that? She must be dreaming. In a world created by the mind but complete and convincing as that perceived by waking eyes, mind frightens itself, talks to itself, teaches itself, punishes itself...

She crossed the cobbles, passed into a warm animal smelling
gloom. It was nearly dark in here, and littered with the tidy
untidiness of a well-used work place. She could make out pots
and tins and brushes on shelves, a confusion of metal and leather
hanging along one wall. There was a dim raggedy strip of red
and blue on one upright: ah, rosettes. Something moved behind a
partition, a bright-coloured shadow. The other stalls were empty.
Otto looked for the way out: a hidden exit that would get her past
BREAKTHRU's beaters, a trapdoor. The figure she had taken for
Paddy Maguire suddenly reappeared. It reached over and flicked a
lightswitch on the whitewashed wall.

Otto gasped.

She was not afraid but the shock was visceral, not to be argued
with. It plastered her against the whitewash, made her teeth shake
in her head as Luci advanced. He was dressed as he had been that
night in Clerkenwell, in dun breeches cut for fashion not for riding
and a white shirt. His feet were bare. Through the white cotton
she could see dark stains over his ribcage. He came up close,
and fingered the lapel of her jacket. His eyes were very bright,
insufferably knowing as ever.

Dear me Otto. And would you be as quick in my grave?

'If you mean me and James, Luci – it *was* the right thing to
do this time.'

It was absurd. But if her mind felt it had to produce this phantom,
then apparently she must answer it.

Yes, you must, said the ghost. You dumb materialist, don't you
understand yet what it means if the world is in your mind? It does
not mean I am your property, Otto.

He opened the loosebox and lead out the bright shadow. She was a
short-backed, long-legged chestnut mare, gleaming with health and
strength; and brilliant eyed.

Her name's Calpurnia. She's the Maguire's pride and joy. She's
very fast and very tough and never tires. I've ridden her point to
point, so I speak as one who knows. You can ride, can't you Otto?

She gaped.

'Not for years-'

You'll manage. Cal is a sweetheart.

The sweetheart danced and kicked about playfully as Luci exchanged her halter for a saddle and bridle. He led her out into the
yard. The clash of iron-shod hooves on the cobble seemed hideously

loud. Calpurnia described a small neat circle while Otto hopped about frantically. Up aloft at last. She felt the breath and heat and weight of the animal beneath her. Luci stood holding Calpurnia's bridle.

James had said the house was haunted.

'Luci – has James seen you?'

The voice she had made up for her phantom spoke. Of course he has. He doesn't tell you everything.

She had conjured Luci to the life, with real pain in those insolent green eyes. On an impulse she leaned down – pity for the dreamed dead: Luci flinched away.

Oh no. Mustn't touch.

He held the mare's soft muzzle between his hands. It was the right thing to do and so is this. Remember what you decided, you have to get unfrightened. You have to make peace with what you don't like about your enemy as well as what you do.

I'm a mare, Otter. Mount me.

She had forgotten how noisy, how awkward and painful horse-riding was. Her thighs clutched the animal's ribs. She kept her hands down at the base of Calpurnia's neck, inelegantly gripping the reins and the front of the saddle at once. The mare looked so delicate, but her big heavy feet smacked up clods of earth from the bridleway. Coppiced oaks thick with dead and dying leaves blurred by on either side. Otto ducked low. She must be through the ring of beaters, they weren't expecting this. Gaining confidence she stuck in her heels. Calpurnia reacted like a smooth running engine. At first Otto thought she would come off, but the mare's gait was too even for that disaster. It was pure exhilaration. They were heading north but the direction wasn't important. Any road, any town would do: where she could find what resources there might be in this chaos – a car, petrol. Wonderful though she was, obviously Calpurnia couldn't run all the way.

I'm a mare, Luci had said. Mount me. She made sense of what she had said to herself through the ghost. Since everything in my mind is contaminated I have to neutralise *all* my fears to escape from Kairos-as-fear. To get out of this trap I have to fuck with Luci. What was it about him that made her so angry? Bright flesh dressed up in metal and leather, poser clothes and all that shines and glitters: sexy power. It was so easy for him to manipulate the animal world, world-animal: he was part of it and it belonged to him.

236

Slick muscles punched and clenched between her thighs, Luci's face glanced back, flecked with foam, banded in metal and leather... *What am I doing???* She was in danger of losing hold of reality again. All that awful bad-dream drugged business from last night when she first reached Standards flooding back...

There came a sound, louder than the various noises of horse-riding. It rattled down through the fuzzy trees: chakachakachaka. Otto heard it, recognised it: too late for her far from perfect control over the animal. She and Calpurnia came bursting out of the wood. They had to cross three fields to get back under cover. Prayed the helicopter was nothing to do with her. No such luck. She looked up: yelled 'Don't – '. Whoever was riding there fired anyway, a rapid violent spray of sound.

Calpurnia wasn't hit but she was frantic. She put down her vivid head and bolted, laid out on the cold rushing air of time. Otto had lost the stirrups, she hadn't a hope. In the last moments she screamed to herself – this is my dream. I can control it. But she could not. Backbone snapping, hands clutching hopelessly: a gate loomed up across the path. Calpurnia rose and Otto fell, between two worlds, with force enough to break her neck.

4

Nothing More Than Watching the Ephemeral Colours as They Fade on a Sunset Sky

On his way to the top of the oak stairs James noticed he was still carrying the shotgun. He laid it by the wall, gently.

Nothing stirred in the populated silence of the old house, no faces turned to him: neither Luci nor his mother nor any of the others, older; nameless. Otto herself had vanished the moment he closed the bedroom door. It wasn't that he had imagined her presence, no not at all: or rather, that description didn't devalue a meeting the way it once did. She was no more herself and no less than any of his other visitors.

He had a feeling that what had come to find him was the war. If so he had decided to stick to his pacifism, shabby though it was: for a strange reason, for the sake of those children in uniform by the roadside long ago. They had been adults then, they had grown younger and younger like his plump, shiny cheeked parents in the photographs. *Live like human beings! We are giving our souls for you!* That's a gift no human being can give to another. But he did owe those boys his life. This life, of course, not the other one, undamaged, which he had never known. So if he didn't make a very inspiring conchie, that was fair.

Down the dark stairway. He picked his way between a thousand different versions. His eyes had become kaleidoscope lenses: but as he'd told Otto, if you don't think about it you find you get there. The physical world still existed but he was seeing it more fully and from many different angles, like the landscape that slides away as the plane rises. It wasn't one of the experiences Natural Death returnees spoke of – but then, this was a different order of dying.

238

It amazed him that Otto could contemplate halting such a process. He understood what she was telling him: and yes, there was a sense in which what was happening had 'started' a few days ago. But how could there be any way back?

As soon as he saw the two on the doorstep he remembered. Africa was dead, there was no war for him to go to. This was the summons he'd been waiting for.

The shorter of the two men was made of red brick. His arms stood out from his sides bulkily, propped on gym-built muscle and layers of expensive cold weather clothing. He looked as if he was on his way to join a sober young arbitrageurs' expedition to the North Pole. The other was tall, his face a sallow slab with deep grooves framing a sour, habitual smile.

'We'd like to come inside, Sir. We have a few questions to ask you.'

The transparent pretence made him smile in genuine amusement: and then suddenly, he remembered Otto.

'Ah, I'm afraid the restaurant's closed.'

The slab faced man moved in closer. 'We'll come in anyway I think, Sir.'

'I could do you a morning coffee, I suppose – '

They weren't going to take much more of this, in fact none.

'Just a moment – what is this? Are you the police? What's wrong?'

'We're repatriation officers,' explained slab face, dead pan. 'We've come to fetch you, darkie. We're going to take you back where you belong.'

James smiled sweetly: then apparently became aware that he had trodden on something sharp. He managed not to look up at the east wing.

His room smelled of sleep and warmth and woodsmoke, and sex perhaps. The gold and white swirled walls were stained where he'd thrown a bottle of wine at one of his earlier visitors, and scrawled where he had tried to write himself messages in that long-short time of undivided experience before Otto appeared in her final guise.

Slab face grimaced. 'I hate the smell of them.'

The smell of ghosts? Oh no, niggers probably.

They kicked the litter on the floor about and soon discovered the remains of a meal for two.

'She was here all right.'

'She can run but she can't think.'

'It's fucking bizarre that she can move at all, after carrying that amount of K about in her handbag.'

If he had believed for a moment that Otter was real, in this sense...James stood frowning stupidly. It was almost incredible that that fragile charade of drugs and terrorists should still have meaning. It seemed that the construction business went on, even to the very end.

They watched him, grinning.

'Okay, James. Other people will take care of Mrs Murray: she won't be far, will she. Get dressed. We're going back to town.'

He remembered that BREAKTHRU personnel were supposed to be immune to the Kairos. But not entirely untouched, for though they didn't seem at all confused these plain-clothes angels were very frightened: he felt that like an unpleasant itching, like an allergy to their presence. And therefore very dangerous...

He slipped off the robe with a show of unconcern. But it had been an error of judgement to tease these two stalwart hets with a desirable male body. The Kairos heightened almost unbearably their professional, habitual fear of everything and everyone: it helped to see any stranger as a woman, as meat. The brick-coloured one smiled slowly, slab face pursed his lips. James was spreadeagled, violently penetrated. His mouth dried, scrotum tightened, his prick began to fill.

'Look at that, it turns him on,' said one angel to the other.

'And I don't know about you, but I was thinking of big fat broken bottles.'

'Amazing, innit-'

James dressed calmly, a phrase that Otto had used running through his mind, *the voluptuous paranoia machine*. As part of that operation he had consented to Luci's death, been content to see his parents suffer brutally if only he could have his share. He was glad that the machine was being dismantled, it was about time...

Nothing, nothing, nothing.

He only knew when the room returned that it had been gone: for an immeasurable instant. He wondered whether the angels had had the same experience.

'What *is* that?' snarled the one with the red skin and the voice of a city luncher.

'Just shut up about it, will you, Hugo.'

As they reached the car, several figures in dark coveralls were coming across the lawn. They disappeared into Standards.

James stopped.

'You know, this is your boss's house. Are you sure he wants it treated badly?'

Hugo grinned. 'Get in the car, James. It's none of your concern.'

He had produced a handgun, spatter finished in silver and sexy purple: this season's weapon, packaged no doubt with matching posing pouch.

Shaking his head, laughing, James got into the car.

They handcuffed him to a metal grip on the roof and drove off. The driver tried to report their success but his phone was uncooperative, producing only a frenetic crackling sound.

'Give it a rest, Mack. Bloody silly we'll look if the remaining forces of law and order tune in. They might want to take our undesirable alien away.'

He was re-entering the world, the falling world. He was going to his brother. Ever since Luci's death he had been moving through the layers of his life. He couldn't tell if he was rising or falling but he knew that making peace with what Otter meant, profound and painful as that had seemed, was not so deep as this. Sex was not so deep a fissure. I don't know what I could have done but I know I didn't do it, so now I must. He envisioned all the billions – if there were billions still 'alive' by this stage – labouring through their own private versions of the great *uncovering*...

The car pulled up in an underground parking bay. There was dark green durable carpeting around the double parking slot, trompe l'oeil picture-painted walls. James recognised the basement of that expensive little house in Camden where Gerry Howard had lived with Pietro during their brief marriage. The house had been bought by Xav, which probably meant by BREAKTHRU, and signed over to Pietro for some ingenious financial reason.

The journey had had no duration, but that sort of elision no longer worried him. Wasn't it always so? There are points of consciousness and journeys of intention we make between them. One invents the rest, to preserve the illusion of a continuous surface. All that was happening was that autonomous functions became conscious and required effort, as the end approached. The basement spread itself in prismed shadows. He wondered what would happen if he decided to step out into Gerry and Pietro's annulment party?

But he wouldn't do that. He was with the angels of his own free will.

Mack leaned over, unhooked the cuffs and fastened them again. Hugo hit James in the face.

'Don't try it!' he shouted. 'You won't get away that easily, black cunt.'

The lift doors opened in the lobby. James had a glimpse into a fashionably garish kitchen full of joke camouflage: a fridge done up to look like a welsh dresser. He saw Pietro and the housekeeper – a thin girl with a white face and dark hair, she had Gerry's daughter in her arms. The clothes of all three looked as if they hadn't been changed for weeks. They had the blurred grainy faces of hostages in a film made in a cellar. Briefly the older child appeared, running towards his father, sobbing loudly.

The lift rose, the scene slipped out of sight.

Xav was waiting on the first floor, in a room that held a desk, some media hardware, a fibre optic mural on one wall. A minimal staircase of white glass ribs, like a sectioned nautilus, spiralled through it and upwards to the bedrooms. The insolent little rock star had deteriorated. His stencils were growing out. His pink spooklock had become a greasy tail, dancing in agitation against a grimy, sweat-stained collar.

James supposed his own face looked like that. He could feel the pull of muscle around his mouth and eyes: if he was doing it on purpose he would call this one abject terror. He supposed he had been experiencing abject terror for days. He had become used to it, found a new base line. He stared at his brother. What was he to do now? He must make peace, but how the devil did one make peace with Francis Xavier?

'James! Wake up! They're coming for me, the company. They think I'm doing this on purpose. I want that stuff back. This isn't funny any more – '

It was crazy. Surely even the most besotted crypto-fascist gangsters must have noticed the scale of the events that had overtaken their plotting. But perhaps they *could not* see the truth. Xav and his vengeful colleagues were as much under the influence of 'K' as anyone else, and were helplessly acting out their own scenario of fear; and would keep it up until the heavens opened.

An extraordinary light lay on the room, like sunset clouds reflected on water.

'Look, this has gone far enough. All I wanted was a nice bit of temporary mayhem. How was I to know you alternative types were so scared of so much – !'

On the gently angled writing surface, James read upside down a scatter of random characters. Xav slapped the keyboard, but the screen wouldn't be still. He snapped his fingers in James's face, gabbling at him furiously.

'I know what you think. You think this is going to wear off soon, and everyone can go back to what they were doing. You're wrong. This is reality now. What you want is what you get: and this is what you stupid cunts wanted. We're all going to die, minds first, of a new kind of radiation sickness. That means several billion people James. You could have settled for a bit of mass hallucination, a riot or two and a Cabinet reshuffle. Oh no, you had to go for winding up the whole firm. That's what's happening, on a last in first out basis. Consciousness goes. The less complicated parts keep on walking and talking shitting copulating. Then they suddenly fall apart, it looks like at great speed: it's actually something to do with time, what happens to time. This I have seen, in our clinical trials. Maybe the collapse of the non-conscious world stops after we're all gone, this isn't clear. Doesn't fucking matter much, does it.'

It was getting difficult to concentrate. Scraps of memory and reflection kept drawing him away. This light made him feel he was gazing out over a long long shore where the tide has receded so far that sky and sea and sand fade together into one bare luminescence...

He leaned forward solemnly.

'I forgive you, Francis.'

'What the fuck are you talking about?'

'Luci is dead,' explained James patiently. 'There are plenty of other reasons, but especially for your share in that.'

Francis Xavier stared. He jerked his body back from the desk with a squawk of horrified, delighted laughter.

'Oh *Ker-ist!*'

In one corner of the room the various components of a cable system lay scattered. The screen of an eviscerated tv lay on its side. A middle-aged woman suddenly appeared there, huddled behind a newsdesk and mouthing silently. She looked hideous. Her eyes were like cinders, her mouth seemed to bleed. She bore an uncanny resemblance to Francis Xavier: the new model of humanity.

Xav had left the desk. He was by the window shutter switch on the wall, playing with it nervously. 'Oh, I'm really going to hurt you, little black brother. I don't mean me personally. I mean big jobs, professionals. You know you won't take much of that, you know what you are like. Stop pissing around.'

Nothing had happened. Neither the miracle that Otter still believed in, nor that other END of the Kairos experience. But it must be coming soon. New terror shook him, distantly. He had done the only thing left for him to do, in this world. There was nothing more. And still he could talk, still he could see his brother: exactly the same Xav as always. Hardly evil, that seemed an absurd overstatement, merely incurably obnoxious. Like the man said – the poor we have always with us...

'Francis, this is pointless. If you did define what you call the Kairos by injecting the world with a massive dose of fear, then what would be the use of *threatening* me, as an attempt to restore normality? But it makes no difference. You can't lose control. You never had any control.'

His brother glared frantically.

'Oh yes I can lose it. It's only a kid and Otto's mentally incompetent yob girlfriend. But *in their version* we don't find them. Don't you understand? God, you'll make me believe in racial superiority. That unwashed little loony is sharper than you.'

Suddenly the little boy started crying again. The housekeeper's voice said clearly as if beside them – 'Hush Guido, hush. Papa's not angry. He's just, he can't – ' The lift whined and footsteps clattered eerily loud. Xav was listening like a gundog. A car snarled up out of the parking bay: he flicked the shutters and peered out.

'Bastards. I told them to watch those kids. I wanted them. Kids can handle a big dose of K – better, in some ways better...'

He turned on James once more, his gold fringed weasel eyes holes in a skull.

Gone.

They were clutching each other on a – bombsite, was it? The air smelled of roast meat and smokestacks. James screamed. This time it was too much, tearing self loose from the line of time, trying to force it into its non-existence, sixty years ago...

Back. Xav dragged his hands away, flushing. He sniggered.

'You could wake up with my cock in your arse next, James. By the way, you know I was there don't you with you and super-dyke.

244

We spill over, we spill into each other as we rot. I didn't know you had it in you. In her, I should say.'

Perhaps the end of change was coming now. Lucidity was slipping again: the room, *this scene* seething with kaleidoscope meaning. The cure for civilisation as we know it, the collapse of patriarchy: Francis Xavier had been a faithful servant of both, good for nothing else, and he was beginning to disintegrate. The desk, the fibre optic galaxies, the battered video, Francis was smeared all over them like glutinous lace. James felt him, self, too, sliding away into this multifoliate presence...

'James!' screamed the lace-man. 'I have a jet waiting! We're going to New Zealand. You can have a seat, just give the Kairos back to me-'

'Not far enough – ' James giggled. 'You said yourself nothing could stop it from spreading – '

Xav turned. The whole room, his body, was shaking between terror and fury. James went on trying to explain but his words now came tumbling out of Xav's mouth by mistake: a rotting melting gush of nonsense syllables and animal sounds.

'Shut up – '

Outside in the street a car drew up, and another. Instantly Francis Xavier slapped the switch on the wall. That light of cloud on water vanished, replaced almost instantly by brilliant artificial whiteness. Xav scuttled across the floor like a crab. James in him, in the multifoliate see things have no words the opening mouth cunt door. Xav was peering out around it listening, out of him came a thin high keening noise. He scuttled back to the desk, threw up black lizards. Oh shit, oh shit, those goons can't trust them, James.

James, take a lizard.

How could Xav still walk and talk? He understood that what he saw – Xav spreading like lace over the furniture – was a kind of euphemism. All that fun-use of the Kairos must be catching up with him. It had always been Francis's ambition to do without conscience alltogether...but what a way to go, brain rotten with his grisly superdrug and BREAKTHRU's debt collectors at the door.

I can't. I'm handcuffed.

Keening loudly the Xav part of James bent over him, released him. A lizard grew suddenly along his arm, dipping greedy suckers into the flesh to feed. Down in the depths there was a resonant thumping. Louder, louder and then an ominous hot high whine. Heat seared skin.

Christ, they're torching the doors out.

James recognised the lizard and dropped it in disgust. He was outraged. He knew he wasn't innocent, he was part of the organisation, but he was damned if he was going to die with a weapon in his hands...

I won't you can't make me.

Xav didn't plead, not a word. He simply picked up the lizard and thrust it back into James's hands. His eyes were red. His lips had pulled away from his teeth, the muzzle extended, the long canines jutting. It was the mask of a hedgerow beast of prey, puny and savage: insane with fear but incapable of submission. Poor Xav, poor friendless beast.

The hot whine had become a hammering sound, beating like regular thunder. James felt himself poised, sick with uncertainty, hanging between the different orders of destruction...

Is this the Apocalypse or the big jobs catching up with Xav?

He was struck by the appalling notion that he could choose...

No, you're not going to drag me into this. I don't care how much trouble you're in. Only a fool forgets...

James sighed.

'Francis,' he said, taking the ridiculously overcapable firearm (although he had no idea how to use it). 'What I most resent is your capacity for putting me in the wrong. Always always whatever you do to me I come off with the obscure feeling that somehow it is still my fault. Did anyone ever ask Abel what had happened to Cain? I'll bet Someone did. I'm definitely the victim here and on the point of every kind of death yet apparently I'm still expected to be my brother's keeper. All right Xav, I suppose we're in this together. What d'you want me to do?'

One of the two men who had fetched James from Standards came in. There was a furious, incoherent exchange. The goon-angel saw James armed and began to yell at Xav hysterically.

Now I've done it, thought James. Now I've really done it...

He could not remember what.

The house was full of noise.

'You stay up here and hold them off!'

Francis and his goon dived down the nautilus spiral: vanished and the white glass exploded from below in a burst of automatic rifle fire.

Oh, typical. One might as well offer pity and loyalty to a rabid rat.

James crouched behind the stylish colourcast housing of printer and copier, and noticed something strange. The exfoliation of reality had ceased. At the end with Otter he had glimpsed his lost illusion of a single world: this was something different. The room was still. The unlimited multiplicity had not vanished, but it troubled him no more than it had worried him, a week or a month or a year ago, to believe that anything he touched was a swarm of dancing atoms. Why, of course, he thought. This is the way to live with Kairos. You just have to know what you're doing.

The door burst open. James meant to use the sub-machine-gun, or whatever it was, no matter how little Xav could ever know or care. But its technology defeated him. Brandishing the useless weapon fiercely, he launched himself at Xav's enemies: after all, he was dead anyway...A shattering impact caught him, and propelled him into fire and dark.

Δ

Otto lay on the hard ground. She clambered to her feet and staggered through a screen of trees into the open. The chestnut mare had disappeared, so had the helicopter. Across the colourless sky she saw a long complex trail like a river system in a satellite picture, or a line of cross stitching in grey silk on paler grey. She closed her eyes, the split remained. She put up her hands and felt her head carefully. The connection of skull with spine did not seem right at all. She remembered her verdict in front of the bathroom mirror. Oh, I am dead.

She did not have the courage to go back and look to see if there was a body lying on the bridleway.

She sat down. Between her knees the grey grass winked up at her, a million stars. Dead as a dog.

This morning (call it morning) she had woken up with the most powerful intuition. Xav had told Candide that his little dog was being vivisected in a BREAKTHRU laboratory. Candide had refused to believe that Vera was dead. Obviously, then, he had to rescue her. Where did he go to for help, when his mother was no use to him? He went to Sandy. The two of them were in Birmingham now. They must have been caught up in the Kairos explosion, but they were still alive. How did she know that? Because BREAKTHRU had lost control of Kairos. When Otto and James took the drug, they took horror, because that was what it was since Candide lost his darling. They had no chance of remaining in control. But last time Otto had met Sandy Brize she wasn't in a mood to be frightened. She was an ice cold existentialist, bent on psychic suicide.

Sandy, plunged into the abyss of fear but unafraid, was the focus of this terrifying disintegration. The only way to stop it was to reach her, to tell her what she was doing.

But how could Otto reach Birmingham now, on foot? The world, seeded with epidemic schizophrenia, was expanding moment by moment. Already it was flat again. The Americas and Japan had disappeared out of this continuum into their separate unreachable universes. To travel two hundred miles, without benefit of wealth or influence, was more than the average woman could expect to achieve in a lifetime. She could have wept in grief and frustration. The loss of her own life, even Candide's life, was nothing beside this devastation. For even if you believe in the most simplistic Darwinian model it must occur to you eventually that it is the survival of the unfittest that counts. Preserve your variables, the growing points, the margin where change is possible. The time that matters is the time when conditions are so benign that the freaks survive. The future opened before her, utopia's inheritance. Tribes of dirty gypsies wandered their little lands, forgetting each other's languages: the women breeding incessantly, senselessly, rearing one in ten and dying old at thirty. The whole delicate, intricate, damnable confection of this man's world crushed like a sugar rose: and all the work to do again...

She began to walk up the grey field, limping stubbornly northward. She was fairly sure the helicopter team wasn't coming back. The angels were crazy as anyone: each of those scary beaters in the wood flailing about in a lunatic world of his own. As long as she didn't actually bump into one –

Nothing, nothing –

Otto came to herself clinging to a fencepost, shaking. She limped on again, gasping from that momentary earthquake. The horse would have carried her to the nearest town, instead she'd have to walk there that was all. Better not even try to hitch a lift, that would be asking for trouble.

She saw a red thing in the sky to her left, the paring of a fingernail rising above the trees. It was the winter sun. She stared, overjoyed. If she could see the dawn again, surely the Kairos effect was fading. But what was it doing rising to the left of her northward path? Stupid: you're heading the wrong way. With an exclamation of impatience she turned and began to stumble down the pasture. Below her in its clearing lay the white house called Standards, and the Maguires' stables beyond. Otto's heart began to pound. The sun reached its low noon and descended into the East. A cone of shadow lifted out of the oakwood and marched over her: and the sun followed after, rising fractionally higher in the South West than it had before.

Otto pushed her fists into her eyes. Control the dream, control it! You mustn't go under again. You must survive to reach Sandy or no one will survive at all. The horror of what Kairos was doing inside that soft defenceless grey mass. The exquisite filigree continents, their coastlines barely charted by science: lost in a bursting, imploding proliferation. Excess of cells seeping through the cross-stitched fissures in bone. O, I am dying, I am dying cried the melting sugar rose.

Get a grip. Use your reason. If time were running backwards you wouldn't be in this field, would you. You'd be with James, or else in that foul detention place. And instantly she was. A hundred million perceived locations poured in on her. In the hospital room, she held James in her arms driving out fear to the beat, beat, beat of their joined bodies. Soldier's eyes in purdah. Golden wings and a wind torn flag over Grosvenor Square. Sandy on the beach at Croyde, body surfing : a burning stretching tearing between her thighs the whole cosmos a ring of muscle ripping up from its bed higher than houses curving back CRASHING down, sigh, sigh, sigh, salt mouth bruised exultant...

Otto in the November field. She had bitten her lip again as the world fell. White out, she whispered. All the colours of the rainbow. Have to try to stick with one. And the absolute impossibility of travelling anywhere in this state made her start to cry.

Where had Luci gone? Where was the chestnut mare?

She had blundered into the Maguires' stable yard and stolen a horse, conjuring up Luci's ghost for company while she was doing it...

No, that wasn't what happened. Nothing, nothing, nothing.

Otto keened and whimpered. She knew what she must accept, but she couldn't do it. Whatever happened inside her skull, somehow through everything she had managed to preserve the integrity of the outside, of that out there. Every time the real state of things made itself known to her she fled, fugue. She could only bear it by calling it the ultimate horror, the thing that has to be stopped...It was impossible. Never in this world could there be a drug that did the things the Kairos did. And yet it was true. She was (risked white out –) had access to, all the information there was. It was as the angel had told them, long ago. Anything one of us knows, we all know now. But then Sandy knows, but then everything is all right. No it isn't how can 'everything' possibly be all right if I am not with Sandy...*I have to get unfrightened.* Oh no, oh no, is that what the death of the world turns on? The intolerable complexity and grotesque simplicity folded into each other so horribly: alp on earwig.

And again, the pulse of utter nothingness...

That sobered her. Stop fighting. Mind and world are one. Don't think about how: it works any way you can make it work. Go to Sandy.

I can't.

But you must.

Δ

> oh saddle to me my milk white steed
> And go and fetch me my pony oh
> For I must ride to seek my bride
> Who is gone with the raggle taggle gypsies oh

'It isn't real, Otter.'

The Hampshire field had vanished. She was with Sandy, they were sitting at a battered kitchen counter on two breakfast bar stools. Through the window beside them was an airy view of clouds and sky, and a distant cityscape stretched out far below.

She had entered into the middle of a conversation which had been going on for some time. In the course of it, Sandy's mysterious remark was explained: she would remember the explanation soon. She had the feeling she herself had just been sounding off as usual, laying down the law about something or other. Sandy's clear eyes had that patient, amused look they sometimes developed. How beautiful she was, even now: bedraggled and distinctly gamey after following the gypsies for so long. How could you lead me such a dance! You wait till I get you home! The reproaches would come no doubt, she never could resist them. But there was no hurry. There would always be enough storms and enough reconciliations in this long running conversation to satisfy even Otto's doubting and greedy heart.

At the other end of the room a group of women, three young men and an old one were talking earnestly. The older man was one of those eccentrics the radical fringe has to put up with because no one else will: you knew him by his witless bullshitter smile. And now Otto saw that this was an AL shelter. Gruesome propaganda plastered the sagging doors of the fitted cupboards. Rescued victims from what seemed to have been a recent raid lined most of the counters in open cages: hamsters and rabbits and some very smart looking rats, who were obviously following the round table discussion with keen interest. The ambience, quite apart from Sandy's contribution, was a mediaeval combination of petshop and unwashed humanity.

'Pretty soon, there will be no more women and no more men either,' said a young white woman with purple female nation scars. 'The chemical identity will break down.'

'Will we all be like transexuals?'

'No – stupid. There'll be no gender at all.'

'They're not like wild animals are they?' broke in the bullshitter, indefatigably. 'I mean, while mankind is going through these changes, who's going to have time to feed a hamster? You've got to be realistic. You've got to be cruel to be kind.'

Everybody groaned and made retching noises at this last repellent sentiment.

Otto could not tell if the emotion that flooded her was genuine euphoria or merely the absence of the mind-killing terror that had been, a moment ago, her mode of being. She saw and heard the animal libbers and the explanation of her release dawned on her while she was still looking around the room or else it was still materialising: and then there was Candide, filthy and wildhaired. He was down on the floor, he was playing, or rather refereeing a boisterous game of tag between a small Jack Russell terrier with one brown ear, and a huge white rabbit. The rabbit boxed the terrier's ears and showed enormous teeth. She heard the terrier yapping and Candide laughing.

Otto began to laugh, helplessly.

'You rescued the dog!' she cried. 'O God, Sand, you rescued the dog! Sandy, you're brilliant! I never would have thought of that, never in a million years!'

251

Candide looked up.

'Oh, hello Mum.'

He charged over, covered in embarrassment, and thumped his head into her midriff.

'Sorry if you were worried.'

She laughed until the tears ran down her face, and hugged him hard for as long as they could both stand the unseemly demonstration.

'I did now – ' said Sandy, very earnestly. 'Originally I didn't, originally she was dead when we got here. But that became a dream. I might have guessed as soon as I saw the white stones what had happened. The future can change the past.'

Candide hauled Vera up on the counter between Sandy's stool and Otto's where there were no tempting cages. He ruffled the coarse hair on her stumpy little foreleg.

'Otter, can you see the join? It was her paw you know. I'm certain.'

Sandy shook her head scornfully. 'There isn't any mark, don't be daft.'

'I know there isn't. The blackmail bits were samples of another world. That you and me unmade, Sand.'

It was ludicrous, it was awesome: to think what this noisy, self-important little bundle of flesh had been, for the duration of the nightmare. Candide's obnoxious pet – surrogate for the whole, the whole good bad and indifferent sum of things. But already such thoughts seemed the merest psychedelic image-spinning. The Kairos experience was receding from her, losing its grip.

'What are you talking about, Sandy? Of course you rescued the dog, here she is.'

'I told you. This isn't real. I made it up. I couldn't let our Candide cry like that, even though I never liked the beast. So I changed everything. I may even have changed it twice: it's quite likely that the AL people had started mercy-killing their refugees before we got here.'

A couple of times that she could remember, she had come near to recognising that Candide's loss and grief were vital, the edge where the world had changed. But it hadn't occurred to her that anything could be done about those things. They were fact. Otto was not troubled by the wonderful woman's cagey way of putting things. She could barely begin to imagine the kind of strain Sand had been under, holding the Kairos and not knowing it.

She was wondering how the debt of her 'astral travel' would be paid, now that everything was back the way it had been before. Perhaps the only gap was in her consciousness. She had covered the distance somehow, a dazed automaton, and woken up here. She might start remembering the journey soon. The next few days, come to think of it, were going to be quite extraordinary. Everyone would be finding out whether they had lost an hour or a weekend or a month in Kairos. There would be incredible chaos on the markets, and real news from the war zones again.

'Sandy – don't look so anxious. There's nothing to be afraid of. It was all, like you said, a bad dream. And it's over, it's over!'

'Is it?'

What an odd tone of voice –

'Sandy?'

It'll take a while for her to recover –

The high rise kitchen was very brightly lit. It's strange how artificial light can seem, so easily, when darkness is always natural however it is made. The people at the table had stopped talking. Even Candide and Vera were quiet.

Sandy took something out of her coat pocket and held it on her palm. Her expression was not exactly anxious. It was very familiar: cool and cerebral and quite without mercy.

'If everything is back the way it was before, Otter, then what is this? And what do you suggest I should do with it?'

The lull between the waves was over. Here comes another one. And just when you didn't think there could be anything bigger, anything more terrifying than the last –

Here it comes. Here it comes.

△

James noticed that the house had become very quiet. His head hurt terribly. When he moved, nausea engulfed him: he heaved himself up and vomited down a cliff of leaf green enamel. He was in a bathroom. He must have been thrown in here unconscious by the BREAKTHRU heavies who came after Xav. How good of them to make the distinction.

He was not afraid any more. To be free of fear was very, very strange. It gave him a new perspective on life. He wondered if freedom came from having picked up the gun at last. But that didn't seem right. What else had he done? Nothing at all, as far as he could remember: a performance of masterly inactivity. He ran water to wash away the vomit and sat on the side of Pietro's bath holding his head. When he was able he got up, left the room and walked out of the house. It was a cold day. There was a city Sunday morning feeling, the residual presence of a defunct and irrelevant day of rest. He passed a newsagent's and thought he would buy a paper: the couple were outside taking down their grilles. The woman, wrapped in a droopy woollen cardigan over her sari, smiled at him.

'Good morning,' said James.

'Good morning. Yes – good, good morning.'

She bowed over her folded hands: the man did likewise, both of them grinning effusively.

It was then that James realised that his brother must be dead.

He had left the door of the house ajar: not that he had had any choice, the thick plate of colourcast metal was burned through. He searched everywhere. There were burns and bloodstains all over the decor, but no bodies in evidence. At last he pushed open a sliding closet door in the biggest bedroom and something moved inside. Xav fell out as if he was blind drunk. James caught the body in his arms and laid it on the floor.

Xav's face looked no more human in the rictus of death than it had in his last hour of life. James closed the wide open eyes. He was kneeling there, wondering how he would break this to Bernie and Margot and trying to think not too sentimentally about the space between the stirrup and the ground, when he heard a step behind him. He turned to see who it was: and his heart stopped.

He stood up too fast. Pain cracked his temples.

'Well don't just stand there, James,' said the familiar voice, lightly, affectionately, unkindly, 'lookin' like Bambi in a thunderstorm. I'm here, I'm real. Touch me.'

Δ

The wave was coming, building from immensely far.

Otto had forgotten about the Kairos. What could they do, what could anybody do with that stuff? It was dangerous in a way without precedent. It could not be contained. She had desperate thoughts of taking the little black tube, wrapping it in a subcontinent of lead and concrete, sinking it in the deepest ocean trench: and what would that achieve but to give it greater stature, greater power than Xav had ever imagined?

The animal libbers and the female nation women seemed to be talking again quietly. Otto was aware of them as background. She had an inconsequent feeling that she and Sandy had been up here in Birmingham at an event, a conference: it had been absorbing and pleasurable...must remember to buy the crêche team a drink...She didn't want this party to end. It was her exactly, it was the way she was made...

Sandy was picking at the seal. She had it open. She uncapped the tube and pulled out a three lobed capsule: a horse pill, almost too large to be swallowed.

'I know what you're thinking, Otter,' she said – and grinned: language was full of pitfalls. 'You think we can't, the two of us, do this, it's too big a responsibility. But there's no need to worry. Did I say I changed things? It was a figure of speech. As you know right now this moment I am still in the dark wood with the bird singing and Vera dead. I don't do things. No one does things: they are. All of them. If this is the way things turned out, they always were going to turn out this way, in our version, if you see what I mean. Like I said to Luci – what is and human perception, they're one and the same entity. But I had the idea, you know, that I was walking to the south pole of time. And I've reached journey's end.'

'Sandy, don't even think it – ' cried Otto in horror. 'It would kill you – !'

But Sandy climbed up on her stool. She pushed the top light of the window open: and Otto couldn't make out why, she was herself so torn between rational panic and totally inappropriate calm.

'Sand? What are you doing?'

A gust of cold fresh air rushed into the room.

Sandy looked over her shoulder. 'I'm not convinced – ' she admitted, in her normal voice. 'Maybe I'm imagining it all or maybe I'm merely going to give this crummy estate another weird drug experience. How can I ever know for certain? All I know is that this is what I do. But supposing it is real, Otter. Are you sure you can tell the difference, between something dying and something being born?'

'Sandy don't-' screamed Otto.

Too late. A mass of tiny transparent crystals fell out into the high-rise breezes, and at once broke apart and vanished with a sweet faint sound. As Otto pulled Sandy back from the open window the sweet note began to grow and grow: never louder, always clearer, until it filled all the sky.

On The Beach

They met the boys at the station, under a grimy little red framed information screen. As they met, Otto gave James a long thoughtful look; but said nothing. They walked down to the sea. It was early February, a bright day with even a touch of warmth in the sun. They talked of the ceasefire and its slender chances, the expensive convalescence of James's car; of the aftermath of the raid in Camden and whether James was going to be a witness at the murder trial. Their opinions divided on the future of BREAKTHRU. James said the company would disappear completely. Luci thought, and Otto agreed, that the kind of people who became angels would not be disillusioned by a little thing like a gangland killing. Otto complained bitterly about her insurance claim, and spoke of her expanding empire. She now employed an accounts clerk. A Mrs Eliot, a neighbour whose family badly needed the money. The strange thing was, she used to be senile before Kairos. The drug had apparently cured her.

'Yes, I've heard some stories like that.'

'Only anecdotes I suppose, so far. Maybe someone'll do a study eventually, if they mount up.'

The Nouprims leaned their elbows on the eau de nil railings and gazed. Mid morning on a winter weekday, the promenade was quiet. A few old ladies walked their little dogs. Parents of toddlers pushed buggies. An old man sat on a bench alone, reading a newspaper with a discontented air.

'Well, Luci?' asked Otto. '*Was* it the late quartets, as we've always been led to believe?'

Luci shook his head. 'Nothing like. No Beethoven at all: it was one of these modern johnnies – Messiaen, I think.'

It was the first time the four of them had met since the Kairos event. In the days just after that bizarre adventure they had not felt like rushing into each other's arms. There was an intense and very natural impulse, which was shared by the whole world, to pretend that nothing much had happened.

'So now there is an enthralling correspondence going on,' said James to Sandy, 'between the police and the forelady or whatever her title is, of this Polish place where they make antique Triumph parts – '

'Will you ever see you motor again, though?'

'I doubt it.'

A tiny girl scorched past them on a midget BMX with trainer wheels. She was singing in a high squeaky voice, the hook from that old Collins anthem. *I may not get there, get there with you. But I have SEEN, the promised land...*

'Anyway, did you get your job back?'

Sandy chuckled. 'You're always worried about me being out of work, James. No I didn't, I got a better one. I'm mending roads. It's very sexy, we take turns to drive an antique tar spreader, it makes a fantastic noise.'

The theory Luci liked best, about the event which had been for them Francis Xavier's surreal act of terrorism, suggested that the BREAKTHRU company hadn't been responsible at all. It was clear by now that their experiences had been only one small manifestation of a general, worldwide period of mass hallucinations. Discussion of its meaning would run and run, but Luci favoured the idea of a cosmic event affecting the whole (relatively) local area. Perhaps in its sidereal orbit, the galaxy passed through such 'areas' of turbulence quite frequently, but simply had not happened to meet one for the last two or three million years; and that was why it had come as such a surprise. Or else, intriguingly, there *had been* times in the past when signs were seen in heaven, pillars of cloud and fire, extraordinary behaviour of all kinds: but later generations would naturally dismiss these reports... or award them a different value.

'But wouldn't something so major have been predicted by – oh, by all sorts of high-tec stuff?'

'Maybe it was,' said James. 'In the other place, the one Sandy didn't like. How is one to find out?'

'Ugh.'

Sandy smiled wickedly. 'Well, I still think it was the end of the universe.'

'No reason why not. Once you've decided there will be strange effects, which there might well be around the Big Flip, what's the loss of a few trillion perceived years? This phase was supposed to be unsuitable for intelligent beings. But according to Umbriel the Universe and human consciousness are now one and the same – if they ever weren't. I expect that might make a difference.'

Down below Candide and Vera scampered about on the pebbles.

Luci scratched his ribs slyly. 'And we all know what poor James thinks...'

James assumed a dignified expression –

Otto turned her back on the sea and watched an elderly lady getting down, with an air of conscious and painful virtue, to scoop up her doggy's mess.

'I think it's better just to forget it, all of you. Let the place heal over. And accept the world as it is, the way we always did.'

Her friends glanced at each other, and smiled.

'So what did we come down for Otter? So you could show off your new shop windows? You were very portentous on the phone.'

Otto looked embarrassed. 'Oh, nothing special, Lu. I just think we ought to see more of each other, or how can we organise...taking over the world, you know.'

They descended to the shingle. Vera was tearing in and out of the water, yapping hysterically. Candide generously sought to involve James and Luci in the fun: he felt it wasn't fair to keep her wonderful bouncing wetness all to himself. Otto wandered. She picked up pebbles and dropped them. The sea lay like a steel mirror, reflecting faithfully an ocean of bright silence overhead. Kneeling by the water's edge she sat back on her heels. On her palm there were five oval stones: two white, one liver coloured and two blue-grey. She looked down at them, covertly, until they disappeared and the hand became transparent. And still she didn't know why something so simple should make her so afraid. The ever present murmur of the human ocean whispered, on the threshold of her consciousness. 'Never get back there,' she muttered. 'It's gone forever. I have to keep imagining things now. Never stand on solid ground again.' And what next? Stand for parliament, or walk through walls? She had to admit, in support of James's theory, that this world was scarey and strange enough to be the antechamber of the Land of the Dead.

At least I remember. There'll be those who will not.

She looked up, over her shoulder, into the eyes of the old man on the bench. He had put down his newspaper. He was staring at Otto. Everyone along the promenade was staring: a myriad viewpoints breaking, multifoliate, inescapable.

'I walked to the end of time,' whispered Sandy, gazing out to sea. 'And everything turned around. Now we go home.'

James was standing a few paces away, watching her. She lifted her shoulders a little: and he nodded.

There will be time, the visitor said. This is just a warning. The little waves sighed on the shingle, retreating and retreating.

Otto jumped up and whistled to the boy and the dog.

'Let's go and find something to eat. I'm so hungry.'

So they strolled back up the promenade looking for early ice cream and Otto allowed herself to be teased at length, over her cowardice in the face of the extraordinary and her dreams of conquest.

Otto did have something important to tell the Nouprims. (Sandy might have guessed; if so she was being discreet.) But she had decided to wait until they were all feeling a little stronger.

Acknowledgements

This book was conceived ten years ago. I intended to revise it for this edition, but in the end I made only a few tiny changes; mostly removing obsolete political labels (EEC; the Soviets; the FDR; White South Africa). In ten years, things get lost, but this is a list of sources, as far as I remember.

The Golden Age of Children's Literature: *The Jungle Book*, Rudyard Kipling; *The Wind in the Willows*, Kenneth Grahame; *The Chronicles of Narnia*, C. S. Lewis; The *Swallows and Amazons* series, Arthur Ransome; *Escape to Persia*, Katherine Hull & Pamela Whitlock (Jonathan Cape, 1938).

End of History FX: *Ulysses*, James Joyce; *Finnegans Wake*, James Joyce; *The Tragedy of Charles II*, Hester Chapman (Jonathan Cape, 1964); *The Flying Inn*, G. K. Chesterton (Methuen, 1914); *Ideology and Utopia*, Karl Mannheim ed. Turner (Routledge, 1984); 'Violence and Metaphysics' from *Writing and Difference*, Jacques Derrida, tr. Alan Bass (Routledge, 1978); Max Delbruck, *Mind From Matter* (Blackwell Scientific, 1986); Lynn Margulis and others on the deep history of symbiosis, various articles in *New Scientist* & elsewhere. **Plus:** *The Marriage of Figaro*, Mozart; *Quattuor pour la fin du temps*, Messiaen.

Some quotations:
The Ford Cortina song, p11: adapted from a revue sketch performed at Brighton Pavilion Theatre *c*.1981; Luci's prayer, p11: from the *Salve Regina*, Liturgy of the Roman Catholic Church; Otto's reflection on the children at play, p43: from 'In Time of "The Breaking of Nations"', Thomas Hardy; James's recitation for his godfather, p51: from 'Windhover', Gerard Manley Hopkins; Xav's BREAKTHRU

manifesto, p69: misappropriated fragments from *Finnegans Wake* James Joyce; James's unease about a revivalist meeting, p81: from Acts Ch11, v15; Otto's accusation of her father, p176: from 'A Dead Statesman', Rudyard Kipling; Sandy's reference to 'the worst of all bad names', p181: from 'Father and Child', W. B. Yeats; James greets the Apocalypse, p196: from the Sequence, Liturgy of the Feast of Pentecost, Roman Catholic Church. Luci on the nature of reality, p203: from the Latin gospel of John Ch1, v1; Otto in pursuit of Sandy, p250: from *The Raggle Taggle Gypsies*, traditional.